Praise for Patrick Taylor's Irish Country Novels

"Taylor masterfully charts the small victories and defeats of Irish village life."
—Irish America

"Wraps you in the sensations of a vanished time and place."
—The Vancouver Sun

"Gentle humor, deeply emotional stories drawn from everyday life."
—Kirkus Reviews

"Taylor adds another delightful chapter to his heartwarming Irish Country series. . . . Interweaving several story strands to craft a cozy patchwork quilt of a novel, Taylor ensures that hearts will be warmed as myriad problems are tackled with love, kindness, and gentle humor."
—Booklist on *An Irish Country Love Story*

"Deeply steeped in Irish country life and meticulous in detail, the story is the perfect companion for a comfy fire and a cup of tea or a pint of bitter. A totally wonderful read!"
—Library Journal (starred review) on
An Irish Doctor in Peace and at War

"The author laces his heartwarming moments with liberal doses of whiskey and colorful Ulster invectives."
—Chicago Sun-Times

"Both hilarious and heartwarming."
—The Roanoke Times

BY PATRICK TAYLOR

An Irish Country Doctor
An Irish Country Village
An Irish Country Christmas
An Irish Country Girl
An Irish Country Courtship
A Dublin Student Doctor
An Irish Country Wedding
Fingal O'Reilly, Irish Doctor
The Wily O'Reilly
An Irish Doctor in Peace and at War
An Irish Doctor in Love and at Sea
An Irish Country Love Story
An Irish Country Practice
An Irish Country Cottage

Home Is the Sailor (e-original)

An Irish Country Cookbook

Only Wounded
Pray for Us Sinners
Now and in the Hour of Our Death

An
Irish Country
Practice

PATRICK TAYLOR

A Tom Doherty Associates Book

New York

To Carolyn Bateman
to celebrate twenty years of publishing together,
with my heartfelt thanks and admiration

Acknowledgments

I would like to thank a large number of people, some of whom have worked with me from the beginning and without whose unstinting help and encouragement I could not have written this series. They are:

In North America
Simon Hally, Carolyn Bateman, Tom Doherty, Paul Stevens, Kristin Sevick, Irene Gallo, Gregory Manchess, Patty Garcia, Alexis Saarela, and Chistina MacDonald, all of whom have contributed enormously to the literary and technical aspects of bringing the work from rough draft to bookshelf.

Natalia Aponte and Victoria Lea, my literary agents.

Don Kalancha, Joe Maier, and Michael Tadman, who keep me right in contractual matters.

In the United Kingdom and Ireland
Jessica and Rosie Buchman, my foreign rights agents.

The librarians of the Royal College of Physicians of Ireland, the Royal College of Surgeons in Ireland, and The Rotunda Hospital and her staff.

For this work only
My friends and colleagues who contributed special expertise in the writing of this work are highlighted in the author's note.

To you all, Doctor Fingal Flahertie O'Reilly MB, DSC, and I tender our most heartfelt gratitude and thanks.

Author's Note

It doesn't seem like a year since I was adding an author's note to the final draft of book eleven, *An Irish Country Love Story,* but it is, almost to the day. And now it's that time again because *An Irish Country Practice* is ready to go to the publisher and some explanation is required of events between these covers.

I wish to thank those who helped get my facts right, name the real people who play supporting roles, and finally pay tribute to a remarkable man, a classmate, who has allowed me to base one character on his young life.

The work opens with the televised running of the Grand National horse race in 1967. I have tried to reproduce some of the commentators' words verbatim as taken from archival film.

In this novel, technical accuracy could not have been achieved without a great deal of help freely given.

On matters non-medical, I was greatly assisted by Sergeant Mike Bradshaw, late of the Royal Ulster Constabulary, who advised me on the correct arrest procedure by an officer of that force and about the workings of the magistrate's court in Northern Ireland in the late 1960s.

Unfortunately, enquiries to the two Ulster law faculties were not answered, so if some of the other legal matters described here are inaccurate in any way, the fault is mine despite extensive perusal of the relevant acts of Parliament by my wife. Dorothy was a senior civil servant in the Northern Ireland legislative branch.

I must thank many in health care. Dana Doheny of that part of the

Porphyria Consortium at the Icahn School of Medicine at Mount Sinai Hospital in New York City who put me in touch with Dr. Manisha Balwani, also at Mount Sinai, who explained the subtleties of that condition. Drs. Fred Alexander and Jimmy Sloan, contemporaries at Queen's University Belfast, fine pathologists and friends, corrected my misconceptions about oat cell lung cancer. Dr. Tom Baskett, retired professor of obstetrics and gynaecology, a classmate and my friend of longest standing, along with his wife, Yvette, who had been a nursing sister at Belfast's Royal Victoria Hospital, reminded a failing memory about the physical layout of the wards of that institution.

For the purposes of the story, I have altered by three years the timing of the opening of the university's Department of General Practice at Queen's, but I have been aided in understanding its initial workings by Dr. Lewis Miller, a classmate and friend and one of the first graduates of that programme and later one of its faculty. More details were added by Professor Margaret Cupples, currently of the department. Thank you both and forgive me, Lewis, for stealing your name for a central actor in this work.

As an aside, there are a lot of characters in twelve novels. It helps me to remember them if I give them names of people I have known. I was at school with a Guffer, and a Dapper Frew, who you will meet on these pages. Nicknames were nearly universal back then. I was known as "Spud," a moniker usually reserved for Murphys. Guffer and Dapper here are fictional, and with one exception that will be described later I do not use my friends in their entirety as characters. There is only one thing worse than using a friend in a novel—and that is not using a friend. I think Oscar Wilde might have said that.

There are on these pages real people who did exist. Joe Togneri taught me how to sail. He was a remarkable man who bore his kyphoscoliosis (humped back) with courage and dignity. John Crosslé of Holywood designed and built the famous Crosslé Special Formula Ford racing car. The Duffy Family Circus is still in operation.

The following were senior consultants when I was a student. They are of course used fictionally, but they all taught me a very great deal. Dr. Teddy MacIlrath, radiology; Mister John Bingham, thoracic surgery;

Dr. John Millar, neurology; John Henry Biggart, later Sir John, dean of the faculty. I did not know Professor George Irwin, the first head of the Department of General Practice, who was appointed after I had emigrated. The details of their distinguished careers can all be found in *The Royal Victoria Hospital Belfast: A History 1797–1997* by Professor Richard Clark, who was also one of my seniors and who gives an anaesthetic in chapter 31.

The rest of the characters inhabiting these pages are figments of my imagination, except Dr. Connor Nelson. His real name is Colin Nelson but, to avoid confusion with Colin Brown, I changed the name. Colin Nelson and I were in the class that started in 1958 at Queen's. He was a reserved young man, older than the rest of us, and with a pronounced limp, the result of childhood poliomyelitis. We graduated together in 1964. I specialised in gynaecology, he in ophthalmology. We both immigrated to Canada, but to different sides of the country and, apart from meeting at occasional class reunions in Belfast, I am sorry to say lost touch until last year when I discovered that, like me, he had retired from practice and was living a short drive and ferry ride from us.

He was immediately invited over, and while he was here he asked shyly if I would mind reading something he had written? The upshot was that I was privileged to be shown his autobiography, written for him and his family. I was humbled by his struggle to become a doctor. I have told his story in this work with his full permission and as a tribute to his courage.

And that's it. Dr. Fingal O'Reilly and I tender our most sincere gratitude to all who helped. I trust the real people will forgive us and hope Colin, as I hope you the reader, will enjoy these pages.

PATRICK TAYLOR
Saltspring Island
British Columbia
Canada
June 2016

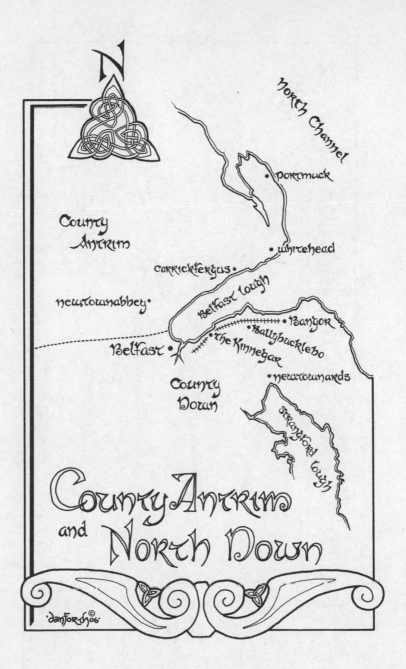

N

North Channel

portmuck

County
Antrim

whitehead

carrickfergus

newtownabbey

Belfast lough

Banjor

Belfast

Ballybucklebo

the Kinnegar

newtownards

County
Down

Strangford lough

County Antrim
and North Down

danforth 06

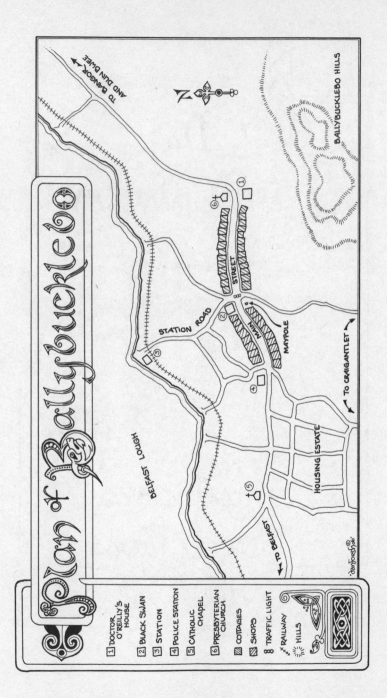

Plan of Ballybuckleboo

TO BANGOR
AND DUN B'JEE

N

BALLYBUCKLEBO HILLS

STREET

STATION ROAD

MAIN

MAYPOLE

TO CRAIGANTLET

BELFAST LOUGH

HOUSING ESTATE

TO BELFAST

1 DOCTOR O'REILLY'S HOUSE
2 BLACK SWAN
3 STATION
4 POLICE STATION
5 CATHOLIC CHAPEL
6 PRESBYTERIAN CHURCH
COTTAGES
SHOPS
8 TRAFFIC LIGHT
RAILWAY
HILLS

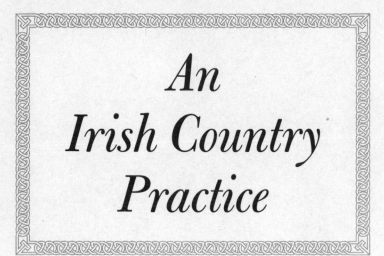

An
Irish Country
Practice

1

Pulling in One's Horse as He Is Leaping

Fingal Flahertie O'Reilly, *Doctor* Fingal Flahertie O'Reilly, took the stairs two at a time, a tin of Erinmore Flake in one hand, and went straight into the upstairs lounge at Number One Main to pour himself a Jameson. As he unscrewed the cap from the bottle, the extension phone rang. "I'm home from the tobacconist, Kitty," he yelled in his best quarterdeck voice. "I'll answer it."

"All right, but hurry, Fingal, the race is about to begin," came her voice from the television room as O'Reilly answered the phone.

"Finn?"

"Lars. You're back."

"Yes, Myrna and I got home from Villefranche last Saturday. We had a wonderful time. Sorry I haven't called sooner but it's been—excuse me—" O'Reilly heard a mighty sneeze through the phone line. "Sorry about that. A touch of hay fever."

"Hay fever in April?" O'Reilly laughed.

"It's been bedlam around here, with . . . with . . . work mostly. Look, I know it's short notice, but I wonder, can you and Kitty pop down to Portaferry tomorrow for lunch? There's something I need to discuss with you both and I'd rather not do it over the phone."

"Nothing serious, I hope." Was the usually reticent Lars, Fingal's elder brother, having trouble with his romance with Lady Myrna Ferguson, the Marquis of Ballybucklebo's widowed sister? She and Lars had been in his summer house in France for a fortnight.

"No, no, nothing serious. We're both fine. It's just . . . I'll explain tomorrow. Can you come?"

"I'll ask Kitty," O'Reilly said, "phone you back. The Grand National's about to run and I've a houseful of guests. But I'm pretty sure we're free."

"Fine." The phone went dead. O'Reilly shook his head, replaced the receiver, and returned to the sideboard to finish pouring his drink. Grasping his glass, he went down to a lower landing where a photograph of his old battleship, HMS *Warspite,* hung on one wall and went into the room. "I'm back," he announced to the little group seated in a semicircle around the Phillips black-and-white and plunked himself down between Kitty and Barry Laverty. "Who was on the phone?" she asked.

"Lars. He's home. They had a wonderful time and he'd like us down for lunch tomorrow."

"Lovely. I can't wait to hear all about it," she said.

"Great," O'Reilly said. "I'll let him know after the race." He peered at the screen and then at his watch. "Should be starting soon." And when it's over, he thought, with a twenty-pound bet to win on the favourite, Honey End, at odds of fifteen to two, my return should be 170 pounds. More than enough for the new record player he coveted. Sure the sound was good from his old Pye Black Box. But ever since he'd heard Mozart's Symphony No. 39 in E-flat major on one of the new long-playing recordings at Solly Lipsitz's Belfast music shop, O'Reilly had wanted to own a stereo player. They were not cheap, but he was going to get one courtesy of Honey End.

He grinned and rubbed his hands. All the touts and tipsters were extolling the virtues of the animal. It seemed like such a sure thing, he hadn't even bothered investing another twenty quid in case the horse only placed.

On-screen was the ever-suave Peter O'Sullevan, a BBC commentator born in Kerry but raised in England. "Welcome on this Saturday, April the eighth, 1967, to Aintree Racecourse and the one hundred and twenty-first running, here on Merseyside just outside Liverpool, of the famous Grand National steeplechase, a race of four miles, two furlongs, and seventy-four yards. In all, the horses must clear thirty obstacles before racing for the finish line. Quite the test of endurance for horse and jockey."

"It is that." O'Reilly sipped his Jameson and surveyed his friends. O'Reilly's housekeeper, Kinky Auchinleck, sat next to her second husband, Archie, at the left end of the semicircle. O'Reilly knew how much she enjoyed watching horse racing, and particularly the annual running of the National. He'd invited the Auchinlecks round. "So, Kinky," he said, beaming at her, "are you two having a flutter?"

"We are, so." Her dark eyes looked serious as she patted her silver chignon and stroked O'Reilly's white cat, Lady Macbeth, who was curled up on Kinky's lap. "There's a nice little black Irish gelding called Foinavon. We have four pounds on the animal to win at a hundred to one." Her County Cork brogue was as soft and melodious as when she had left her home in Ring thirty-eight years ago to come north. She sipped an orange squash.

Archie, a usually reserved man, smiled and nodded, holding a glass of Harp lager in both hands.

O'Reilly made a mental note to find some pretence to add the money she surely was going to lose to her next pay packet. It was a lot of money for a milkman and his wife. O'Reilly'd not miss it from the profit he was going to make. "And you, Nonie?"

Doctor Nonie Stevenson, the practice's new assistant, sat beside Archie. She'd been on call and busy last night, not rising from her attic bedroom until noon. She'd cooked herself a late breakfast and happily accepted an invitation to stay and watch the race. She had no plans, she'd told him, until that evening, when she and her new boyfriend were going to see *The Sand Pebbles* at Belfast's Hippodrome. She held her favourite tipple, what she called a "Cuba Libre." O'Reilly himself had little time for the fashionable rum and Coke mixes or Babychams favoured by modern young women, but he was a considerate host and kept his sideboard well stocked.

She grinned at him. "Four bob each way on Red Alligator at thirty to one."

"Last of the big spenders, Nonie?" Barry asked, and laughed.

She smiled at him. "Trying to save a bit for my mum's fiftieth birthday present. I'll be happy to collect at those odds if my horse comes first, second, or even third . . . It'll help, but I can afford to lose four shillings if it doesn't."

"Fair play to you, Nonie," O'Reilly said. Her mum's fiftieth? Damn it all, he'd be fifty-seven in October. Where had the years gone? He shook his head. "I'm sorry you're only going to place. Nothing can beat Honey End." He sipped his whiskey and glanced at Kitty.

Kitty O'Reilly née O'Hallorhan sat between Nonie and O'Reilly. Her eyes, a soft grey flecked with amber, shone when she said, "Fingal's got twenty quid on the favourite. I haven't made up my mind where I'd like him to take me for a holiday yet, but it'll be somewhere warm and sunny."

O'Reilly spluttered on his whiskey. A few drops got into the back of his nose and his sneeze must have been heard in Carrickfergus on the far shore of Belfast Lough.

Lady Macbeth let out a yowl like a banshee with her arm caught in a combine harvester and, tail fluffed up, fled from the room. He hauled out a red-spotted hanky and honked into it before saying, "Will it, by God? I actually had some thoughts about replacing my record player, but I'm sure we can agree on a good use for my winnings."

He saw Kinky's almost imperceptible shake of her head. He knew the Corkwoman was fey, but she always said her ma had told her the gift was never to be used for personal gain, and Kinky had never done so. Mind you, she had a brother-in-law, Malachy Aherne, whose last name in Irish, Echtigerna, meant "lord of the horses," and she always swore she'd learnt from him how to pick winners. Could she be right today? Nah. Honey End was a sure thing. He'd done his research about the race. "Honey End's a stallion out of Fair Donation by Honeyway and they've pedigrees going back to the 1880s. Her jockey, Josh Gifford, has been National Hunt champion twice already and he's only twenty-six. I wish your horse good luck, Kinky, but I think mine's going to give yours a run for your money."

"I know what you're thinking, Doctor dear, that three jockeys turned down the chance to ride Foinavon and that the owner, Mister Cyril Watkins, has so little faith in his own horse he's not even at the course today, so. But isn't it just the fun of watching the race and cheering on your horse?"

"It is indeed, Kinky. Best of luck."

She smiled and turned back to the television, where Peter O'Sullevan was saying, "And now over to Michael O'Hehir. He and his camera crew will be covering the track between Becher's Brook and Valentine's. Michael?"

O'Hehir, a Dublin man with a thick brogue, said, "Thank you, Peter. Good afternoon, ladies and gentlemen. Welcome to Aintree and the famous, or should I say infamous, Becher's Brook, named for Captain Becher, who fell here during the first-ever Grand National in 1839 and took shelter in the water from the other horses."

Behind him the camera panned across an eight-foot-wide brook with the fence set three feet back from the water.

"This is a particularly difficult jump because the landing area is three feet lower than the takeoff."

Sue Nolan, Barry Laverty's fiancée, sat to Barry's right, cradling a small sherry. "More horses have fallen at that fence than any other two put together. I love horses, you all know that, and I'm no protester, but I wish the racecourse owners would make that jump simpler."

"It had better not make my pick, Kirtle Lad, go down," Barry said. "I've a pound on the horse, and if it wins you and I are going for a slap-up dinner at the Culloden, Sue."

"Yum," she said, and winked at him as he took a sip of his white lemonade. He was on call today and ready to leave if the phone rang.

"What about you, Ronald?" said O'Reilly. Doctor Ronald Hercules Fitzpatrick, a classmate from medical school in the '30s, was a GP in the Kinnegar and now a member of the combined on-call rota. He was nursing a shandy. His prominent Adam's apple bobbed as he spoke. "I don't usually bet," he said, and blushed. "At one time in my younger days, I managed to run up a considerable debt on horses and dogs."

O'Reilly sat back in his chair. "You, Ronald? A gambling man? I had no idea."

"It started in medical school and it's not something I've wanted to advertise, but I am proud to say I was able to delve into my interest in things Japanese, found some aspects of Buddhism a great comfort, and with their help overcame my silliness." He coughed. "Having said that, I have allowed myself a wager. I too have picked Foinavon." He laughed a dry, cackling noise. "Long odds always did appeal."

"More power to your wheel, Ronald," O'Reilly said, "but you'll be out of luck today. It's Honey End. Just you watch." Then his gaze went back to the screen. The camera showed the horses behind the start line. Jockeys clad in the racing silks of their owners, hard-peaked hats, jodhpurs, and English riding boots jostled for position at the start line. The course was open. There were none of the fancy starting gates favoured by the Americans. A flag was hoisted on a raised platform at the start.

"They're under starter's orders," O'Sullevan said. Horses and riders settled. The flag flashed down and forty-four horses bounded forward. O'Sullevan yelled, "They're off," then adopted the horse-racing commentator's breathless cadences and inflexions. "Aaaand it's Rondettos in the lead by a nose. Rondettos. Kirtle Lad's next aaaand, I think, yes, yes, it's Leedsy, Leedsy close behind in third. There's a group two lengths back and Honey End the favourite—"

"Go on, you boy-you," O'Reilly yelled.

"There's quite a bunch farther back," O'Sullevan said, "as they come to the first fence, aaaand bringing up the rear is Foinavon."

O'Reilly stole a glance at Kinky, who was sitting, hands in lap, with a tiny smile on her face.

"Oh dear," continued O'Sullevan. "Popham Down's been hampered at the first."

O'Reilly had seen another horse obstructing the now-fallen animal.

"Aaaand Popham Down's jockey, Macer Gifford, has been unseated. He's all right, walking away, but the horse is back up and continuing to run with the pack."

O'Reilly became oblivious to those around him as the horses soared over jumps and charged along the straight from fence to fence, sod flying from their pounding hooves. In his mind he could hear the thunder of hooves, the great beasts snorting. He imagined he could smell their sweat. Across from the racetrack tall terrace houses behind the track seemed to flash away in the opposite direction.

At each fence, some horses refused or pulled up. Others fell, threw their jockeys, or were brought down in collision with another animal. Riderless horses charged on with the rest. Some, no longer burdened by a rider, were right at the front.

"The field is thinning, but Honey End is still going strong," said O'Sullevan.

O'Reilly winked at Kitty.

"As are Kirtle Lad and—"

"Go on, boy," Sue called, bouncing in her seat.

Barry grinned.

"Several riderless horses are up with the front runners, Red Alligator, Greek Scholar, Aussie. Poor old Foinavon is manfully trying but is well back."

O'Reilly stole another look at Kinky. He hated to see her being disappointed, but she was expressionless. Had she, perhaps, used her gift of the sight? He couldn't believe it. Not Kinky.

In what seemed like no time, the cameras had switched to Becher's Brook for the second time and Michael O'Hehir's Dublin twang took over the commentary. "Of a field of forty-four, twenty-eight competitors have safely cleared Becher's and are heading for fence twenty-three. The riderless Popham Down leads the field from near the left-hand boundary."

"What?" O'Reilly yelled. He leaned forward and stared at the screen. "Holy thundering Mother of God." Something was going horribly wrong. The leading riderless horse had turned to its right just before the twenty-third jump and had run directly across the bows of the rest. Horses reared, stopped dead. Some were running the wrong way. Honey End's jockey, Josh Gifford, had been unseated in the fray but was hanging on to the reins, frantically trying to remount. "Bloody hell. Get on your horse, you great bollix," O'Reilly yelled. "It's my twenty quid at stake."

As calmly as if he were commentating on the usually sedate Oxford versus Cambridge Boat Race, O'Hehir said, "Rutherfords has been hampered, and so has Castle Falls; Rondetto has fallen, Princeful has fallen, Norther has fallen, Kirtle Lad has fallen."

"Damnation," said Barry.

"The Fossa has fallen. There's a right pileup. Leedsy has climbed over the fence and left his jockey there. And now, with all this mayhem, Foinavon has gone off on his own. He's about fifty lengths in front of everything else."

O'Reilly had watched it all in wonder. Foinavon had been so far behind, his jockey had been able to avoid the melée at jump twenty-three and find a way clear in which to jump. The black gelding was now well on its way to Canal Turn. And still not another single horse had cleared twenty-three. Riderless mounts milled about. Unhorsed jockeys ran along the track.

"Come on. Come on," O'Reilly growled. Josh Gifford, Honey End's jockey, had now remounted, and yes, yes, Honey End had cleared the fence and was in furious pursuit of Foinavon. "Oh, for a horse with wings," O'Reilly said, hoping that Honey End could be able to catch Foinavon before the finish, but fearing he might soon be feeling an ache in his wallet.

"Shakespeare, *Cymbelline,* Act two," Barry said, "Imogen." He grinned at O'Reilly. "At least your horse is likely to finish. Might win yet. Mine's a dead duck."

"Thanks, Barry," O'Reilly said, looking at Kinky. Her features were composed and he would have expected no less. Kinky Auchinleck was too much of a lady to gloat.

"That was tough luck, Barry," Nonie said.

Barry shrugged. "My dad always said, 'Never lend or bet more than you can afford to lose, son.'"

"And that, I think," said O'Hehir from the television, "is the last horse that's going to clear twenty-three. And now back to Peter O'Sullevan at the finish."

"Thank you, Michael. Aaand it's Foinavon just clearing the Chair, the final jump. I don't know how his jockey has done it, but somehow the gelding has found the reserves for a final burst of speed, because he is being pressed by Honey End, who is catching up, but still lags by about fifteen lengths."

"Come on, Foinavon—" yelled Sue, then stopped and turned to O'Reilly. "For Kinky and Ronald."

O'Reilly glanced from Kinky, who had a gentle smile on her face, to Ronald, who was leaning so far forward that he almost touched the screen.

The room broke into a chant of "Go on Foinavon" that ended only when O'Sullevan said, "Aaand it's Foinavon, Foinavon, at one hundred to one crossing the finish line to win this year's Grand National, Honey End second at fifteen to two, and Red Alligator in third place at thirty to one . . ." Everyone in the room clapped.

O'Reilly rose now, ignoring the post-race festivities on the screen. "Well done, Kinky. That's a tidy sum you've won. Congratulations." Indeed it was. Four hundred pounds was probably close to a year's wages for Archie. He drank to her. "And to you, Nonie. And to you, Ronald. But if you don't mind a bit of free medical advice from one friend to another, if you've had trouble with gambling before, don't go back to it."

For a moment Ronald seemed not to hear O'Reilly, then blurted, "I'll not. I promise, Fingal." He swallowed and his voice had a dreamy tone. "But it was fun. Great fun."

Kitty crossed to bend and give Kinky a hug. "We are delighted for you and Archie."

"Thank you, Kitty. But there's something I want to say." She stood, her voice low and very serious. For someone who had just won four hundred pounds, she looked sad, not jubilant.

She used the gift and now she's ashamed, O'Reilly thought.

"You all know, except saving your presences, Doctors Nolan and Fitzpatrick, that I do be fey . . ."

"Good gracious," Fitzpatrick said. "Well, I never."

Nonie's hand flew to her mouth.

"I got the gift from my ma. I have told Doctor O'Reilly it is never to be used for personal gain. I want to reassure you all that it was not. I told no one else the winner, even though the horse's name came to me a month ago. It saddened me to know my doctors, except Doctor Stevenson, were going to lose money and I do be pleased for Doctor Fitzpatrick. I ask for your trust because this time I did look ahead again. Now, the gift's not a telescope. I don't see everything and when I do I usually only see things in blurs, but just this morning I saw something very specific, that in this village there was going to be a desperate need for about four hundred pounds, so I said to Archie when I told him, 'I know we weren't going to bet because I saw the winner, but now I think we should.'"

"And I agreed," Archie said.

"Archie and I will take back our stake money, but not a penny more. The rest will be kept in the bank until I find out who needs the money badly. Now, if it please you all, Archie did place our bet at Ladbroke's in Belfast. When the need comes for the money to be spent, we do not want it known that it came from our wager, or indeed from us."

"That's very gracious of you, Kinky," Kitty said.

"Thank you, Kitty. Now I wondered about coming today, but," she looked around the small semicircle, "Archie and I think of you all as our family here at Number One Main," she giggled, "and you, Doctor Fitzpatrick, as a close cousin . . ."

"I'm flattered," he said.

"But it does be said if more than one knows a secret it is no longer a secret." She allowed herself a little smile. "In our case, Archie and I count as one, so. "

Archie nodded in agreement.

"Thank you for telling us, Kinky," O'Reilly said. "I'm sure I can speak for everyone here. You have our complete trust. Always have."

There was a general murmuring of assent.

"Thank you all," Kinky said, "and I'm sorry for your losing, Doctor Laverty. And your loss, Doctor O'Reilly, sir, would have been less if you did bet both ways, so."

O'Reilly shook his shaggy head and harumphed before saying, " 'Fraid not." He was about to ask, as a good host, if anyone wanted another drink, but the insistent double ringing of the telephone extension in the lounge interrupted.

"That's probably for me," said Barry. "Maybe a dejected patient who lost more money than you, Fingal." With a swift kiss to the top of Sue's copper-haired head, he left.

"No rest for the wicked," O'Reilly said, sipping his drink and thinking, not for the first time, how pleasant life had become since he had first taken young Barry Laverty as an assistant in 1964, then as a partner in '66. O'Reilly glanced at Kitty. Now if only he could get her to slow down too. He'd been working on that for several months but with little progress.

Barry stuck his head round the door. "Mrs. Galvin's a bit off colour. Doesn't sound too serious. And here's Saturday's post." Barry dropped an envelope into O'Reilly's lap. Stamped on the outside was the coat of arms of Queen's University, beneath it the words "Department of General Practice." He shoved it into an inside pocket of his sports jacket. It could wait.

"You mean Seamus Galvin's mum? That buck eejit of a carpenter who took his family to California three years ago?" O'Reilly asked.

"That's her," Barry said. "See you all soon." He vanished.

Fingal O'Reilly lifted his glass to his departing friend and colleague, then rose and switched off the telly. It had been a great start to the afternoon. Close friends enjoying the race, Nonie and Ronald making a bob or two. And he was delighted to know Kinky and Archie had made a killing for a mysterious good cause. O'Reilly would have given all his winnings—if he had won—to find out what Kinky and Archie's "good cause" was, but fully understood that he must bide until she was good and ready to tell him.

Cries and Falls into a Cough

Barry smiled to himself as he steered Brunhilde, his lime green Volkswagen Beetle, onto the Bangor to Belfast Road. When first he'd come to Ballybucklebo, he'd been impressed by how Fingal O'Reilly seemed to have an encyclopaedic knowledge of all his patients. Three years later, it pleased Barry to recall that Mrs. Anne Galvin was fifty-seven, mother of two grown sons, a heavy smoker, and played the uileann pipes. He'd seen her last year when she'd complained of not being able to read the Mills & Boon romances she loved so much. It had taken only a few moments of an eye examination to satisfy himself she had neither cataracts, damage to the lenses, nor glaucoma. He'd sent her to an optician for spectacles. He smiled again. It seemed he was developing his own encyclopaedia of patients. It meant he knew them as people, not anonymous cases.

The traffic light was red. A Massey-Ferguson MF35 tractor led the line of traffic coming the other way, its engine burbling and blue exhaust fumes staining the air outside the Mucky Duck.

He wondered what might be wrong with Anne. Her husband, George, known to everyone as "Guffer," had sounded worried. She'd had a cough for four days and it was getting so bad, he'd said, she sometimes couldn't stop. It was one such fit of coughing that had got him on the phone ten minutes ago. Probably bronchitis—it was much commoner in smokers—but things like pneumonia would have to be excluded too. Not much to go on, and although it was not a bells-clanging, sirens-screaming emergency, Fingal O'Reilly was not a "take two aspirins and come in to the surgery on Monday" kind of doctor and neither was Barry. He'd take a history, examine Anne before determining the severity of whatever was wrong, and with a bit of luck prescribe a treatment that wouldn't require hospital admission.

The light changed, the traffic moved on, and Barry had a flash of memory about the first time he'd seen Anne's son, Seamus Galvin. It was 1964, and Barry had applied for the position of assistant to one Doctor Fingal Flahertie O'Reilly. He'd driven in this very car down to Bally-bucklebo from Belfast for the interview. He'd rung the bell at the surgery door, the door had immediately opened, and he'd been confronted by a huge man carrying a smaller one by the collar of his jacket and the seat of his moleskin trousers. The ogre had hurled the smaller man into a rosebush outside the door and pitched a shoe and sock at him, yell-ing, "The next time, Seamus Galvin, you dirty bugger . . . The next time you come here after hours, on my day off, and want me to look at your ankle, wash your bloody feet."

Seamus Galvin, carpenter by trade, had been the notorious manu-facturer of a flock of wooden rocking ducks that the hapless entrepre-neur had hoped would be his ticket to financial success. Barry was sure he'd faithfully remembered the tirade word for word. He shook his head and turned left to climb the hill to the council housing estate of low-rent homes.

He'd almost turned tail and run that afternoon, but he hadn't, thank goodness. He was still here in Ballybucklebo, and Fingal Flahertie O'Reilly, on closer acquaintance, had turned out to be much less of an ogre than he first appeared. But Seamus Galvin and his young family had left the village for the sunny climes, citrus trees, and swimming pools of Palm Desert, California, hoping for a more prosperous life. O'Reilly got a card from them every Christmas.

Barry took the first narrow street on the right. Most of the houses in the village, some more than two hundred years old, had grown up higgledy-piggledy along old cowpaths or bordering the main street. The housing estate, in sharp contrast, had been laid out with that peculiar geometric soulessness much loved by postwar town planners. Streets crossed each other at exactly ninety degrees. Rows of identical narrow terrace houses marched in ranks. No front gardens. No flowers. No shrubs. No trees. Tiny cement-paved backyards were separated by high, moss-covered, redbrick walls. In the winter months, the place was wrapped in a noisome miasma from the dozens of coal fires that were the only heat source of each damp home. In summer, most of the streets and yards were in permanent shadow from the Ballybucklebo Hills to the south. Places like this were ideal breeding grounds for bronchitis, pneumonias, rheumatic fever, and until the widespread introduction of the BCG vaccine after the Second World War, tuberculosis.

He parked at the kerb and got out. Seamus and Mary had lived in one of these two-up, two-down, outside-privy, jerry-built terrace houses. The Galvin seniors' own two-storey home was much the same, its façade of grey stucco peeling like a bad sunburn. Blistered brown paint adorned the sash-window frames and front door. But the windowpanes sparkled, the sandstone doorstep had been scrubbed, and the brass letterbox flap shone. Clearly Mrs. Galvin was house-proud. He knocked on the door.

Guffer Galvin, a short man, bald as a billiard ball, grey eyes with laugh lines at their corners, answered. "How's about ye, Doc. Thanks for coming so quick. Sorry til drag yiz out on a Saturday. Come on on in."

Barry followed into a linoleum-floored hall. He smelled floor polish and stale cigarette smoke.

"The missus isn't feeling at herself so I've her upstairs in our bed. First on the right. I'll wait in the parlour, so I will."

"Thanks, Mister Galvin." Barry headed up the narrow stairs where a frayed tartan stair carpet was held in place by polished brass carpet rods. The door on the right was open. He knocked on it and said, "Mrs. Galvin? It's Doctor Laverty." He could hear her wheezing.

"Come in, sir," she said. Barry was reminded of the harsh song of a corncrake. Her voice wasn't the soft contralto he remembered from their first meeting. "Thanks for coming."

He went into a tiny room where chintz curtains were drawn back so he could see across to rooftops, some with broken slates. Spindly TV aerials sprouted from the side chimneys.

"You'll have til sit on the bed," she said. "It's a bit cramped in here."

Barry did. "How are you?" he asked. She lay propped up on pillows and wore a pink bed jacket over a red flannel nightie, a book open at her side. Her pale grey-blond hair was curled and rolled in a style fashionable in the 1940s, giving her the look of an aging, bespectacled Bette Davis. Her National Health Service wire-rimmed granny glasses covered pale blue eyes. Her cheeks were flushed and she was sweating, but not profusely, her breathing rate steady, not increased as it would be with pneumonia. He took her wrist.

"I've been worser, so I have," she said, "but I've had a chest cold for the last four days. An ould niggly cough, you know. I've took my granny's Dublin mixture—porter, milk, and sugar—but it never done me no good. I was going til come til the surgery on Monday, but about half an hour ago I had a real hacking fit, so I did." She wheezed as she inhaled. "I thought it was never going til stop, so I asked Guffer til send for yiz." She handed him her bunched-up hanky. "I kept that for yiz til see."

Her pulse was one hundred, raised from the normal eighty-eight, her skin warm. At this point, he still could not exclude pneumonia. He took the hanky, but before examining its contents, he fished a thermometer out of his inside pocket. "Here," he said after he'd shaken down the mercury, "pop this into your armpit."

"Right, sir." She coughed again, moist and hacking. "Sorry," she said. "Can I have my hanky back, please?" She hawked and spat into it.

"Tell me about the cough."

"Och, Doctor dear, sure haven't I smoked like a chimney since I was fourteen? All the girls in the linen mill did. I've had a smoker's cough for donkey's years." She smiled. "Just like my oul da, God rest him, used to say, 'My idea of breakfast is a cup of sweet tea, a cigarette, a good cough, and a spit til clear the pipes.'"

"I'm sorry to hear about your father." Family history might be important. "What did he die of?"

"He'd a heart attack, sir, going on ten years back."

"I am sorry." Smoking might have caused it, but it was no help with this present case. "About your usual smoker's cough, do you bring up anything every day?"

"Aye." She looked down as if ashamed to be discussing such a thing. "Clear phlegm, but only in the mornings."

"I see." Pretty well every smoker brought up the mucus that had accumulated in the lungs overnight. Barry had before he'd quit four years ago. The worst had happened in the few weeks after his last cigarette. As the cilia, mobile hairlike protuberances from the cells lining the air passages, recovered from the paralysing effects of the smoke, their renewed vigour moved a lot of mucus upward. He was better off not smoking, but quitting was one of the hardest things he had ever done.

"And have you ever coughed up blood?"

"Blood? Not at all, and if I had, you or himself, your Doctor O'Reilly, would have known about it quick. But the stuff I'm bringing up now has a different colour. See for yourself." She handed him the hanky.

He took a look. No frank blood. No blood tingeing the yellow mucus on the bright white hanky. That yellowness suggested infection, but probably confined to the bronchi and not affecting the lungs. He leant forward and retrieved the thermometer. "Your temperature's up, at one hundred point two, but that's not a killing matter." Pneumonia usually caused a much greater elevation, which led to a feeling of being cold. "Any shivering fits?"

"Not at all, sir, just the cough, and the goo coming up, and a burning pain behind here." She pointed at her breastbone. Her laugh was embarrassed. "It gets worse when I have a fag."

"You really should try to quit, you know," said Barry, having a vision of a certain King Canute ordering the tide not to come in.

"Oh, aye, don't I know it," she said without emotion, "but I've been smoking for more than forty years, Doctor. When I started, the *craic* was, 'Do you know what the big chimney said til the wee chimney?'"

"No."

"'Yiz is too young til be smoking . . .'"

Barry, who had heard the old chestnut as a boy, chuckled.

"Sure everyone smoked."

Barry nodded. She'd only quit, if ever, when she wanted to. He was nearly certain that she was suffering from acute bronchitis. Given that she was a smoker, he would have given serious consideration to a diagnosis of lung cancer. After all, heavy smoking had been implicated as a cause as long ago as 1953. But usually with that disease the cough was dry, not productive, and often accompanied by haemoptysis, coughing up blood. An examination would still be required, but he was sure it would be simply to confirm his belief—and his relief.

He hated dealing with potentially lethal diseases, and now, after nearly three years in practice, he was still trying to decide whether a completely honest answer or a little prevarication initially was kinder. He'd been taught as a student to be perfectly truthful with the nearest next of kin, but to shield the victim. He smiled inwardly. He'd not be having to decide here today. "Right," he said. "Let's have a look."

"Yes, sir."

He turned his back as she started to unbutton her bed jacket.

Barry examined her with the routine steps of inspection, palpation, percussion, and auscultation. The only additional positive findings were widespread rhonchi, musical squeaks that came up his stethoscope as Anne exhaled. He was as certain of his diagnosis as O'Reilly had been that his horse was going to win or, Barry corrected himself, Kinky had been.

"Nothing really to worry about. I'll give Guffer a yell, ask him to come up so I can explain to you both what's wrong and what we're going to do."

She was wracked with another coughing fit, but nodded her agreement.

He rose and took a step to the doorway. "Mister Galvin, come on up." Barry glanced at the book on the bed. "I see you still enjoy a good romance, Mrs. Galvin."

"Thanks to these—" she said, touching the glasses on her nose, then coughed, holding her chest and grimacing. "Thanks to these specs." The cough subsided and she relaxed into her pillow. "This here one takes place in some big plantation in Africa. The hero's lovely, so he is."

Guffer appeared and stood at the end of the bed. "You going to be all right, girl? I heard you coughing just now."

"Aye," she said, "and nice young Doctor Laverty here's going til explain it til us."

Barry nodded. "Anne, I'm sure you've got a touch of acute bronchitis."

"Boys-a-dear," Guffer said. "Is that like the brownkitees? There's a quare bit of it about at the shipyards."

Barry knew the man was a welder at Harland and Wolff's.

"One and the same, Mister Galvin," he said, "and your wife should be right as rain in a few days. I'm going to give you a scrip for the black bottle . . ."

"Dead on," said Guffer. "I'll nip down til the chemist in a wee minute."

The locals put great faith in *mist morph et ipecac*. The morphine was an excellent cough suppressant, which overrode the mild expectorant effects of the ipecacuanha.

"Yeugh," Anne said, and screwed up her face.

The ipecacuanha gave it its black colour and foul taste, thus, it was widely believed, enhancing the medicine's effectiveness. "Take two teaspoonsful every six hours." Barry took out his pad and scribbled the prescription.

"Thank you, sir." Guffer accepted the piece of paper. "Thanks very much. He's going til have you right in no time, love."

"Have you an electric kettle?"

"Aye."

"Bring it up, get the room steamy. That'll help. Light diet. Plenty of fluids . . ."

"I'll get you Lucozade when I'm at the chemist's," Guffer said.

"Good. And you'll be better in four or five days. I'll pop in tomorrow, and you know to send for us if you're worried."

"Excuse me, Doctor," Guffer said. "Now, I'm not trying to teach my granny how til suck eggs, but would them antibiotics be any use, like?"

Barry shook his head. "Mister Galvin, I'm a GP, not an infectious disease specialist, but the profs taught us when I was a student that antibiotics don't help coughs, colds, the flu, or acute bronchitis. And, you know, people can have severe reactions to those medicines. Safer to avoid them."

"Fair enough, but you don't mind me asking, sir?"

"Not at all, Mister Galvin." Barry half turned to go, but noticed a photo in a silver frame on the dresser. A young man, a pretty wife, a toddler, and babe in arms. "Is that Seamus and his family?" Barry still remembered with pleasure his first home delivery in Ballybucklebo, Seamus and Mary's little boy, named Barry Fingal Galvin in honour of his attending physicians. "Young Barry's growing like a weed, and I see they've got another."

"Wee girl called Colleen, and another one on the way, so they have," Anne said, and Barry detected sadness in her voice. She sighed. "Seamus writes twice a month. He's doing very good. He went out for til work for his big brother Pat, who owned a construction company. Pat's wife Jeannie is a lovely Dublin girl. Couldn't stand America, wanted to come home, so Pat had to sell the company to a Yankee. They moved back to Dublin a year ago, but Seamus loves it out there. He stayed on. He hasn't missed a day's work since he started."

"We're quare nor proud of him—of both of them," Guffer said.

"Och, we are, right enough," said Anne. "But hasn't it always been like this? Poor Irishmen leaving home for Liverpool or America or Canada and the ones across the Atlantic never ever getting home again."

"Aye," said Guffer, clearly to comfort his wife, "but that was back when there was sailing ships or liners and covered wagons and trains. There's jet planes now, so there is."

"Seamus never lets on in his letters," Anne said, "but I'm sure he's homesick."

"And Anne's very brave too," Guffer said. "She never moans about it, but I know fine well she misses our son, because I do, and what granny wouldn't want til see her grandchildren?" He looked fondly at his wife.

"That Maureen, she has her head screwed on good and tight." Anne coughed. "They will come home—one day. Maybe only for a visit, like, but I know they will." There was a catch in her voice.

"Aye," said Guffer, "but we have til get you better first. I'll get my bike out and—"

"Stick it in the back of my car, Mister Galvin," Barry said. "I'll give you a lift to the chemist and I'll pop by tomorrow just to be sure you're on the mend, Anne."

3

Walk Up and Down with Me

"That did be a very lovely afternoon, so," said Kinky, gently decanting Lady Macbeth from her lap and standing. "Thank you very much, Doctor and Kitty, for having us." Kinky and Archie had stayed after Ronald and Sue had left.

"Our pleasure," Kitty said. "We are delighted with your win." She smiled. "And Fingal and I will respect your request, won't we, dear?"

"Of course," O'Reilly said. "And will we see you on Monday morning as usual, Kinky? Or now that you're a rich woman, perhaps you'll have better things to do."

"You will see me, sir," Kinky said. "Even if I were the richest woman in all the six counties, I would still be here at Number One Main on Monday morning." Kinky gave O'Reilly a penetrating look and then she laughed and took her husband's hand. "Come along, Archie. The walk home will do us good, and I do have braised lamb shanks for our tea, bye. They are marinating now." She smiled at O'Reilly. "We'll see ourselves out. *Slán agat,* sir." The Irish leaver's good-bye.

"*Slán leat,*" O'Reilly gave the customary reply from the one staying behind. "Archie's a lucky duck," he said. O'Reilly could practically taste the delicate flavour of lamb accented by garlic, bay, rosemary, and thyme that Kinky used for the dish. Enough to make a fellah salivate. He sighed.

"Don't sigh, Fingal," Kitty said. "What do you think's on for our supper tonight?"

"I dunno."

"How many legs does a lamb have?"

"Usually four."

"And the other two are in our kitchen waiting to be popped in the oven. Kinky prepared them yesterday. And there's champ and spring cabbage and a roly-poly jam pudding for dessert."

"Lovely," he said, "and bugger the horse racing. Water under the bridge." He grabbed her, swung her to her feet, and kissed her soundly. "With you, Kitty O'Reilly, for a wife who I love dearly, Kinky still doing her magic in the kitchen, a partner I'd trust with my life doing my work for me, and a new assistant, I'm the luckiest man in all Ireland."

She laughed. "But if you don't get a bit of exercise, you'll not only be the luckiest, Fingal Flahertie O'Reilly, you'll be the tubbiest too. Let's take Arthur for a walk."

"You're on," said O'Reilly. "We'll head up into the Ballybucklebo Hills. It'll make a change from the shore, and Arthur'll be in his element pushing rabbits out of the whin bushes."

"I'll just be a jiffy," she said, heading for the hall, "I need to change. High heels and hills don't go very well together." He heard her light tread on the stairs and he took out his briar, filled it from his recent purchase, lit up, and puffed his contentment in blue clouds to the ceiling of the cosy room.

O'Reilly stopped at the end of a rutted lane in front of a rusty five-bar gate in a tall blackthorn hedge. The white flowers shone in the sun's rays. Before he could move, Kitty said, "I'll open the gate," and hopped out.

Arthur, sensing they had nearly arrived, intensified his usual refrain of throaty mutterings that had begun as soon as the Rover had left the main road for this country lane.

"Wheest, dog," O'Reilly said as he drove past Kitty at the gate to park in a grassy field. Waste of breath, he thought. It was the otherwise perfectly behaved gun dog's only flaw. He could never control his excitement when he realised he was in the country. O'Reilly found it endearing because it mirrored his own love of the outdoors. "Come on, old fellah," he said, climbing out of the Rover and opening the back door for Arthur.

O'Reilly inhaled the aroma of a stand of spruce trees off to his left and the distinctive odour of red fox. One must have passed by here recently or perhaps there was a den nearby. He reckoned a vixen might have newborn cubs. "Heel," he said to an excited Arthur, who had probably got the scent too, because his nose was to the ground, tail thrashing.

Arthur sighed and tucked in. O'Reilly walked to where Kitty stood after closing the gate. She was frowning and her right eyebrow was raised in a question. "Er, Fingal? What on earth is that?" She pointed.

A bicycle was propped against the hedge, but this was no ordinary velocipede. Someone had decorated it in multihued splendour. He laughed. "A biblical scholar would assume it belonged to Jacob to complement his coat of many colours, but, and I'm sure it'll come as no surprise, that machine is the property of one Donal Donnelly."

"Oh," Kitty said with a smile, "I suppose I should have guessed."

"It used to be black and rusty, but he got the idea of redoing it with the contents of some nearly finished cans of paint."

She looked more closely. "You know," she said, "he could probably exhibit it in a modern art gallery. It's like something Jackson Pollock would have done with his 'drip' technique. Give the thing a title like 'Rigid Rainbow.'"

O'Reilly laughed and said, "For God's sake, don't tell Donal. He'll start a production line and sell them for five quid a piece. You know what he's like." O'Reilly glanced round. "If Donal's bike's here, it's a fair bet so's Donal. Probably giving his greyhound Bluebird a run." He took her hand. "Come on, let's get our legs stretched."

They set off uphill across the grassy field.

"Hey on out."

A joyous Arthur ran off, nose to the ground, quartering from left to right, right to left.

Overhead a flock of argumentative black jackdaws flapped lazily across a sky done in pastels. Blue bird's-eye speedwell and red dove's-foot cranesbill flowered between the blades of grass. They only grew in land that was ploughed very infrequently.

Arthur crashed into a clump of yellow whins and out rushed two rabbits, grey-brown fur, long ears, bounding and jinking, heading for a warren farther uphill that O'Reilly had known about for years. He and Arthur occasionally came out here to shoot a rabbit for the pot.

Arthur, as a well-behaved gundog should, did not tear after the creatures, but sat so as not to obstruct his master's shot, which of course never came. Arthur looked up at O'Reilly. The panting dog shook his head as if to say, "Sometimes, boss, I wonder why I bother."

The rabbits had reached safety. "Hey on out, boy," and the big Lab trotted off again. There was a stiffness in the movements of his hind legs.

"He's having fun," Kitty said.

"But," said O'Reilly, "a couple of years ago he'd have raced off as fast as those rabbits. He's like me and my old gramophone. He's getting on. He's not as fast as he used to be."

Kitty squeezed O'Reilly's hand. "And you may not be boxing or playing rugby football anymore, but there's many a good tune played on an old fiddle."

"And there's life in my old dog yet. As long as he's fit, he'll have fun."

Kitty chuckled. "Sometimes, Doctor O'Reilly," she said, "you have a one-track mind."

He stopped, grabbed her, and kissed her. Hard. "Not true, Mrs. O'Reilly." He kissed her again. "There are lots of other things I think about," and he gave her bottom a squeeze.

Kitty burst out laughing. "A man of many appetites," she said, "and I do love you, but control yourself." She kissed him then he felt the tip of her tongue in his ear and heard her whisper, "Later." She looked past him. "Oh, Lord. Behave yourself, Fingal. Your friend Donal has just appeared from the spruce wood." She stepped back.

Sure enough, Donal Donnelly, sucking on a straw, tweed duncher set at a rakish angle over his carroty thatch, was striding at an angle downhill toward them. He carried a small sack in his right hand.

"How's about youse, Doctor and Mrs. O'Reilly," Donal called as he drew near. He was grinning from ear to ear, but was now holding the sack behind his back.

"Very well, Donal," O'Reilly said. "And yourself, and Julie, and wee Tori?" *What was in that sack?*

"We're all grand, thank you, sir. Julie's near halfway til her due date and Tori's walking by herself. She can use a spoon too. She's growing fast, so she is." He frowned. "I'm not sure she understands she's going til have a wee brother."

O'Reilly didn't want to spoil Donal's unshakeable belief by telling him that the birth ratio of boys to girls was about 101 to 100. An even-odds bet.

Arthur trotted up to see what was going on, accepted being patted by Donal, and sat at O'Reilly's feet, otter tail making lazy half circles through the grass.

"No Bluebird with you today, Donal?" Kitty asked. "Is she all right?"

"She's grand, but I left her at home." He shook his head. "I didn't want her messing things up, and I come over til ask you a wee favour, and all, sir. About Arthur."

"Arthur?" O'Reilly frowned, shrugged, and said, "Ask away."

"Could you, like, keep him out of the wee spruce wood, sir?"

O'Reilly was starting to put two and two together. Donal did not want dogs in the wood. Why? It marched with the Marquis of Ballybucklebo's estate. Technically, Donal wasn't on the marquis's land, although the birds had undoubtedly been bred by the marquis's gamekeeper. But game birds paid no heed to boundaries, and Donal Donnelly had been known to pay attention to game birds.

"Please, sir." Donal was beginning to look sheepish.

"Would this have anything to do with pheasants, Donal?"

"Och, Doctor O'Reilly." Donal hung his head.

"Tell," O'Reilly said. To be honest, if Donal were trying to "borrow" a few of John MacNeill's pheasants, they'd hardly be missed, and they would be added food on the table for Donal and his growing family. "Donal?" O'Reilly was more interested in how exactly Donal was going to do it.

Donal took a deep breath. His expression performed the usual localised Saint Vitus' dance that always accompanied his coming to a decision. "You'll not tell nobody nothing, sir? Please?"

O'Reilly guffawed. "Sure amn't I your doctor, Donal? I'm not allowed to tell anybody what a patient tells me."

Kitty said, "That goes for nurses too."

"Stickin' out a mile," Donal said with a vast buck-toothed grin. He produced the sack. "This here's barley, so it is." He opened the neck.

O'Reilly nearly banged his head into Kitty's as they both leant forward to peer in at the beige-coloured grains.

"I've been baiting the wood for a week, so I have, and when I come out last night for til see—the moon's been a waning crescent all week, so its dead dark and tomorrow night it's a new moon—anyroad, six birds was roosting in the trees and—"

"You're setting the real bait for tonight?" O'Reilly had caught a whiff of what might have been whiskey coming from the sack.

"Yes, sir."

"Not soaked in good Jameson or Bushmills, I hope?"

A look of horror crossed Donal's face. "Indeed no, sir. Not at all. That would be hearsay, so it would."

"I think you mean heresy," Kitty corrected gently.

"Right enough, heresy. No. I used Scotch whisky, it's only fit for cooking with anyway, til soak the grain. I'd not waste good Irish."

"That is a relief," said O'Reilly. "So please explain to Mrs. O'Reilly how this all works."

Donal took a deep breath. "Do you see," he said, "you get the birds used til coming for the grain, then when they are, you set out the whisky-soaked stuff. Along comes your birds, gobble gobble, up a tree til roost, off til sleepy-byes, but the birds is getting hammered."

Kitty chuckled. "I've heard of 'drunk as a lord' and 'drunk as a skunk,' but—"

"It's as properly and potently pissed as a paralytic pheasant, Missus," Donal said.

O'Reilly and Kitty laughed.

"And them birds can't lock their feet, so they need to keep a grip to stay on the roost while they are asleep. When the drink gets to the pheasant, the talons open up and the birds drop off their perches like ripe apples from the trees in September."

Kitty clapped her hands and laughed out loud. "Donal," she said, "if it wasn't, I am sure, illegal, it would be brilliant."

"Aye," said Donal, "and the best bit is when you wring the bird's neck . . ."

Kitty shuddered.

"They're still stocious and they don't feel nothing."

"I am glad to hear it," Kitty said.

"Just one more thing," O'Reilly said. "Do you take cocks and hens?"

Donal blew out his cheeks. His eyes blazed. He snorted and came close to stamping his foot. Clearly his honour had been impugned. "Dear God, I'd never take a hen. Not never. Them's for breeding for next season." He grinned. "Once they get over tomorrow morning's hangovers."

Or being breakfast for the fox, O'Reilly thought. Mind you, being a meal for one was an occupational hazard of being a bird.

Donal, still indignant, said, "A man who'd take a hen would steal his oul granny's last farthing, so he would."

O'Reilly laughed. "I apologise, Donal. I always knew you were one of nature's gentlemen, but I had to ask."

Donal, obviously mollified, said, "That's all right then. No offence taken." He closed the sack. "It was grand seeing youse both," he said, "and old Arthur." He patted the dog's head and was rewarded with a Lab grin. "Now, if youse'll excuse me?" He nodded in the direction of the spruce. "I'll be off." He began to stride away.

O'Reilly called after him. "Donal. One small thing. It's not illegal to take the marquis's birds if they're not on his property, but they are out of season. Don't get caught."

"Me?" His laugh rang across the field. "Catch me? Not a snowball's chance." Donal's parting wave was cheery as he disappeared among the trees.

"I hope not," O'Reilly said, turning to Kitty. "Taking game birds out of season is not taken lightly in these parts. A hundred years ago, you'd get a one-way trip to Terra Australis Incognita, the great unknown southland, to sample the delights of Botany Bay." He sang,

> . . . Sure she'll wait and hope and pray
> for her love in Botany Bay
> it's so lonely 'round the fields of Athenry

"Now it's just a dirty great fine." He patted his pockets, looking for his new Erinmore tobacco. A rustling of paper came from over his inside breast pocket. Pipe forgotten, he fished out an envelope. "I forgot all about this letter. It was in the post today. With all the excitement I never got round to reading it." Stamped on the outside was the coat of arms of Queen's University with its red hand for Ulster, seahorse for Belfast, book for learning, and harp for Ireland, surrounding the royal crown. Beneath it were the words "Department of General Practice." What on earth could they want with him? He was no academic. He was a country GP and proud of it.

He used a finger to tear the flap open.

"Is it important?" Kitty asked.

"Hang on." He read,

Dear Doctor O'Reilly,
    As professor of the newly formed department of general practice of the medical faculty of the Queen's University of Belfast . . .

O'Reilly read on silently and said, "There's lot of going on in here about 'the exciting dawn of a new speciality' and their plans for future GPs. Sounds to me like the death of the old GPs like me and Barry." He read on. "Ah," he said. "There's the rub."

I have been advised by two senior colleagues, Sir Donald Cromie and Mister Charles Greer, that you are an exemplary practitioner and someone to whose practice we would wish to consider attaching GP trainees . . .

He shook his head. "Me? A teacher? I dunno, Kitty. The new professor, George Irwin, wants me to go up to the Royal for a meeting with him next week." He shoved the letter back inside his jacket, dragged out his well-used half-smoked briar, and lit up. He'd used that tactic for years when he wanted to collect his thoughts.

"Think about it, Fingal," said Kitty. "Go to the meeting, hear what they've to say, and then decide. You might just enjoy it, you know. My mother always says mixing with young people keeps her young."

He laughed. "And sure isn't that why I keep you around, Kitty O'Reilly née O'Hallorhan? Come on. Give me a kiss and we'll get on our way."

Hand in hand they tramped uphill.

"You're probably right. I might enjoy it. There'd be no harm in finding out." He had to help Arthur over a stile in a dry stone wall before mounting the step and offering his hand to Kitty.

"Thanks," Kitty said, taking the hand and clambering up as O'Reilly leapt down on the other side.

She jumped down beside him. "There is one thing though, if you do decide to accept a trainee."

"Oh?"

"Well, Barry will be moving out once he's married."

"True."

"And Kinky has her own home now and Nonie only sleeps in on her night on call. We're going to have a lot more privacy."

O'Reilly patted the pocket that contained the letter and took a puff from his briar. "That's true," he said absently. He was thinking ahead to his meeting with George Irwin. "I'm sure having a youngster working with us, being taught, may slow things down at first, but once they can work independently, take call, I'm going to have more time off. You know, Mrs. O'Reilly, you and I could be spending more time together out in the country like we are now. Particularly if you slowed down a bit too."

She smiled. "You mean take on fewer hours at the hospital? We've talked about it before, and trust me, Fingal, I will think about it."

Not quite the answer he had been hoping for, but not a flat refusal either. He'd keep working at it. "And I heard what you said about taking a holiday on my then hoped-for but now nonexistent winnings. I don't see why we shouldn't, you know." A new gramophone could wait.

"You are a pet, old bear," she said. "Paris perhaps? I'd love to go to the Louvre."

"I'll think about it. I went to Paris in '59 to watch Ireland play France at the rugby," he said, echoing her words. "But what is the 'one thing,' if I accept a trainee?"

She stopped walking and turned to him. "I'd rather they didn't lodge with us. We'll have a lot more privacy once Barry finds a house and moves . . ." She grinned and raised one eyebrow.

Was she hinting that . . . ? He felt a frisson. She laughed out loud and pointed to the crest of the ridge forty yards away.

"But later. I'll race you to the top now. Ready? Steady. Go."

Legs pounding, wind burning in his unfit lungs, Fingal O'Reilly ran after her. By God, that had been no hint. That was the second time this afternoon she'd said "Later." And he loved her very dearly for it. Would he take her to Paris soon? Too bloody true he would.

4

Giving Your Heart to a Dog

Lars stood in bright sunlight on the sandstone steps of his ivy-covered house on Portaferry's Shore Road. "Welcome, you two. Pleasant drive down?"

"Very. Strangford Lough was at its best, and it's lovely to see you, my dear," Kitty said.

They followed Lars along the hall and into a spacious living room with some of the late Mrs. O'Reilly's oil paintings on the walls. A large picture window, which now replaced the original three tall narrow Georgian ones, gave views over the Strangford Narrows to the left, the lough to the right, and the eight hundred mostly landscaped acres of the Castleward Estate, until recently home of the Viscounts Bangor since the 1760s.

O'Reilly stood at the window. He never tired of watching the crabbing progress of the little car ferry from Portaferry, Port á Fheire, the landing place of the ferry, to Strangford Town. He knew the current in the Narrows was strong and could run at ten knots at peak flow.

Lars showed Kitty to an armchair and O'Reilly turned reluctantly from the view and took one beside hers. "Sun's over the yardarm," Lars said. "Drinks?"

"Sherry, please, and I'm sure Fingal will have a Jameson."

"So am I. Sure, that is," Lars said. "I've known him for a long time." He started pouring.

O'Reilly noticed an almost finished packet of Cadbury's chocolate digestive biscuits on a plate beside the core of an apple. A teapot and mug kept them company on a tray on a coffee table. He frowned. Lars was not a fussy man but it wasn't like him not to clear off when he'd finished.

Lars gave Kitty her sherry, O'Reilly his whiskey, and stood with his back to the window. He raised his glass. "Your health."

"*Sláinte.*"

"Cheers."

O'Reilly thought his brother would, like courtiers of old, indulge himself in the usual social pleasantries before coming to the crux of the matter. It would be typical of Lars to keep the conversation light, beat about the bush for a while before taking the leap. Fair enough. He took a sip of his Jameson and settled into the chair. He could wait.

Lars took a deep breath. "Thank you both for coming. I hinted that what I need advice about is urgent, and I'd like to get right down to brass tacks."

"Would you lads like to be on your own?" Kitty said, starting to rise from her chair.

"Not at all, Kitty," Lars said. "I very much want you to be a part of this." He swallowed. "I'm sorry to have been so mysterious," he said, "not wanting to talk about it over the phone."

"Some things need to be discussed together," O'Reilly said. "What's bothering you, Lars?"

"It involves Myrna," he said, and sighed. "I'm going to have to hurt her and I'd hate to."

"Now how would you do that, Lars?" she asked gently.

O'Reilly heard the concern in her voice.

Lars walked over to the window, stared out, then turned. "May I ask you a medical question, Finn?"

Medical question? What could something medical do to hurt Myrna? He wasn't sure he liked where this was going. "Fire away."

"As a doctor, Finn, what would you say if I told you every time I go near something my skin itches, my eyes water, and my nose runs?"

"I'd say you were allergic to it."

"I thought you might," Lars said. "All very embarrassing." He shook his head.

For a second O'Reilly seriously wondered if his brother was becoming allergic to Lady Myrna O'Neill, the woman he so recently had fallen in love with. The adage from the immunologists was, "You can be allergic to anything under the sun—including the sun," but he'd never heard of a person allergy. Was his brother about to make medical history?

"And could one have been exposed to—I believe you physicians call the noxious matter an allergen . . ."

"That's right."

"Could one have been exposed to the allergen for years without any difficulties and then, for no apparent reason, be struck down out of the blue, as it were?"

"Happens all the time," O'Reilly said.

"Thank God. I thought perhaps I was imagining it." Lars inhaled deeply. Shrugged. "Myrna and I came back here last Saturday after we got home from France. We went for a walk over the fields, just like you and I did once when we saw old Willie Caulwell using his ferrets to catch rabbits. Myrna and I passed by Barney's grave."

"Barney was Lars's springer spaniel," O'Reilly explained to Kitty.

"I told her what a great dog he'd been. That I still missed him. She was sympathetic, very sympathetic, and last Wednesday she showed up unexpectedly." He started for the door. "Will you please come with me?"

A puzzled O'Reilly and a frowning Kitty followed.

Lars stopped in front of the kitchen door and listened. Silence.

"What is it, Lars?" said O'Reilly.

From behind the door came a series of high-pitched yips and the sound of claws scrabbling on wood.

"I'd like you to go in," Lars said, ushering them into the kitchen, but hanging back, holding the door almost closed.

Immediately a ball of canine brown fur, all feet and ears, wagging its whole body, hurled itself at O'Reilly's legs, then reared up and put its forepaws on O'Reilly's thigh.

Lars, speaking through the crack in the doorframe, said, "Meet Kenny. He's a chocolate Labrador, pedigree as long as your arm. His full name's Carlow Charger of Kilkenny. Myrna went to great lengths to find him, and I shudder to think what she must have paid. She's daft about the little chap. He's three months old. I confess he soon found a place in my heart too—"

Hearing his name, Kenny redoubled the rate of his tail-wagging and gave a series of excited yips.

"Until yesterday afternoon." Lars sneezed mightily. His eyes reddened. "Oh Lord," he said, "it's starting again. I'm an exile from my own kitchen. I gave him the run of the room yesterday, last night, and this morning. Thank the Lord for the Portaferry Arms or I'd have starved.

"I managed to put up with it long enough to leave him plenty of puppy chow, water, toys, a chewy rawhide 'bone.' They need to chew at that age to bring on their teeth. Puppy papers." He cleared his throat. "I did my best for the little chap, then I bolted and phoned you." He sighed. "Without company, the poor wee thing must have been lonely, but at least at that age they sleep a lot."

O'Reilly saw the bowls and doggy toys scattered hither and yon and not just puddles on the papers.

"You see my dilemma?"

"I do," said Kitty.

"I fear I must let the dog go, but Myrna will be so disappointed, she'll miss the beast, and I'd not want to do anything to hurt her. She said she'd picked a Lab rather than a springer because Labs are more docile, easier to train."

"It's hardly your fault you're allergic," O'Reilly said, getting down on his haunches to pet the wiggling brown ball. "Antihistamines might work short term. A really bad attack will respond to adrenaline injections, but the best treatment is to avoid the allergen completely."

Lars sneezed again and scratched at his left forearm. "Please excuse me." He fled, closing the door behind him.

"Well, Kitty, it's hardly a diagnostic mystery. Lars is allergic to the animal," O'Reilly said.

Kitty squatted, clicked her tongue. "The effects wouldn't be particularly dangerous, I suppose, but they would be thoroughly unpleasant." The pup ran to her, lay down, and rolled on his back. She tickled his tummy. "Poor Lars," said Kitty. "All those years without a dog and now that he has one . . . Oh, you're so cute, Kilkenny," she said, grinning mightily.

"He's a cute problem," O'Reilly said. "I know my brother. He's worried he'll upset Myrna if he has to give the dog up, but medically I can't see any way out." He scratched his chin.

"You could explain the medical aspects to Myrna. She's an intelligent woman. She'll be disappointed, but she'll understand, I'm certain."

"I agree. I wonder if Lars isn't being a bit pessimistic about how she'll react?" Pleased as he always was to see his brother, O'Reilly didn't quite see why this couldn't have been discussed over the phone.

"And if she knows Kenny's going to a good home? That might please her too. She could see the wee button regularly." Kitty picked up the pup and held the wriggling bundle in front of her face, to be rewarded with a series of loving licks. There was deep fondness in her voice when she said, "Kinky would call him a wee dote. I think he's adorable."

O'Reilly frowned. What was Kitty hinting? His eyes widened. "No," he said. "Oooh no." He backed toward the door. His old friends from medical school used to call him the Wily O'Reilly, but this time it looked like he'd been well and truly outmanoeuvred by his elder brother. Lars had wanted Kitty to see the pup and fall in love—and you can't do that over the phone. "My love, aren't Arthur and Lady Macbeth a big enough menagerie at Number One? And what with Barry and Nonie, Kinky, and possibly a student in the house, the place will be a circus. And I thought," O'Reilly said, arching an eyebrow, "you wanted more privacy."

"Don't be silly," Kitty said, "one little puppy won't make that much difference, and Arthur Guinness will be delighted with the company. Probably make him feel five years younger. Probably make us feel ten years younger."

"I'm not worried about old Arthur," O'Reilly said, "but what about Lady Macbeth?"

A faint cry of "Finn" came from the direction of the hall.

"Hang on to the pup, Kitty," said O'Reilly, and opened the kitchen door. There was no sign of Lars. "Lars? Lars?" No reply, but O'Reilly could hear a faint rapid wheezing coming from the lounge. An allergy to dog dandruff or hair could bring on an asthmatic attack. "Quick,

Kitty," O'Reilly called. "Shut Kenny in, then go get my bag from the car and give me a hand."

"Right." She left at the run.

He found Lars slumped in an armchair, head thrown back, eyes watering. His lips were a slatey blue. Cyanosis from oxygen deprivation. There was pleading in his eyes as he looked into O'Reilly's and gasped, "Can't—" wheeze, "can't breathe." He was having more difficulty exhaling than inhaling, typical of the partial obstruction caused by a bronchial muscle spasm. O'Reilly began undoing the top buttons of his brother's shirt, then took his pulse. Rapid at one hundred per minute, but not a serious tachycardia. O'Reilly knew his brother had no previous history of asthma, nor was there any reason to suspect this attack had been brought on by infection. He said, perfectly confident in his diagnosis without any need for auscultating Lars's chest with a stethoscope, "You're having an asthmatic attack brought on by your allergy. I'll have you right as rain in a few minutes."

Lars nodded.

Kitty arrived, clutching the worn leather medical bag in her arms. "Adrenaline one to one thousand for subcutaneous injection?"

"Please."

Kitty opened the bag and began her preparations. "I'm going to give you a slow injection, brother. It may make your heart rate even faster. If you feel palpitations, tell me and I'll stop at once."

Lars nodded and wheezed on.

"Here." Kitty handed O'Reilly a syringe and a cotton-wool ball soaked in methylated spirits. "Point five millilitres."

"Thanks." O'Reilly rolled up Lars's shirtsleeve, swabbed the skin on the inside of his arm, pinched up a fold, and slid the needle in. He began to increase the pressure on the plunger. To reduce the risk of severe tachycardia, he was going to use Hurst's method of injecting: 1 minim, of which there were 8.5 in the syringe, per minute until the attack ceased.

Kitty and Lars said nothing as they watched O'Reilly slowly and steadily push the needle's plunger. There was no sound in the house. Even Kenny's whimpers and yips had subsided. Five minutes later, with less than half the amount left in the syringe, Lars's wheezing eased and stopped.

O'Reilly withdrew the needle. "There," he said. "Feeling better?"

Lars drew in a slow, even breath. "I don't think I ever truly appreciated breathing until I couldn't," said Lars. "Thank you very much, you two." He swallowed and managed a weak smile. "Sometimes it comes in handy to have medics in the family."

"And for once," O'Reilly said, hiding his concern for his brother, "the old saw 'doctors who treat their own family have idiots for patients' is not true. I'm going to give you a prescription for isoprenaline sulphate, twenty milligrams. If you ever get another attack, pop half a tablet under your tongue."

"I hope I never have to use it, but thanks." Lars buttoned his shirt sleeve and began to do up his collar.

"But we don't think you will have to use it, do we, Fingal?" Kitty said. "I'm sure you'd agree that Myrna can hardly be upset with Lars now. Asthmatic attacks are a serious condition." Her smile was beatific. "The source of the problem must be removed, and I honestly think—"

You clever minx, O'Reilly thought.

"I honestly think we could have little Kenny in our family. Don't you? We can take him with us when we go."

O'Reilly grinned. Game, set, and match to Lars and Kitty O'Reilly. "If that's all right with Lars?"

"All right? I should be eternally grateful," Lars said, "and I'm sure Myrna will be relieved too, that the little lad will still be in the family, so to speak." He laughed as he did up the buttons of his shirt. "Now, I'm feeling much better. Perhaps we should finish our pre-luncheon drinks and head on down to the Arms?"

"That," said O'Reilly with an innocent smile, "is a splendid idea, but you've just had adrenaline, big brother. I'd suggest we finish ours, but that you heel tap until we get to the pub." Lars was by no means a bowsey, but it still gave O'Reilly a little secret pleasure to get one back at the big brother who had just pulled a fast one with an allergenic pup.

5

The Weaker Vessel

Barry was driving as fast as he dared along the rutted lane to Lewis and Gracie Miller's seaside bungalow. Gracie's panicked words had come tumbling over the phone not fifteen minutes before. "It's my Lewis. He's slumped over the kitchen table and he won't wake up." A muffled sob. "For God's sake, come as quick as you can. Please." The line had gone dead.

Had he had a heart attack? A stroke? Internal bleeding? For a man in his early eighties, all were possible and all very urgent.

O'Reilly, no slouch when it came to breaking speed limits, would have been proud of how fast Barry had raced out to his patient. He would assess Lewis and then decide if an ambulance was needed. If he'd had a heart attack then he'd need the newly introduced cardiac flying squad with its portable defibrillator. But Barry knew it would be irresponsible to tie it up if Lewis had some other condition.

He parked outside the low back wall, grabbed his doctor's bag from the passenger's seat, and hurried through the back garden to the door.

It opened. "Thank God you've come, sir." Gracie was a small woman but she grabbed Barry by the arm with surprising strength and hurried him into her cosy kitchen redolent of roasting chicken before slamming the door. She wrung her reddened hands. A single tear trickled under her tortoiseshell-framed spectacles and down her wrinkled cheek. Wisps of iron-grey hair straggled from her bun. "He's still out like a light, Doctor, but he's breathing."

"Good. That's good, Gracie." Barry gently detached her hand from his arm, then tore off his overcoat and duncher and flung them on a chair beside the kitchen table, where Lewis had his head cradled between a plate of biscuits and a side plate that lay overturned on a rumpled red tablecloth. The retired postman's head was turned to one side, his spectacles half-dislodged from the bridge of his nose. His sandy hair was tousled and Barry saw beads of sweat on pink patches of scalp.

"I'm terrible sorry, sir. I should've tidied up, but I was too scared to do nothing, so I was. All I wanted was for you til get here." She sniffled, wrung her hands. "I didn't know what til do."

"It's all right, Gracie," Barry said. "There was nothing you could do, but send for me."

"Right enough." He heard relief in her voice. "I've been talking to him, like. I don't think he can hear me, but I keep asking him to wake up."

Barry ignored the cold tea dribbling from a smashed teacup on the tiled floor at Lewis's carpet-slippered feet. The man's trousers were soaked too. Thank the Lord he was still breathing and it was deep and regular. The tongue of a patient who had passed out could block the airway and cause suffocation, but was not a risk here. Barry held Lewis's wrist to take his pulse. His skin was clammy. Barry counted a steady ninety-two firm beats per minute. It would be racing and thready if there were major internal bleeding, and irregular if there were atrial fibrillation associated with a heart attack. Barry felt a little less concerned.

It would be better if the patient could be moved to a couch or bed, but Barry doubted if he and Gracie could carry Lewis between them so decided to leave the man where he was.

"Can you tell me what happened, Gracie?"

"Him and me was having a wee cup of tea in our hands. He kind of moaned, then he says, 'Holy Mother, I can't see nothing from my left eye' and fell forward. He dropped his teacup. I screamed and I asked him what was wrong, but he never said nothing. I shook him, but he wouldn't wake up, so I ran til the phone . . ."

"You did exactly the right thing," Barry said. And what she had told him had given him enough to formulate a working diagnosis. A heart attack was unlikely. No crushing chest pain or pain radiating up into the jaw or down an arm. Nor was the pulse rate irregular. It was possible that Lewis Miller had had a bleed from a brain blood vessel or a thrombosis of one, either referred to colloquially as a "stroke," but the loss of sight in one eye was more suggestive of disease of the left internal carotid artery, the great vessel which with its partner on the right were the major suppliers of oxygenated blood to the brain. If it were narrowed by fatty plaques of atheroma, blood flow would be impeded and an early sign of that was loss of sight on the same side as the vessel. It was a condition from which quite a few sufferers survived the first attack without permanent nerve damage.

No matter the exact diagnosis, there was little any doctor could do in the home for any of the potential causes. Lewis Miller would need to be admitted to hospital to establish a firm diagnosis and receive expert nursing. "Gracie," he said, "I think Lewis may have had a thing like a wee stroke."

"Dear God, that's desperate." She bit her knuckles. "Oh, Doctor, will he die?"

I don't know. He might, Barry thought, but he couldn't bring himself to give an honest answer. Not yet anyway. The truth was he simply didn't know. He put his hands on Gracie's shoulders and looked into her eyes, seeing the pleading in their depths. "I think the big artery, here"—he put two fingers on the side of Lewis's neck—"may be a bit narrow, but I don't think he'll die."

She took a deep breath. "Thank you, Doctor."

Sometimes comfort was kinder than the truth. "But we'll need to get him up to the Royal Victoria Hospital in Belfast. I'll arrange that right away."

"Phone's in the hall, sir."

Barry rang the Royal. "Come on, come on." Hospital switchboards were notorious for their slowness in answering. As he waited, he looked out through the glass panels of the front door of the bungalow, a house he'd started thinking of as his own. He and Sue were hoping to buy it once the Millers finally decided to sell. The lough was powder blue with ranks of white etchings and the Antrim Hills, purple in the distance, blended with a baby blue sky. Sue was going to love it here.

"Get a move on," he muttered, and for a second wondered if he were talking to the switchboard or most uncharitably encouraging the Millers to sell. He knew Gracie had had some hesitations and now with Lewis . . . Stop it, he told himself. Trying to predict the future is a waste of time and energy. Concentrate on your patient.

"Royal Victoria Hospital switchboard."

Barry soon learned that wards 5 and 6 were on "take in" today, accepting emergencies on a twenty-four-hour rotational basis with other medical wards. He asked to speak with the duty registrar, explained the situation, and was told an ambulance would be dispatched and a neurologist consulted, if need be, after the patient had been assessed. "Just keep his airway clear. There's not much more GPs can do." That last with a touch of condescension. "Thank you, gotta go, it's Bedlam here. Good-bye."

Not much more I can do? Barry blew out a deep breath as he replaced the receiver none too gently. Some of these self-satisfied specialist trainees, who only had to be knowledgeable in their own narrow field, should spend a bit of time in general practice. Might help them understand the difficulties of practising without access to all the sophisticated equipment in a hospital.

And, damn it, there was more he could do, Barry thought as he headed back to the kitchen. Make Lewis comfortable, examine him in greater detail. It might be professional pride, but GPs weren't mere signposts to direct the sick to the right specialist. Barry took satisfaction from making accurate diagnoses with the limited resources at his disposal. And he could support Gracie until the ambulance arrived.

"Doctor. Come quick." Had the man taken a turn for the worse?

Barry entered the kitchen at a trot to find Lewis sitting upright and Gracie resettling his spectacles over his grey eyes. "Glory be, he's woke up there now, Doctor, but I can't make out what he's saying."

Spittle ran from the drooping right corner of Lewis's mouth.

Gracie wiped it off with a hanky.

His face lacked all expression and he said in a monotone, "I muh ha fawn aheep," which Barry interpreted as "I must have fallen asleep." Dysphasia, difficulty in speaking, could be associated with a stroke caused by either a clot in a blood vessel in the brain or bleeding into the brain or disease of the carotid artery. Following a stroke, it never fully recovered. It might, though, if the artery were the cause.

"You had a wee turn, Lewis," Barry said, "but you're on the mend."

"Ank oo."

"Is Lewis right-or left-handed, Gracie?"

"Right," she said, "I'm the cack-handed one." Her giggle was one of nervousness. She held up her left hand. "I had it tied behind me back at school when I was wee, so I did, so I could learn til write with my right hand. I do, so I do, but I'm still a leftie for the rest."

"Poor you," Barry said. "It's important for me to know about Lewis. Thank you." The information of his right-sided dominance would help Barry piece the puzzle together. He knelt beside the man's chair. "Lewis, I'm going to ask you to do a few things. All right?"

"Awight."

Barry grasped his patient's left hand. "Squeeze my hand." The grip was firm, but the same request was met by a feeble response when the right hand was tested. At least this was only paresis, weakness of voluntary movement, rather than paralysis, complete loss of activity. "How does your left side feel?"

"Fine."

"And your right?"

"I've tebbil pins a eedles." Although slurred, his speech was improving and there was no sign of the intellectual impairment that often accompanied such an episode. That was a good sign. Paraesthesiae, heightened sensations, on the one side was also typical of cerebral damage or at least temporary oxygen deprivation. Whatever was afflicting Lewis was doing so on the left side of his brain, which received nerve signals directly from the left eye and in a right-handed patient controlled speech, interpreted sensations from the right side of the body, and sent control messages along the nerves to make the right limbs move. The key to deciding if the underlying cause was a stroke or narrowing of the left carotid artery would be the speed of recovery of function.

Barry felt optimistic that the root cause lay in the artery and that there was the possibility of a full recovery in the short term. "I'm sure," he said, "that the worst is over."

"Thank God for that," Gracie said, and began to cry softly. "I don't know what I'd do without the oul' fellah." She put a trembling hand on her husband's shoulder and he reached up to grasp it with his left hand.

Barry knew the Millers had been married for sixty years. Although he and Sue were only on the threshold of their marriage, he couldn't bear the thought of life without her either. What Gracie was going through he could only imagine. His heart ached for the Millers. Recovery from a stroke would be slow and was never complete. Even if his diagnosis was right and full recovery was possible, there was at least a 10 percent risk of a full-blown lethal interruption of blood supply to the brain within the next forty-eight hours. Once again he decided to keep that information to himself. Let Gracie have her bit of comfort.

Modern medicine could diagnose carotid narrowing by angiography, injecting radio opaque material into the artery and taking a series of X-rays. He had heard that an American surgeon, Doctor Michael DeBakey, had operated successfully on such a patient in 1953, but here in Ulster in 1967 no one was doing such procedures. He sighed. In fairness, he supposed Lewis was already ahead of the odds. Average life expectancy for a man was about seventy years, but Barry knew that Gracie Miller was not thinking about actuarial tables. She was thinking about the prospect of life without her husband of sixty years, and the thought must be terrifying. Barry sighed. He did not have much more comfort to offer, but he could keep her occupied and get Lewis tucked up warm and comfortable while they waited another half hour for the ambulance. "Gracie, have you a wheen of pillows and a rug?"

"I do, sir. I'll run away off and grab a clatter and we can make my oul fellah more comfy. I'll be back in a wee minute."

"Great," Barry said.

She was smiling as she left.

"Doctor," Lewis said, "thank you for coming. I was scared skinny I'd gone blind, but"— he managed a weak chuckle— "for a man that's had a cataract fixed I'm seeing bravely now, so I am, and my right side's stopped tingling. That was bloody awful, so it was." Barry felt himself relax a little more. This was a rapid recovery. Lewis's speech was showing no signs of its earlier distortion.

Lewis yawned mightily. He said, "I think I'll just take a wee nap," and slowly drifted off to snore softly.

Barry was not concerned, but wished he could make a completely accurate diagnosis, although there were no definitive tests or imaging techniques that would give an exact diagnosis in this case. Indeed, it had been the *craic* when he'd been a student that neurology, the specialty dealing with nervous diseases, was often a competition between the clinician and the pathologist for the correct diagnosis. Barry would bet a great deal that his patient's "turn" had been temporary reduction of blood flow to the brain due to a narrow artery. And it was satisfying to be able to think that. But what the future held for the man, Barry Laverty had no idea. And if they were honest with themselves, the specialists didn't either. Even under the best circumstances, it couldn't be rosy for any man of eighty-two years.

Barry had once before been so dissatisfied with how little GPs could do, he had flirted with the notion of specialising, spending six months as a trainee obstetrician. But in the end, the satisfaction of working closely with patients had won out. Today, though, that arrogant registrar had hit a raw nerve. Barry remembered one of his classmates who had been convinced he could make a much bigger contribution in the long run by going into research. Finding a way to prevent diseases rather than trying to treat them one by one. The man was finishing his Ph.D. this year. Barry shook his head. Nah. Living here, accepted as an important part of village society, having a colleague like Fingal, on the verge of wedded bliss—and starting a family. The thought sent a trill of sensation through Barry's stomach, whether of excitement or panic he wasn't sure. Sue was certainly bound and determined that soon after they'd moved in here, one bedroom would become a nursery. He frowned and let the thought go. Gracie had returned. "I'll give you a hand," he said, holding Lewis forward so she could tuck a pillow behind his back.

"Thanks a million, Doctor," she said, spreading a tartan rug over her husband's lap and legs. "I'll just have til baby you for a wee while, dear," she said, and there was such intense love in her voice, Barry suddenly felt like an intruder and had to look away.

6

Touch Not the Cat

O'Reilly sat in the Rover with Kitty cuddling a sleeping Kenny beside him. "I hope we don't come to regret my suggestion of bringing Kenny home with us," she whispered. "I'm sure he's going to be all right with Arthur." Kitty pursed her lips. "But Lady Macbeth?"

Is this how Kitty had looked holding a baby when she'd worked in that orphanage in Tenerife before the war? His heart swelled and he stroked his index finger lightly over her cheek, then over the velvet fur of the puppy's head.

"I have a plan."

"You always have a plan, Fingal O'Reilly. The most resourceful man I know. It's one of the reasons I fell in love with you." She paused. "Then and now."

He turned off the engine and gave her a grateful look. "I suggest you find her ladyship, bring her into the kitchen. I'll introduce Arthur to what I hope is going to be his new friend. Then we'll collect all Kenny's bits and pieces. My plan is to leave Kenny with Arthur and take the things with Kenny's scent on them into the kitchen. See how her ladyship reacts."

"Fine by me," Kitty said. "The wee dote." She kissed the top of Kenny's head, then handed over the drowsy puppy. "Here."

They got out and headed for the back gate. The moment Kitty opened it, Arthur Guinness stuck his head out of his kennel, grinned, and trotted out to greet his people, tail going to and fro like an overheated semaphore.

"Hello, Arthur," said Kitty, patting the big dog's head.

"Lie down, sir," said O'Reilly.

Obediently, the Labrador sat, then flopped onto his tummy, front legs stretched out in front of him, tail still going like the hammers of hell. He sniffed and stared at the bundle in O'Reilly's arms. Arthur cocked his head to one side, his eyebrows working up and down.

O'Reilly squatted and offered Kenny for Arthur to sniff. He raised his muzzle, sniffed twice, and nodded. Kenny woke up and O'Reilly set him on the grass. The puppy wobbled, found his too-big feet, and when he saw Arthur his hackles rose, his legs stiffened, his tail stuck out, and he gave a belligerent "yip."

"Male pups are already instinctively ready to try to become pack leader," O'Reilly said. "Don't think it's going to work with old Arthur."

Arthur Guinness grumbled low in his throat, let his upper lip curl and a sliver of white canine tooth show.

The impertinent pup, realising he was having ideas well above his station, whimpered and rolled wriggling onto his back in abject submission.

Arthur lowered his square head—and licked the pup's tummy.

Kenny squirmed upright, leapt back stiff-legged, and charged, tail going so hard it moved his whole rear quarters.

"Feisty little devil," Kitty said.

Arthur put one forepaw on the pup's head. For a moment Kenny stood still then took one step back and licked the paw.

"Ah, truce. Let's see what happens now," O'Reilly said. He started to walk across the grass. "Heel." Arthur followed and Kenny bounded after like a small dinghy in the wake of a large keelboat. "Seems to me," said O'Reilly, "they've established who's master." He stopped. "Sit."

Arthur obeyed, but the puppy charged, yipping around Arthur, O'Reilly, and Kitty before pushing between Arthur's front legs, turning round, sitting, and panting.

"Well," Kitty said, surveying the pair, "that's one step over. You three wait here." She headed for the house.

O'Reilly said, "Stay," and wandered off back up the garden. He turned. Arthur hadn't budged, but Kenny was staring at O'Reilly, clearly wanting to run to him but confused that Arthur hadn't. "Stay," O'Reilly repeated.

Kenny must have taken that for an invitation. He started off, but Arthur leant forward and, with the gentleness he used when retrieving a bird, lifted Kenny by the scruff of his neck, brought him back, and set him on the grass.

Good Lord. Arthur Guinness was instructing the wee fellah.

"Come." Arthur used his muzzle to nudge Kenny toward their master and followed the little lad to O'Reilly's side.

"Sit." Arthur immediately obeyed and, after looking at his mentor, Kenny followed suit. O'Reilly guffawed. "Good dogs," he said in the same level tones he'd used for years to reward Arthur for obeying commands. It was really all it took to train such an amenable breed: consistency, firmness, and love, with occasional tangible rewards for everything done right.

"What were you laughing at?" Kitty asked, returning from the house.

O'Reilly explained.

"Pity the Arthur Guinness School of Animal Training never worked with Lady Macbeth. She was snoozing in an armchair. I had to wake her. She was not amused and is now sulking in the kitchen."

O'Reilly laughed. "Hang on to him, will you, love?" He set the basket on the ground and took from it a piece of dog chow and a rubber squash ball. "Arthur." O'Reilly tossed the ball to the end of the garden. "Hi lost."

Off Arthur went, and returned with the ball in his mouth. He sat and dutifully offered the ball to O'Reilly. "Good dog." O'Reilly repeated the exercise twice using the command and noting how closely Kenny was paying attention. "Put Kenny down please, Kitty."

The pup made a beeline for Arthur, who lowered his head so greeting sniffs could be exchanged. O'Reilly stood beside Kenny. "Sit." As he spoke, O'Reilly used his hand to exert gentle pressure on Kenny's rump.

Arthur obeyed at once.

The little dog hesitated but, giving in to the pressure of O'Reilly's hand, followed suit.

"Good dog." O'Reilly patted Kenny and gave him the piece of food.

"Now," he said to Kitty, "watch this. Arthur. Stay." He let Kenny sniff the ball, threw it, and before O'Reilly could say "Hi lost," the chocolate Lab pup had raced off. The instinct to retrieve was deeply bred into the species. Kenny picked it up, turned, and headed back to O'Reilly.

It was a tussle to get Kenny to release the ball, but after a tugging match it was finally surrendered. "Good dog," O'Reilly said, but no food. The retrieve had not been perfect. "It's going to be fun training that one," O'Reilly said, "and I think Arthur's going to want to help."

Kitty laughed. "Old dog teaching young dog. Might just work with old GPs and young ones too. You will be going up to the Department of General Practice this week, won't you?"

"Indeed I will," said O'Reilly. He spoke to the dogs. "Be good, you two. Come on, Kitty. Let's see if Lady Macbeth is in a better mood." They headed for the back door.

The little white cat was eating from her bowl in front of the range. She turned to look, then returned to eating.

"Here goes," said O'Reilly, setting Kenny's basket on the tiled floor close to the little feline. "What's that, your ladyship?" O'Reilly asked.

The cat climbed into the basket, sniffed, arched her back, and growled. Her tail expanded, but not to the full glory she achieved when truly scared or angry. She examined Kenny's ball, a rubber bone, and a small beige teddy bear. Although a cat can't shrug and say "so?" her posture conveyed those sentiments. She lay down, curled up, and promptly fell asleep.

"Begob," said O'Reilly with a grin, "we're going to get away with it. Wait here." He turned and in moments had returned carrying Kenny. He didn't bother closing the door completely behind him.

He set Kenny down beside his basket and stepped back.

The pup's brow wrinkled and he approached slowly. He cocked his head, took a step forward, then another. His tail began to wag. He put one paw into the basket and nudged the sleeping cat.

Lady Macbeth's eyes opened—wide. She stood up, back arched like a long bow at full stretch, tail fluffed like an electrified toilet brush, and screeched. The hairs on the back of O'Reilly's neck rose.

Kenny leapt backward in time to avoid a slash from Lady Macbeth's right front paw, all four wickedly sharp claws fully extended. He howled, a piteous, keening noise.

Before O'Reilly could grab the pup and hoist him out of harm's way, the door burst open and Arthur Guinness stalked in. This time his growl was full-throated, both canines were fully exposed, and his hackles were up. He stalked stiff-legged, stood over a whimpering Kenny, and gave a vast "woof," daring the cat to attack.

Lady Macbeth gave both dogs her most disdainful look, sheathed her claws, furled her tail, straightened her back, sat, hoisted one leg, and began to lick her backside. The message was clear: "Dogs do *not* frighten me and this is *my* kitchen."

"Phew," said Kitty, "for a minute I thought her ladyship was going to maul Kenny."

O'Reilly chuckled. "I never knew male dogs could show maternal instinct, but old Arthur certainly did." He looked fondly at the big Lab, who was licking Kenny to comfort him. "But it hasn't solved our problem. I'd intended to put Kenny's stuff in the kitchen where he'd be cosy at night." He pointed to Lady Macbeth, who had clearly taken possession of Kenny's basket. "If we do, we'll have to give her ladyship the run of the rest of the house."

Kitty said, "I don't think so. Watch."

O'Reilly turned.

Arthur was heading slowly for the door with Kenny walking at the big dog's shoulder. O'Reilly and Kitty followed.

When they reached Arthur's doghouse, he looked back at O'Reilly and Kitty as if to say, "Don't worry about it," picked Kenny up by the scruff, and lifted the pup over the threshold.

"I'll be damned," said O'Reilly as Arthur climbed in after the pup.

"I," said Kitty with a catch in her voice, "will have to go and get a hanky." She sniffed. "I've never seen anything so lovely in my life."

And Fingal Flahertie O'Reilly, ex-boxer, ex-rugby player, couldn't answer. He was going to need a hanky himself.

"Have a pew, Cissie," Barry said, indicating one of the two hard wooden chairs. He was taking surgery on this Tuesday morning and Cissie Sloan was his last but one.

Cissie parked her not inconsiderable form, and the torrent began. "How's about ye, Doctor dear. Fit and well you're looking. I think thon Miss Nolan's doing you a power of good, so I do. You know, I seen her yesterday at MacNeill Primary. Thon wee lassie has the loveliest hair I've ever seen in my puff—"

"Thank you, Cissie, but—"

"And have yiz heard about Bertie Bishop? I hear tell he put in a bid for til build more houses on the council estate, but he never got it, so he never. Flo says he's a much nicer man since he had thon heart attack, seen the light so to speak, but," she leant forward and lowered her voice, "*I* think he's losing his edge. There was never a tougher businessman than Bertie, but now? See him? See him? He's going soft, so he is." She sat back and folded her arms.

Barry wondered if it were true. It could have implications for more than the Bishops. His workers needed their jobs. He sighed and let Cissie blether on. She was a good-hearted woman and was here today so Barry could keep an eye on her myxoedema, deficiency of thyroid hormone, that he'd diagnosed two and a half years ago.

". . . anyroad, I hear poor Lewis Miller was took poorly and had til go til the Royal on Sunday. Me and Flo's going til look in on Gracie the day. She's no spring chicken and she'll be worried sick, so she will. Flo's made up some chicken soup, Kinky's recipe, and—"

"That's very kind of you both. I'm sure it will be appreciated, but, Cissie, I need to ask you a question or two about how you are."

"Fire away."

"Still no muscle cramps, tiredness?"

"Not—"

Barry didn't wait for the "at all" but charged on. "Feeling the cold? Drowsy? Bowels? Monthlies?"

"Warm as toast, bright as a bee, and them others? Been right as rain since you found out I was short of them wee thingies in my blood. I take my pills every day, so I do and, just like clockwork I—"

"You sound pretty fit to me, Cissie." She was evincing none of the usual symptoms of myxoedema. From where he sat at the rolltop desk, Barry could see that her skin was pale, not yellow. The puffiness he'd noticed when he made the diagnosis had gone. Her eyebrows had grown back.

"Can you hop up on the couch?"

She laughed. "I'm no great hopper, but I can climb," and she did, sitting with legs swinging.

Barry started to take her pulse.

"Dis yiz hear about—"

"Hang on, Cissie. I've lost count." Which wasn't true. Her pulse was perfectly normal. If she were short of thyroid hormone, it would be slow and her blood pressure low. "Take off your coat, please."

Cissie must have remembered the routine. She had worn a short-sleeved blouse so Barry could wrap the cuff round her upper arm.

"It's one twenty over eighty. Spot on. Turn to one side." He palpated her neck. No sign of thyroid gland enlargement. He was happy enough to confirm normal thyroid function on clinical grounds. The definitive diagnosis involved measuring the uptake of radioactive iodine by the thyroid, and the less radioactive material injected into an individual the better. "I think the pills are still doing the trick," he said.

"Dead on," she said, "and will I have til have any blood tests? I don't like them needles. Did you hear about Alice Maloney? Put a needle straight through her thumb on Friday fixing Maggie Houston's best hat. It's a wonder she didn't get the blood poisoning—"

Before Barry had arrived in the village, the bi-weekly *Ballybucklebo and Townland Chronicle* had operated for a few years but had eventually folded. By the time it had gone to print, the locals already knew the news anyway. "No, no blood tests, Cissie," he said, perhaps a little more sharply than he should have. "I'll give you another scrip for six months and I want to see you a week or so before it runs out."

"Fair enough, sir." She got off the couch and started putting on her coat as Barry rapidly wrote a prescription for sodium l-thyroxine tablets, 0.3 mgm to be taken daily. "Here, and come and see me if you don't feel at yourself between now and then." He had her by the elbow and was steering her to the door.

"Thanks very much, Doctor, but I must tell you a wee thing. It'll only take but a moment, but it's to do with one of your doctors."

Barry bit back a sigh. "Cissie, it's probably none of my business."

"Sure it is, Doctor dear. I was at the off-licence til get a few bottles of stout, about three o'clock on Saturday, so it was. Who comes in but Doctor Fitzpatrick. All smiles. Now, no harm til him, but we all know he's a dry ould stick and probably'd wrestle a bear for a ha'penny. Anyroad, your man's buying two bottles of them expensive French champagnes. Two. Says he til Hughie, him that runs the place next door to the Duck for Willie Dunleavy, 'I've just done rather well on the National.' What do yiz think of that, sir?"

Barry reckoned that it was out of character, but why shouldn't the man celebrate? And two bottles. Could there be someone else in the good doctor's life? Barry said, "I say good for him, Cissie. Now, I've another patient—"

"I'm away off, sir. If I don't see yiz through the window, I'll see yiz through the week." She chortled at her own humour.

Good old Cissie. He grinned. She was a decent sort, but best taken in small doses.

He headed for the surgery and returned with Julie Donnelly, carrying a wicker shopping basket on one arm, its contents covered by a red-checkered cloth.

Her bump was obvious under her blue woollen pullover. "Great day, so it is," she said. "I seen Anne Galvin at the grocers there now. She said you'd fixed up her bronchitis and it was so sunny she reckoned she was fit to go out."

Barry smiled. Acute bronchitis could resolve very quickly so he was not surprised, but he would pop round anyway on Thursday as planned. "How are you, Julie?"

"I'm early for my visit, sir," she said, handing him a plastic specimen bottle, setting her basket on a chair, and without having to be told climbing up onto the examining couch. "I'm twenty-seven weeks now and I know I shouldn't come in until twenty-eight, but Mister Bishop's business is slowing down a wee bit so he's given a wheen of his workers next week off. Me and Donal and Tori'd like to go down to Rasharkin to see my family. We haven't since Christmas. I hope you don't mind. He doesn't get much holidays."

So Cissie had been right about Bertie. "I'm glad you're able to get away. And I don't mind a bit you coming early." He thought of how important families were and of Anne Galvin missing hers in America. "You were doing fine three weeks ago. Anything different now?"

She opened her skirt and adjusted it so he could examine her. "I'm bigger, my back hurts if I stand too long, I have to pee more often, and the bairn's kicking the living bejasus out of me, but sure I had all that with Tori too." She rolled up her right sleeve. "Will the cuff fit?"

"It will." Barry put on the blood pressure cuff. "One thirty over eighty-five. Up a tad but nothing to worry about." He was not concerned. Julie had no untoward symptoms. Any pregnancy could go sour at any time, but she was young. Healthy. Granted she'd miscarried her first, but she'd sailed through her second so far, and second, third, and fourth pregnancies were usually the most straightforward. "Let's see your tummy."

She lay on the couch and Barry palpated her abdomen. The fundus, the top of the uterus, might be a bit higher than he would have anticipated, but some women did "carry high." He could make out a foetal head at the top of the uterus. "The wean's bottom-first today, but that's nothing to worry about." And wouldn't be unless it persisted until much later in the pregnancy. Only three percent of babies were breech births. "They toss around a lot at this stage." He found the baby's back and placed his Pinard stethoscope over the foetal heart. "One hundred and forty-four. Spot on," he said, straightening up. He moved along the couch and palpated her ankles, pressing in with his thumb. When he removed it there was no remaining pit, so no fluid, oedema, in the tissues. Good. "Everything looks pretty good. I'll test your urine while you're getting dressed."

He did, with the use of two dipsticks. No sugar. No albumen. So no need to worry about gestational diabetes or pre-eclamptic toxaemia, a combination of high blood pressure, swollen ankles, and albuminuria. It was ill understood, but if untreated could interfere with foetal growth and in severe cases cause fits in the mother. "Fine," he said.

"Just need to weigh you." He glanced at the notes, then at the scales. "Three-pound gain in three weeks? Perfect." He returned to the desk to fill in her chart. "You are taking your iron, folic acid, cod liver oil, and orange juice?"

"Aye. I'm not fond of the cod liver oil, but sure if it's for the wean?" She smiled.

"Come back in three weeks then," Barry said.

She nodded. "I'll do that." She removed the cloth from her basket and handed Barry a greaseproof-paper-wrapped parcel. "It's a wee gift for himself and Mrs. O'Reilly. A cock pheasant. Donal brung it home Saturday. The bird's plucked and cleaned, like. I know it's a bit naughty of Donal, but it does help with the housekeeping."

"I'm sure Doctor and Mrs. O'Reilly will be delighted," Barry said, accepting the parcel.

"You won't tell no one, Doctor?" Julie said.

"Not a soul," Barry said, understanding how with a family like the Donnellys money was always tight, "and you do know you'll be getting a maternity grant of sixteen pounds when you deliver, and another three pounds seven and six a week for eighteen weeks starting eleven weeks before you're due."

"That's dead on, so it is." She lowered her voice. "Mister Bishop's been generous. The week off's with pay, but . . ." She pursed her lips. "Donal and I worry a bit about the future of the boss's business."

So did Barry, but he said, "Mister Bertie Bishop's been around here for a long time. I'm sure it'll only be temporary. Donal and the lads'll be back to work in no time."

"I'm sure you're right, sir."

Barry rose and showed her to the door. He wandered back to the kitchen. The door was shut, but he knew why.

"Just a minute." Kinky's voice came through the door when he knocked.

He heard a couple of yips then, "Come in."

Kinky stood with her back to the range, cuddling a wriggling Kenny. Barry shut the door. It kept the pup in and Lady Macbeth out.

Kinky set him on the floor and he immediately ran over to Barry to be petted.

Barry handed Kinky the parcel. "A gift from the Donnellys. A pheasant. Donal got it Saturday." He bent and patted Kenny's head.

"Grand, so," Kinky said. "Three days old? They'll be just right tomorrow night roasted. Sage-and-onion stuffing, roast potatoes, and red cabbage." She shook her head. "But they do be out of season." She tutted. "I know Donal's no dozer, but if he's not careful he's going to get caught and summonsed, and I do hear the new resident magistrate is tough. Very tough."

"Donal?" Barry said. "I think he's big enough and ugly enough to look after himself."

"Well, I do hope so," Kinky said, "for it would be a stiff fine, and him with another mouth to feed soon."

And for a moment Barry wondered if Kinky's winnings might be going to be needed very close to home.

7

Teach Me To Feel Another's Woe

"Please have a seat, Doctor O'Reilly." The young secretary in the outer office of the department of general practice whipped off her glasses and offered him a wide and open smile. "Would you like some tea? Coffee?"

"Thank you, but I'm fine." He reckoned she was about twenty-five, with fair hair and blue eyes. Her accent definitely came more from the roomy mansions of Malone Road than the tenements of the Shankill. Bernard Shaw's Professor Higgins would have enjoyed Belfast, so different were the tones of the upper-and lower-class districts.

"Professor Irwin, I'm afraid, is running a bit late. He's meeting with the dean but had the dean's secretary phone me and ask me to explain and apologise."

"That's perfectly all right," O'Reilly said, and smiled. Although he hated unpunctuality, there was no need to take it out on this young woman, and George Irwin had at least had the courtesy to apologise. "I can wait. Don't let me hold you up."

"Thank you, sir. I'm sure he won't be long, and I do have a lot to do." She returned her pair of gold-framed spectacles to the bridge of her button nose and began typing furiously.

O'Reilly sat for a while listening to the clatter of the keys, the *ting* and clack of the carriage return. Twice she stopped to answer the phone. He glanced at his watch. His appointment was for eleven and it was already ten past. He had arranged to meet two of his closest friends from his student days at Trinity College Dublin, now surgeons who worked here.

Charlie Greer and Sir Donald Cromie would be waiting for him at noon in O'Kane's Oak Bar on Grosvenor Road opposite the gates to the hospital. He didn't want to be late.

The outer door flew open and a man of medium height wearing a black academic gown dashed in.

He thrust out his hand. "Doctor O'Reilly? George Irwin. Sorry I'm late. Do come in. Molly, coffee and biscuits, please."

O'Reilly stood and shook hands.

The professor's silver hair was parted to the left, with short sideburns coming halfway down beside large ears. Thick eyebrows arched over dark eyes. He strode to his inner office.

O'Reilly followed him into the small room. A functional Formica-topped table sat serving as a desk in front of a window. The tabletop was overflowing with books and manuscripts, an in-and-out tray, and a telephone. A bookcase occupying one wall was stuffed with medical texts and bound issues of *The Journal of the College of General Practitioners* arranged by year of publication. On another he noticed Professor Irwin's framed diplomas: his medical degree, his Member of the College of General Practitioners certificate, and the crest of the Royal College of General Practitioners with its motto, *Cum Scientia Caritas.* O'Reilly had no trouble translating. Science with compassion. Latin had been one prerequisite for admission to medical school, both at Trinity—where in O'Reilly's day one lecture a week had been delivered in that language—and here at Queen's University.

The professor pulled off his gown. "Bloody archaic tradition," he said, hanging it on a hook behind the door. "Have a pew." He indicated a small sofa with dark linen-covered cushions in front of his desk.

"Thank you for coming, Doctor. And thank you, Molly." He cleared room on his desktop, then sat down behind it. "Pop it there." The secretary set down a small tray. Coffee, cups, milk, sugar, and McVitie's chocolate digestive biscuits. "Help yourself."

O'Reilly took half a cup of coffee, with milk and sugar, and two biscuits. He had a soft spot for chocolate digestives.

"Molly knows my habits," the professor said as she left and closed the door. "She keeps a pot of coffee on the go." He raised his cup as might a man raise his glass in a pub. "Now. To business, and I'm George, by the way. Do you prefer Doctor O'Reilly or Fingal?"

Here was a courteous and probably humble man. Many professors were jealous of their rank and would never have dreamed of asking lesser mortals their preference. "Fingal's fine." O'Reilly sat back and crossed his tweed-covered legs. He was interested to hear what the man was going to say, but had decided on the day he'd opened his letter not to make any firm commitments until he'd had time to think, to talk it over with Kitty, then with his partner and associates.

"Let me give you some history. This is a brand-new department. The National Health Service was brought in in 1948—"

"Don't I know it?" said O'Reilly. "Don't I work in it?"

"Of course you do, Fingal. I wasn't thinking. So you well know the effect it's had."

"I do. I used to get paid by the patient's fee for service. Well-to-do people like the local gentry or successful business owners paid directly. The marquis paid for his servants or folks had work-related insurance. Colleagues got 'professional courtesy'—free treatment. Now the ministry pays me so much a head every year for each patient registered with my practice, whether I never see them or have them in once a week. The change hasn't affected me much, but I hear it's really altered things for doctors in the city. I don't know the details though. I haven't paid much attention to the financial aspects of medicine, I'm afraid."

George Irwin laughed. "Then you're a lucky man. There certainly has been a change. The private, fee-paying patients like your marquis have vanished for the GP. Everyone has taken advantage of the Health Service's low premiums and apparently 'free' medical services from GPs. That's cost a lot of city GPs money. There's private insurance and lots of the wealthy do pay premiums, but the companies only cover specialist care and hospital costs."

O'Reilly frowned. "I thought specialists like Charlie Greer got a salary for looking after folks in hospital and the state-insured folks weren't charged."

"True, but if you were having an operation, would you like to go on a waiting list and recover in a twenty-six-bed ward or have your operation that week and recover in a private room like today's private patients do?"

"I know my friends Charlie and Cromie, fair play to them, do work in the private Musgrave and Clark clinic for patients who have extra private insurance."

"The specialists are doing very well, but a lot of GPs have started feeling hard done by. No more private patients. And because they think of the service as 'free'"—he emphasised the word—"patients don't put up with a cold until it gets better. Now they demand to be seen, insist on a home visit, and often in the middle of the night. I think the lack of respect is more galling for many than the drop in income."

"Most country patients aren't like that, thank the Lord," O'Reilly said.

"I'm glad to hear it. But if that's not enough," George said, "the paperwork has increased. Letters for sick leave. Physical examinations before certain government employment. I'll not go on. You know about it as well as I do."

"I hate filling out forms," O'Reilly growled.

"And of course there's the financial pressure."

Now that's never bothered me, thought O'Reilly. Even before the National Health Service and its guaranteed payment per patient on his list he had been happy to collect what fees he could. He'd charge the marquis or Bertie and Flo Bishop lots, but see the likes of Maggie Mac-Corkle for free, take payment in kind, a couple stone of spuds, a goose, a string of plaice. He remembered Seamus Galvin, before he'd emigrated, arriving at the door with a brace of lobsters. O'Reilly'd always believed doctors were meant to look after people first and worry about money later.

George continued. "We decided it was time to become specialists in our own right, the equals of consultants, not simply triage officers sending the patients to the right consultant. To do so we needed our own college. I was on the steering committee. Foundation memberships were offered in 1953 to those doctors who met a set of criteria. Within six weeks more than one thousand, six hundred had joined."

"I got a letter, but I didn't apply," said O'Reilly. "I'm not very political. I told you I hate filling in forms, and surely to God after thirty-one years since qualification, no one's going to take away my licence, are they?"

George laughed. "No, Fingal, they're not. I hear from your friends and some other GPs that you are a first-class physician."

O'Reilly cleared his throat, grunted, and looked down. He didn't need to be told that he bloody well knew his job. And flattery always made him cringe. He supposed it was his Victorian upbringing.

George Irwin shook his head. His voice was firm. "Charlie Greer warned me you might shrink from praise, and Charlie's known you since 1931. I admire modesty, but I don't hand out credit unless I believe it's due. Your reputation is solid." He fixed O'Reilly with a steely stare. "And I want your help."

Polite George Irwin might be, but O'Reilly realised the man was determined and did not like being contradicted, even if only by a grunt.

"We got our Royal Arms in '62 so we are recognised as being on a par with the other royal colleges: physic, surgery, and obstetrics and gynaecology. We moved our headquarters to Kensington in London and now we're going a step farther. All across the United Kingdom of Great Britain and Northern Ireland, we're going to start insisting on formal training in university faculties for new GPs. Our department is the fifth to be established."

O'Reilly noted the man did not say "my." In that one word he had defined his position. Academic medicine, O'Reilly knew, was full of little Caesars building their empires, polishing their reputations, regarding their department as a private fiefdom. Clearly George Irwin was not one of them. Cromie had said as much when O'Reilly had phoned his old friend to enquire about the new professor. Charlie had assured O'Reilly that George Irwin was a good head.

"And I'd like to have you a part of it." He sat back in his chair and steepled his fingers. "Tell me, Fingal. Do you think GP as a specialty is a good idea?"

That caught O'Reilly off guard. He inhaled, pulled out his pipe. Lighting up always gave him time to think. He saw George's look of disapproval and shoved the briar back in his jacket pocket. "When I got your letter, I automatically said to my wife, 'That's the end of old GPs like me,' and I'm not sure what I actually meant. I've done my job my way for a long time. I'm not used to change, and yet in the last couple of years I've taken on associates, seen less of my patients, have more time off. My own general practice is changing. Medicine has changed enormously in the last thirty years. I've tried to keep up." He hesitated, working out the rest of his answer.

George sat back in his chair and said nothing.

O'Reilly frowned. "I think you and your colleagues will be steering a narrow course. On one hand there's resentment about the way today's GP can be regarded as second class by some of the more arrogant specialists. I understand that, but if the only reason for a college and extra training is to salve your collective *amour propre,* no, I'm not in favour." He inhaled.

"Please go on," George said.

"But if at the heart of your endeavours you want to make better GPs, who to the best of their ability look after their patients with . . . what's your motto, 'Science and compassion'? Then, yes. I'd fully support that." He grinned. "Do that—improve our services to our patients—and the respect is bound to follow."

George smiled. "You're not only a first-class physician, Fingal O'Reilly, whether you like to be told it or not, you are a thoughtful man, and I like the way you think. I believe you will be a valuable asset, so let me explain how the training will work."

"Fire away. Convince me."

"The course will last for one year and will be a combination of approaches. Formal instruction will be given here at the Royal until we get our own facility away from the teaching hospital. Much of what today's student sees there is not germane to what we actually do in our work. We also want to attach students to working general practices, and not only in the city. We do understand that rural practice differs in many ways."

O'Reilly sipped his coffee and leant forward. "What exactly do you expect the trainee to do during the attachment?"

"Initially follow the principal, sit in on surgeries, make home visits. Everything under supervision during the working weekday and availability for call when you are on call. We'll leave it up to the trainer to decide when the trainee is fit to be left to work unsupervised."

The man was describing exactly how O'Reilly had worked with Barry back in '64. "That doesn't sound too difficult," he said, but he remembered the reaction of some of his patients who had demanded to see "the real doctor." "The odd country patient can be picky about which doctor they see, though. What if one says, 'I don't want a learner near me'?"

"Patients are not given a choice in the teaching hospitals. And medical students are also used as cheap labour, admitting patients, taking blood samples, setting up drips, suturing. We think your patients should be given a choice, asked if they mind seeing a younger doctor in training. If they refuse . . ."

The implication was obvious. "Makes sense to me," O'Reilly said. He smiled. It had been fun working closely with Barry. The idea of another apprentice really was appealing.

"It should eventually lighten your workload when the trainee starts working independently."

More chances to spend time with Kitty and his friends. Give Barry and Nonie Stevenson and Ronald Fitzpatrick less night and weekend work too. He frowned, but on the other hand a five-doctor on-call rota? It would certainly dilute the personal approach he and more recently he and Barry used to have with the customers.

"I'm afraid there are one or two snags," George said. "I'm working on them. That was one reason for my meeting with the dean earlier, but the faculty of medicine budget is very tight. I'm afraid there's no title or stipend attached to the position of trainer."

O'Reilly shrugged, then laughed. "To me, 'Professor Fingal Flahertie O'Reilly' would be about as incongruous as 'His Lordship Donal Donnelly, Earl of Ballybucklebo.'"

George Irwin looked puzzled.

"One of my friends in the village. Carpenter, pheasant poacher, fixer of greyhound races, and abstract expressionist decorator of bicycles."

George laughed. "Colourful place, this village of yours."

"It is that." O'Reilly's smile faded. His voice became serious. "George, I have to tell you I am interested and I also feel I have an obligation.

About two and a half thousand years ago, on the Greek island of Cos, a physician named Hippocrates included in his oath, 'I will teach my art without reward or agreement; and I will impart all my acquirement, instructions, and whatever I know, to my master's children, as to my own; and likewise to all my pupils.' Money's not important to me, but passing on what I've learned over the past wheen of years is."

George Irwin sat back in his chair. "I'm glad. I remember that oath too. It's part of the reason I'm sitting in this chair today, so thank you, Fingal. Now, I know how you feel about paperwork, but we will want regular written reports on the trainee's progress."

O'Reilly laughed. "And you're the bloke who said you folks formed a college in part because of unreasonable administrative pressure?"

George laughed. "Touché. We will keep it to a minimum, I promise."

"All right. I'm going to hold you to that."

"Fair enough. More coffee?" George said, pouring himself a cup.

"No thanks," said O'Reilly, "but I will have another bikky." He laughed. "George. I think I might well like to participate."

"I hope you will."

"But the decision isn't entirely mine to make. I have a partner, an assistant, and an associate. I'll have to talk to them first."

"Of course."

"And there's the matter of accommodation," O'Reilly said, remembering Kitty saying she'd rather not have a permanent resident. "I have a spare room where the learner can sleep when on call, but—"

"You'd rather not be a landlord as well as a mentor?"

"That's right."

"The man I'm thinking of can easily drive down from Dundonald, where he has a flat."

"Grand. I'll discuss all of this with the interested parties"—there would be a bit more work for Kinky too—"and if they say yes, when would you send us our first trainee?"

"As soon as possible. I have a most interesting candidate. Doctor Connor Nelson. He's a bit older than the usual graduate. He finished his houseman's year last year and has been doing locums. Naturally I'll expect you to approve of him before you accept him."

"Thank you. You can tell me more and give me his phone number if and when my lot decide to go ahead," O'Reilly said, rising. "It's been a pleasure meeting you, George. I'll give you a ring by the middle of next week. How's that?"

George rose and offered his hand, which O'Reilly shook. "Splendid. I'll look forward to hearing from you."

As O'Reilly walked along the hospital road past the Clinical Sciences Building, he pictured Arthur Guinness taking Kenny under his wing. It made him chuckle. In his day, student learners had been known as pupils, "pups" for short. He sighed. He'd never had his own child to teach. The war had seen to that. Fingal O'Reilly had made his peace with that loss. And now here was another chance to teach a young "pup." And at least, he thought, he'd not have to house-train the fellow.

8

Let Age Approve of Youth

O'Reilly collected a walking stick from the hall stand and headed for the back garden. The April sunshine warmed him. Overhead, fluffy clouds meandered over the Ballybucklebo Hills, casting shadows to dapple the coppices where wood pigeons' liquid cooing mellowed the harsh cawing of rooks. Somewhere in the distance a donkey's bray, loud and discordant, split the evening. Donal had been round earlier to mow the lawn, a bargain at ten shillings a cut, and the air was redolent of freshly cut grass. O'Reilly took a deep draught of the sweet-smelling air and sighed.

The meeting just now had gone very well. Barry, Nonie Stevenson, and Ronald Fitzpatrick had unanimously agreed to take on the trainee, Connor Nelson, in May. O'Reilly was particularly pleased that the money questions, the rocks upon which many otherwise amicable medical arrangements foundered, had been answered satisfactorily. O'Reilly would phone this Connor Nelson tomorrow and see when he could meet with himself as principal and Barry as a partner. Somewhere pleasant. Maybe the Crawfordsburn for dinner?

O'Reilly smiled. Nonie had left in a rush and in a cloud of Je Reviens. She had a date in Belfast at six. She'd been wearing more makeup than usual, including the now-popular false eyelashes, and sporting a neatly tailored powder blue jacket over a white silky blouse, a miniskirt, dark hose, and heels. Some new fellow was taking her to see *Georgy Girl* starring Lynn Redgrave and James Mason. Och well, O'Reilly thought, gather ye rosebuds while ye may.

Barry was deep in conversation with Ronald and would join O'Reilly later for a quick pint in the Duck. Kitty wouldn't be home for at least an hour, but last night she'd said the GP in training, as long as he would not be a permanent resident, would be welcome, and Kinky had brushed aside any concerns about her having extra work to do. The woman thrived on looking after people.

O'Reilly was sure he was going to enjoy helping the younger colleague, but now he had other teaching to do. He'd time to give Kenny another lesson. He'd been working with the pup twice a day since bringing him home last Sunday.

Lars had already done a good job of teaching the vital foundation to all training: respect for the human who had become the pup's pack leader. Kenny had been housebroken, and had learned simple rules like not jumping up on people. He also recognised two critical words: "no" and "good."

"Come," O'Reilly called.

Arthur piled out of his doghouse and, with Kenny at his shoulder, trotted across the lawn toward where O'Reilly stood.

"Sit," O'Reilly said. Down went Arthur's backside.

Kenny hesitated, looked at O'Reilly, back at Arthur, and kept trotting until he reached his master.

O'Reilly bent, clipped a leash to Kenny's collar, then, repeating "sit" with exactly the same tone, pushed down on the pup's rump. "Sit."

Down it went.

"Good," said O'Reilly. "Good."

Kenny wagged his tail.

"Heel," he said, then gave a gentle tug on Kenny's leash and strode toward the far end of the garden, collecting Arthur from where he sat. The three of them went through the gate and into the back lane.

Arthur tucked in on O'Reilly's right. Kenny tried to run ahead, but sharp tugs on the leash and a tiny tap with the walking stick on his nose kept him in position.

"Heel," said O'Reilly, removing the stick.

Kenny stayed put.

"Good," said O'Reilly, and headed for the traffic light, stopping only to wish Alice Moloney, the dressmaker, a good evening and answering her polite but eager inquiries after the health of one Doctor Ronald Fitzpatrick, who she'd met last month at the party at Number One Main. O'Reilly would take the two dogs down to the beach to give Kenny ten minutes more training then let both dogs play for a while before heading to the Duck to show off his newest protégé.

"Evening, Doctor. Usual for you and Arthur?" Willie Dunleavy greeted O'Reilly as he entered the Duck, breathing in the fumes of tobacco smoke and beer. Willie's welcome was echoed by the other patrons.

"Evening all," O'Reilly called, "and yes, please, Willie."

"How's about ye, Doc," said Donal Donnelly, wandering over from where he sat with Gerry Shanks, "and who'd this be?" He bent and patted Kenny.

"Carlow Charger of Kilkenny," O'Reilly said, "Kenny for short."

"Handsome wee fellow, right enough. Going til be big when he grows intil his ears and his feet. Are him and ould Arthur mates, like?"

"They are, just like your Bluebird and Colin Brown's Murphy." O'Reilly remembered the last time he'd seen Donal's greyhound and grinned. "And by the way, thanks for the, ahem, gift."

Donal winked, ran a finger alongside his nose, and lowered his voice. "There's a brave wheen more where that one came from." He frowned. "And it's not just the sport now. The oul do-re-mi's a bit tight. My Julie's hair's gone a bit tatty now she's in the family way, so that photographer fellow's not using her as a model. But I'll say no more."

He didn't get the chance anyway. Willie set O'Reilly's pint on a nearby empty table and a bowl of Smithwick's beneath. "There y'are, sir. That'll be five bob."

O'Reilly paid, ushered Arthur and Kenny under the table, and took a chair. "Sit," he said. Both dogs obeyed, but O'Reilly kept ahold of Kenny's leash. "Good." He peered under. Arthur had lowered his head and had started lapping. Kenny cocked his head to one side and watched. His eyebrows twitched. He lowered his muzzle, sniffed, jerked back, and made a snorting noise. Smithwick's, it seemed, was not to the pup's taste. "Have you water, Willie?" O'Reilly asked.

"Right away."

O'Reilly took a pull on his pint of Guinness and looked round. All the regulars. There was the usual hum of conversation, but no bursts of laughter punctuated the chat. Somehow the good old Duck seemed subdued this evening.

Bertie Bishop sat alone at a table next to O'Reilly. "Evening, Doctor. New pup?"

"Aye. My brother gave him to me."

"The solicitor?"

"That's right."

Bertie sighed. "Does he take people til court, like?"

Willie appeared and put a small bowl beside Arthur's.

Kenny began to drink.

"I should think so too," said Willie, gazing down at Kenny. "Yiz is far too young to be drinking beer." He laughed. "No charge for that, sir." He left.

"Sorry, Bertie," O'Reilly said. "No, Lars doesn't. He prefers conveyancing, wills, that kind of stuff. You need a lawyer?"

Bertie pursed his lips. "I might." He sighed. "You mind the council's going til bypass the village til the south?"

"I certainly do. And your company is part of the consortium that should be doing it."

Bertie's shoulders slumped. He sighed. "Should's right, but . . ." He glanced round the room. "Just between you and me and the wall, we were meant til start next month, but there's a delay in the sale of the land, and I had til turn down two other jobs so we were all set to go. But now?"

O'Reilly felt for Bertie. It had been years now, but O'Reilly still remembered his first months back in 1946 when he'd been trying to establish his practice. That sinking feeling in the pit of his stomach when the money that was coming in wasn't enough to cover what was going out. "And I hear from Barry you're giving all your workers next week off. With pay. That's generous." O'Reilly drank.

"Och, not really. They all get paid holidays in July anyway. I've just moved them up. I hope I can keep them all on, they're good lads, but if we don't get started on the bypass soon . . ." Bertie's sigh was vast. He finished his pint. He stood. "Anyroad," he said, "I have til be running along. Say hello to Mrs. O'Reilly."

"And to Flo." O'Reilly took another pull and watched the retreating councillor's back. Perhaps the prospect of imminent unemployment for some men in here had something to do with the relative quiet. It would hit Donal Donnelly hard now with another mouth soon to feed. For a moment O'Reilly wondered whether Donal's or perhaps Bertie's impending financial difficulties might be the "desperate need for four hundred pounds" that Kinky had foreseen?

O'Reilly was still ruminating when the batwing doors reopened and in walked Barry accompanied by—wonder of wonders—Ronald Fitzpatrick. "Over here." He waved.

Both men came and sat.

Kenny tried to put his paws on Barry's knees.

"No," said O'Reilly. "Sit."

Kenny obeyed.

"Good." O'Reilly turned to his colleagues. "My shout. What'll it be?"

"Pint, please," Barry said.

"Me too," Ronald said. "I had one the other night. I could get a taste for the stuff."

"You could do worse," O'Reilly said, pointing at his nearly empty glass and holding up three fingers.

Willie nodded and started to pour.

"I hear," said Barry, "that champagne has been in order too." He laughed. "Cissie Sloan told me."

"Honestly. That woman. We hardly need the BBC news," Ronald Fitzpatrick said with a lot more lightness than was customary for the lugubrious man. "And yes, I did have a glass or two of bubbly. I really did quite well on Foinavon." He laughed his hoarse cackle.

As O'Reilly laughed too, he remembered Ronald admitting to having difficulties gambling as a young man. Could a big win have shoved him off the straight and narrow? O'Reilly pursed his lips but then relaxed.

Nah, not likely. "Ronald," O'Reilly said, "I lost twenty quid. Do you mind me asking how much you won?"

Ronald Fitzpatrick laughed. "Quite a bit," he said. "I bet on the tote."

O'Reilly was familiar with the totaliser, a form of pari-mutuel betting. The bettor's stake was not put on the horse at odds the bookies were offering. Winners received a percentage of the total amount wagered by all the losing bettors, minus the tote's cut, divided by the number of people who had bet on the winning horse. Often the payout was higher if few people had done so. In this case, Foinavon, regarded as having no chance, had attracted few bets, so a large sum was available for the animal's backers.

"It paid off at four hundred and forty-four to one. And I'd ten pounds on," Ronald Fitzpatrick said.

"What?" O'Reilly's mind whirred doing the calculation. Holy Mother of God. "You won four thousand, four hundred and forty pounds?" O'Reilly's voice rose. "Four thousand, four hundred and forty pounds? Holy Moses, that's about twice what I make in a year—and yours is tax free."

"I'd rather not appear smug, Fingal, but . . . yes. Yes, I did."

O'Reilly whistled. And he'd thought Kinky and Archie had done well. Remembering how Ronald Fitzpatrick had bristled last year when the O'Reillys had been genuinely concerned for the man's health, O'Reilly hesitated, but he'd known enough compulsive gamblers to want to stop Ronald heading down that road if he could. "Now don't get cross," he said, "but I hope—"

"Of course not." Fitzpatrick's reply was friendly, if a little speedy. "Once bitten, twice shy."

O'Reilly was distracted by a high-pitched "yip" and a throaty "grrrr" coming from under the table. He peered beneath.

Mary Dunleavy's Chihuahua, Brian Boru, had tried to scare Kenny, and big protective Arthur, even though he and Brian were friends, was having none of it.

Willie, like Aladdin's genie coming out of his bottle, appeared at the table. He grabbed Brian and tucked the little dog under his arm. "You be nice to my guests, boy, or I'll send you back to Mexico." Willie vanished through the door behind the bar that led to the Dunleavys' living quarters. He was back sans dog in no time. "Sorry about that. Here you are, gents," he said, depositing three black pints with their creamy heads. "Seven and six, please."

"Allow me," said Ronald.

"Certainly, King Croesus," Barry said.

As Ronald paid, O'Reilly said, "King of Lydia, from 595 BC until his defeat by the Persian Cyrus the Great in 546. Reputedly issued the first gold coins."

"Lord," said Ronald, "not only could Cissie replace the BBC news. The *Encyclopaedia Britannica* would get a run for its money from Fingal Flahertie O'Reilly."

O'Reilly bowed his head and raised his glass to Ronald.

Ronald lifted his glass in turn. "Cheers," he said, and swallowed a third at one go.

"Here. Go easy," O'Reilly said with a smile. "You're not used to it. Keep up at that rate and you'll be flying." A sea change had come over this usually dry, reserved man. O'Reilly had seen this kind of thing before. Middle-aged men suddenly behaving like teenagers.

"I'll be good," Ronald said, and sank another third.

O'Reilly shook his head. He didn't want to intrude, but later he'd have a word with Barry. O'Reilly would speak to Kitty too. A gentle eye would be kept on Ronald Hercules Fitzpatrick. Just in case he did start to slip. Just in case.

9

A Little Sleep, a Little Slumber

"Honestly I still can't find anything physically wrong," Barry said from behind the rolltop desk in the surgery as Eileen Lindsay finished buttoning up her blouse. "It's too bad the simple things I suggested two months ago and the chloral hydrate I gave you last month aren't working. I think we'll need to try something a bit stronger."

"Please do, sir," she said. "My oul' brain just keeps going round and round half the night." She sighed. "Working full time shifting in the linen mill. Rearing Sammy, and Mary, and Willie all on my own."

Barry smiled when he remembered how the little divils had tried to help out an impoverished Santa Claus at Christmas a few years ago.

"At least Willie's going on twelve now and he can mind his wee brother and sister after school till I get home." She sighed. "But then there's the shopping, the housework, cooking. I'm running around like a bee on a hot brick and I don't seem til be able til get over, or if I do, I wake up a couple of hours later."

"I know it's difficult for you, Eileen." And he truly felt for her. It must be no fun being a single mother.

"I know that, sir, and I know you're doing your best." She managed a small smile. "And I have tried all the things you suggested. I don't smoke—never did, even though most of the girls at the mill do. I don't take a drink before bedtime except the warm milk you told me til try. I go to the bathroom before I get intil bed." She took one of the patients' chairs and held her handbag in both hands on her lap. "I think that chloral stuff did help a wee bit at first, but now?" She shook her head and looked down. "Honest to God, I'd kill til get through the whole night, so I would."

Her brown hair was neatly cut, she wore little makeup, and would have been an attractive young woman but for the dark bags under her bloodshot blue eyes. Barry knew life had not been easy for Eileen. Her husband had left her four years ago. The local poulterer, Johnny Jordan, who had walked out with her before her marriage, had tried and failed to rekindle the old flame two years ago. Barry was glad there was more that he could offer her; more potent sleeping pills like the barbiturates or perhaps one of the benzodiazepines like Librium, introduced in 1960, or the newer Valium? "I'll write you a scrip for some capsules." He turned back to the desk and started to fill in a prescription for Nembutal 0.1 gram, a quickly metabolised barbiturate that should not leave her feeling drowsy the next day.

Someone was knocking on the surgery door.

"Come in."

Kinky appeared. "I do not wish to interfere, Eileen, but we do have an emergency in the waiting room, so. If you could see to Eileen quickly, sir? I'll fetch the patient."

"Right." Barry handed Eileen the prescription.

"Thank you, sir," Eileen said as she rose and hustled to the door. Barry called after her, "Take one capsule half an hour before bedtime. Come and see me in a month if they're not helping." He turned to see Kinky accompanying Maggie Houston and her husband, Sonny, supporting a tearful woman whom Barry vaguely recognised. "Come in," he said. "Sonny, can you help the patient up on the couch? Maggie, have a pew. Kinky, thank you very much." She left and closed the door.

Sonny helped the woman up. The head of the table was inclined so she could lie with her torso at forty-five degrees. He joined Maggie on the other patient's chair.

Barry approached the small woman with tousled auburn hair. Her left eye was pale blue, but her right eye was closed and blackened. Hester Doran. He'd last seen her in February at a borough council meeting. She was the wife of one of the councillors, Hubert Doran. The horrid man had voted against O'Reilly's best interests, but had been defeated, got his comeuppance. Before she'd left the meeting she'd approached O'Reilly and asked to be taken back as one of his patients. "Hello, Mrs. Doran," Barry said. "I'm sorry for your troubles. Let's see what we can do to make you more comfy."

She was supporting her left wrist with her right hand.

"Can you tell me what happened?"

She sobbed and gulped in deep lungfuls of air. She wouldn't meet his gaze.

Barry frowned. "Sonny? Maggie? Can either of you help?"

"Aye," Sonny said. "We were having our elevenses when the dogs started carrying on. There was a ring at the door, and when I answered it, Hester was there. We're neighbours, you know."

A shuddering sob came from the couch.

Barry didn't let himself be distracted. He wanted to get as much information as quickly as possible.

"She was in floods, poor craytur. Maggie helped me get her calmed down. Hester said she'd been up wee stepladders in the kitchen, had hit her face on an open cupboard door, fallen off the ladder, and had stuck out her arm to break her fall."

That explained the black eye. The rest of the history was highly suggestive of a Colles fracture of the wrist, named for the Dublin doctor Abraham Colles, who had first described it in 1814. No wonder she was in tears. Broken bones hurt like the blazes.

"She said she heard the bone snap," Maggie said with a shudder.

"We put her in my motor and brought her straight here. She said her husband, Hubert, was out. Maggie and me'll go and see him after you've sorted things out."

"Thanks, Sonny," Barry said. "That's most helpful." He moved closer to the examining couch.

Hester looked up at him. Her good eye held pleading. She sniffled and said, "It hurts," and there was pain in her voice.

"I know," he said, "and I need you to be brave, Hester, and help me." She nodded weakly.

"Sonny's told me you had a fall."

She nodded again.

"And did you hit your head on the floor?"

She shook her head.

"What day is it?"

"Friday, April the fourteenth," she whispered.

"Where are you?"

"Doctor O'Reilly's surgery."

"Thank you." Good. She was not disorientated in time and place so it was unlikely that she had sustained a concussion. Until the bruising round the eye went down it would be impossible to assess any damage to the bones of the face, but she would have to go to hospital. If the surgeons were concerned, they could arrange a facial X-ray. For the moment Barry would concentrate on the wrist.

He could see a bony protuberance under the skin one inch above where the wrist joined the hand, on the thumb side. That was the end of the ulna, the biggest of the two forearm bones, and it had been displaced sideways from its fellow, the radius. Hester's wrist, if looked at from the side, had the contours of a dinner fork if the forearm were the handle and the hand the tines. "I'm afraid you've got a bust wrist, Hester," he said. "I'm going to send you to the Royal."

She hiccupped, took a deep breath. "It's all my fault," she said.

"You fell, that's all. Anyone could take a tumble."

Barry shook his head. "Hester, I'm going to give you a jag and then splint the wrist." Even when splinted, any jolting in the ambulance might rub the displaced bone ends together and the pain would be awful. "Maggie, could you nip through to the kitchen? Ask Kinky to call the ambulance?"

"Yes, sir." As she left he noticed a yellow primrose keeping a bluebell company in her hatband.

It took moments to prepare a quarter grain of morphine and inject it into Hester's right deltoid, the big muscle that sits atop the shoulder. "I'll need your help in a minute, Sonny." Barry rummaged in a drawer where O'Reilly kept splints and bandages, finding what was needed. Barry glanced at his watch. Another five minutes for the narcotic to work.

"You're going to start feeling drowsy, Hester," he said. "They'll have you fixed in no time at the Royal. Set the bones. Put on a cast. Keep you in overnight, and Mister Doran will be able to take you home in the morning."

She shook her head. Ulsterfolk were superstitious and it was widely believed that being discharged on a Saturday was unlucky and often led to early re-admission.

"Now, Sonny," Barry said, "I need a hand. Hester, I'm going to splint your wrist now that the painkiller has taken effect. Mister Houston is going to support it. Don't be scared."

Barry showed Sonny how to hold Hester's fingers so she could remove her other hand without disturbing the broken wrist. It took a very short time for Barry to apply a wooden splint and bandage it firmly in place. He quietly blessed his dad for having Barry join the Sea Scouts as a lad. Making slings was not taught at medical school, but Barry's scoutmaster would have been proud of his student's efforts with a triangular bandage. "There," he said. "Just have to wait for the ambulance now. I'm going to put you in our dining room because the waiting room's still half full. Sonny, could you and Maggie keep Hester company until it gets here?"

"Our pleasure," Sonny said. "If you'll help me get Hester over there, sir, then I'll get Maggie."

"Of course."

Together they helped Hester, now groggy from the morphine, into the other room. She muttered a slurred, "Thank you."

"Not be long," Sonny said and, true to his word, he and Maggie soon returned.

Barry headed for the kitchen to speak to Kinky, pausing to peek into the waiting room. Not as busy as he had anticipated. The less urgent cases would have gone home to come back next week in the hope they'd not have to wait too long. "Kinky," he said, "please let me know when the ambulance gets here. I need to tell the crew that Hester's had morphine."

"I will, sir." She tutted and shook her head. "Poor Hester was a patient here for a brave while before her husband and himself, Doctor O'Reilly, had their big falling-out. She was a desperate one for having the accidents. She told me once she's been accident-prone ever since she was a little girl, falling off slides, skinning her knees." She tutted. "Enough of my blethering. Run along now, sir, and see to the sick and suffering. There do be potted herrings for lunch."

10

Ere His Race Be Run

The big Rover purred along the Kirkubbin to Portaferry Road.

"Five more minutes to the Rubane Road, Kitty, and then another five to Kirkistown racetrack. You remember we came down here last year to watch Donal Donnelly race his greyhound, Bluebird?"

"And it bucketed with rain? I remember all right." Kitty laughed. "I'll bet Donal Donnelly does too—no pun intended. It's good to know not all of the man's ploys work out quite the way he plans."

O'Reilly grinned remembering Donal's face streaming with rain and rife with frustration. It had not been one of Donal's finer moments. "Brother Lars was there too, that day, and I'll bet he and Myrna are at the racetrack long before us today," he said. "My big brother's car mad. Always has been. He told me that the first race starts at one thirty and there'll be four races. We'll be there in plenty of time."

"I wonder how things are going between them," said Kitty, turning toward the view of Strangford Lough to their right.

"Lars said they were fine, remember? While we were having lunch at the Portaferry Arms. The day we collected Kenny."

"I'm looking forward to seeing them both again," Kitty said, "and I've never been to a car race. Should be fun. I certainly enjoyed going for a spin in your brother's E-Type Jaguar back then."

O'Reilly grinned. Kitty had thrown him for a loop when she started holding forth on engine capacities of various models of the famous sports car. "I'd never known you were an automobile enthusiast. Even now I'm finding hidden depth in you, my love."

"And I you. And long may it continue."

A contented O'Reilly glanced past her to look over to the lough. The tide was going out over the acres of mudflats and its shining surface was barely ruffled, so any breeze must be gentle. In the early-afternoon hazy distance, the Mourne Mountains bulked midnight-hued against a light blue sky, and the sun's golden path stretched from Strangford Town on the far shore to sparkle on the nearby pools left by the receding tide. A mixed flock of emerald-headed mallard and buff-pated widgeon paddled along in the shallows, birds dabbling, heads down, paddles churning, backsides in the air. Glaucous gulls wheeled above, soaring and screeching like a party of arguing fishwives.

Strangford Lough today was living up to its Irish name, Loch Cuan, "the peaceful lough," but in the winter he knew it well when the southerly gales tore the waters to a vicious, spume-laden chop. Then it was the Vikings' Strangfjorthr, "the turbulent lough." "Begod," he said half to himself, "I do love this bit of Ireland. I was thirteen when our uncle Hedley started bringing Lars and me here to teach us to be wildfowlers." He shook his head. "That was in 1921, the year the Ulster parliament opened at Stormont and a truce was declared in the war between Britain and De Valera's Irish Republicans. Professor O'Reilly, God rest him, had insisted his sons take an interest in current affairs."

"In 1921? Eleven years before we met at Sir Patrick Dun's Hospital. That was much more important than Irish politics," Kitty said, and squeezed his thigh.

"I should have married you back then." He shook his head. "Where the hell did the years go?" As he indicated left and braked for the turn, his right knee complained by sending a stabbing pain down his shin. He reflexively sucked in his breath.

"You all right?" Kitty asked.

"Old age and decrepitude," he said, and laughed. "Ancient rugby battle scar acting up again. Did it playing against Old Belvedere in '36. You've got to expect the odd twinge."

"Poor old bear," she said, and there was sympathy in her voice. "Still, if you stay on the perch as long as Konrad Adenauer, and I for one hope you do, you've a wheen of years left. He died last Tuesday. There was an article on him today in the *Belfast Newsletter*. He was ninety-one."

"Sorry to hear that he's gone," said O'Reilly, and he was. He'd admired how the German chancellor had dragged his country up from the Nazi depths after the war. "But with respect to me and my imminent descent into senility, in the immortal words of Groucho Marx, 'A man's only as old as the woman he feels.'"

"Eejit."

Kitty was still chuckling when O'Reilly pulled off the road and onto a lane leading to a field full of parked cars. He stopped beside a man in a grocer's coat and wound down the window. "I know," he said. "I was here before. Two pound ten. Highway bloody robbery." But he paid up and parked not far from Lars's red E-type. The old aerodrome's paint-peeling control tower, reminder that what was now a racetrack had been a Hurricane fighter station during the war, stood behind the parking lot. O'Reilly got out and trotted round to open Kitty's door and help her out of the car. She was looking particularly smart in brown brogues, slim hunter green pants, a cream wool sweater, and black blazer. As always, his heart expanded with pleasure when she tucked her arm under his. "Come on," he said. "Let's go and look for big brother. I'll bet you he's at the start/finish chatting with some of the drivers."

Arm in arm, they walked over the turf, following others in the crowd of spectators to the mile-and-a-half circuit. The area for spectators was separated from the track by hay bales and oil barrels full of cement. An ancient red fire engine carrying galvanised buckets, and a Saint John's ambulance were parked on the grass in the middle of the track. Farther on past the back straight in a gorse-spotted field outside the old aerodrome, cows went about their business untroubled by the sound of highly tuned engines being run up, tested, and fine-tuned again. Overall hung the stink of high-octane exhaust fumes.

"There they are," O'Reilly said, pointing. He quickened his pace.

On the track before the start line, fifteen strange-looking cars were lined up three abreast in five ranks. They were all low-slung one-seaters with their wheels not under the chassis like ordinary motorcars, but rather sticking out to the sides. Each was truncated and low at the back with an inverted U steel roll bar behind an open cockpit and had an oval air intake that fronted a long snout in place of the usual radiator grille.

Lars and Myrna stood beside one with the number "6" painted on the bonnet, chatting to a man in oil-stained overalls. Lars raised his voice over the grumbling of engines. "Finn, Kitty, great to see you."

"And you and Myrna," Kitty said. "Your fortnight away did you good, because fit and well you're both looking."

"It was very pleasant," Myrna said, "and it's good to be back." She lowered her voice. "But I'm here under protest. I really don't like these things. Too noisy and smelly."

O'Reilly and Kitty exchanged glances.

Lars, apparently not hearing her comment, turned to the mechanic and said, "Doctor and Mrs. O'Reilly, I'd like you to meet a good friend of mine, Mister John Crosslé from Holywood."

Pleasantries were exchanged. The mechanic appeared to be in his midthirties and had a long narrow face topped with an unruly mop of dark hair with no parting, piercing dark eyes, and a long nose. "John runs the Crosslé Car Company. This is one of his cars. It's a 16F model."

"I'm curious, John," Kitty said, "is this some kind of international class? Are all the cars the same?"

"Aye," he said, "it's called the international Formula Ford class. They all have to be built around a 1600cc Ford four-cylinder, push-rods engine."

"Good acceleration?"

"Zero to sixty in six seconds."

"Impressive," Kitty said.

"You're dead on," John said. "We'll be hosting our first Formula Ford championship next year."

"I think I'd like to see that," Kitty said. "How fast will these cars go?"

O'Reilly shook his head and smiled. While his interests were legion, he'd never understood why some folks, Kitty included, could get so worked up over things like cars. As far as he was concerned they were needed, but the depth of his knowledge was restricted to putting petrol in one end, oil in the other, and water in the radiator. When they refused to go, you consulted a mechanic.

"I've had her up to one hundred and twenty on the straight," John said.

Kitty whistled. "That's amazing."

"You interested in cars, Mrs. O'Reilly?" He was clearly surprised.

"Just a bit," she said, "and it's Kitty."

"Not many women are, Kitty."

O'Reilly saw Myrna vigorously nodding in agreement. She said, "I'm certainly not. In fact, they worry me."

"Ah, but, and saving your presence, Myrna, and your well-known dislike of things mechanical, Kitty's not just any woman, John," Lars said.

"Thank you, Lars," Kitty said, blushing. "I don't know why, but I find speed exhilarating."

"Do you now? Not when I'm driving," O'Reilly said. "How many times have I heard 'Slow down, Fingal'?" and he laughed. Then he frowned. Scratched his head. Was he detecting friction between his brother and Myrna? He remembered how when they'd first met, they'd fallen out because of Lars's conservationist leanings over hunting and shooting, but had agreed to differ on that subject.

"Anyway," Lars said, "we'll be moving on so we can watch the races. Good luck, John." Lars led the way. "John's driving his car today. It's the prototype. He hopes to get into full production in a couple of years."

"I remember him starting up his company in 1957," Kitty said. "He had been a motorbike racing champion, hadn't he? But he said he'd rather race on four wheels so he built his own racing car."

Lars nodded. "I hope he does well today, and I want us to have a good vantage point so we can see all the action. We'll get the best view from here at the start line. It's a testing track. Starts with a straight, goes down into Debtor's Dip. Lots of speed on the back straight before they get onto the right-handed turn at Maguire's Hairpin just before the finish. It's going to be great."

"I'm not sure machines will replace racehorses for real excitement," Myrna said. "Like this year's Grand National."

Lars snorted and said, "That's what the cavalry generals said when they first saw tanks in 1916. You'll see."

They were now in the middle of a small crowd of racing fans, tucked behind the hay bales. O'Reilly grabbed Kitty's hand so they'd not become separated.

"Sometimes, Lars O'Reilly," Myrna said, "I think you like being argumentative for the sake of being—well—argumentative, and I'm not sure it's an entirely admirable trait. I'll take a horse over a motorcar anytime. And I'm not just talking about race cars. There are more and more of the damn smelly ordinary things cluttering up the roads. More good land being paved over. Bloody great motorways all over Britain since the first one in '59. The Germans started it with their *autobahnen* before the war. Our own M1's going from Belfast to Dungannon and it'll be finished next year."

Lars inhaled. Deeply. Then said, "You can't stop progress, Myrna. I suppose you'd rather take a horse and cart to Queen's every day rather than that smart little Austin you drive. On the old Dungannon Road it took more than an hour to do the journey. No more than forty-five minutes once the M1 is finished. It already has a six-mile straight." He grinned. "It's naughty, but I've done the ton more than once there in the Jag."

Myrna shook her head. "I would, actually, prefer a horse and trap, but we'd never get there alive. Especially if there are people like you driving at one hundred miles an hour on the roads. That speed holds not the least attraction for me, and there's a price for this car worship. I'd have thought with your bird conservationism"—Not again, O'Reilly thought—"you'd have a care for the dozens of badgers, hedgehogs, hares, and rabbits killed on the roads. Have you ever seen a hare caught in headlights? The poor thing is terrified. And how much nesting hedgerow is being destroyed?"

O'Reilly was torn. He didn't really want to prolong the argument, but in fairness to Myrna said, "I think Myrna has a point, and it's not just roads and cars. Houses going up everywhere. Farmland paved over. You all know I love the countryside and the shore." He sighed. "But Lars has a point too. It is very hard to slow down progress."

Kitty said, "I agree about progress, it's both inevitable and heartbreaking in a way, but still . . ." She glanced up at the cars at the start. "I can't help admire the grace of those race cars, the skill of the drivers. I'm sure watching is going to be thrilling."

No one spoke for several moments.

O'Reilly glanced at Kitty and inclined his head. In love Lars and Myrna might be, but they certainly knew how to spar. Had things really gone smoothly in France? To change the subject, he said, "I'm sure the pair of you will be pleased to hear Kenny's training is progressing. I've got him retrieving now and he and Arthur are the best of friends."

"Poor Lars. He rattles round in that big house like a pea on a drum," Myrna said. "Kenny was meant to be a companion." She shook her head in Lars's direction.

Hardly fair, O'Reilly thought. It wasn't his brother's fault that he'd developed an allergy.

"Thank you both for taking him in," Myrna said. "I know it's clichéd, but I am glad he's gone to a good home."

"We are very fond of him," Kitty said, "and—"

"Sorry to interrupt," Lars said, "but the drivers are getting into their cars. It'll be a standing start. Drivers aboard, engines running, but the cars not moving, green flag dropped and off they go."

O'Reilly heard the engine notes rising and falling as drivers revved their engines.

"Green flag's up," Lars said, barely controlling the excitement in his voice.

O'Reilly realised he was catching the feeling from his big brother and craned forward.

The flag was snatched down.

Engines screamed up an octave as fifteen racing cars hurtled off, everyone, it seemed, vying for the inside position. One after another they disappeared into the dip only to reappear tearing along another straight.

O'Reilly heard the deepening notes as drivers changed down to negotiate a right-turn, left-turn complex, then up again for another straight. Behind the cars, which were beginning to spread out, hung a cloud of exhaust fumes.

"That top right-hand bend," Lars said, "is called Fisherman's. The men from Portavogie used to dry their nets on a fence there. I can just make it out and, terrific, John's in second place."

Kitty was jumping up and down beside O'Reilly. Her grin was vast. "Boy, this is exciting."

O'Reilly glanced at Myrna. She was inspecting the nails of her left hand, her expression cold.

The engine noise grew louder as the cars changed gears and drew closer at the final hairpin before the home straight. As each one approached and tore past where Lars had placed his little party, the notes seemed to rise as the car approached and fall as it went away. The Doppler effect.

O'Reilly saw John Crosslé's number 6 swing wide and pass the leading car. "Go on you-boy-yuh," he yelled—as if a driver could hear over the row.

"Bit hard on the ears this, Lars," Myrna shouted, hands clapped over hers. She was frowning. "I am going to get a headache if I have to listen to this for much longer."

Lars stooped so he could hear her better.

"How long does it go on?"

"The meet'll finish at about five, but we don't have to stay for it all," Lars said, straightening up and returning his attention to the track.

"Lars," Myrna yelled, "I'd really like to go home. Now."

Oh-oh, O'Reilly thought. Now what?

Lars turned, bent, and O'Reilly heard his brother say, "Myrna, I'm sorry I brought you."

Now was that an apology or an expression of regret?

"Can you stick it out until the end of this race? It'll be about thirty more laps. Only about another twenty minutes. I'd really like to know if John wins. Then I'll drive you home."

"Oh, very well. If I must, I must."

"Thank you."

Myrna leant over and said in O'Reilly's inclined ear, "Sometimes, Fingal, I think your brother and I are more different than I originally believed."

Brakes screeched, O'Reilly inhaled the stink of tyre rubber burning and heard the clangour of metal on concrete as a car overturned at the apex of the nearby hairpin bend, burst through the wall of hay bales, and slewed onto the grass on this side of the track.

O'Reilly reflexively started running to it. From the corner of his eye he saw the fire engine and ambulance speeding to the wreck, stewards flagging other cars down. He hoped to God the driver was all right and just had time to wonder if anything else had crashed this afternoon.

11

My Stomach's Not Good

Barry struggled up from sleep as deep as the Irish Sea. The phone extension in his quarters was ringing. He piled out of bed and grabbed the receiver. "Doctor Laverty."

"Come quick." It was a boy's high-pitched voice. A terrified boy's voice.

Barry blinked. "Who's speaking?" He rubbed his eyes with his free hand.

"It's Sammy Lindsay. It's my mammy. She's come over all queer, so she has, and I don't know what to do." A sob came over the wires.

Barry still wasn't quite awake. "What's wrong with her?" Stupid question to ask an eleven-year-old, he told himself.

"She's talking, but I can't understand all of what she's going on about, but she says her tummy hurts and she's—she's thrown off, and—" More sobs, then, "Me and Mary and Willie don't know what to do."

"I'm on my way, Sammy. Try not to be scared. I'll be there soon."

Barry rang off, grabbed the phone book, and looked up the number of the tobacconist's on the estate. They lived over their shop and once before Barry had used their phone to call an ambulance. Not all the council houses had phones. He dialled.

"Do you know what the hell time it is?" answered a man who was clearly not happy about being woken up at this hour.

"Mister Jackson, it's Doctor Laverty." There was no time for apologies. "It's an emergency. Can you and your wife run down to Eileen Lindsay's. She's ill, very ill, and her kids are all alone. I'm on my way. Thank you."

He didn't wait for a reply, and as Barry threw on his clothes he offered up thanks for how the villagers could be relied upon to come to each other's aid.

It took less than ten minutes to get to Comber Gardens in the council estate where the Lindsays lived at number 31. Barry had ignored the red traffic light. At three thirty on a Tuesday morning, the roads were deserted.

He hammered on the door.

Bloody hell. He'd just been trying to help the poor woman's insomnia. Vomiting, stomachache, bouts of delirium. The symptoms could be due to a host of conditions, but the most likely culprit was the medication Barry'd prescribed. Though rare, this side effect usually manifested itself within twenty-four to forty-eight hours of starting the drug. A simple urine test would tell, and if that wasn't possible, the history and physical findings would be pretty convincing.

The door was flung open by an unshaven, unkempt Tom Jackson, who wore a duffle coat over his pyjamas. "Thank God you're here, sir. Come on on in."

Barry remembered the little house from more than two years ago when young Sammy had contracted Henoch-Schönlein purpura, an autoimmune response causing joint pains and blotchy rashes following a mild upper-respiratory infection. He'd made a complete recovery in time for Christmas.

"The missus has Eileen tucked up in bed, first on the right upstairs, and she's stayed with her because she's blethering on about all kinds of things. I'm keeping the youngsters company in the sitting room."

"Good man," Barry said, "and thanks for coming."

Tom shrugged. "Away off and chase yourself, sir. Sure, aren't them and us neighbours?"

And, Barry thought, that was all that needed to be said. "I'll head up and see her." He started to climb the stairs as Tom went back to the small parlour. Barry could hear two women's voices. One querulous, the other soothing.

"You're leaving me and the kiddies? You're going to England?" Eileen's words were strong. Aggressive. "What am I going to do? What about me?" The "me" rose in pitch. The strength was gone now. It was a touching, pleading sound.

In her delirium, Eileen Lindsay seemed to be reliving a conversation she'd had with her husband when he'd left her in 1962.

"There there, Eileen, lamb. Hush now. Lie down. You'll tire yourself out."

Eileen spat, "Bastard. Selfish bastard. Go on then, get out. Get out—" The strangled sobbing tore at Barry's heart. He and Patricia Spence hadn't even been engaged, but he would never forget how he'd felt the night he'd discovered their love affair was over.

The little bedroom was lit by a single overhead bulb in a pink lampshade and a light on a bedside table. There was a strong smell of vomit coming from an enamel bowl set on the dressing table. Eileen Lindsay had propped herself up on her elbows, and Daphne Jackson was still trying to persuade her neighbour to lie down. She was holding one of Eileen's hands. "Hello, Doctor," Daphne said. "Am I dead glad til see you! Poor Eileen's gone astray in the head, so she has. Talking and talking." Daphne whispered, "She thinks I'm her sister, Jean. She lives in Brisbane. And she keeps grabbing her tummy like it's sore. She's boked twice." Daphne inclined her head to the bowl.

Eileen's eyes were staring and clearly she did not recognise him. Nevertheless he said, "Hello, Eileen. Sorry you're not so well."

"Is that you, Johnny. Is it?" At least her words were calmer. She sighed and lay back on her pillows.

She must think I'm Johnny Jordan, the man who'd tried to romance her after Christmas 1964.

A tear slipped down her cheek. "I've tried. God knows I have. I really have." She shook her head. Her words were flat. Affection? Guilt? Barry wasn't sure. "You're a good man, so you are, but Johnny. I don't love you . . . and I won't pretend."

She certainly could have made life a lot easier for herself and her three kids if she'd married Johnny Jordan, but from what Barry knew of

Eileen, a marriage of convenience would have been totally out of character. More of an idealist than a realist.

And she certainly wasn't in touch with reality now. He wasn't going to get any history from this patient. Not while she was delirious. He sat on the bed and took her pulse. One hundred and ten. Too fast and very strong. Her skin was hot to the touch. Barry took a cuff and his stethoscope from his bag. Her blood pressure was 160 over 98. That was too high, her pulse was too fast, and she had a fever. It was adding up. "Don't be scared, Eileen," Barry said, and tried to look under her lower lip. A sign for one possible cause of her illness would be visible there. Lead poisoning, which he thought unlikely, often produced a stippled blue line where the teeth left the gums. He could see nothing.

She tore her head back and shouted, "Take your hands off me, Jim Taggart. You think any of us shifters is fair game just because you're the foreman. Especially a woman whose husband's run off? You touch me again, you hoor's git, and I'll bloody well geld you."

Barry could imagine the scene in the linen mill. Eileen Lindsay was a tough young woman and a fighter. She had to be to raise three kids single-handed. But even if she didn't want to be touched right now, he had to examine her. "Daphne, give me a hand, will you?"

Between them they pulled down the bedclothes so he could see Eileen's abdomen.

"Thanks."

Barry said softly, "I'm your doctor, Eileen. Don't be frightened."

She started keening a low, harsh sound, then said, "The rent's due on Tuesday. We don't get paid til Friday. What'll I do?"

Barry shook his head. While Daphne sat on a chair by the bed, he inspected Eileen's abdomen. He saw nothing out of the ordinary. She didn't seem to mind his gentle palpation, so there was no question of peritonitis. He listened with his stethoscope and was rewarded with hearing loud borborygmi, the gurgling noises the bowel makes when it is pushing its contents along. Eileen writhed and clutched her tummy. He straightened up and removed the earpieces. She was having colicky pains all right.

She seemed to calm down, then smiled broadly. "Honest to God, Mister Callaghan, you can wait til Friday for the rent? You're one of God's angels, so you are."

Was it any wonder, Barry thought, with all these pressures surfacing, all the stress Eileen Lindsay was living under day to day, that she was having difficulty sleeping?

"Is she—is she going til be all right, Doctor?" Daphne asked.

"I think so." Barry turned to her. "I'd know better if I could get a urine sample, but even without it—" He could get one by passing a catheter into her bladder, but would rather not. "I'm pretty sure I know what ails her. She's reacting to her medication."

"Medication? Poor wee lamb," Daphne said.

"She'll have to go to the Royal. I'll go and phone if you'll keep an eye to her."

"Her phone's in the hall."

"Thanks."

As Barry went downstairs, he set to remembering all he knew about the rare side effect of barbiturates called porphyria. It was a disturbance in the metabolism of a family of chemicals from which haem was derived. Haem combined with iron to form haemoglobin, so vital in red cells for carrying oxygen. One in every 25,000 people was genetically predisposed to the disorder. In some, it appeared in childhood. In others, the defect lay dormant until provoked by some external stimulus. One of the possible external stimuli was barbiturates, and last Friday Barry had prescribed Nembutal 0.1 gram to be taken half an hour before Eileen's bedtime. He remembered how he'd rushed out the door because Hester Dolan and her broken wrist were waiting in the outer office. Barry had not warned Eileen of any potential side effects of the medicine he'd prescribed. Damnation. This was a classic case of iatrogenic, or doctor-caused, disease.

He dialled and waited. Damn, damn, damn. He spoke through gritted teeth to the necessary people, made the arrangements, and went back upstairs. Wasn't the unwritten law of medicine *primum non nocere,* first do no harm? And yet in fairness to himself, his well-meant prescription would not have affected 24,999 other people. And he was a mature enough physician to recognise that.

"I think she's calming down a bit, sir," Daphne said when she saw him in the doorway.

Eileen was lying on her pillows, eyes closed, her breathing regular and deep, but by the time he had crossed the small room to her bedside she was sitting up, grabbing her belly, and sobbing, "Oh God, it hurts. It hurts."

His textbook had said that the pain of porphyria could be excruciating. And yet it had been drummed into them as students never to give painkillers until a firm diagnosis had been made. An absolute diagnosis could only be made by chemical analysis of her blood and urine.

He rummaged in his bag as he convinced himself that giving a painkiller would not interfere with the diagnostic process at the Royal.

Eileen moaned and Daphne murmured, "There, there, love."

"I'm going to give her a jag in just a minute." He drew 100 mgm of pethidine into a syringe. "This will only sting for a second," he said, rolling up the sleeve of her nightgown and giving the drug intramuscularly.

It took several minutes for an obvious effect to be noticeable, but soon her breathing was deep and regular again.

Barry knew he was halfway to solving one of Eileen Lindsay's problems—the medical one. But what to do about her children? "Daphne," he said, "I know you and Tom have a shop to run—"

"Never you worry about it. Me and him'll see to them the day, get them their brekky and off til school, and—" She frowned.

The Jacksons worked as a team. He understood that while they could afford to help out today, they would not be able to provide a long-term solution. He said, "When Sammy was sick Maggie Houston came and babysat. I'll ask her if she'd help out again."

While he waited for the ambulance, he'd fill out the forms to make sure she got her sickness benefit and that her employer understood her absence from work. The Lord knew money was tight enough for Eileen, poor creature. As if coping with the desertion by her husband, raising three kiddies, and working full time wasn't enough to cope with, his attempt to let her get a decent night's sleep had made her sick enough to end up in hospital. He just hoped they could do more for Eileen Lindsay than a country GP.

12

Of Some Distressful Stroke

Barry let himself into the warm kitchen at eleven the next morning. And a good thing it was warm too. Rain was rattling off the kitchen window, staccato, never-ending drum beats to underscore something bubbling in a pot on the stovetop.

"You're up?" Kinky said, turning from the stove.

"I am," he said, and inhaled. Whatever she was cooking was a delight to the nose. "That smells delicious."

"For himself and Kitty's dinner," she said. "Parsnip and apple soup. Kitty will only have to heat it up, so, and there'll be beef and dumplings to follow."

"Pity you're married to Archie," Barry said with a grin. "The way you feed us I might just forgo Sue if you'd marry me."

She laughed. "Go away, Barry Laverty. You're quite astray in the head about Miss Nolan."

"I am," said Barry, "but you are a marvellous cook, Kinky."

"Thank you." She made a little bow. "It does be nice to be appreciated, bye." She sipped a taste from a spoon. "Coming on a treat."

"I'm off—"

"For your bath, I imagine, and to make a phone call about last night's case. You must be famished, bye."

Barry opened his mouth but no words came out. Kinky's powers of deduction were especially keen this morning. "How—how did—? Never mind." He smiled.

"I do have a fresh batch of soda farls. I'll make you my Kinky's eggs Benedict."

Barry grinned. Her soda farl topped with a rasher and a lightly poached egg and smothered in Hollandaise sauce was a thing of beauty. "That would be wonderful."

And fifteen minutes later it was. Oh it was. He mopped dark orange-yellow egg yolk and creamy sauce Hollandaise up with a piece of fried soda farl.

"That," she said, "will do you for breakfast and lunch, seeing it's eleven thirty now."

"It will," Barry said, "and keep me full until this evening. I'm taking Sue to the Culloden for dinner." He sliced off a piece of rasher and popped it in his mouth. Delicious. And decent of Kinky to make it for him.

"Busy night last night," Kinky said. It wasn't a question.

"Yes. I'm afraid Eileen Lindsay was taken poorly."

"She went off by ambulance," Kinky said, then paused dramatically. "Aggie Arbuthnot popped in to bring me a dozen eggs, so. You're eating one of them now."

Barry grinned, mopped up more yolk, and shook his head. He had long since stopped marvelling at the speed of Ballybucklebo's jungle—no, that was the wrong word—its rustic telegraph.

"And will Eileen be all right?"

"It was the Royal I was phoning just now. She's more comfortable this morning. She's got a thing called porphyria. There's no cure."

Kinky tutted. "The poor wee soul."

He heard the deep sympathy in her voice. "But if she avoids things that bring it on, she'll be all right once she's got over this attack."

Kinky folded her arms. "It will be difficult for her to manage with three kiddies and her the only breadwinner."

"Aye. It will." Was this perhaps the "need" Kinky had foreseen for her four-hundred-pound winnings on Foinavon? He popped in the last slice of tomato, then carried his plate to the sink. "I'm going out, but I'll wash my things first."

"Leave that. I'll see to it," Kinky said.

"Kinky, cooking breakfast for late-sleeping doctors is not exactly in your job description. You were kind enough to make me breakfast, the least I can do—"

"It's your day off, and besides, I can't have you underfoot while I'm finishing up this soup. Now run along and get dressed like a good doctor."

And Barry did as he was bid.

He was back in the kitchen ten minutes later, putting on his Burberry raincoat and cramming a paddy hat on his head. He listened to the rain still rattling off the windows. The late Al Jolson may have waxed lyrical about "April Showers." Clearly the man hadn't experienced what Ulster could offer. More like a blooming monsoon.

"And where might you be going to on an afternoon like this? And why aren't you tucked up in the lounge with a cup of tea and your book. That John D. MacDonald one about a Mister McGee that you've been talking about?"

"Eileen's going to need help. She'll be in hospital at least until Saturday."

"Och, the dear."

"The Jacksons can hold the fort today, but they've got their shop to look after. I thought maybe Sonny and Maggie might help out the way they did when Sammy was sick."

Kinky nodded. "Hearts of corn, those two. I'm sure they will."

A gust shook the kitchen windows.

"Keep yourself well wrapped up, Barry Laverty. I'll make some beef tea for when you come home."

"Thanks, Kinky," Barry said. "I'm off." And having a distinct image of Scott's South Polar Party straining into the Antarctic blast, he let himself out and hunched his shoulders against the storm.

"Come in out of that, Doctor," Sonny Houston said. "And let me take your hat and coat."

As always, barks and yips came from the kitchen where the Houston dogs were penned when visitors called.

"Come into the parlour." He led the way. "Look who's come to call, Maggie," Sonny said.

"How's about ye?" Maggie asked. "Take the weight off your feet." She sat by a roaring fire with what looked like a large atlas open to a map of Australia and the one-eyed, one-eared General Sir Bernard Law Montgomery purring on top of it. "Very well, thanks, Maggie," he said. "And all the better for seeing you and Sonny."

"And what can we do for you, Doctor," said Sonny. "As much as we're delighted by your visit, I imagine this is more than just a social call."

"I've come to ask for another favour for Eileen Lindsay. She's had to be admitted to the Royal. She's okay, but she's probably going to be in there until at least Saturday."

"Gracious me," said Maggie. "As if the poor soul doesn't have enough to contend with. That deadbeat wastrel of a husband of hers taking himself off to England—"

"Now Maggie dear, no one can know what happens inside a marriage except those involved."

Maggie sniffed. "For a man who spent his life sifting through people's rubbish, Sonny has no interest in gossip."

"It's not rubbish. It's called a midden and it's important to archaeologists. But you're quite right about gossip and rumour. Now, how can we help?" Sonny asked.

Typical of the man, Barry thought. "Her weans, Sammy, Mary, and Willie, need looking after until Eileen's back on her feet."

"What do you think, Maggie?" Sonny asked.

"They're a bunch of wee dotes, so they are." She frowned. "But we've the dogs and the General til look after." She hesitated then smiled her toothless-as-an-oyster smile. "But don't we have two spare rooms and couldn't you run them to school and pick them up, Sonny?"

"With no difficulty. It is a bit of a walk from here." He beamed. "And do you know what, Doctor? Tom Duffy's Circus will be in Bangor on Saturday. A trip there might help cheer them up. We'll do it."

Before Barry could say thank you, Maggie had stood up, decanting the General and the atlas onto the floor. "You and Sonny work out the details. I'll make us a wee cup of tea in our hands. The kettle's on and I've some new plum cake."

Barry's heart sank. Even Arthur Guinness turned his nose up at the indigestible stuff.

"But I've fresh scones too, Kinky's recipe, if you'd prefer."

"That would be lovely, Maggie," Barry said, swallowing down the acid taste that always developed in his mouth when he thought of Maggie's tea. The stuff could tan rawhide, but trapped as he was by courtesy, he'd choke down a cup before leaving.

"Maggie and I'll go over after school today and work things out with the Jacksons, but the little ones will be perfectly fine with us. Maggie and I didn't have kiddies so we've no grandchildren. It'll be a kind of being granny and grampa, and I know Maggie will really enjoy that."

"I will, too," Maggie said, depositing her tray on a table. "And I'll tell you a thing, young Doctor Barry Laverty. We all know yis and Miss Nolan's getting wed in July. Make sure the pair of youse has lots of weans or youse'll end up like me and my ould goat." Her voice was honeyed with affection. "Mammy and daddy to a clatter of daft dogs and a belligerent pussycat. Now," she picked up the teapot, "I'll pour."

Barry sighed. He remembered that walk along the banks of the Braid River with Sue in February, when they'd discussed starting a family. He'd confessed he was torn then, and he still was. He wished to hell he could be enthusiastic, but, unlike Sue, deep down he found the prospect of parenthood daunting.

"Here's your tea, sir." Maggie gave Barry a cup. "Help yourself til—"

The phone rang in the hall.

"I'll answer it," Sonny said, and rose.

Barry was on the verge of accepting a scone when Sonny reappeared. "It's Kinky for you, Doctor, and she says it's urgent."

"Right." Barry ran to the hall and grabbed the phone. "Kinky?"

"It's Gracie Miller. She says Lewis has taken another turn. Doctor O'Reilly's in the surgery sewing up a bad cut and Nonie's just left to see someone in Helen's Bay."

"I'm on my way." Barry stuck his head into the lounge. "Thanks for helping with the Lindsay kids, you two. I've got an emergency. Gotta go." He grabbed his coat and hat and without bothering to put them on tore into the pelting rain and down the path.

Brunhilde, as Volkswagens were reputed to do, started at once. As Barry accelerated, he recalled that an angiogram had confirmed a narrowing of the left internal carotid artery in Lewis's neck. Over the years a build-up developed, called atheroma, of fat—he guiltily thought of the fry he'd just enjoyed in Kinky's kitchen—white blood cells and calcium under the inner wall of the vessel. Lewis had been discharged on the fifteenth, twelve days ago, and the low dose of Coumadin he'd been prescribed, an oral anticoagulant, had stabilised. The senior consultant who had looked after Lewis—Doctor Harold Millar—had said in his letter to Barry that it was unclear if anticoagulants really helped, but it was the best he could do.

Barry wished his specialist colleague could do more. Ultimately nothing was going to prevent the inevitable: either more attacks like the last one or, perish the thought, some of the atheroma breaking free, travelling to the brain, and causing death of brain tissue. That outcome would be categorized as a stroke and the severity of the residual damage would depend upon how much brain function was lost—if Lewis survived.

The sooner Barry got to their bungalow, the better.

Gracie met him at the back door. She was in floods of tears, fragile and pale. "You have to do something, sir. Come quick." She ran back into the kitchen. "It's not like the last time. Lewis never said nothing. He just collapsed in a heap."

Barry slammed the door against the gale and gave silent thanks that the kitchen was toasty. He'd got himself soaked for a second time on his way from the car.

Gracie stood wringing her hands over her husband, who lay crumpled on his right side on the floor. He wore a shirt under a sleeveless pullover, trousers, slippers, and socks. His spectacles had skidded across the tiles.

Barry knelt beside the fallen man and set his bag on the floor. He made sure Lewis was breathing regularly and deeply. His pulse was slow, but there was no evidence of any arrhythmia. "Lewis?" Barry said into the man's ear. "Lewis?" But there was no sign he had heard. Barry pushed the patient gently so he lay on his back. His eyelids were closed. Barry opened the right eye. He pulled a pencil torch from his inside jacket pocket and shone the beam into the eye. The pupil constricted. He repeated the process on the left. No response. It was the left carotid that was damaged. It supplied the left part of the brain that received visual signals from the left eye.

"Is he—Is he dead, Doctor?" Gracie asked. Her voice quavered.

"No," Barry said, "but he's unconscious. I just need to do a quick examination." Loss of consciousness wasn't always a sign of a stroke, but Barry was seriously worried. He lifted Lewis's right arm, bent it at the elbow, and supported it by cupping it in his own left palm. He pulled a patella hammer from his bag. The instrument looked like a tomahawk with a steel handle and triangular red rubber head. He tapped it against the tendon of the biceps. No response. He moved to kneel beside Lewis's left knee, flexed it, and tested the patellar tendon reflex between the kneecap and the shin bone. Nothing. Barry took off the man's right shoe and sock. His toenails were yellow and horny and the ball of the foot and heel callused. All those years as a postman had left their mark. Barry found his keys and rubbed the tip of one along from the heel to the front of the big toe side of the sole. The toe bent upward into what was known as a positive Babinski reflex, named for the French physician who had described it in 1896. This, along with the loss of reflexes, was indicating left-sided cerebral damage. Barry inhaled deeply, then said, "Pillows and blankets, please, Gracie."

"Yes, Doctor."

It was going to be back to the Royal for Lewis Miller, and this time whether or not he'd be coming out was unclear. And if he did survive, how damaged would he be? That was the job of the specialist to assess if Lewis recovered consciousness.

"Here y'are." Gracie gave Barry a pillow that he slipped under Lewis's head and a pink blanket to cover the man.

Barry rose. "You stay with him, Gracie. I'll need to phone."

"Will he live, sir?" The pleading in her voice was heartbreaking.

"I hope so," Barry said, "but I must phone."

There was a bed for Lewis on ward 22, the neurology ward. The ambulance would arrive in about twenty minutes.

Barry looked down at the man, feeling helpless and knowing he could easily slip into feelings of guilt if he didn't recognise that doctors were only human and could not cure everything. And certainly not cerebral damage. His care now must be for Gracie. He took her by the elbow and led her to a kitchen chair. "Sit down, Gracie," he said, helping her to do so. "Can I make you a cup of tea?"

She nodded, her eyes never leaving her husband. "The kettle's full. There's matches by the stove."

The coal-gas burner lit with a *pop*. He put the kettle over the light blue flames. "Gracie," he said, "I'm pretty sure Lewis has had a stroke."

She wailed suddenly, a high-pitched keening, then collected herself, and said, her voice cracking, "Och, no. Och, please no."

Barry moved to her side, putting his arm round her shoulder. "I'm sorry. I'm so sorry."

She shuddered as she inhaled. "I'm going to lose him, so I am."

"We don't know that," Barry said.

The kettle whistled.

"I'll make the tea," he said.

As he warmed the pot, spooned in the leaves, poured in the boiling water and let it sit, he heard her gentle sobbing.

Barry knelt beside Lewis. He was still breathing and his pulse was steady. His right eye responded to light, but the left did not. This was no simple repeat of his last episode.

"I'm afraid he's no better, but he's no worse."

Gracie cried quietly.

Barry stood and returned to the stove. "Milk and sugar?" It seemed incongruous that mere feet away an old man lay close to death and here Barry was making tea, but in Ulster, tea was the universal comforter.

"Just milk."

Barry took the cup to Gracie. "Here you are, love."

"Thank you." She sipped. "And thank you for coming so quick. I-I know there's not much you can do."

Or anyone else, Barry thought, but kept that thought to himself. "Would you like me to phone your daughter, Joy? Isn't she in Portrush?"

Gracie sniffed. "It's all right," she said, "I'll call her in a wee minute. I'm sure you must be busy and if you want to run along, sir . . ."

Barry shook his head. "I'll stay until the ambulance comes."

"Thank you." Gracie pulled in a deep breath, and glanced at Lewis, who was snoring gently. "He looks like he's asleep. So peaceful." And she managed the ghost of a smile. Her gaze took in the whole kitchen. She must have noticed the way the storm was hurling the rain against the window. "Boys-a-dear," she said, "thon's a powerful blow." She looked straight back at Barry. "Manys the gale him and me've sat through in this house, all cosy in the wee lounge by the fire. Maybe a wee hot-half to keep away the dew." There was a dreamy tone to her voice.

Barry recognised the thought as selfish, but that was the scene, starring Barry and Sue Laverty in this bungalow, that he'd pictured ever since Dapper Frew had shown him the house. Which should be coming up for sale this month. Should be. But now? He banished the thought and knelt beside Lewis. He could detect no change. Barry sighed. "He's no worse," he said.

Gracie nodded. Sipped her tea. "And the summers, with wee Joy in her pram in the garden. When she was seven, she had a pet tortoise . . ."

Barry reckoned if it was comforting Gracie to remember happy days, he'd not interfere.

"D'yiz know, Doctor, and I'll have to get Lewis's say-so when he's all better, like, but I don't think I could bear to move away. I think him and me should see out our days where we started. What do you think?"

Barry flinched. He wasn't going to be able to buy his dream home for Sue. And he certainly was not going to try to dissuade Gracie. "I think that's—"

He was interrupted by a hammering on the kitchen door. The ambulance had arrived.

"Excuse me," he said, crossing the floor to open the door to two blue-uniformed Northern Ireland Hospitals Authority attendants.

"This the Mill—? Course it is. How's about ye, Doctor Laverty? The dispatcher said it was one of your patients."

"Come in, Tommy." He recognised the man. They'd gone out together on an obstetrical flying squad case when Barry had been a student. "And shut the door behind you." Barry stood aside and let the attendants place Lewis on a stretcher. They lifted him. "Get the door, Doc?"

Barry hesitated. Gracie had risen. She stood by the stretcher, bent, and kissed Lewis's forehead. "I love you, husband," she said. "And I always will. Please don't go and die on me. Please." The yearning tore at Barry. He turned his back and opened the door, unsure whether it was rain or tears that coursed down his cheeks.

13

The Warmest Welcome, at an Inn

The elderly black-and-white Vauxhall Victor in front of him was creeping along the narrow road, and for once O'Reilly was in no hurry. Barry was driving and the pace allowed O'Reilly to appreciate how the late-evening sun limned the little hedged fields, some dotted with white sheep, some green and fallow, others scattered with small herds of cows. The long right-hand corner was on an escarpment above a valley leading back toward Helen's Bay. A garage with three petrol pumps and a mini-mart stood at the crown of the bend. The road then veered to the left, running straight and narrow for a quarter of a mile through the little village of Crawfordsburn.

He'd always had a soft spot for the village. In those early years in Ballybucklebo after the war, desperate to get away from the empty house, he'd gone for drives when petrol rationing allowed and had sometimes ended up here, having a quiet drink at The Old Inn.

The grey, two-storey building housing the Orange Order's "Crawfordsburn Chosen Few Temperance Lodge 1091" wasn't exactly welcoming for a man who enjoyed his pint. But next door stood a terrace of low cottages, some grey stucco, some whitewashed, all with slate roofs. For some reason, despite being in a village, they had reminded him of happier times as a young doctor in Dublin with their scrubbed front steps and gleaming windows. Outside one hung a sign, "Irish Cottage Crafts," where O'Reilly had bought his first paddy hat.

The inn had been a welcome respite for him. No one here knew him as the local doctor, a far cry from the Duck back in Ballybucklebo. There it had taken a couple of years for the locals to accept him as one of their own. Here the staff had been cheerful and kind, and even during the worst of the rationing had managed to serve up decent meals.

Tonight a middle-aged couple strolled along the narrow footpath that separated the original one-storey whitewashed inn building from the road. A row of tall bay windows with shiny black-enamelled frames was overhung by the reed thatch eaves.

Adjoining the low building was a much more recent addition, an Irish-Georgian two-storey structure topped with twin steeply pitched roofs. The inn had been an integral part of the area since 1614. Donaghadee, eight miles to the east, had been an important cross-channel port, and what had then been called The Old Ship Inn was where coaches running between Belfast to the west and Donaghadee to the east had changed horses.

Barry indicated for a left turn into the inn's car park. Past it stood the village post office facing the gardens and the low pavilion of the exclusive Crawfordsburn Country Club, its façade pseudo-Tudor with black beams against whitewash.

They got out to listen to the happy burbling of the burn that ran through a ravine behind the inn. That burn and an early Scottish lowland settler named Crawford had given the village its name.

From a hedge bordering the stream, the falsetto notes of a song thrush, each phrase repeated three times, welcomed the soft evening. April was drawing to a close, the buds would soon be bursting, the sticky horse chestnut ones first. Spring was well on its way. The month and the chestnut trees struck a chord and O'Reilly sang, a low rumbling sound,

April in Paris, chestnuts in blossom . . .

He had resolved to take Kitty for a fortnight to Paris sometime soon, but not until the new trainee, if he passed scrutiny this evening, had become settled in.

"You're in good form, Fingal."

O'Reilly turned to see Barry swinging the door shut on Brunhilde. "And why not? It's Friday. We both have the night off. The inn always serves a great dinner, and we're going to meet our potential junior colleague, Doctor Connor Nelson."

"Do you know much about him?"

O'Reilly shook his head. "Charlie Greer and Cromie speak highly of the man. They both had him as a student. I had lunch with them after I met with George Irwin ten days ago."

"So we're sussing him out, seeing if we'll feel comfortable working with him?"

O'Reilly nodded. "George has recommended him, so our job tonight isn't to grill him on his technical ability or how he feels about taking night call. He's a trainee after all and until I say so, he'll be working under supervision. We just want to know how easy he'll be to get along with. Nelson was a few years behind you. Know anything about him?"

"Can't say I do, but you know the structure at Queens. Third years don't speak to second years, who don't mix with first years."

O'Reilly nodded. There were class distinctions as rigidly marked as the Hindu caste system in all walks of Ulster life.

Barry shrugged. "Anyway, you want us to form our own first impression."

"Right. The one thing you don't get a second chance to make." O'Reilly stopped outside the inn's front door. "Do you know," he said, "this old place has lodged Peter the Great, Tsar of all the Russias, Dick Turpin the highwayman, Dean Swift, Charles Dickens, and C. S. Lewis."

"And the wise and eminent Doctor Fingal Flahertie O'Reilly," Barry said with a bow, letting O'Reilly go first.

O'Reilly laughed and thought about himself as he had been when he'd first started coming here, a widower, married only six months. Grieving and weary after six long years of war. The new young doctor in Ballybucklebo, desperate for acceptance. Barry too, had lacked self-confidence when first he'd come. Changed days now.

O'Reilly went down the three steps into the inn's carpeted hall before the reception desk. Hanging on the back wall was a fine pastel portrait of a previous owner, a woman known to all her regulars as "Mrs. White."

"Evening, Doctors." Peter, the night manager, a tall, solemn man wearing a dark business suit, greeted them from behind the reception desk. "We've a table for three in the dining room for you, but would you like to go through to the bar first? There's a table there for you too. Kelly the barman will give you menus."

"Thank you," O'Reilly said. "Our guest is a Doctor Nelson. He'll be here any minute."

"I'll bring him through, sir."

O'Reilly led the way along a narrow hall and through a swing door to a crowded room with a low, dark-beamed ceiling. Although the air was heavy with tobacco smoke, it was a very different crowd from the locals at the Duck. No dunchers and frayed collarless shirts. Business-suited men in white shirts, old school ties, and highly polished shoes would duck in here on their way home to Bangor from their offices in Belfast for a quick one. Of the couples, the well-coiffed ladies wore cocktail dresses, sipping aperitifs before going through to dinner. The hum of conversation was muted and overheard snatches dealt more with holidays in Spain, business matters, the stock market, or cricket than racing greyhounds or the prospects of Linfield or Glentoran Football Clubs. A well-occupied long bar was immediately to his right.

"Bout ye, Doctor. How's it going?" Kelly the barman said from behind a row of four shining brass pump handles.

O'Reilly smiled. "Pretty much the way it's been going for the last twenty-one years that you've been pouring me drinks."

"That long? My God." Kelly laughed. "I'll be ready for my pension soon, so I will." He pointed to a table set in the bow of a mullioned bay window. "That one there's for youse."

"Thank you."

"And what would youse like?"

"Barry?"

"Pint, please."

Kelly nodded. "And the usual for yourself, sir?"

"Please." O'Reilly followed Barry and they took their seats. Before Kelly could deliver their order, Peter appeared in the doorway, accompanied by a younger man. Medium height, receding ginger hair, a high forehead. A sharp nose separated two lively eyes. O'Reilly guessed the man to be in his late twenties. Old for a recent graduate? As he walked across the bar toward their table, O'Reilly noticed the newcomer was dragging his left leg. His lips were set in firm resolution, and there was a determined thrust to his chin despite his difficulty.

O'Reilly and Barry rose and O'Reilly offered his hand. "Doctor Nelson?"

The man nodded.

"Fingal O'Reilly, and this is my partner, Barry Laverty. Have a pew." Barry and he shook hands.

"Thank you," the man sat, "and thank you for inviting me to dinner." His gaze wandered round the room. "Very swanky," he said. "Very p-posh."

Just a tinge of working class in the man's accent, O'Reilly noticed, a certain hesitation in his speech. "Good of you to come down from Dundonald. Would you like a drink?"

Doctor Nelson smiled. "Ordinarily I'd go a pint, but I'm here because I really want the job. I'll have a white lemonade, please."

O'Reilly glanced at Barry, who was nodding and, O'Reilly was sure, drawing the same conclusion. This was a serious young man who was too astute to be caught out by the *in vino veritas* school of job interviews. Good.

Kelly arrived with three menus, a pint, and O'Reilly's Jameson.

"Thanks," O'Reilly said, "and a white lemonade for Doctor Nelson." Kelly withdrew.

"Now, sir," Doctor Nelson said, "you introduced yourself and your partner as Fingal and Barry. I-I don't make much of a fuss about titles . . ." That hesitation again. "M-my friends call me Connor or Con."

"Good man, Con," Barry said. "Except in front of the customers, we're pretty informal."

O'Reilly nodded approval. "Tell us a bit about yourself."

The man shrugged. "Not much to tell, really. I was b-born in 1938 in the Royal Maternity . . ."

That made him twenty-nine now. He'd qualified in 1965, so he'd have been twenty-seven then, at a time when most medical students graduated at twenty-two or -three. O'Reilly wondered what had delayed the man's progress, but he wasn't going to ask outright. He'd wait to see what came out as the conversation progressed.

Con Nelson pursed his lips. "I'm sure you saw me limping. I had polio in 1943. I was in Purdysburn Fever Hospital for six months." Nelson inhaled. "I still remember a Doctor Drew there. He was the kindest man I ever met." He sighed. "I really looked up to him."

O'Reilly nodded. Perhaps some seeds had been sown then?

"Then I was laid up in a plaster of Paris for a year. The polio held up my schooling for a while."

And that, O'Reilly thought, accounted for some but not all of the delay in Nelson's going to Queens. O'Reilly remembered the bitter struggles with his father, who had wanted his son to be a nuclear physicist and refused to pay for his education. That had held O'Reilly back four years before he could start at Trinity College School of Physic in 1931. It had been a five-year course back then. Now it was six. He'd been twenty-eight when he'd graduated. He felt a certain sympathy for Connor Nelson.

"Your lemonade, sir," said Kelly, appearing with the drink and disappearing as discreetly.

"Cheers," said O'Reilly, and drank, accompanied by the others.

"So why general practice?" Barry asked.

Con Nelson looked thoughtful, inhaled, then said, "I'd to take a wee bit of time g-getting into Queens, so now that I'm qualified, I want to practice." He stared at the tabletop for a moment then looked up first at Barry then at O'Reilly. "I'm from a kitchen house on Rydalmere Street . . ."

O'Reilly nodded. Working-class housing in Belfast was only a step up from the tenements in the Liberties of Dublin where he'd started in general practice in '36. Even among the working class, there was a kind of stratification. A parlour house had an extra room and was regarded as superior to a kitchen house. It spoke volumes for this man's honesty that he didn't try to conceal his roots. And very few children from those neighbourhoods stayed in school past sixteen. Boys either got a job or started an apprenticeship, and it was received wisdom that it was a waste of time educating girls, who'd only get married anyway. Polio. Poverty. Connor Nelson had certainly overcome a lot of obstacles. O'Reilly was warming to this man.

"Rydalmere Street is a long way from medical school," O'Reilly prompted when Connor's silence continued.

The young man nodded slowly. "I'll not tell a lie. It was tough. Daddy didn't have a job for a b-brave while, we lived with my grampa on a wee three-quarters-of-an-acre farm at Stockdam." His smile was of fond reminiscence. "We had pigs and goats, chickens, dogs and cats. Then Daddy got taken on at Maguire and Patterson's match factory working five and a half days a week for ten pounds six shillings. Not bad money." Connor Nelson's face clouded. "Daddy died. They said it was generalised atherosclerosis, but I think it was overwork. He was laid up for six months, then took pneumonia and was admitted to Purdysburn hospital. Doctor Drew was still there. He remembered me, comforted me when . . . I was with Daddy when he died the next day. I was sixteen."

"Most young men in your position would have left school by then," O'Reilly said.

Con nodded. "M-Mammy pushed me on. Made me stay in Grosvenor High School until I was seventeen. To get my senior certificate." He sipped his lemonade. "Although, to tell you the truth I didn't work very hard that last year at school, after Daddy died. The heart had gone out of me."

O'Reilly said, "It's hard to lose a father when you're young. I know."

"Thank you, Fingal."

"And grieving takes time," Barry said. He paused, looked about to say something, and stopped. Then, squaring his shoulders, he said, "If I've got this right, you left school in 1955, but you started Queens in '59, right?" O'Reilly noticed the question "why?" was left unsaid.

Connor Nelson nodded. "I had no idea what I wanted to do when I left school. Ever since I was in Purdysburn hospital with the polio and watched Doctor Drew, I thought maybe that's what I would do, but— och . . ."

O'Reilly understood. This was a boy from the backstreets of Belfast.

"And I fell behind in maths and science in my last year at school.

I found out later you needed them for medicine. And to get your fees paid by the state, you needed a sixty percent average in your school-leaving exams. With the pass mark at forty percent, that's a brave high average to go to Queens for free. I didn't have it, and Mammy and me didn't have the money for the fees anyway, so I went to w-work. And anyroad, d'you ever hear this one? 'God bless the squire and his relations, And keep us all in our proper stations.' I was a working-class boy. People like me don't have professions. Being a doctor wasn't for the likes of me." He stared down at the tabletop. "I thought I had to accept that."

Aye, O'Reilly thought. Bloody class system. The Americans have that right. Oh, there was a form of one based on celebrity or wealth, but O'Reilly had been over there during the war and seen how anyone with gumption could rise in the world. He'd been told how actor James Cagney's family had come from the lowest slums of New York, but in spite of that, two of his brothers had gone on to be physicians.

"But you didn't accept it," said Barry.

The man shook his head. "I got a job as a civil servant. At least I didn't have to go and work in the shipyards or—a match factory. Mammy was pleased. I worked in the Registry of Deeds copying documents all day." He made a self-deprecatory laugh. "It was very boring. I couldn't do that all my life. I started to get a notion I wanted to have a profession. I thought about medicine but, och . . . I didn't have the marks and we couldn't afford the fees so there was no use day-dreaming. I wasn't going to win an Olympic gold medal either."

O'Reilly was listening carefully. There was no bitterness in the man's speech.

Connor took a deep draught of his lemonade. "My great-great-great grandfather had been a Methodist minister. I took a notion that kind of thing might suit me. So I wrote the exams to be a lay preacher. I didn't need any more schooling or money to do that, and I passed . . ." A smile of pride crossed his face, then faded. "But then I still had a powerful s-stammer. You could hardly preach a sermon if you tripped over all of your words, could you?"

Mmmm, O'Reilly thought. While he would judge no man for his

faith, there was no room for proselytising in the practice. Doctors, in O'Reilly's opinion, had no place in patients' religion or politics, particularly here in Ulster where the old Orange and Green currents still ran strongly beneath an apparently tranquil surface. He sipped his Jameson.

Connor Nelson sighed. "By then I'd started asking myself, why shouldn't I be a doctor? If I was smart enough to pass the exams for preaching, why not try for medical school? Maybe it wasn't expected for a boy like me . . ." He looked directly into O'Reilly's eyes. "But there was no law against it neither, and I began to see I had wanted it ever since I was wee and in hospital. I still didn't have the marks, though, or the money. It started to get me down until I heard a thing from one of the ministers. The Methodist Missionary Society would pay for your medical education if you became a medical missionary."

O'Reilly's frown deepened and he could see that agnostic Barry was looking puzzled too.

"I applied. No luck." Connor Nelson chuckled. "I think they saw through me. I don't think I'd have been very good at converting the heathen."

O'Reilly glanced at Barry, saw a look of relief akin to the one he was feeling cross Barry's face. Clearly the man was no evangelical. "So what did you do?" he asked.

Connor Nelson took a deep breath. "I quit my job and got thirty-two shillings and sixpence a week unemployment while M-Mammy paid for the rent, my elocution classes, and my fees for Renshaw's Academy."

Certainly, O'Reilly thought, while there was still a touch of the Donegal Road accent in Con's voice and an occasional repeat of a letter, his teachers had done a fine job. Almost as good as Professor Higgins had done with Eliza Doolittle.

"Renshaw's? On Botanic Avenue?" Barry said. "I know that place. It gives intensive instruction in subjects its pupils need to go to university or join one of the services."

"That's right. I passed all three subjects I needed," Con shook his head, "but I still didn't get sixty percent. Like I said, I hadn't been good at maths and sciences at school. Still no Queens. At least not paid for by the state."

O'Reilly was intrigued. He even ignored his whiskey.

"I wasn't going to give up. I made one last attempt. I got a job as an assistant technician with the Linen Research Council in Lambeg." He smiled. "They paid a good wage and gave me two and a half days off every week to go to Belfast Technical College." His grin started small but grew. "I studied physics and chemistry and biology in June 1959 and I passed them all and my average was sixty-two percent. A seventy in biology pulled up my fifty-three in physics. And I still had the Latin from the exams I'd done at school. I got into Queens." Then he grew solemn. "Mammy could hardly stop crying when I got my results, she was so proud." He nodded to himself. "And so she should have been. All the sacrifices she made for me."

"Begod," said O'Reilly, clapping the man on the shoulder, "I never heard the like for persistence." He laughed. "Except maybe the spider that Robert the Bruce watched build and rebuild her web."

Connor looked from O'Reilly to Barry, then down to the table. "I know my marks weren't that good to begin with, but I've done well at Queens. Never failed a single exam."

O'Reilly thought fondly of his closest friend, Bob Beresford, who'd made a profession of failing medical school. Poor old Bob. Dead these twenty-three years.

"I don't like to boast, but I won the prize for ophthalmology in finals."

"Good for you," Barry said, "and fair play. You're not boasting, just telling us about a real achievement."

"Absolutely right," said O'Reilly, who was impressed by the young man's honesty, determination, and natural modesty. "Will we take Connor Nelson as a trainee, Barry?"

"Like a shot," Barry said.

"Welcome to the practice." O'Reilly offered a hand, which was shaken. "We'll show you the ropes on Monday, May the second."

There was a shake in Connor Nelson's voice when he said, "Thank you, Fingal. Thank you, Barry. I promise you won't regret it."

"I might," said O'Reilly, "if you ever delay my dinner again." He picked up one of the menus. "Now you two decide what you'd like to eat, and, Con?"

"Yes, Fingal?"

"I was impressed when you wanted to keep your wits about you, but you're over the hurdle. Will you take a jar to celebrate?"

"I will, Fingal. Gladly. Mine's a pint."

O'Reilly raised his whiskey. "And may you take many more with me and Barry for as long as you work at Number One Main Street, Ballybucklebo."

14

All the Fun of the Fair

"Roll up, roll up. See death-defying aerialists. Laugh at the clowns. See the world's strongest man lift five men at once."

The clown, dressed in fuzzy silver wig, bulbous red nose, baggy polka-dotted pants, and enormous shoes, cried in a thick Belfast docklands accent. "Be amazed when the lion tamer puts his head in the lion's mouth. Be more amazed when he takes it out again."

Sue Nolan laughed and the clown doffed the small black bowler perched on his wig. "What a great way to spend our Saturday off," she said with a sigh. "You know when I was ten, I wanted to run away and join a circus."

"I'm very glad you didn't," Barry said, taking her hand.

"Mum and Dad used to take my brother and me to Hunter's Circus in the Belfast Hippodrome after Christmas, but it was indoors." She looked around wide-eyed at a single enormous, lozenge-shaped tent supported by two poles that stuck out through holes at each end of the roof. The tips of the poles carried long, multicoloured banners. "Where shall we go first, Barry?"

"Go to the fun fair," roared the clown from behind them. "Try the coconut shy. Win a prize. Every time she bumps—she bounces. Roll up. Roll up."

They looked at each other and laughed. "The oracle has spoken," said Barry. "Let's go to the fun fair." He'd already noticed several families with children clutching stuffed animals. "I'll try to win you a prize."

"All right. Win me a teddy bear and I'll call him Barry," she said, then whispered, "He can sleep with me when you're unavailable. Oh, Barry, we're going to have lots of fun today. It'll bring out the kiddy in us." She skipped happily on the springy grass. "It's been years since I've been to a circus."

"Decent of the marquis, letting the Duffy circus use his ten-acre field," he said, having to quicken his stride to keep up with her. "The MacNeill family have hosted the Duffy family on this field since the 1880s. One of them, John Duffy, an acrobat, was known as the 'Irish Barnum,' you know."

"I said it would bring out the kiddy in us, not the history master." She was looking at him sternly and he forced a smile. He thought he'd been looking forward to today, and the weather was perfect for it. A warm sun looked down from a cloudless sky and the air was scented with . . . Barry sniffed and wondered who got the job of dunging out the elephant's cage.

It was hard to get into the spirit of things, though, when one of his patients might be close to death. Three days it had been since Lewis Miller's stroke and, according to a registrar in the Royal, the patient was not one bit improved. Barry felt for Gracie, and, selfish though it might be, for him and Sue as well. He hadn't told her yet that they might not be able to buy the bungalow.

A roundabout with its garishly painted horses spun. Kiddies on their wooden saddles bobbed up and down. A small Ferris wheel slowly rotated. Rows of attractions lined a wide, grassy thoroughfare along which a young woman was giving a youngster a donkey ride. Duffy's had been touring Ireland for almost ninety years and was still a family business. The circus had become an annual local fixture.

Barry caught up to Sue, took her hand, and headed across the field. As they approached the roundabout, Barry waved back at Eileen Lindsay's three kids, Sammy, Willie, and Mary, as they whirled past.

"They all attend MacNeill Memorial, you know," Sue said. "Sammy'll be going to the Bangor technical school when he's fourteen, to be prepared to learn a trade. He's not academically gifted like Colin Brown, but he still likes to learn." She smiled. "I do love teaching . . ." There was a tone in her voice that sent a pang through Barry's heart.

Barry knew very well what she was thinking. She loved teaching, but she'd love being a mother even more. It wasn't something he wanted to discuss today. "Their mum's been sick," he said, feeling awkward. "Sonny and Maggie are looking after them." He remembered that Eileen Lindsay was to have been discharged this morning. He hoped she was recovering well, but he'd try not to think about that either. "Sonny told me he would bring them here. There he is waiting for the ride to finish."

Sonny turned, in that curious way people sometimes do when they're being observed, and must have seen them. He beamed in their direction.

"We should speak to him," Sue said. "Come on."

"All right." Politeness demanded they do, but he had wanted this afternoon to be for him and Sue, and not have his concern for his patients intrude.

They walked to where Sonny was standing.

"Afternoon, Sonny." Barry had to raise his voice to be heard over the music of the roundabout's steam-driven calliope, the children's laughter and delighted squeals, the calling of hucksters from other stalls.

Sonny lifted his hat. "Afternoon, Doctor. Miss Nolan. How nice to see you both. Lovely day. The little Lindsays are having great fun."

"So I see," Sue said. "I hope Duffy's stays in business for a long time. One day I'd like to bring our kids here."

"I hope you do. I was never lucky enough to have children of my own." He shook his head. "Now, Doctor, I must tell you I picked up Eileen from the hospital this morning. She's much better. Maggie's keeping her company at our house. She's going to stay with us for a few days."

"I'm delighted to hear it," Barry said.

The three breathless Lindsay children arrived. Sammy, the oldest and clearly their spokesman, said, "Hello, Miss Nolan. Doctor. That was wheeker, Mister Houston, so it was. Can we go on the Ferris wheel now? Can we? Can we?"

Sonny tousled the boy's hair. "Willie and Mary are too wee, and I don't think your ma would want you taking the ride on your own, would she?"

"Aaaaaaaw, but we wanna. We wanna." Sammy kicked a grassy tussock and eyed his sister with a stony gaze.

Tears trickled from Mary's eyes as she said, "I don't. I'm scared to go."

Willie's lower lip began to quiver. "Me too."

"They're such babies," said Sammy in disgust. "I wanna go on the Ferris wheel."

Barry watched Sammy, who was continuing to kick the ground, his face resolute. As "Doctor Laverty" he was perfectly relaxed with children as patients, talking to them easily to discover where things hurt. In general practice, it was mostly the typical childhood illnesses of mumps, measles, and chicken pox, broken bones, coughs and flu. He'd never considered paediatrics as a specialty because he hated seeing children suffer, and his own upbringing as an only child had left him with very little understanding of child-rearing. He'd been brought up solely by his mother until he was five, and then by her and his ex-naval father, who had put great store in fair but rapid discipline and the philosophy that "children should be seen, but not heard." Corporal punishment had been the order of the day at Barry's boarding school. He waited to see how the puzzled-looking, childless Sonny would deal with this. Sammy, as far as Barry was concerned, should be spoken to harshly for upsetting his younger sister and brother and told off about the evils of selfishness.

But before Sonny could speak, Sue knelt beside Mary. She looked deep into the little girl's sapphire blue eyes and said, "Don't be scared, Mary. If Mister Houston would like, you and Willie can come with us, can't they, Barry?"

Barry nodded. What else could he do?

"And Sammy can have his ride with Mister Houston, if that's all right?"

"Dead on," said Sammy.

Mary stopped crying, wiped her nose on the sleeve of her cardigan, and said, "I think you're very nice, Miss Nolan."

"Thank you, Mary," Sue said. "And Sammy, do you think it was very nice of you to be so selfish? Make Mary cry?"

Sammy hung his head. His voice was small. "Sorry, Mary. I am. So I am."

"Thank you," Sue said. She stood.

"I think it's an excellent idea." Sonny surveyed the Ferris wheel as it revolved slowly, and laughed. "I reckon my old ticker can handle the pace. I'm looking forward to this. Come along, Sammy, my boy. We'll meet you, Doctor, and your adoptive brood at—at . . ." Sonny stared round the fairground. "At the candy floss stand in about fifteen minutes."

And Barry, not particularly relishing his role as surrogate daddy, followed on behind Sue and her two charges.

The wide path between the two rows of tents and booths was thronged with families. Barry noticed a lot more youngsters clutching stuffed toys, and he'd not forgotten his promise to win a teddy for Sue.

Barry and Sue were kept busy exchanging greetings with villagers. The whole population of Ballybucklebo seemed to have turned out for this beloved local tradition. They passed Madame Rosalita's tent, advertising "Fortunes told, palms read, Tarot readings." I'd give a lot to get a glimpse into the future right now, he thought.

Sue hurried the children past the "Salome and her Dance of the Seven Veils" tent. "Not for little eyes," she said.

"Agreed." But what would keep the children amused until they could be returned to Sonny? Perhaps there was a petting zoo somewhere?

The air rang with calls of shills trying to entice customers to the various attractions, the music of the calliope was unceasing, and from farther away where the field dipped into a hollow came a ferocious roaring.

Mary screamed and clung to Sue.

Willie stuck out his chin, Barry guessed, to show he was a big boy and not one bit scared.

Sue turned and grinned at Barry. "What on earth was that?"

"Donal, who has been going to the show for years, told me their top act is the animal trainer. He gets in a cage with some lions and a Bengal tiger. I think that was the tiger."

Sue shuddered. "Lady Macbeth's enough cat for this girl." She bent to Mary. "But it can't hurt you, dear. It's in a very stout cage."

Barry was impressed at how good she was with the children. Would he be when the time came?

"Doctor Laverty," Willie said, "please could me and Mary go for a ride on one of them wee donkeys, like?"

Mary said, "Pretty please."

Barry looked at Sue. "What do you think?" Personally, he had no desire to have to explain to Eileen Lindsay why one of her precious kiddies had fallen off and broken an arm. On the other hand, he'd told Sue he would win her a teddy bear, and that would be easier to do without the kids looking on.

"Why not?" Sue said.

"All right." Barry spoke to the nearby donkeys' handlers, paid, and turned over the children to the care of the two young women. He waited to see the little ones mounted and led off at a sedate walk.

To his left was a stall with more stuffed prizes, including a big teddy bear like the ones he'd seen earlier. Hopeful punters were throwing tennis balls at pyramids of grey wooden milk bottles at the back of the booth.

"Try your luck, sir? Win a prize for the beautiful lady? A shilling for t'ree tries. Knock all de bottles down." He demonstrated by sweeping the pile closest to him off with his hand. "See? Nothing to it. Go on, sir. Big strong man like you? No problem." The man had a thick Northside Dublin accent.

"Right," Barry said.

"Twelve brown pennies or one shiny shilling buys you t'ree balls. That'll be all a fellah like you'll need, sir." He didn't bother to rebuild the fallen pyramid.

Barry paid, picked up one ball, sighted, threw side-arm—and missed. He did that twice more.

"Good try, Barry," Sue said.

He frowned, passed over another shilling—and failed again. "Right. Hold this, please." He took off his sports jacket and handed it to Sue.

After eight more shillings, twenty-four more balls, a lot of sweat, two hits, but no luck dislodging the whole pile, he confessed defeat. "Sorry about that," he said to Sue, accepting his coat and carrying it folded over his arm.

"You're still my hero," she said, then whispered, "and I'd rather have you beside me than a stuffed bear anyway." She blew him a kiss just as Willie and Mary returned on their donkeys, were helped down, and ran over to Barry and Sue.

"Thank you very much, sir," Willie and Mary said together.

Barry sighed. "My pleasure. Come on, then," he said. "Time we met Mister Houston and Sammy." He could see them standing at the nearby stall that purveyed sweeties, ice-cream cones and sliders, toffee apples, and candy floss.

In no time each little Lindsay had been handed a quarter of an ounce of clove rock, a toffee apple, and a whirl of pink spun sugar on a stick.

"I think he's spoiling them rotten," Barry whispered to Sue, but she said, "Let him. Their mum's been in hospital, Barry, and the poor old boy never had kids of his own." The look she gave Barry held a great deal of meaning.

"I think we should be heading back to the big top," Sonny said. "The show will start soon." He beamed at his charges. "And if we all go together we can sit together. Won't that be nice?"

The answers of the children were muffled by mouthfuls of candy floss.

Barry's enthusiasm for such an arrangement was hardly overpowering, but he was spared the need to answer by the appearance of Donal and Julie Donnelly. Donal was carrying a teddy bear like the one Barry had wanted to win for Sue. "How's about youse, all?" Donal said. "Tori's at her granny's. She's too wee yet for circuses."

"I see you won a teddy for her," Barry said. Clearly other people had been successful.

"Away off and chase yourself, Doctor. I used til work on one of them throw-a-ball-at-the-bottles stalls. No one ever wins. Two of the bottles is glued til the shelf, so they are."

"You're kidding."

"I never kid about such things, Doc. Conning is serious business."

"Well, no wonder I didn't win. So did you win the bear at that booth where you aim the air rifles at Ping-Pong balls bouncing up and down on jets of water?"

"Not at all. There's a fellah with a barrow over there"—Donal pointed with his bear—"selling them for twelve and six."

15

Examine Well Your Blood

"Well, thank you." O'Reilly accepted the damp teddy bear from Kenny, who had appeared from the doghouse bearing the offering as soon as O'Reilly closed the kitchen door behind him. The pup had trotted straight to his master, sat, and presented his "retrieve." O'Reilly patted the pup's head. "Good."

Arthur stood nearby, supervising as usual, head cocked at an angle, tail lazily swinging from side to side.

In the two weeks since Kenny had moved into Number One, he had already mastered "sit" and "heel," and was improving on "stay," but with the natural impatience of the young still had a habit of running to O'Reilly before being given permission.

"Heel. You'll both get your run after I've finished seeing my patient." O'Reilly set the toy on the grass and headed for the Rover. Both dogs tucked in as directed. He opened the car door. "In."

Arthur went first. Even though he had grown, it was a scramble for Kenny, but Arthur took him by the scruff and helped him up.

Anne Galvin's husband, Guffer, had phoned earlier to request a home visit. Fingal drove off, his eyes on the road but his thoughts on Anne— how Barry had seen her two weeks ago for acute bronchitis, a cut-and-dried case. From what Guffer had said, it seemed Anne was having a recurrence. That was quite common and not very serious.

O'Reilly exchanged waves with half a dozen people before turning left to climb the hill to the council housing estate. He sighed as it came into view. He supposed Bertie Bishop had built the rows of identical, gardenless terrace houses according to the directions of town planners. The place had no heart, no soul, and more so today. Children who would have been outside bringing life to the street with their cries and laughter must have been at the circus. Even an early-afternoon sun just past its zenith barely penetrated the narrow streets. Three little girls, not lucky enough to be at the circus, were skipping a rope and chanting,

> One potato, two potato, three potato, four
> Five potato, six potato, seven potato, more.

O'Reilly recognised the Harrison twins, Ingrid and Astrid, and their cousin Gillian MacAllister. Their fathers both worked for Bertie Bishop, who still hadn't started work on the new road. Their two weeks' paid holiday would soon be over and the men would be going on the "burroo," local parlance for "the bureau," the department that paid out weekly unemployment insurance. There was probably no money for circus shows and candy floss.

He parked in front of the Galvins' two-storey home and wound down the driver's window to ensure a good flow of fresh air for the dogs. O'Reilly grabbed his bag and got out. One door down, a woman wearing a calico pinafore sat on the sill of the second-storey window, backside protruding into thin air. The sash was pulled down onto her thighs to anchor her in place. She was washing the panes with soapy water and cleaning them off with a piece of chamois leather. "How are ye, Doc," she called down. "Great day."

"Grand altogether, Myrtle, thanks. You be careful up there."

"Way off and chase yourself, Doc. Haven't I been washing windys like this for forty years." Before he could knock on the Galvins' door, the air was rent with a howling so loud Myrtle dropped her shammy, which landed with a splat on the narrow footpath. The sound was coming from the Rover. O'Reilly turned to see Kenny standing on the backseat, paws against the window, head thrown back. It was the first time the pup had been left alone in the car with only Arthur for company. The wee mite must be terrified.

"I thought it was the banshee, so I did. Don't worry about the shammy. I've got another."

"Sorry, Myrtle." O'Reilly retraced his steps and opened the car's back door. Kenny immediately shut up, but tried to lick O'Reilly's face.

"No. Lie down."

The pup obeyed, and Arthur looked at O'Reilly as if to say, "He's only a kid, boss. Don't be cross."

"Stay," said O'Reilly, and closed the door.

The howling began at once and Kenny was once more on his hind legs.

Before O'Reilly could open the door to admonish Kenny, there was a tap on his shoulder. He turned to see Guffer Galvin.

"Scuse me, Doc, but the missus sent me out til see what all the row was about. Your pup?"

"Aye. I thought he'd be all right with Arthur there."

"We heard you'd a new one. Anne says—and she knows a brave bit about dogs, her da ran Jack Russells all the time she lived at home—she says very young pups can get upset in strange places if they're left on their own. She says just bring him in with you."

O'Reilly hesitated. A dog at a consultation? It was hardly by the book, but Kenny showed no sign of calming down and doors were opening all along the street as folks rubbernecked, wanting to know the cause of the disturbance. "Right, take my bag, Guffer." O'Reilly opened the door. "Stay, Arthur." He grabbed a now-silent Kenny and followed the man indoors.

"Just set him down, Doc. Here's your bag. I'm afraid the missus's brownkitees is back. She's hacking away again. Has been for a couple of days, and it's worser than her oul smoker's cough."

O'Reilly nodded and put Kenny on the linoleum.

The pup sat at once.

"I've her teed up in the parlour. Said she wasn't sick enough til go til bed. Young Doctor Laverty seen her a fortnight back. He said there was no need for a chest X-ray, give her the black bottle and, right enough, she was well mended in four days."

The much-valued black bottle, *Mist morph et ipecac*. "Fair enough. Let's go and see her."

"In here." Guffer opened a door to the right of the hall. "I'll leave you and the wee tyke to do your jobs, sir." He bent down and stroked Kenny's head. "I'll be in the kitchen."

O'Reilly nodded. A man may not attend his wife's examination, but, he smiled, apparently chocolate Labrador puppies did.

The parlour was tidy. A single sash window looked out onto the narrow street. A white roll-up blind hung above. The floor was carpeted. An unlit fire lay in a small black grate and three ceramic mallard, garishly painted and decreasing in size, flew up at an angle on the whitewashed chimney-breast.

Anne Galvin sat in an armchair, one of a frayed maroon three-piece lounge suite. She had her feet up on a pouffe and was tucked up under a tartan rug. She coughed and said, "Afternoon, Doctor O'Reilly." She peered at him from pale blue eyes behind her wire-rimmed granny glasses. "And is this the wee one Cissie Sloan told me about? Handsome lad. What's his name?" She coughed again, a dry, rasping sound.

"Kenny."

"Can I pet him? Please?"

Kenny was not a lap dog. He'd be a working animal when he grew up, but there was such pleading in Anne's voice.

"I love dogs, but wouldn't be fair to have one here on the estate."

"All right," O'Reilly said. He lifted Kenny and set him in Anne's lap. How she managed to have a simultaneous coughing fit and keep a huge smile on her face amazed him.

Kenny seemed unfazed by the coughing and tried to lick her face.

"No, Kenny," she said firmly. "No."

The pup obeyed.

"Good," she said. "Good."

O'Reilly nodded. This woman did know about dogs, and if Kenny was a comfort to her, why not let him stay?

"Thanks for coming, sir. Sorry to drag you out on a Saturday." Her right hand stroked the top of Kenny's head.

"Rubbish. It's what we're here for. How are you, Anne?" He set his bag on a table beside her chair and perched himself on its arm.

"Och," she said, "I've been better. I'm not all shivery like last time."

So she probably didn't have a fever, making pneumonia and acute bronchitis unlikely.

"I've a bit of the rheumaticks, but doesn't everybody my age?"

O'Reilly nodded. It was true. Vague muscle and joint aches were prevalent among the denizens of the damp, draughty council houses.

"And the coughing's not the same as when young Doctor Laverty was here. Once I've had my morning coughing over and a good spit, nothing comes up, I'm still hacking away." She punctuated her remarks with a dry cough. "See what I mean? I'd still a toty-wee bit of the medicine he give me a couple of weeks back so I took it, but it never done me no good. I'm not wheezing as much, but—" Her gaze held O'Reilly's eyes. "I've been coughing up a taste of blood today. That's why I asked Guffer til send for you." She lowered her voice. "I never told him about the blood." She stroked Kenny a little faster.

Kenny wriggled but made no other attempt to move.

O'Reilly heard her anxiety for herself and her concern for her husband and kept his face impassive. What she had just described did not gel with simple acute bronchitis, where the sputum could be blood-tinged but the cough was moist. And what he'd been taught back in his Trinity days had not changed, particularly now when the relationship between smoking and lung cancer had been established. Haemoptysis, coughing up blood by itself, had to be taken very seriously, because it might be a symptom of either pulmonary tuberculosis or lung cancer. There were other causes, but those two must be excluded. "Are you sure you're coughing it up?" he asked, dropping a hand to take her pulse. Her skin was cool to the touch. Blood was always worrying and could be vomited up in a number of gastrointestinal conditions, as well as coughed up.

"Aye. Dead sure. It's bright red. Frothy, like." She forced a smile. "It's only a toty-wee taste. Not much."

O'Reilly nodded. He did not like the sound of this. Her pulse was a steady eighty beats per minute. "Have you noticed any other things?"

She shook her head. "I told you I'm a bit creaky, but"—she managed weak smile—"what can't be cured must be endured. If it was just a bit of a cough, I'd have tholed it because there's nothing else wrong . . . except the blood." She inhaled a jerky breath, pursed her lips, and coughed again.

"Right," he said, producing his stethoscope. "Can I pull up your blouse at the back?"

"Aye, certainly."

"And it's all right if you want to hang on to the pup."

"Thank you." She sat forward.

"Uh-huh," O'Reilly said when he'd finished a thorough examination of her chest and found nothing. The rate of breathing was not increased. No dull areas to percussion. No tender spots. Lots of air going in and out as she breathed. No wheezes, whistles, or hirstles of any kind. He straightened up. Put his stethoscope back in his jacket pocket. But still the blood called for an X-ray. And soon. "You can tuck in your blouse now, Anne."

As she did, he said, "I'll nip through. Get Guffer so I can explain things to you both."

"Doctor," Anne said, "I know blood's serious. I'd an uncle who got . . ." She didn't say the word aloud but mouthed "cancer." "Please don't say nothing til Guffer until you've all the answers. Please."

O'Reilly nodded. He was not unfamiliar with this present dilemma. Anne deliberately wanted to keep any possible bad news from her husband to spare him worry until either the cloud had passed or there was something to be concerned about. Yet O'Reilly had always believed in being honest with patients. He had never accepted the received wisdom that if a diagnosis of cancer had been made, only the closest relative should be told, not the patient. "Stay, Kenny," he said, and headed for the Galvins' kitchen.

His nose told him there was something cooking involving ginger. "I'm all done, Guffer," O'Reilly said, sticking his head round the kitchen door. "Come on through."

Guffer set down a copy of *Reader's Digest* and followed O'Reilly back to the parlour.

Both men remained standing, with Anne's gaze shifting from face to face.

O'Reilly cleared his throat. "I'm not quite sure what's up. It's not the bronchitis back."

"I'm glad to hear that," Guffer said. "I'd a notion she should've got antibiotics, so I had. I asked Doctor Laverty. He said no, and if it's not come back, I was probably wrong."

O'Reilly shook his head. He should support Barry immediately but chose to be more circumspect. "Guffer," he said, "no good doctor, and Doctor Laverty is a good one, minds being asked questions." Just please don't ask me the wrong one this afternoon, he thought, and directed his gaze to Anne. "I'm stumped this time," which was nearly true, but he did have two serious conditions in the forefront of his mind, "and I don't want to go off at half cock. Anne needs an X-ray, and I'll arrange that for Monday morning. I'll need to use your phone."

"In the hall," Guffer said.

"In case you're wondering why not today, us GPs are expected not to clog up the X-ray department at weekends." And despite a widely believed notion that cancer must be diagnosed immediately, two days would make not a pick of difference to the final outcome.

He went to the hall, and after the usual delays was connected with a sympathetic unit clerk, made the arrangements, and left a message asking his friend Teddy MacIlrath, a senior radiologist, to read the plates himself as a favour to Fingal and phone the results through to Number One.

He returned.

Guffer was standing beside his wife, holding her left hand while she went on stroking Kenny with her right.

O'Reilly rummaged in his bag for the necessary form. As he wrote, he said, "All set. Be at the Royal on Monday at ten. Here. Take this form with you. The X-ray won't take long and I or Doctor Laverty will give you the results as soon as we have them. Probably by Monday afternoon. All right?"

Before Guffer could speak, Anne looked O'Reilly right in the eye and said, "That'll be dead on, sir. We'll bide patiently. Isn't that right, Guffer?"

"Aye. I suppose so, but I'd like til know—"

"Guffer," Anne said, "let Doctor O'Reilly get on with his job. Please."

O'Reilly knew that the worst thing for patients and loved ones was dealing with uncertainty.

Guffer said, "Aye. Well." He sounded confused.

"I'll get the answers as soon as I can. I promise."

Anne coughed. "That would be grand—" Another cough stopped her. When she recovered, she said, "Wouldn't it, Guffer?"

"Aye."

O'Reilly produced a small bottle from his bag. "This is *linctus pholocodeine*, Anne. One teaspoon at bedtime might help you get a night's sleep."

"Thanks very much, sir," Anne said. "For everything."

O'Reilly detected a hint of emphasis on that word. "My pleasure," he said. "And now I'll be running along." He closed and picked up his bag.

"Thanks for letting me pet Kenny," Anne said. "Can he come and see me again, please?" She inclined her head. "Please?"

O'Reilly said, "I don't see why not." He heard her thanks as he picked the pup up and headed for the door. "If it gets any worse, but I don't think it will, send for me at once."

"I will." She turned to Guffer. "And we'll say nothing til our sons until we know exactly what ails me." She smiled. "I'm a tough oul duck, you know. I'm sure it'll all blow over soon."

And as O'Reilly closed the front door behind him he hoped to God she was right.

"Hey on out." O'Reilly had let the dogs out of the car at the end of a bridle path at the bottom of the Ballybucklebo Hills. Both sat at his feet without being told. Now, on command, Arthur put his nose to the ground and began quartering, tail waving like a flag. Kenny, who for the last two weeks had watched Arthur, had soon started to imitate his big friend. He was clearly in no doubt about what to do today.

He'd let them both work off a bit of steam first then give Kenny another lesson in retrieving. There was a dummy, a length of wood wrapped in old carpet, in the boot. He watched the dogs. Kenny had overtaken Arthur. They were having fun, but no doubt about it, old Arthur wasn't as young as he used to be. Andrew Marvell had been right about "time's wingèd chariot drawing near" and O'Reilly thought again of Anne Galvin. He hoped he was wrong and that she'd still get her full span.

He looked around the small grassy field and inhaled the piney scent from the trees and the almond aroma of the yellow whin flowers. The only sounds were the pattering of the dogs' paws, the burbling of a couple of woodpigeons, and—he strained to hear. Yes. Yes. Faint, but distinct:

"Cuckoo. Cuckoo."

The birds had returned from wintering in Central Africa on a migration that included a nonstop flight over the Sahara Desert and the Med. He remembered one in early 1940, perhaps more exhausted than the rest, seeking respite on the top of *Warspite*'s gun turret. The bird had renewed its resources and flown off just as he was doing now, getting away from the practice for a few minutes, trying to let his interest in his dogs give him a break from worrying about Anne Galvin. Worrying would change nothing.

The dogs were approaching the edge of the pine wood. "Come in. Come in." And both stopped in their tracks, turned, and galloped back. Kenny beat Arthur by a nose.

He'd used this spot years ago when he'd been training Arthur. It was one of those places that folks out for a walk didn't seem to use much, and so having his educational efforts interrupted by other dogs had been unlikely. It still was.

O'Reilly fished out his briar and lit up. "Sit."

Both dogs did.

"Good. Now. Stay." He walked over to the car, opened the boot, and took out the dummy and Kenny's leash.

Both dogs watched his every move but stayed where they were.

"Good. Now, young Kenny, after being spoiled rotten by Anne, you are going to work for your keep." O'Reilly bent and clipped on Kenny's leash. "Kenny. Stay."

The pup looked at O'Reilly. The adoration in the young dog's eyes would have softened Pharaoh's hard heart. It melted O'Reilly's. No wonder he'd had such a soothing effect on Anne Galvin. He repeated, "Kenny. Stay," and hurled the dummy overhand to the edge of the clearing.

Arthur leant forward, his breath coming in shorter pants.

"Kenny. Stay. Arthur. Hi lost."

Arthur bounded off.

Kenny lifted his backside as if to follow.

"Stay."

Bottom hit grass.

"Good dog. Good dog." O'Reilly slipped Kenny a piece of puppy chow as Arthur arrived, dummy in mouth, and sat at O'Reilly's feet.

Before he could accept the dummy, O'Reilly heard a hail of, "Hello, Fingal," from behind him and turned to see John MacNeill, Marquis of Ballybucklebo, sitting astride Ruby, Myrna's mare. "Hello, John. Come on over." O'Reilly took the dummy from Arthur. "Good. You take a breather, Arthur Guinness. Lie down." The big Lab flopped onto the grass and put his head on his outstretched front legs.

Ruby and the marquis ambled slowly over to join O'Reilly and the dogs. "So, this is the pup I've been hearing about?" said the marquis.

"Yes, this indeed is Kenny, but if you'll excuse me for a moment? Kenny. Stay." O'Reilly hurled again, bent, and undid the leash. "Good. Now, Kenny, hi lost."

The pup took off like a rocket.

"Sorry about that, but Kenny got 'stay' right for the first time ever and I didn't want to stretch his patience."

"I completely understand. Please don't let me interrupt. Lovely afternoon. Did you hear the cuckoo?"

"I did."

"Sure sign summer's on the way." The marquis leaned over and patted the mare's cheek. "I've recently discovered the cuckoo is from the same family as the American roadrunner."

O'Reilly chuckled. "Ours don't go 'meep-meep,' like their Yankee cousin in that cartoon."

"And ours don't have to worry about coyotes either." John laughed and shifted in the saddle. "I was just out giving old Ruby a bit of exercise. We come here quite often. Myrna's job at Queens keeps her pretty busy during the term weeks and she's in Dublin this weekend. Some chemistry convention at Trinity." He laughed. "Can't have Ruby here getting fat like one of Thelwell's ponies."

O'Reilly knew his friend was alluding to Norman Thelwell, an immensely popular British cartoonist who drew chubby little girls astride even chubbier ponies, which often peered through long fringes of mane.

Kenny arrived back, and far from tussling over the dummy as he had over a rubber ball two weeks ago, sat and presented it to O'Reilly. "Good." He patted Kenny's head.

He sent the pup out on another retrieve. "I've not spoken to Lars recently. Is he in Dublin with her?"

"No. I think originally he was meant to be." The marquis shook his head. "I'm not entirely sure what's going on there. None of my business, really. I don't see nearly as much of your brother now he's got the paperwork for the transfer of the estate to the National Trust all sewn up." He frowned and shook his head again.

O'Reilly accepted the dummy from a now-panting Kenny and sent him out again. "John, are you hinting that all isn't well between them?" The last time he'd seen Myrna and his brother they'd had a falling-out at the car races. Hardly much of a reason for a major split, but in his years in practice, O'Reilly had seen affairs founder over less. "I hope not," he said. "I thought things were going swimmingly when they got back from Villefranche."

"I'm sure it'll all blow over," John said. "Now, I really must be getting back. Meeting with the National Trust folks this afternoon at Ballybucklebo House. You remember the day we met you and Kitty at the Transport and Folk Museum?"

"At the horse-shoeing?"

"That's it. We were meeting with the museum people. They agreed to accept two of my eighteenth-century labourers' cottages. We need to sort out the details of getting them from my estate to the museum grounds." He started to turn Ruby's head, then half turned in the saddle. "And please do give my regards to Kitty. Hope to see you both soon, Fingal. I'm going over to London tomorrow, but I'll be back by lunchtime on Wednesday. Wednesday evening?"

"I'll need to ask Kitty, but I'll let your staff know."

"Grand." And without further ado, the marquis put his mount into a smart trot and was disappearing round a bend in the path when a panting Kenny came back.

"Good," said O'Reilly, accepting the dummy. "Right, you two. Very well done, but it's time to head home. See if Kitty's got any more work for me." He took a deep breath and let it out slowly, hoping his worries about Anne, and his brother and Myrna, would dissolve into the pine-scented air. Then he let the two dogs into the backseat and closed the door.

16

Vesti la Giubba. Put on Your Costume

Barry and Sue bought their tickets and waited in the short queue behind Sonny and the Lindsay children. The two youngest were standing quietly, trying to see into the tent, but Sammy, who had demolished his candy floss, was now biting great chunks out of his toffee apple and chewing with his mouth open. His face was sticky with bits of apple and confectioner's sugar.

Barry hadn't been fazed for years by the often unpleasant sights of medicine, but he still had an aversion to seeing what was in people's mouths as they ate. He shuddered and half turned away from Sammy. He knew the paediatric developmental milestones: when a baby crawled, said its first words, walked. But he hadn't a clue how long this unpleasant phase that Sammy Lindsay was exhibiting would have to be tolerated by parents.

Donal Donnelly and Julie were queuing up behind. "It's a great show, you know, Doc," Donal said. "There's a trained sea lion. The first time I seen him he played 'Twinkle Twinkle Little Star' on bicycle horns. You know, them ones with the rubber bulbs? He squeezed them with his mouth. I near laughed my leg off, so I did." Donal's eyes twinkled.

"Little amuses the innocent," Julie said, but she was smiling and Barry heard the affection in her voice and knew she was teasing Donal.

"Ooof." Julie grabbed her tummy. "If you're right, Donal Donnelly, your wee boy's going til be a centre forward. Thon was a powerful kick."

"We'll find out in July," Barry said, and watched as Sue regarded Julie with wonder and longing.

The queue had moved and Sonny was giving in his tickets.

Sammy dropped the stick and the core of his toffee apple on the ground and immediately hauled out his packet of clove rock. The peppery smell mingled with the animal odours coming from inside the tent.

Barry wondered if there was some way he and Sue could sit with Donal and Julie, but as Barry showed their tickets to the ringmaster, Sonny said, "Just follow the usherette, Doctor. We need to stick together."

A heavily made-up young woman in silver soft shoes, fishnet tights, and a high-cut silver leotard was leading Sonny and the children.

"I recognise her," said Barry. "I've seen her picture on a poster. She's the flyer, the acrobat who performs between two catchers on flying trapezes."

Sue glanced up. "I'm glad to see there's a safety net."

"Me too. I don't want to be giving first aid today."

Barry and Sue arrived at their seats. He was not overjoyed to discover he was sitting beside Sammy Lindsay, who was shoving another piece of clove rock into his mouth.

Sonny waved from near the far end of the row.

Barry waved back.

Sammy offered the packet. "Want a sweetie, Doctor?"

"No thank you, Sammy."

"Och, go on, go on. Have one."

"No-thank-you." Barry made each word distinct. He shook his head and turned to Sue. "Comfy enough?"

"Just fine, although these seats are a little hard on the derrière."

Barry whispered in her ear, "If it gets too sore, I'll make it better after the show, back at your flat."

Sue's chuckle was throaty. "I'll hold you to that," she said, and winked.

Barry grinned. Finally, his day off was beginning to head in the right direction. He was alone, after a fashion, with Sue and the show was about to begin.

"I'm going to enjoy this." Sue nodded at the red raised circle surrounding the ring. "You really can smell the sawdust." She loosened the top two buttons of her blouse. "Boy, it's muggy in here."

"It is," Barry said as he undid his tie and glanced at a hint of cleavage.

Sammy was nudging Barry. He had no choice but to turn. He forced a smile. Allowances had to be made for children. "Yes, Sammy?"

"Mister Houston says would you and Miss Nolan like an ice cream? See over thonder?"

Barry looked to where a young woman stood in an aisle between tiers of benches. She wore a red short-skirted tunic and a striped pageboy hat cocked to one side of a blond bouffant hairdo. A tray in front of her waist, attached to a strap around her neck, contained wrapped ice creams, ice lollipops, and the popular fruit drink Kia-Ora.

"I'm going to have a Walls chokky ice, so I am."

The thought of the ice cream's oily texture did not appeal, but Barry turned to Sue. "Sonny's offering to buy us an ice cream?"

She shook her head. "Not for me, thanks. Got to think of my figure."

"No," Barry said, "that's my job, and I think a great deal about it." He turned back to Sammy. "Please thank Mister Houston, but no thanks."

A sudden beating on the side drum heralded the band, which broke enthusiastically into that classic of all classic circus tunes, "Entry of the Gladiators," a screamer march intended to whip the audience up. Even Barry, who was a little tone deaf, could appreciate the enthusiasm of the musicians. He tried not to smile when the music developed into a race between the trombonist and the rest of the ensemble to finish first. The trombonist won, the band came second, and the bass drummer a reluctant third, hitting two extra beats after everyone else had finished.

Sammy started cheering in a series of high-pitched "Yoooooooo"'s.

Barry sighed. Perhaps the lad would settle down soon.

A curtain rose at the far side and a single white-faced clown entered the ring. Under a white conical dunce's cap, his alabaster makeup was highlighted by huge crimson lips and ebony eyebrows. His white Pierrot suit was covered with sparkling sequins. The jacket was short, the trousers swollen at the hip and tapering to cuffless ends halfway down his calves. He bore a shining brass trumpet and put it to his lips.

Barry thrilled to the pure, clipped but soaring notes of Verdi's "Triumphal March" from Aida. He slid a bit closer to Sue because Sammy just wouldn't sit still.

The clown led a stately procession round the ring. He was followed by an Indian elephant with the trapeze flyer, who moments ago had been the usherette, sitting like a mahout on its neck. The great beast curled its trunk upward and drowned out the music with an ear-piercing trumpeting while simultaneously depositing a heap of elephant apples, much to the great amusement of the children and a loud raspberry from Sammy. A man and a woman, each wearing tall red top hats and bright green tailcoats and trousers, strode in on ten-foot-high stilts.

Four French poodles, all wearing tutus, followed. Each on command from their tutu-clad trainer rose on its hind legs and pirouetted before jumping through a ring held by the young woman.

Three ponies, each with plumes on their heads, were led round by another ballerina. A cheer went up as the sea lion galumphed into view and began to honk raucously and clap its front flippers.

"That'll make Donal Donnelly happy," Barry said.

"I think a lot of things make Donal happy. I like that man's philosophy of life," said Sue.

Barry thought he heard something in her tone and turned sharply to look at her face, but it was relaxed and smiling, enjoying the spectacle before them. A troupe of clowns was pushing each other, tripping, falling, doing handsprings. One was trying to juggle four coloured balls and kept dropping them, then chasing them across the sawdust and knocking his companions down.

Sammy was up on his feet, dipping and swaying, mimicking the movements of the clowns. Barry overheard him say to Willie, "Say 'thank you very much' til Mister Houston." There was a sound of paper being torn. The ice cream, no doubt.

Then with a final deafening flourish, the trumpet solo finished and, strutting with all the pride of a Roman emperor, the scarlet-coated ringmaster made his entrance smiling widely and cracking his long horsewhip.

The show was about to begin and Barry, trying hard not to let Sammy annoy him, settled back to enjoy the performance. He felt a small hand tug at his sleeve.

"Doctor, I don't feel so good."

"Watch the clowns, Sammy."

"No, Doc, I'm really peely-wally." Then, without further ado, young Sammy Lindsay threw up in Barry's lap.

Barry leaped to his feet and before he could control himself yelled, "Och, Jaysus." He could feel the warm creep of the vomit seeping through to his skin. "Why anybody, anybody in their right mind, would have a brood of bloody rug rats is utterly beyond me."

17

Laugh, Clown, at Your Broken Love

"Come on, Sue." Barry was on his feet. His crotch and upper thighs were damp and the stink of puke overpowered even the smells of animals and sawdust in the big top. He glanced over at Sammy, who was hunched over and clutching his tummy. "Sonny'll have to see to him. He's not ill. He's just greedy and ate too much, and I can't stay here like this." And not just because he had to get cleaned up. After his last remark about people being out of their minds if they had kids, he had some fences to mend with Sue too.

Barry followed Sue along the row, apologising to the folks who had to stand to let him pass. The ring was being rapidly cleared of the performers who had been part of the opening procession.

In stentorian tones, the ringmaster announced, "Ladies and gentlemen, pray welcome our first act. Madame Barishnikova from deepest Kazakhstan . . ."

More likely her name's Mabel Thompson and she's from the backstreets of Belfast, Barry thought. He was not in the mood to be entertained. Not now.

". . . and the world's leading contortionist. Her act will have you, but mostly her, in knots. Ladies and gentlemen, if you please, a very warm welcome to . . ."

The crowd applauded. There were catcalls and whistles.

Still following Sue, Barry was ignoring the events in the ring, but his head turned instinctively when the entire audience went "oooooh."

Somehow the performer was supporting herself with her palms on the ground. Her arms had passed through the angle between shin and thigh caused by both ankles being locked behind her neck. The sequins of her leotard sparkled in the spotlights' glare.

As Barry turned away, the ringmaster bellowed, "And how, ladies and gentlemen, is Madame Barishnikova going to get out of that, I ask you?"

She's not the only one facing that difficulty, Barry thought, following Sue out into the clean air.

"So what do you suggest we do about you?" Sue's voice was flat. Not entirely controlled.

"My clothes or—?"

"Your clothes. I don't want to talk about the other just now. I imagine you want to go home. Get cleaned up—" She took a deep breath. "—and change."

There were two meanings to that last word, but Sue's inflection had left him in no doubt which was uppermost in her mind.

"Good idea," he said, opening Brunhilde's driver's door. "Can you drive? I'm too sticky." So's my position, he thought. What the hell am I going to do? It's out in the open and I can't force myself to want children.

"Yes." She climbed in.

Barry knew Kitty would probably be home at Number One, and O'Reilly could still be out seeing Anne Galvin. It might be a good idea not to be alone with Sue for a little while. Give her a chance to settle down. He had decided, at least for now, to adopt the "least said, soonest mended" approach. He needed time to collect his thoughts. He got in beside her and she drove off too fast, jouncing over the field that served as a car park.

Little was said on the short drive to Number One.

No dogs greeted them as they walked through the back garden. "Fingal must have taken them out," Barry said. He hoped Kitty would still be at home. He let them into the kitchen and breathed a silent sigh of relief at the sight of Kitty at the sink.

She turned. "Hello, you two. You're back early. Circus not so hot?"

"You might say that," Sue said. Ice was in her voice.

Barry pointed at his trousers. "A little boy threw up on me."

"Oh dear," said Kitty. "Fingal has told me he thought your pants were jinxed. You got them covered in glaur on your very first home visit. Arthur peed on them after your first delivery . . ."

"Barry Fingal Galvin, now in the States," Barry said, wondering how Anne was doing.

". . . and didn't Lady Macbeth throw up on them once?"

"That's all true," Barry said, "and now I must go to my quarters and get them off, clean myself up, and change into something decent. If you'll excuse me?"

As he went into his room he heard Kitty say, "Kettle's on. We'll make some tea and see you upstairs when you're done."

Sue and Kitty were sitting in two of the armchairs in the upstairs lounge. Each had a cup of tea. A silver three-tiered cake stand on the coffee table carried an assortment of fig rolls, McVitie's Jaffa Cakes, and their famous digestive biscuits. O'Reilly had a soft spot for all three, but they only came out at weekends, when Kinky was not at Number One. She took great pride in her home-baked confections and no one wanted to hurt her feelings.

Kitty and Sue both looked up when Barry, wearing clean flannels, a white poplin open-necked shirt, and a blue V-necked sweater, came in. He had heard a low murmur of conversation as he approached the lounge. He wondered what they'd talked about in the five minutes it had taken him to wash and change. He hoped Sue had not repeated his words at the circus to Kitty.

"Ah, Barry," said Kitty. Her smile was open and sincere. "That must feel better. And smell better too. I prefer the scent of Old Spice to your recent attar of . . ." She left the sentence unfinished.

Sue was polite. "Would you like a cup of tea and a biscuit?"

"Please." Barry took the third armchair, dislodging Lady Macbeth before he could do so.

He accepted his cup and helped himself to a Jaffa Cake.

Sue avoided his gaze and a silence hung until they all spoke at once,

Kitty saying, "So the circus was . . ." Barry stammering, "I'm-I'm sorry . . ." and Sue murmuring, "I think I'd like to go . . ."

Silence.

Barry sipped his tea.

Kitty looked from Barry to Sue and back, frowned, then said, "The cat's got your tongue, Barry Laverty. And Sue's not been very talkative either. It's not like either of you. Is there something wrong?"

Barry shook his head. "No," he said. "We're just a bit tired." This was between him and Sue. He finished his tea and Jaffa Cake without tasting either and started to rise. "Come on, Sue. I'll take you—"

"Begob," said O'Reilly as he came through the door, "I thought you two were at the circus."

"We were," said Barry, retaking his seat, "but Sammy Lindsay threw up in my lap. Sonny brought the Lindsay kids to the circus and gave them too many sweets. I came here to get cleaned up. I was just going to take Sue home." He glanced at her but still she would not meet his gaze.

"Good heavens. Too much candy floss, I reckon. Terrible stuff. I just came from seeing their mum. Popped in to see how Maggie was getting on with Eileen. And she'd just had another visit from Hester Nolan. Another little fall, apparently."

"God, I hope she didn't reinjure that wrist," Barry said.

O'Reilly shook his head. "Nothing to send for a doctor for. Bruises mostly. She was gone by the time I arrived. The cast on her wrist probably put her a bit off balance. But Eileen was doing well."

"And Anne?"

O'Reilly helped himself to tea and a couple of fig rolls. He sat on the pouffe, sipped, devoured half of his roll in one bite, and said, "Sue, you're practically a doctor's wife . . ."

Barry hoped to God that was still true.

"You understand confidentiality?"

"Of course."

"I'm worried about Anne," he said. And the concern was in his voice.

Barry flinched. "I thought she only had—"

"Acute bronchitis. I know. And before you start playing your usual game of trying to hold yourself responsible for missing something, Hippocrates himself would have made the same diagnosis you did two weeks ago. She wasn't coughing up blood then. Now she is."

"Oh," Barry said.

"'Oh' is right," O'Reilly said, finishing the other half of his fig roll. "And we'll have to bide until Monday. She'll get a chest X-ray then, and a friend of mine's to phone me with the results."

Barry nodded. He glanced at Kitty, who was nodding her head, frowning, and pursing her lips. She must know what Fingal and Barry were worrying about. Sue was looking baffled.

O'Reilly said, "Barry and Kitty and I are worried that the patient may have cancer."

"That's awful," Sue said. "The poor woman."

O'Reilly shook his head. "I hope I'm wrong, but there's not much we can do until we have the results." He grabbed another fig roll. Half of it vanished. "Now, you said you were going to take Sue home, I believe. Barry, put it out of your mind until Monday. Take your fiancée home. The day's a pup, and speaking of which, Kenny's coming on a treat. The little fellow has all kinds of talents I never suspected, but I'll tell you about that later."

The other half of the roll went. O'Reilly cast a hopeful eye on the Jaffa Cakes and began to stretch out a hand.

Barry saw Kitty's look of disapproval and the hand retreat. That was the kind of husband-and-wife mutual understanding he'd been looking forward to with Sue.

"I'm sorry your day at the circus went bust . . ."

And how, Barry thought.

". . . but there's a good Western with Paul Newman and Diane Cilento, *Hombre,* playing at the Ritz in Belfast."

Barry rose. "Thanks, Fingal. We'll think about it." He looked at Sue.

She stood, brushed crumbs off her jeans, and said, "Thanks for the tea, Kitty. I hope the rest of your weekend's not too busy, Fingal," and headed for the door.

Barry followed. "Cheerio," he said to Fingal and Kitty, who raised her eyebrows but said nothing. By the time he'd reached the landing,

Sue was waiting in the hall. It looked very much as if his hopes that she'd calmed down had not been realised. Barry took a very deep breath and slowly went downstairs.

He could only hope he'd be able to come up with the right words on the short drive from here to her flat so that when they got there they could put all of this behind them. But that hope vanished when Sue opened the passenger-side door and fixed him with a look over the roof of Brunhilde. "Barry, we are not mentioning this on the drive to my apartment. I'll tell you that right now. I don't want us discussing something this important while you're driving. It's not safe." She disappeared into the car, and not for the first time did Barry wonder why medical students had to spend the better part of eighteen months dissecting a cadaver and not one hour on clinical psychology. If ever he could have used some practical expertise, it was now.

By the time Barry had closed the door to Sue's flat, he thought he might explode from the tension of not speaking throughout the drive to Holywood. "Look, Sue, I'm sorry—" But that was as far as he got.

Sue's gormless springer spaniel, Max, barked loudly and hurled himself at Barry. The dog reared up on his hind legs and slammed his front paws into Barry's crotch.

"Christ." The entire question of having children might very well have become academic, Barry thought, as he tried to push the animal away and haul in a great lungful of air. "Get down."

Sue grabbed the dog by his collar. "Down, Max. Down. Bad dog. Sorry about that, Barry."

Barry was beyond speech. He massaged where the dog had tackled him and waited for the pain to subside.

She dragged the beast off and shut him in the kitchen. She came back. "I truly am sorry. Are you all right?"

The most severe pain had passed. "I will be in a few minutes." At least physically. "No need to apologise." She was making no move toward her sitting room. Barry struggled to find the right words. "Look, Sue, about what I said at the circus."

Sue folded her arms across her chest. "Yes, about what you said at the circus. Go on."

"I was furious. It just slipped out."

There was no change in her expression. She said nothing.

Barry ploughed on. "We've talked about this before. I was truthful. I said I had reservations."

"But you agreed that after a reasonable wait we would start a family. Didn't you?"

He couldn't meet her gaze, but said quietly, "Yes. Yes, I did."

"Yet what you yelled didn't exactly sound like the words of a man who had a few reservations. They sounded like a man who can think of nothing worse than being a father." She let her arms fall to hang by her sides. "You are still having second thoughts, aren't you?"

Barry pursed his lips and nodded. "I did not enjoy the company of Sammy Lindsay today."

Sue took a deep breath. "Sammy Lindsay was just being a little boy. Being a parent isn't all about having a day of fun at the circus." She paused. "Better it's out in the open, now."

The implication "than after we've taken our vows" was not lost on Barry. "We'll work it out," he said, and stepped closer to her, but she took a pace back. "I love you, Sue."

"And I love you, Barry, but I couldn't face a childless future." She shook her head. "I simply couldn't."

He didn't know what to say. The silence hung and lengthened until finally she said, "I think . . . I think . . ." Now her words came in a rush. "I think perhaps we both need a break."

"You mean break off our engagement?" Barry's heart shrank in him. No.

"No," she said. "You lost your temper, and I can understand why, but it brought out something that has made me very upset."

Again he tried to move to her to comfort her and again she moved away.

"I'm not thinking very straight just now. I'd like to be left alone. And I think you need to do some soul-searching too. I love you, Barry. I'll say nothing to anyone else. Let all the arrangements stand. But . . ." her voice took on a sharp edge, "I need time to myself."

Barry wasn't sure what to do. Every instinct called to him. "Take her in your arms. Tell her you love her. Tell her what she wants to hear," but another small voice said, "Do what she wants. Let her have her time." He said, "Very well," and moved to the door. "When will I hear from you again?"

She shook her head. "Soon," she said, "but right now please go."

He left and closed the door, but before he could take his first step toward the car, his soul was torn by the sounds of sobbing.

18

'Til I Took Up to Poaching

"Blether," mumbled O'Reilly, groping back to consciousness. Somebody was pushing the night bell outside the front door and the sound had pierced the silence of the old house, jangling up from the first-floor landing. He slipped out from under the covers, trying not to disturb Kitty.

She muttered in her sleep and rolled onto her other side as he slid his feet into carpet slippers and padded across the floor to where his dressing gown hung on a peg at the back of the door.

The bell's insistent clamour grated on his nerves. "Whoever it is, if you push any harder you'll break the bloody thing."

The villagers rarely disturbed his sleep unless something was badly wrong. He yawned mightily, recalling his time in the Augier Street dispensary practice in 1936 when the telephoneless residents of the Liberties in Dublin would come to the practice at any time of day or night. That was thirty-one years ago now and village life here in the north had softened him.

He switched on the hall light and opened the door.

In the light spilling from the hall and the brilliance of a full moon overhead, he saw a despondent-looking Donal Donnelly, his carroty hair hidden under a rolled-up woollen balaclava. Beside him was Constable Malcolm Mulligan, clutching a brown canvas game bag. O'Reilly shook the last of the sleep from his shaggy head and sighed. Donal Donnelly had been caught—he looked down at Donal's left hand, wrapped in a bloodstained rag—literally red-handed.

"I'm desperate sorry for til disturb you, sir, at two o'clock of a Sunday morning," the officer said, "but your man here has cut his hand, so he has."

"Bring him through to the surgery." O'Reilly opened its door and turned on the lights. The officer closed the surgery door. "I know it's unusual, sir, but I'm afraid Mister Donnelly has til be identified, arrested, and cautioned. You and me know who he is. I've arrested him, but I can't caution him until I'm satisfied he's healthy and understands. I'd rather not let him out of my sight until I can do that. After he's all fixed up."

"I understand, Constable Mulligan," O'Reilly said, "but I give you my word"— He fixed Donal Donnelly with a stare not unlike that of the mythical Balor, the one-eyed Fomorian giant whose glare could destroy armies— "until I've finished with him, he'll not be leaving this surgery, at least not standing up, will you, you great glipe?"

Donal shrank away. "No, sir. I will not, sir. Honest til God."

O'Reilly realized his anger was not because he'd been hauled out of a warm bed. He was angry that Donal Donnelly had been careless enough to break the eleventh commandment: "Thou shalt not get caught."

"Make yourself comfortable in the dining room, Constable Mulligan," O'Reilly said. "It won't take long to patch Donnelly up."

"It's very irregular, sir."

"Come on, Malcolm," O'Reilly said. "I know you've your procedures, but we both know Donal's not going to do a runner. On a bike at two A.M.?"

The policeman looked serious. "Right enough." He turned to his prisoner. "Now you do as you're bid by the doctor, and then I'll caution you and let you go home."

"Yes, sir." Donal was meekness personified.

Constable Mulligan left, closing the door behind him.

"I'm awful sorry, sir."

O'Reilly shook his sleep-tousled head again. "Can't be helped. But by god, Donal, you are an eejit. Getting nabbed by Mulligan. We've only got one peeler in the area. Did you take a fit of the head staggers?"

"I must of. I was a bit stupid."

"All right. Come on then. Let's get that cut of yours seen to. You can tell me your tale of woe and stupidity while I'm working. Come on over to the sink."

Donal obeyed.

"Stick your bad paw over the basin. Right. Let's get that rag off." He unwound it and dropped it into a pedal bin. A cut stretched diagonally for three inches across the palm from the ball of the thumb in the direction of the base of the little finger. "It's going to need stitches," O'Reilly said. "Wriggle your fingers and thumb."

Donal did.

"Good. No tendon damage. You'll live to poach another day, and go on working as a carpenter, but it's going to be sutured."

Donal sniffed. "Aye." He shrugged. "Won't be the first stitches I've had. There's few chippies don't cut themselves. It's an occupational gizzard, so it is. Goes with the job."

"Hazard, Donal," O'Reilly said.

"Aye," said Donal. "Right enough. I've got birds on the brain."

O'Reilly was tempted to remark that on occasion, Donal Donnelly was a bird brain, but said, "Now go and sit back in that chair. I need to get ready, and while I am, tell me what happened." He slipped on a surgical mask, then took a sterile pack from a nearby shelf and set it on a small stainless steel table on wheels.

"Some bugger grassed," Donal said. "You know thon wee coppice?"

"Where Mrs. O'Reilly and I met you a couple of weeks back? Um, bird-watching, I believe." O'Reilly opened the pack. Its green sterile towel covered the tabletop. Inside were a sterile towel with a centre opening, a stainless-steel kidney dish, forceps, a needle driver, a pack of sutures, scissors, swabs and swab holder, and a preloaded hypodermic containing local anaesthetic.

"Aye," Donal said. "Tomorrow, the two weeks of paid holiday is up and Mister Bishop's heard there'll be a month delay before the road job will start. Fair play. He's not made of money. It's me and the lads for the burroo next week. Julie and me's got a bit put aside, but I'm afraid the ould do-re-mi's going to get a bit tight."

"I can imagine. And there's not much other work around, is there?" O'Reilly opened a pack containing a sterile towel and rubber gloves.

Donal shook his head.

O'Reilly poured disinfectant into the kidney dish on the trolley and pushed the trolley over to Donal. "And don't tell me. You were helping out with the provisions."

Donal frowned. "It's a man's duty til provide for his family, so it is." O'Reilly, who now was scrubbing his hands, heard the sincerity in Donal's voice. "I'd spent the thirty bob I'd won playing poker last week. The dosh went at the circus this afternoon."

O'Reilly dried his hands on the sterile towel. Some men, and Donal was one of them, couldn't resist betting on things even if they were hard up. O'Reilly gave a fleeting thought to Ronald Fitzpatrick. Had he been behaving himself in that regard? He shook his head and pulled on the rubber gloves. O'Reilly couldn't help but have a sneaking admiration for how the man before him now was trying to meet his obligations. Perhaps, he thought, it appeals to the not-so-well-hidden sense in your own soul that some laws were meant to be broken?

He walked over to where Donal sat. "Shove your hand onto the table, Donal. Palm up." To satisfy O'Reilly's curiosity and to distract Donal from what initially was going to be uncomfortable, O'Reilly continued, "And while I'm working I want to hear the rest of your story. Now this will be cold and might sting a bit." He used the syringe to spray a small amount of local onto the raw edges of the wound. It would numb the exposed flesh a little so the washing and actual deeper injections would be less painful. He'd learned the trick from Barry three years ago.

Donal sucked his breath in and said, "Do you keep that stuff in the fridge, sir?"

"Actually we do sometimes. We'll give it a minute or two to work. Now, come on. What happened?"

"I done a couple of stupid things." Donal hung his head then looked up at O'Reilly. "I'd been out you-know-where doing a bit more 'bird-watching' last night. Feeding them whisky-soaked grain. Then I popped intil the Duck. Julie had given me a couple of bob for a pint." Donal smiled. "She's quare and smart about the housekeeping money."

There was pride in the man's voice. "Anyroad, Dapper Frew was in, him single and it being Saturday night, so him and me was colloguing and he asked where I'd been. I should have told him, 'A policeman wouldn't ask you that,' but did I tell him til mind his own business? No, I didn't. I let slip, on the QT, like, what I was up til and where I'd been. I'd trust Dapper with my life, so I would."

"So would I," O'Reilly said. "Sound man, Dapper. Now, Donal, I'm going to wash it with disinfectant. But go on." O'Reilly bent to his work using the sponge holder loaded with Dettol to wipe away old clots. A small trickle of fresh blood started.

"I don't know if I'd been overheard, but Dapper whispers til me, 'Donal, don't look now, but see yer man Hubert Doran . . .'"

O'Reilly muttered, "Gobshite," under his breath, then said, "Hold your hand still. I'm going to put in the local. Go on." He began to inject one lip of the cut with Xylocaine. "I didn't think Doran went into the Duck much."

"I heard he's been coming more often since that wee bit of trouble at borough council last month. Trying to get in folks' good books again."

"Some chance," O'Reilly said, starting on the other lip of the cut.

"I kept staring ahead. Dapper says, 'I know Doran and I hope he wasn't listening til you. He's a sleekit bugger. Always eavesdropping. Don't you go out again tonight, Donal.'" He sucked in his breath. "I felt that one a bit, sir."

"Sorry. I'm all done freezing. It'll only take a couple of minutes for the whole wound to go numb." He laid the towel with the central hole over Donal's palm so only the wound was accessible.

"Fair enough. Anyroad, Julie's parents are coming up from Rasharkin today and she wanted til give them something special for dinner. So I reckoned I'd chance it anyway."

O'Reilly nodded.

Donal sighed. "That was my first mistake. I should have heeded Dapper."

"You should have," O'Reilly said. He could picture Doran, who had been forced to resign from the borough council for lying. Was the man trying to rebuild his stock by being an upright citizen reporting a possible crime? If so, he was a sillier bugger than O'Reilly'd thought. You'd think an Irishman would know about the utter contempt in which informers were held in this country. More likely, he was getting back at Donal for the remarks he'd made at that fateful council meeting.

"Tell me if you can feel that," said O'Reilly, and jabbed the needle along the length of the edges of the wound.

"Just a wee bit of pressure, sir. It's all froze, so it is."

"Good," said O'Reilly. "I'll get the stitches in now." He opened the packet of sutures swaged to curved needles and loaded the needle driver. "And what was your second mistake?"

"I reckoned if—if Doran had tipped off the peeler, he'd probably be expecting me til get out there as soon as I left the pub. He'd need to set an ambush. I know how Malcolm Mulligan works. You're dead on, Doc, he's single-handed, he can't stay in any one place for too long. He has his rounds til make."

O'Reilly took the first stitch and cut it short with the scissors. "Go on."

"I didn't think he'd stay. So I went home, but out again to do the wee job after one in the morning."

O'Reilly clipped the second stitch and kept working. "Wasn't the moon a bit bright? It's full tonight."

"Bright as bloody day, but it wouldn't matter if there was none there til see me." Donal blew out his cheeks and expelled an exasperated breath. "More fool me. I'd just got my brace of birds and shoved them in my bag when up pops the bloody peeler from out of a fern thicket." Donal hesitated. "Malcolm Mulligan's a good head. He's just doing his job. Anyroad, I took off like a liltie. I had my balaclava down and hoped I'd not been recognised. Your man came pounding after, yelling, 'Come back here, you. You're only making it worse for yourself.'"

"That's the last stitch, Donal," O'Reilly said, and straightened up. He had a vivid image of a startled Donal, only his eyes showing from the eyeholes in his mask, slung bag bouncing on his hip, charging out of the wood and across the field, chasing his own moon shadow, breath burning in his chest, and the heavyset police constable in hot pursuit, boots pounding on the ground, arms pumping.

"I'd have got to my bike, and maybe could have got away, but I got stuck in a barbed-wire fence, so I did. That's where I cut my hand. And that's where Malcolm got me. He hauled off my balaclava. Says he, 'So it is yourself, Donal.' He had to take another breath, then says he, 'I hate til do this to you, Donal Donnelly, but I'm going til arrest you for taking game birds out of season.' Then he saw my hand. 'That's not so good. Come on, we'll get you fixed up first,' and he brung me here."

"I see." O'Reilly realised how difficult it must be for the policeman to arrest one of his neighbours, an out-of-work man with a family, for stealing a couple of birds. Malcolm was a humane man. O'Reilly removed the sterile towel and bandaged the hand. "All done," he said.

"Thank you, Doctor," Donal said. "I don't know what I'm going to tell Julie, so I don't."

"The truth," O'Reilly said. "She's a very understanding lass, your Julie." He stripped off his gloves into the pedal bin. Kinky'd tidy up in here tomorrow before surgery hours. "One last thing. I'll have to give you a lockjaw jag."

Donal sighed. "I suppose if you must, you must."

The deed was swiftly done.

"Now come on, Donal. I have to give you back to Malcolm."

"Fair enough, sir, and thanks for fixing me up."

"Here." O'Reilly gave Donal a dozen Panadol. "Take one every six hours. It's going to throb once the local wears off. And come back in a week. I'll take your stitches out." O'Reilly led Donal through to the dining room where Constable Mulligan was sitting on a chair reading. He leapt to his feet, thrusting *Analog* magazine, a science-fiction digest, into his tunic pocket. "All done, sir?"

"He's all yours, Officer."

Constable Mulligan's voice was full of concern. "And are you all right, Donal?"

"I'll live." He pointed at his torn trouser legs. "I'm not sure they will." He shook his head. "What now?"

"Doctor, you'll agree that this here's Donal Donnelly?"

"To the life, Constable."

"Thank you." He licked a pencil and scribbled in his notebook. "And, Donal, do you understand what I'm saying til you?"

"Aye, certainly. Some might think I'm a stook short of a haystack, but I know fine what you're about, so I do."

O'Reilly harrumphed and Constable Mulligan drew himself up to his full height. "Donal Donnelly, I arrest you under the Northern Ireland Game Preservation Act of 1928 for taking game birds, namely two cock pheasants, out of season. You have the right to remain silent but anything you say may be taken down in writing and used as evidence against you. Understand?"

"Aye."

"Good." Mulligan closed his notebook. "Right. I'm off til the station til write up my report. You'll get a summons to appear at the petty sessions in Bangor Courthouse in about a month." He turned to O'Reilly. "And you'll be asked, sir, to come as witness to what happened here tonight. You are proof that Donal got all due process in his arrest"—he held out the game bag and opened the flap—"and that this here bag had two cock pheasants in it." He closed the bag.

"Fair enough."

"Can I go home now, Constable?" said Donal, a touch of the plaintive child in his voice.

"Aye, certainly. I'll release you on your own recognizances. That's a promise that you'll show up on the court date. You'll not need bail."

"Thank God for that," Donal said. "I'm away on home. Thanks for fixing me up, Doc, and it's all right, Malcolm. No hard feelings."

O'Reilly was still chuckling as he turned out lights and made his way back to bed.

"So," said Kitty as he snuggled under the blankets, "saved another life?"

O'Reilly grunted, then said, "Bloody Donal Donnelly got nicked pinching pheasants by PC Mulligan because that piece of human slime Hubert Doran grassed."

"Doran? Oh dear. Poor Donal."

"He'd cut his hand so I had to sew him up." He moved closer to Kitty, enjoying her nearness, her warmth. "And I'll have to go to court as a witness when the case comes up."

"Indeed you will, pet, but not tonight." She yawned mightily, kissed his cheek, and said, her words already slurred, "It's a God-awful hour and time for sleep."

19

The White Sail's Shaking

"So, let's get this yoke afloat, hey." Jack Mills's County Antrim accent was as thick as—Barry inhaled deeply—as thick as Sue's father's. Barry had slept little last night, had been tossing and awake when the bell rang in the small hours. He'd heard O'Reilly going downstairs but was surprised by how little curiosity he had for the event. He seemed to have no room in his head but for thoughts of Sue and his God-awful gaffe.

Wearing a kapok life jacket over his yellow oilskins, Barry took hold of the starboard gunwale of Andy Jackson's loaned GP14, *Shearwater*. Andy was visiting his family in Donaghadee this afternoon and had been happy for Barry to use her. "You right? Ready to go?" Barry asked.

"Aye." Jack, similarly clad, lifted the car-hitch end of the boat trailer and started to push. Strong as an ox, that man. The two rubber tyres bumped over the dinghy park and up onto a concrete ramp leading down into the waters of Ballyholme Bay.

Barry walked alongside, steadying the little craft heading stern first for the water. He looked under the boom to his parents' seafront three-storey house on the Ballyholme Esplanade and wondered what Mum and Dad would be up to today. He often dropped in on them when he was out this way, but today he didn't have the heart for it, and his mother would have had the truth out of him in about five minutes. He walked straight into the rapidly deepening water. He wanted to get afloat and think of other things. Holding on to the gunwale as the dinghy floated free, he felt the wind on his cheeks, the salt-sea smell in his nostrils, and the chill on his legs up to his knees. I hope this will clear the cobwebs, he thought, help me to start thinking straight. When the time's ripe, I'll ask Jack's advice. The already hoisted foresail flapped with a series of cracks in the stiff northeast breeze.

In very short order, Jack had taken the trailer back and waded in on the port side. "Jaysus. That would freeze the balls off a brass monkey," he said as he climbed into the boat's cockpit, sat for'ard on the port-side bench, and grabbed a paddle.

Barry clambered over to starboard, sat aft, took a paddle too, and together they worked the dinghy out stern first and away from the shore.

Barry as skipper had to give no orders. He and Jack had sailed Barry's old dinghy *Tarka* together for years when they'd been schoolboys, and Jack had come to Ballyholme for summer holidays. Their friendship went back to 1953. And today Barry needed a friend.

In no time the little boat had turned and made enough distance from the ramp that Barry stopped worrying about being blown ashore. He put her head into the wind so Jack could hoist the mainsail and Barry could drop the centre-board, the dinghy's retractable keel. Barry headed them out toward the waters of Belfast Lough. The brisk breeze coming into Ballyholme Bay carried the almond scent of the gorse flowers on Ballymacormick Point and bittersweet memories of walks he and Sue had taken there among the sheltering whins.

"She's going like the clappers," Barry said to Jack. They had their backsides on the port gunwale as the dinghy sped through the chop. Both men's feet were tucked behind canvas straps in-board and they leant backward over the water to counterbalance the wind in the boat's sails that was making her heel to starboard. Barry held a rope in his right hand and the tiller in his left.

Jack sat ahead of him. His job was to work the ropes called sheets that controlled the triangular foresail. Barry would take care of helming and the single sheet controlling the bigger mainsail. "It's good to be afloat again," he said.

Jack nodded. "For a country boy like me who's not too keen on all the noise and stink of the big city, it's grand. Nothing out here to listen to but the odd gull squawking, the wind in the rigging, the chop and slap of the waves . . ." One broke and threw spray in his face. He laughed. "And the now-soggy crew yelling, 'Bugger it.'"

In spite of how he felt, Barry managed to laugh. Jack Mills, with his mad sense of humour, was a tonic. Barry stared ahead. It would soon be time to change course. The wind met the boat's port side, blowing the mainsail and foresail out to starboard, but as both their sheets had been hauled short the white wings were nearly flat. She was said to be sailing "close hauled,'" or "full and bye," an old square-rigger term.

"Remember that wonderful little hunchbacked man, Joe Togneri? He was the son of Italian immigrants who ran the Coronation Ice Cream Shop in Bangor. He had a small dinghy and taught me to sail her when I was thirteen." A simpler time when girls hadn't become important enough to complicate life, as they were doing now.

"Who'd forget Joe?" Jack said. "One of nature's gentlemen. And then you taught me, a farm boy from Cullybackey, miles from the sea. Thanks, mate."

"'Hold her full and bye, Barry, son,' Joe'd say, then he'd break into one of his innumerable 'come-all-ye,' songs that always began—"

"'Come all ye dryland sailors and listen to me song.'" Jack sang in a good tenor, one he used to sing at student parties. "''Tis only a thousand verses so I won't detain youse long . . .'"

Good old Jack. Barry looked ahead and saw they were getting too close to Ballymacormick. Time to change course. "Ready about?" His warning to prepare for the manoeuvre.

Jack glanced back, grinned, and loosed the sheet until only one turn remained around its anchor point, a cleat. He held the rope in his hand.

Barry nodded and prepared to cast off the main sheet.

"Lee oh." The executive command. Barry pulled the tiller to him and felt the rudder bite.

The little boat responded like a thoroughbred. Her bows swung to port, and as they crossed the wind, he ripped the sheet from between serrated jaws called a jam-cleat and hauled in to control the boom as it swung across the boat.

Jack had let fly his sheet.

To the furious flapping of the headsail, the mainsail's boom swung across the cockpit. Barry paid out line as the boom and sail ran out over the boat's port side. Simultaneously, the hull righted itself before beginning to heel to port as he and Jack crossed the cockpit, got seated, and put their toes back in the opposite straps. When Barry was satisfied with their new course, he yelled, "Sheet home."

With both sails filled, *Shearwater* tried to heel further, but the men counteracted that by leaning backward.

A sudden stronger gust hit. Barry felt his side of the dinghy rise as the low side dipped and the masthead moved closer to the sea's choppy surface. He heard the slapping of waves on the little boat's bow, tasted the chill spray that blew aft. He eased the tiller away from himself, allowing the bows to move closer to the wind so the pressure on the sails lessened and the boat became more vertical. The headsail began to flap and he ignored it until the gust had passed and he had once more brought the dinghy back on course, sails drawing beautifully.

"God, but I love helming a dinghy in these kinds of conditions. Love it." He knew he was grinning like a mad jack o' lantern, but it was okay because Jack was grinning back.

So what if once in a while Barry misjudged and the little boat fell on her side, sails in the water? Experienced sailors could right a dinghy in no time. Then he wondered, was his falling out with Sue just a temporary setback like that sudden gust? Was there a way to bring their lives together back on course too, or had he capsized things irrevocably? He shook his head. He simply didn't know.

Another gust, more easing of the tiller, flapping of sails and wind-blown spume before coming back on course.

"Having fun, skipper?" Jack asked, turning to face Barry. His cheeks were rosy from the wind.

Barry was and he wasn't, and he wanted to talk to his friend about it, but not now. Sailing close-hauled took concentration. "We're nearly out of Ballyholme Bay and into Belfast Lough. As soon as we pass Luke's Point, I'm going to let her fall off the wind and head for Bangor," Barry said. "That'll put the wind on the beam."

"A soldier's wind," Jack said. "Easiest point of sailing, and it'll be the same coming back." He loosed his sheet. "Ready when you are."

Barry pulled the tiller to him and the little boat's bows went in the opposite direction. The sheets of both sails were paid out until Barry was satisfied with their set and the dinghy, with considerably less heel, was racing the waves now, coming in at an angle to her starboard side.

"Want to helm?" Barry asked.

"Love to."

Barry waited until Jack had taken the tiller and wriggled for'ard past his friend.

Jack sat looking up. Good sailors spent a lot of time doing that, to make sure the sails were set to best advantage. "Little more jib, Barry."

He slackened off the sheet until the foresail began to flap, then hauled in, stopping the second the flapping disappeared.

"Perfect," Jack said.

They were now both able to move into the cockpit and sit on the starboard-side bench.

Barry looked ahead. He could see the long finger of Bangor's North Pier with its platoons of ever-hopeful sea-anglers, and behind the pier and on a hill, Bangor—Beannchar, which meant "the place of the pointed hills." The narrow spire of First Bangor Presbyterian Church pointed for the sky.

On the far rocky shore, he spied the white-and-green walls of Pickie Pool, the outdoor seawater swimming baths with their ten-metre diving tower. Barry had learnt to swim there. He could describe this part of County Down with his eyes closed. And just as clearly, he could see Sue's look of yesterday when she'd said, "I think perhaps we both need a break."

"Jack, there's something I want to talk to you about."

Jack stopped staring up and looked straight at Barry. "I wondered when you'd say that. Go on, mate. That's what friends are for. I knew there was something bothering you from the minute I met you today."

"It's Sue." He swallowed. "To get right to the point, she's keen to start a family after we get married." He paused.

Jack, who must have thought his friend had finished, laughed and said, "I don't see too much wrong with that. I've been trying for years not to, you understand." He leered and said, "The fun's in the trying, hey, and if a wee one comes along, sure isn't that the natural course of things once you're married?"

Barry sighed. "I suppose coming from a farm, seeing new baby animals every year, you would think of that as natural. My difficulty is that I'm not so sure. Not sure at all. We'd discussed it a month ago. I'd said it would be fine. Then I started to have second thoughts." He stopped talking. He didn't feel up to telling Jack about the remark that had brought it all to a head.

"I think that's pretty normal, Barry. I've heard lots about maternal instinct, not a whole hell of a lot about paternal—"

"Hang on." Barry hadn't been paying attention to his job and he was distracted by the flapping of the headsail. He adjusted the sheet until the sail was set properly. "Sorry, go on."

"Well, I reckon that rearing the chisslers when they're little is mostly what mothers do. Our job's to bring home the bacon." He glanced up and made a small course correction. "I've not talked this over with Helen, but I can see difficulties for us too. Can you see Helen Hewitt qualifying and then not practicing so she can be a brood mare and babysitter? It's not as if my folks live close enough to Belfast to babysit, and Helen's mum died a few years back. No handy grannies to help out." Jack laughed. "And can you see me staying at home doing the child minding? Helen thinks I'm just a big kid myself, and I think she may be right."

"You, minding the children? Perish the thought." Barry grinned. "My mum might help, but Sue's dad's been sick and her parents live in Broughshane."

"Sure, but your Sue, she's a teacher. She loves kiddies. She'd be fantastic with them, Barry."

Barry checked his sail's set. "She would, won't she?" Barry felt his heart swell at the thought, but as quickly felt a pang of real fear about his own abilities as a father. "She'd have to give up teaching for a while, but I don't think she'd mind."

Jack nodded his agreement. "But these days it's not all black and white either. Men are expected to help out some, change nappies, give bottles in the middle of the night, that sort of thing."

"I'd not mind that. Babies I think can handle, it's once they're older that has me worried." He glanced ahead. "Oh-oh. Look ahead," he said, pointing. "There's a bloody great cabin cruiser coming out of Bangor Bay."

The white vessel was rounding the pier.

"But we're sail and we're on the starboard tack, so we have the right of way on two counts."

"Keep an eye on her."

The throbbing of diesels was becoming louder. Barry looked ahead. The rule of the road was: Distance closing, bearing changing—safety. Distance closing, bearing constant—look out. There was still enough distance, but Barry was starting to become concerned. "Come a few degrees to port," he said. "I'll look after the sails."

Jack made the necessary course correction.

When Barry was satisfied they would be safe, he said, "Bring her back on to the original heading. Good. That's better. The stink-pot'll pass us close to starboard now."

"Good. And to get back to your question," Jack said, "I think there'd be a great deal of satisfaction seeing your offspring take their first steps, speak their first words. When they get older, watching them play sports. Teach them to sail, fish, swim. Watch them do well at school, learning how to play the bagpipes in the school band—"

Jack saw Barry's grimace and laughed. "Well, maybe not that last bit, but before you know it, you'll be a grampa."

Barry smiled. "I suppose so, but it's still pretty scary."

Two immature brown-flecked herring gulls flew overhead, screeching and calling in the way of their kind. Barry could hear the waves crashing on yellow barnacle-encrusted rocks inshore.

"Sure it's scary, mate. This whole bollixed-up thing that's called life is scary. We see it every day in our jobs, people getting sick, having accidents, dying, for God's sake. I don't blame you for being scared. Just shows you think about things, care about things."

"Maybe," Barry said. "Maybe." He looked at his friend and shook his head in wonder. He'd always seen Jack as supremely confident, but perhaps he wasn't. If it was possible, he realized he liked his friend even more. "The last thing she said was she wanted time to be alone to think. You're the expert on the female of the species—"

Jack let out a roar of laughter. "Thanks, mate, if you want to think that."

"I can't just ring her up and say 'I love you' and hope that will make it all better." He looked ahead. The cruiser was still some distance away, moving sedately, but noisily in their general direction.

Jack thought, then said, "You're still sure you want to marry Sue?"

"Absolutely."

"Remember what you advised when Helen wanted to be left in peace to study before the Second MB exam last month?"

"Yes. I said to leave her be. She'd not thank you if you didn't and she failed."

"Right. And Sue's not going to thank you if you don't give her the time she wants. Look. You're head over heels, right?"

"Right."

"You're missing her like blue buggery?"

"Right."

"And how do you think she's feeling?"

Barry shook his head. "Sad. Angry. Disappointed."

"And missing you—a lot."

"I suppose so. I sure as hell hope so." Barry knew what was coming, but he didn't want to be patient. He wanted to go ashore, jump into Brunhilde, and roar up to Holywood. "So you think I should give her the time she's asked for?"

"Yes, and give yourself some time too, Barry, time to let the idea of being a daddy sink in. Now, I'm foundered. Where's that flask of coffee . . ."

Barry cleated home his sheet and ducked under the foredeck overhang. He grabbed a khaki canvas knapsack, fished out a thermos, and filled the cap that served as a cup. He sighed. Jack Mills had certainly expressed himself clearly, but was Barry ready to commit? Because if he was, there was no going back this time or it would all be over.

He backed out from the cramped little space carrying flask and cup and glanced ahead. Holy Mother of God. The engine noises that had steadily been getting louder as the cabin cruiser approached went up to a thundering roar as her skipper, who must have been unaware of *Shearwater*'s presence, slammed into full speed ahead.

Barry watched the big boat rise up on her step. The white foam of her rooster tail could be seen astern higher than the deckhouse, and already the tsunamis of her bow waves and wake were spreading on both sides fore and aft. She passed *Shearwater*'s starboard side too close for Jack to put the dinghy's bows onto the wake and lessen its effect. "Bastard," he yelled at a man in a navy blue reefer jacket steering from aft, captain's cap on his head, drink clutched in one hand. The stink of diesel was overpowering.

"Hang on," Barry yelled, dropping flask and cup into the cockpit.

The bow wave hit like a sledgehammer. The dinghy heeled so far to port Barry thought she was going over. Loose gear crashed about. The sails slatted. Water came in green over the port gunwale. Barry felt his arm muscles groaning as he held on to the boat. Like a fallen horse, *Shearwater* shuddered, tried to come upright, but only half succeeded when the tidal waves of the wake hit. Over she went again. Barry let go and hurled his upper body over the starboard side, hoping to God he was heavy enough to hold the dinghy. He was sure he felt a rib go.

And slowly, slowly, like the rolling of a whale, the dinghy righted herself.

"You all right, Jack?" Breathing hurt Barry's chest.

"Just," he said. He shook his fist at the departing cruiser and echoed Barry's earlier sentiments: "Bastard."

Barry grimaced. "I'm pretty sure I've cracked a rib. We'll have to put about and head back, I'm afraid." Barry started to loosen the jib sheet.

Under Jack's guidance, *Shearwater* came about and headed for home. He said, "I'll get a proper look at that rib once we get ashore. Meantime, can you thole it?"

Barry took shallow breaths. He was in pain, but it was not intolerable. "I think it's just a crack. I'll live."

"It stings. I bust two a couple of years ago playing rugby, but it won't take long to heal—and Barry?"

"Yes."

"All is fair in love and war, you know. I want to see you two back together and happy."

Barry held the side of his chest and said, "So do I."

"It's a bit Machiavellian, but when Sue gets back in touch—and she will—"

"I hope to God you're right."

"The old wounded soldier ploy can really work wonders."

Despite the ache in his heart and the pain in his chest, Barry managed a smile. "Jack Mills, have you ever thought of going into partnership with Donal Donnelly?"

"No," said Jack, "I know nothing about greyhounds and race horses, but when it comes to women, trust your uncle, Barry. Trust your uncle. Now let's get this thing home, and you looked at properly."

20

To Comfort and Relieve

O'Reilly regarded Kinky over his half-moon spectacles. She would not interrupt a consultation in the surgery unless it were very important. "Yes, Kinky?"

"Excuse me, Doctor. Shooey. There does be a Doctor MacIlrath on the telephone. From the Royal Victoria. He says he has to speak to you now, so."

"Sorry, Shooey," he said to the octogenarian who had come in for his six-monthly evaluation of his arthritic knees. Barry had started the older man on enteric-coated aspirin last year. "Let me give you a hand down." O'Reilly helped him off the couch. "I'm finished with your examination, so have a pew. I'll be back in no time."

"Take your time, sir," Shooey said. "I'm in no rush. It's one of the advantages of being in your eighties."

O'Reilly headed for the hall. "Thanks, Kinky." He picked up the receiver. "Hello, Teddy?"

"Fingal, I got your message. I have the plates on the viewing box in front of me."

O'Reilly realised he had crossed his fingers.

"There's some emphysema, not unexpected in a smoker, and a scar of old healed TB in the apex of the left lower lobe. Hang on. Someone's just come in. Occupational hazard in a teaching hospital."

And in another week we'll be a teaching practice, O'Reilly thought. He overheard a short conversation between Teddy and a trainee who needed advice about an urgent orthopaedic intra-operative X-ray. So

Anne Galvin had a healed TB scar? O'Reilly had one in his own left lung. People of his generation, and of Barry's generation too, pretty much all had had TB. Some had succumbed. The natural defences of the majority had fought the invaders off, and the victim developed immunity, but residual scars were often left behind. That had all changed after World War II with the introduction of BCG vaccination of babies shortly after birth. Well, at least he could exclude active TB for Anne Galvin, but that wasn't his greatest concern. Not by a long chalk. He wished his friend would get a move on.

"Sorry about that," Teddy said, "young lassie wasn't quite sure what she was seeing. Back to your patient. That's about it for findings. I don't see any signs of malignancy and, frankly, given the history you put on the requisition form Mrs. Galvin gave us, bronchial carcinoma was top of my diagnostic pops."

O'Reilly uncrossed his fingers and smiled—in part out of a deep sense of relief for Anne Galvin, and in part at the senior radiologist's irreverent way of expressing himself to a colleague. Such seeming insensitivity was a trait common to practitioners of specialities like radiology, pathology, and anaesthesia, which had little or no personal contact with patients. "That," said O'Reilly, "is the best news I've had all week—and it's only Monday. Many thanks, Teddy."

"My pleasure, Fingal. There is one thing though. X-rays are spot on for bones. Once in a blue moon, we miss soft tissue disease. Just to be on the safe side, belt and braces, shoot her back for a follow-up in six months."

"Will do." O'Reilly rang off. That thoroughness was why his friend was so highly regarded. And O'Reilly was pretty sure the follow-up would be exactly what Teddy had said. A precaution. Nothing more. O'Reilly danced a jig step. He was delighted for the Galvins and for Barry, who had been out of sorts at breakfast.

The lad had hurt himself yesterday sailing. Last evening, Jack had examined Barry at the Yacht Club and determined that it looked as if his left seventh rib was cracked, but with no evidence of lung damage. Jack, who was after all well on his way to being a qualified surgeon, had decided an X-ray was unnecessary and had strapped Barry up with elastic adherent bandages here in the surgery. Barry had explained that he was sore but quite able to carry out his duties.

Maybe the news about Anne Galvin would cheer him up at lunchtime. He'd be relieved that, contrary to what he thought, he had not missed making the diagnosis of a lethal illness.

O'Reilly headed back to the surgery.

Hugh Gamble, "Shooey" to all who knew him, was standing up, examining one of the patients' plain wooden chairs and scratching his head. "Boys-a-boys, Doctor," he said, "you've bought a pig in a poke with this here chair, so you have. D'yiz know the front legs is shorter nor the back ones?"

"My goodness," said O'Reilly, "there's a thing, now. Whatever next?" He shook his head in feigned amazement. Of course they bloody well were. Within two weeks of starting his single-handed practice here after the war, he himself had sawn off an inch so the patients kept sliding forward and hence were not tempted to stay too long. Of course, with all the extra help now from Barry and Nonie Stevenson, time was no longer of such importance. "Thanks for telling me. I'll see about getting a new one. Now," he said, "about your knees. I don't see any physical change, and you say you've not noticed any difference."

"Not a bit. Them coated aspirins don't upset my tummy and the joints don't pain me much anymore. If they're still as good by August," he winked, "I'll take myself off to Lisdoonvarna in September." There was a twinkle in his eyes despite the presence of *arci senili,* the lightening of each blue iris round the circumference.

O'Reilly chuckled. "Lios Dúin Bhearna, that hill fort with the gap in the wall, in County Clare? And what's there in September?" As if O'Reilly didn't know, but he wanted to hear what Shooey had to say.

"Sure, isn't it the biggest matchmaking event in all of Europe. D'you know this one, sir?" He sang,

> I dunno, maybe so, for a bachelor is easy and he's free,
> But I've a lot to look after and I'm livin' by meself, and
>   there's no-one lookin' after me.

"'Little Bridget Flynn,'" said O'Reilly. "I know it well. Eighty-two and there's life in you yet, Shooey Gamble, even if you're not running after beagles chasing a hare or a fox anymore."

"I do miss that and och, it's only a gag about me going to Clare, but," Shooey became serious, "Doctor, in all my years, I've learnt if you have your health, it's up to you to keep your mind and your body active, and then you'll not feel old. I don't. Mind you, all my years as a shepherd and the rowing I used til do kept me fit."

"I hear you," O'Reilly said. "And I'll bear that in mind." And by God he would. He'd been spending too much time worrying about his own aging. "You're a shining example, Shooey Gamble." O'Reilly began to head for the door. "One of us'll see you in October." He stood aside to let Shooey out and stood in the doorway for a moment watching the old man toddle down the street, then stop and, with a sweeping gesture, doff his hat to Cissie Sloan. O'Reilly laughed and headed for the waiting room. Perhaps Shooey Gamble would be going to Lisdoonvarna after all.

"I would have appreciated it, Doctor O'Reilly, sir," Kinky fixed him with a glare, "if someone had the courtesy to let me know that Doctor Stevenson would be at some course at the Royal Victoria and would not be in for lunch today." Her eyes flashed and her chins quivered, and not from mirth either. "There does be one perfectly good grilled lamb chop wasted." She stared at O'Reilly's waistline. "And no, sir. I will not be serving you a second chop. I do have perfectly good knives. The meat taken off the bones can be treats for Arthur and Kenny. The bones would be too brittle after cooking, so."

Barry simply sat quietly as she served him his chop, mint sauce, and colcannon. O'Reilly thought briefly about making a jocular reference to it being less than three weeks since her gift had let her predict the winner of the Grand National. Couldn't she just foresee Nonie's absence? He took a quick look at Kinky, whose eyes were still flashing and chins still quivering, and decided it would be less than tactful. He bowed his head. "It was an unforgiveable lapse on my part, Mrs. Auchinleck. Please accept my humble apologies." Although O'Reilly generally worked on the "don't explain or apologise to anyone" principle, he would always make an exception for Mrs. Kinky Auchinleck. "It won't happen again. I promise."

Kinky's sniff would have been described by her as "sthrong enough to drag a piglet across a sty."

"Truly I am." O'Reilly bit into his chop. "And it really is a waste. This lamb melts in the mouth." He sought reinforcements. "Doesn't it, Barry?"

"Absolutely delicious," he said, but O'Reilly heard no great enthusiasm in his young colleague's voice. He'd be sore. At least the news about Anne Galvin's X-ray should cheer the lad up. O'Reilly decided that Barry should have the pleasure of being the bearer of such tidings. He waited until Kinky had stumped off, but something about Barry, perhaps the way he was toying with his lunch, gave O'Reilly pause. "You all right, Barry?"

"Ribs are sore, but it's more than that." Barry sighed. "Sue and I had a falling-out on Saturday, and please, Fingal, I don't want it to go any farther. Not even to Kitty."

O'Reilly, who over the years had become unofficial father confessor to most of the village and townland, nodded. "Do you want to spit it out?"

Barry inhaled. "I dropped a brick. Sue wants children. I'm not sure. I blurted it out at the circus on Saturday. Pretty vehemently. Just as the performance was starting—"

"When young Sammy lost his lunch." It wasn't a question.

"'Fraid so. Sue's upset. She wants time to think about it. I'll not be seeing her for a while."

"Mmmmm," said O'Reilly, and waited.

Barry looked at him. "And you know, Fingal, I'm not one to go crying on everyone's shoulder. I keep my troubles to myself, but I've known Jack Mills since we were thirteen . . ."

"What did he advise?"

"To accept being a parent as a normal part of life. To realise that Sue, by necessity, would probably be doing much of the childrearing and that's her choice, and that there would be all sorts of rewards watching and teaching the young ones to grow. To talk about it with Sue again, but to give her time. Don't rush her." He shrugged. "All wisdom says Jack's right and that I'm being a thran buck eejit . . ."

O'Reilly shook his head. "No, you are not being stubborn, Barry. This," O'Reilly tapped his head, "doesn't always control this," then pointed to the left side of his chest. Only Kinky, Kitty, and Lars knew of O'Reilly's wartime loss. It was his turn to look Barry in the eye and say, "What I'm going to tell you goes no farther."

"Naturally."

"You know I was married once before?"

"Yes. You told me."

And I'm sure Kinky did too, O'Reilly thought. He said, "And you know Deirdre was killed." And now I can talk about it without feeling pain.

"I was sorry to hear it. When you told me. I still am."

O'Reilly took a very deep breath. "I didn't tell you that we'd had a conversation about starting a family. Like you, I wasn't sure. She had to talk me round."

Clearly Barry was paying great attention.

"She was five months pregnant when she was killed."

"My God. I never knew. I'm so sorry, Fingal."

O'Reilly pursed his lips but was relieved that he'd been able to tell Barry. If hearing of O'Reilly's loss could help the young man to work things out, so be it. "I've always thought that regret is a useless emotion. I grieved for my lost wife and family. But I do regret to this day I never had children." Until I got the next best thing to a grown-up son, Barry Laverty, but I'd not tell you that.

Barry sat back. He inhaled and blew out a long breath through pursed lips. "It was hard for you to tell me that, wasn't it, Fingal?"

O'Reilly inclined his head.

"Thank you," Barry said. "Thank you very much." He sat, hands on tabletop, staring out the window, clearly deep in thought, lunch neglected before him.

"By the wee man," Kinky said, bustling into the dining room and looking at Barry's unfinished lunch. "Sometimes I wonder why I bother cooking at all, at all. Was it not all right?"

Barry shook his head. "Sorry, Kinky. I'm afraid I don't seem to have an appetite. I'm a bit worried—"

"About a patient," O'Reilly said. "We both are."

"Well," said Kinky, "in that case I will forgive you, so."

"I'm really sorry, Kinky. It looks delicious, but . . ."

"You do be forgiven. This once." She smiled. "There are going to be two very happy doggies today." She cleared the table and left.

O'Reilly smiled. "That's the pair of us have had to apologise to Kinky today. It's a thing, apologising, a man might just get used to." He sat back and surveyed Barry, who was looking decidedly uncomfortable. "And when you do get your ideas straight about fatherhood and the like and when you do talk to Sue, you might want to apologise there too. I know she'll forgive you."

Barry managed a weak smile. "I hope so. Thanks, Fingal. You've given me a lot to think about."

O'Reilly beamed. "And here's something else to mull over. I told Kinky you're worried about a patient. Anne Galvin, to be exact. I want you—she's your patient after all—to pay her a visit this afternoon. If you're up to it."

Barry winced but said, "I'll not die of a cracked rib. More important, you've got the X-ray report, haven't you?"

O'Reilly nodded and smiled. "Emphysema, healed TB in the left lung, and no, I repeat, no cancer."

"Now that," said Barry with a grin, "is something to cheer about. I'll put her top of my list."

"Teddy wants a follow-up in six months, but we've both examined Anne. I'm sure it'll be clear then too. If Guffer's home, I want you to be circumspect in how you tell her. Anne's rightly concerned she may have cancer, but she's been keeping it from Guffer."

"I understand." Barry frowned. "And I'll play down the need for a follow-up. I'm delighted that there's no evidence of malignancy," he frowned again, "but how do we account for the blood she coughed up?"

O'Reilly shook his head. "Dunno for certain," he said, "and by her account it was very little. It can certainly happen if someone with bronchial or pulmonary inflammation simply coughs too much." He smiled. "Sometimes 'there are more things in heaven and earth, Horatio, than are dreamt of in your philosophy.'" He waited, but Barry seemed in no rush to identify the quotation. Too pleased for Anne? Too worried about Sue? He'd let the hare sit. "We may never know about Anne for sure, but I'm convinced the news is good."

"Fine by me. I'll be on my way."

"And I'd like you to do something else too."

"Oh?"

"Anne Galvin has fallen madly in love with Carlow Charger of Kilkenny. I was surprised, but petting him seemed to calm her when I went out there the last time. She asked could he visit her again. I promised. His training's coming on well. He shouldn't be too much for you to handle."

"I'll be happy to," Barry said, wincing as he rose. "I'm going to head out there right now. I'll bring him home on my way to the next call. I want to see how Gracie Miller's getting on. Her husband's no better."

"Did she ask for a visit?"

Barry shook his head. "But neither did Maggie MacCorkle that first week I started work here. You just thought you should keep an eye on her."

A warm sensation of pride in his friend and protégé bloomed in O'Reilly's chest. Carrying on with a nagging pain in his side and a nagging worry in his heart. Seeing a patient purely from concern. "Great," he said. "And one other thing, Barry. Ronald Fitzpatrick's on call tonight. I know you're worried about Sue. When you're finished this afternoon, how'd you like to pop in at the Duck with me for a couple and then have dinner with Kitty and me? Unless you'd rather be on your own and rest up?"

"I'd like that, Fingal. I'd like that very much. I'll see you in the Duck."

"Good," said O'Reilly. "Go easy on your rib and, as she's going to be making something for Kitty to warm up, for God's sake tell Kinky on your way through the kitchen there'll be an extra mouth for dinner. One bollicking from that Corkwoman's plenty for me for one day."

21

Him That Bringeth Good Tidings

"Come on on in, Doctor." Anne Galvin met Barry at the door. She held a lit cigarette between the index and middle fingers of her right hand. "And I see you've brought my wee friend, Kenny." She stuck the fag in her mouth, then bent and patted the pup's head. A light dusting of ash spilled down her calico pinafore.

"Please come into the sitting room, sir." Barry followed Kenny as he trotted in, sniffing the air.

Anne took a deep breath and frowned. "I can clean all I want, but I can never get the smell of smoke out of the air." She sat, putting a cobweb-laden feather duster on the floor, and sighed. "Can I hold him?"

"Sure."

She took the pup from Barry, and put Kenny in her lap. "Please sit down, sir."

Barry sucked in a quick breath and frowned as he sat in the other armchair.

"How are you feeling, Anne?"

She cocked her head and gave him a long look. "Never mind me. How are you, sir?"

"I'm all right, thanks. I cracked a rib yesterday. It's nothing serious."

"That must sting, sir. I'm very sorry, so I am."

Barry moved to a more comfortable position and managed a smile. "I'll live. Now, please don't worry. I came here to see how you are."

Anne gave Kenny a long stroke, from the top of his head right down to his tail. "How am I? That medicine Doctor O'Reilly give me keeps me from coughing at night. No more blood now."

"I'm glad to hear it." Fingal was probably right about the cause of the haemoptysis. Once the coughing was suppressed, the bleeding had stopped.

"If you've got the results from my X-rays, Doctor Laverty, I think you'll know how I am far better than me, so you will." She took a deep draw on her smoke, let the blue vapours trickle out of her nostrils, and stopped stroking the pup. "Is it serious?"

"You don't have cancer." Barry waited for his words to sink in. "No cancer."

Anne Galvin's eyes widened. "You're sure, Doctor? Certain sure? Honest til God?"

He smiled. Barry saw no reason not to tell her the facts as they stood. "Honest to God. A senior radiology doctor looked at your pictures and phoned Doctor O'Reilly earlier today. The X-ray does show a couple of things, but no cancer. No cancer."

Kenny was whining quietly. Barry had read that dogs can sense human emotions and respond in kind, but the pup was unable to distinguish between sadness and Anne Galvin's sudden tears of happiness and relief.

They trickled down her cheeks and she grinned through them. "I go til church most Sundays like everybody else, but I'm not good living, not very religious, nor nothing like that . . . But . . ." She took a breath that must have reached the soles of her feet, then exhaled. "Thank God. Here's me thinking all weekend I was going til be banjaxed. And what was Guffer going til do then?"

Barry recognised that the question was not for him.

Another deep breath. She stubbed out her cigarette in a half-full ashtray. "Thank God, and thank you and to Doctor O'Reilly, sir." She pulled out a hanky and dabbed her eyes. She spoke to Kenny. "I don't have cancer, Kenny. Praise be." He wagged his tail until his back end wiggled.

"I don't want to worry you, Anne. Doctor O'Reilly and I both agree it's just a precaution, but the specialist thinks you should have another X-ray in six months. It's routine."

Anne smiled. "If you and himself say so, sir, that's good enough for me, so it is." She looked into Barry's eyes.

Her trust humbled Barry.

"It's like I told Doctor O'Reilly when I asked him til keep things til himself, Guffer'd no need to be worried for no good reason." She smiled. "And our two sons, bless 'em, don't need to hear a dicky-bird about any of this, so they don't."

Barry heard the deep affection for her children. "It is good news, but I told you that the X-ray did show a couple of things. I need to explain them."

"Aye. You did say that. Go on, please."

"First of all, you've had TB. Mind I said 'had.'"

"TB? I never have." She shook her head, clearly indignant. "Not never in my whole puff."

Barry was well aware of the stigma attached to the disease. He hesitated for a moment. He had told her about his rib, it would have been difficult not to, but he'd been taught that doctors should not divulge their own personal information to patients. But he was no longer in school. He could make his own decisions. "I have," he said.

Her eyes widened. "Have what?"

"I've had TB."

"Were you in the Whiteabbey Sanatorium?" She leant forward, disturbing Kenny, who had fallen asleep.

Barry shook his head. "No, I didn't even know I'd been infected until I had a test called a Mantoux to see if I should be vaccinated against the disease. Lots of people, Anne, have been attacked by the bacillus, the germ that causes TB, but most of them threw off the disease." A lot of them like her, and probably him, had scars in their lungs, reminders of the old battleground where the defenders had defeated the invading forces. "My test was positive. That meant I was immune to TB. Because vaccination was slow to come to Western Europe and I didn't get one as a baby, the only way I could be immune was to have had the disease. I was lucky. Just like you."

"There's a thing," she said. "So you reckon I did have TB?"

He nodded.

"Aye. Well." She stroked Kenny. "That's just between you and me and the pup here, so it is."

"Of course."

"Thank you." Anne frowned. "And you said there was a couple of things. What else?"

"This is a bit tricky to explain, but your lungs are full of little air sacs called alveoli. You know the seaweed, bladder wrack?"

"The one with all the bubbles?"

"That's the one. Your lungs are a bit like that, although the bubbles, the alveoli, are much smaller and their walls are very thin so the oxygen in the air you inhale can get across them and into your bloodstream. With emphysema, the walls between them break down so there's much bigger bubbles, but far fewer surfaces for the oxygen to get through. The little narrow tubes called bronchioles in your lungs that carry the air to the alveoli get narrowed so it's harder for the air to get in and out. People with it cough a lot and get short of breath." He pointed at the ashtray. "An American doctor, George Walbott, in 1953, showed that smoking is a big cause of what chest doctors call chronic obstructive pulmonary disease. There's no cure and it'll only get worse," he looked her right in the eye, "as long as you go on smoking."

She scratched the top of Kenny's head and he yawned. "Doctor," she said, "I've spent the whole weekend thinking I was going til die. I don't think I was scared for me, but what would Guffer do? And then thinking I'd never get to see my Seamus again, him being all the way in California. I couldn't bear that." She stopped stroking. "But how do I quit?"

Barry smiled. Don't tell the patient personal stuff? He shrugged. "I did. Four years ago."

"You, sir? How?"

"Did you see the film *The Man with the Golden Arm*?"

"With Frank Sinatra, the drug addict going 'cold turkey'? Aye."

"It's the only way. And it's not easy, but it can be done." Barry remembered the first few weeks of intermittently being hit by nearly overwhelming urges for a smoke, headaches, nausea, wanting sweeties, insomnia. "You know Helen Hewitt?" This was no breach of patient confidentiality.

"Alan Hewitt's wee girl? Her that's going for a doctor up at Queens?"

"She quit last year." Barry leant forward. "Anne, if you try to give up the smokes, I'll help you. I've no magic potions, but I'll pop round from time to time to see how you're getting on." He grinned. "Give you a right old tousling if you've fallen from grace. Guffer doesn't smoke, does he?"

"No. Said he'd tried as a youngster but didn't take to it."

"That'll help too. And for a while, don't go to places where everyone is having a fag."

She smiled. "That'll be hard. Just about everybody smokes everywhere. On the bus . . ." She hesitated. "But only upstairs. The pictures is full of smoke, so are the lounge bars. Maybe I'll just stay home with Guffer for a while. Just like the Presbyterian hymn. 'Yield not to temptation for yielding is sin/each victory will help you some other to win'?"

"That's it. It will get easier every day until you can do without cigarettes—for the rest of your life."

"But why would you take time to help me? It's not like I was sick nor nothing."

Barry smiled. "A doctor's job is to help prevent people getting sick too, and if I can get you off the fags . . ." He didn't finish the sentence. "And there's another thing. How many do you smoke a day?"

"Twenty."

"And what do twenty cost?"

Kenny turned round on her lap.

"Two and six."

"So every day you don't smoke, put two and six away. It took me about six weeks to be able to say 'I don't want a cigarette.' That's forty-two days. You'd have saved more than five pounds."

"Right enough. I would, so I would." She glanced at the window. "That's a brave bit, so it is. I could get a wheen of new material and get Miss Moloney til run me up new curtains."

"And every time you look at them it'll help remind you how much smoking costs. Discourage you from starting again." Barry rose, sucking in a short breath. "Do we have a bargain?"

She put the pup on the floor, stood, reached into the pocket of her pinafore, and handed Barry a packet of Player's Navy Cut cigarettes. The front of the package was a seascape with a sailor's head inside a life ring. Barry knew from experience that inside the flap it would bear the motto *It's the tobacco that counts.* "Take you them, sir, and throw them out," she said, offering her hand. "It's a bargain."

Barry shook. "I'll keep you to it if I can. I'll run along now, but I'll pop round soon. Could you help me get Kenny into the car?"

"Aye, certainly." She followed him out and helped put Kenny and Barry's bag in the back of the car.

"You look after yourself, now, Doctor Laverty," she said. "And thank you. I'll be off to finish getting the cobwebs off the landing ceiling."

Barry put the car in gear, feeling pleased. Not only was Anne Galvin on the mend, she was going to try to quit smoking. "Home for you now, Kenny," he said, "and then I'll nip over and see how Gracie Miller is managing." At the thought of the little pebbledash bungalow on the bay and its unhappy inhabitant, Barry felt a pang in his heart as well as in his rib. He wondered what Sue would be doing right now. He looked at this watch. Two thirty on Monday? She'd be teaching an English class. He was none too sanguine about things being as promising as the call he had just made. Still, cracked rib and Sue Nolan notwithstanding, there was a pint of Guinness and some *craic* with Fingal at the Duck later to look forward to.

22

Send Not to Ask for Whom the Bell Tolls

Barry left Kenny romping with Arthur Guinness in the back garden at Number One and, deep in thought, made the short drive to the Millers' bungalow on the little peninsula. Anne Galvin's obvious concern for her husband and sons had given him food for thought.

The last hundred yards were across bumpy ground and he drove slowly to avoid jolting his rib. As he neared the place, he noticed a maroon Hillman Minx parked outside the back garden wall. When he reached the back door, he stood for a minute until the ache in his side became tolerable, then the door was opened to his knock by an unfamiliar woman in her midthirties. She wore black and her eyes were red-rimmed. A shiver of apprehension ran up his spine.

"Good afternoon. Who're you?"

"I'm Doctor Laverty," he said. "The Millers' doctor. I know Lewis has been very ill and in the Royal. I came to see how Mrs. Miller is."

There was a catch in the woman's voice. "I'm afraid my daddy passed away at about three this morning. I'm Joy Graham. Please come in."

Barry inhaled deeply, and regretted it. An electric shock of pain shot through his side and he winced, trying not to show his discomfort. "I didn't know. I'm very sorry." A letter of notification would have been sent to the practice this morning but hadn't arrived by the time Barry had left. Barry stepped into the dimly lit kitchen. It was then he realised that all the curtains and blinds were drawn. "How is your mother?" he asked.

"The doctors at the hospital warned us it might be coming, but it's hard to accept that he's really gone. Mammy's trying to bear up, but she's pretty shattered. She's in the lounge."

They made their way there along the dimly lit hall illuminated by two wall sconces. Here too, the curtains were closed, hiding the front room's spectacular view. With the sun's spring warmth blocked, the place was chilly. A wall mirror had also been covered. In this the Irish shared a custom with the Jews, who masked mirrors during the seven days of shiva, the ritual following a burial. He crossed the room to where the seventy-year-old Gracie Miller, also wearing black as custom demanded, sat in an armchair, staring into an empty fireplace. Her wavy, iron-grey hair was down, not up in its usual bun. She held something in both hands, but in the dim light he couldn't make it out.

"Doctor Laverty's here to see you, Mammy."

She turned and looked up. Like her daughter's, Gracie's eyes behind her tortoiseshell-framed spectacles were red, with dark circles beneath. She wore a small gold crucifix on a chain around her neck. "Doctor. You—you've heard our news then? Thank you for coming. Will you have a seat?"

"Thank you." Barry lowered himself carefully into another armchair while Mrs. Graham took a third. He said, looking from one to the other, "Gracie, Mrs. Graham, please accept my deepest condolences."

"Thank you, sir," Gracie said, and sniffed. "My Lewis was a grand man. A fine husband. A great daddy. I'm missing him sore already, but I can't believe he's really gone." Tears began to trickle down her cheeks and she lifted her glasses and dabbed her eyes with a lace-edged hanky. "I'm sorry." She swallowed, trying to brighten. "The Good Book says in Job, 'Man that is born of woman is of few days and full of trouble.' Lewis has no more troubles now. He's at peace, God love him."

Barry was no stranger to death and yet he never knew the best words to say. The usual "My thoughts and prayers are with you at this time" or "I'm sorry for your troubles" struck him as clichéd platitudes. He saw Gracie shiver. "Are you cold, Gracie?"

"I dunno. I don't feel much at all. I'm numb all over."

Perhaps, Barry thought, he could offer comfort in a more tangible way. "Would you like me to light the fire?"

Gracie looked at her daughter, then at Barry. "Aye," she said. "That would be nice." She pointed to a wicker basket beside the hearth. "The makings is in thon basket." She sighed. "My Lewis always looked after the fire, so he did, so he did."

Barry said to Mrs. Graham, "I think your mother might have a bit of a chill. Perhaps a cup of tea too?"

"Right enough. I'll get the kettle on." She rose and headed for the kitchen.

Barry stood, went across, and knelt by the basket. He pulled out sheets of old newspaper, crumpled them up, and stuffed them into the grate.

"It is good of you to come round," Gracie said, "and Father O'Toole's already been here til comfort us. He remembered Joy from her confirmation when she was a wee girl." Gracie looked into the middle distance. "I remember that day too. August the twenty-seventh, 1944. Lewis and me was so proud we hardly paid any attention to the news that the Germans in Paris had surrendered two days earlier." A tiny smile flickered across her face. Her voice was far away. "Our Joy looking like a beautiful wee bride in her white dress and veil. She was so happy."

Barry paused from laying kindling on top of the paper. Gracie, all unknown, was showing Barry the truth of Jack's words of yesterday. She had shared in her daughter's joy at that moment and now, thirty years later, she was reliving it.

"The father read thon bit from the Psalms before he left today about 'The days of our years are but three score years and ten.' Lewis was seventy-five."

"Father O'Toole's a good man." Barry used tongs to put lumps of coal on top of the kindling, then topped off the pile with a Bord na Móna peat briquette. He turned back to the wicker basket for a second one and flinched and grimaced as his rib complained.

"Are you all right, Doctor?" Gracie asked. There was concern in her voice.

Barry shook his head. "I hurt a rib yesterday. Nothing serious." He put the second briquette beside the first, laid one more piece crosswise on the first two, and stood slowly.

"You take care of yourself, Doctor dear," Gracie said. "We need our doctors, so we do. I could make you up a linseed poultice if you'd like. My granny swore by it, and one time when Lewis ricked his chest muscles picking up a post bag too full of letters, a poultice seen him right in no time."

"Thank you very much, Gracie," Barry said, marvelling at how in the midst of her own grief, Gracie Miller could find it in her to be worried for him. "My doctor strapped it up for me. I should be fine." He stood. "Let's get this lit. Where do you keep the matches?"

"There," she said. "Fornenst the clock on the mantel."

Barry picked up a box of Swift safety matches in their blue box with the bird flying across its front. He crouched, took out a match, and scratched the head along the sandpaper on the box's side. His nose was filled with the smell of phosphorous as the head burst into flame. He put the match to the newspaper and remembered winning his fire-lighting badge as a wolf cub. He'd had to lay, then successfully light a fire using no more than two matches. At the time it had been the most important thing in his young life. Dad and Mum had been proud too.

The paper took and the kindling started crackling.

Mrs. Graham came in with a tea tray, which she set on a table. "Cup of tea, Mammy?"

"Aye. Please."

She poured. "One for you, Doctor?"

Barry shook his head. "No thank you, Mrs. Graham. I had mine at home." He stood.

"Please call me Joy, Doctor."

"I will."

She gave her mother a cup and poured one for herself.

Gracie looked up and patted Joy's hand. "You're a great comfort til me, Joy."

Barry recalled that the Millers had suffered from unexplained infertility and Joy was an only child, unusual in Catholic families in Ireland. Barry himself, though nominally Protestant, was an only child too. His father had been away at sea during the war. Barry had later learned from his mother that she and his dad had decided that as Barry had been nearly six by the time Dad had come home for good, it was too late to have more children. Perhaps he'd feel less insecure about having kids of his own if he'd had brothers and sisters?

He was aware of the gentle smell of burning turf and glanced at the fire. The briquettes were starting to catch, but only a small piece was burning well. "Excuse me," he said, then bent and picked up a new sheet of newspaper, opened it, and held it across the front of the fireplace, leaving a gap at the bottom of the grate so that air was sucked in through the opening. The effect was similar to that of a bellows, increasing the oxygen supply and fanning the flames. He heard a low roaring, saw flames flickering behind the paper.

Barry removed the paper before it caught fire. The coal and the compressed turf were well alight now and already the room was starting to warm up. He folded the paper, replaced it in the wicker basket, and went back to his chair.

"I've seen Lewis doing that with the paper too," Gracie said. There was a catch in her voice, but she sat up straighter and braced her shoulders. "He was a good man, and good-looking too. See." She handed Barry what he now recognised was a wedding photo. A beaming Gracie, who had been a beauty at twenty, was standing in the picture, her white wedding dress high collared and long sleeved, nipped tight at the waist and dropping to a narrow, ankle-length skirt from under which peeped white shoes. There was a huge bow on her left hip. The whole was topped by a now thrown-back veil. Her left elbow rested on the back of a carved wooden chair and she held a bouquet in her right hand. Young Lewis sat in a chair. His dark hair was oiled and parted in the centre. Dark suit over a white shirt. Trousers severely creased. A floral buttonhole in his left lapel. Both hands on his knees. Whereas Gracie was looking directly into the camera, Lewis for some inexplicable reason was glancing off to his left. Barry handed the picture back. "You . . ." He hesitated. Made or make? "Make a very handsome couple," he said.

Gracie set the picture in her lap again. She managed a weak smile. "Aye," she said, "we did. And now I have my memories." She reached out and took Joy's hand. "And I have my family. My grandson Rory's a great lad and wee Betty's as lovely as her mother."

"Mammy," Joy said, and blushed. She moved back to her chair.

"Memories can be good, very good," Barry said, suddenly remembering a day in 1953, the day before he'd gone off to boarding school for the first time. He was thirteen. He and his father passing a rugby ball back and forth. And then, six weeks later, after being confined to the school with no family visits, barely being able to control his excitement when Dad and Mum had picked him up and taken him home to Ballyholme for the half-term holidays. Three whole days with no prefects, no school rules, no algebra, and best of all, Mum's home cooking.

Gracie nodded. "And when there's trouble, family and friends is the most important things of all, so they are. You—and your Miss Nolan—remember that, sir."

"I will," he said. "We will." He swallowed and felt the beginning of a lump in his throat. The fire was well alight now and he remembered his vision of sitting here with Sue, a cosy fire burning in the grate, a storm raging outside. The storm was inside today.

"I'm going til stay here with Mammy," Joy said, "until the lying-in, the wake, the removal, and the funeral's all over. My Des and our children are coming for the wake and funeral."

Barry barely suppressed a shudder. The custom in the Catholic community called for the embalmed departed to lie at home in an open coffin, there to be visited by friends and relations who would pay their last respects and offer comfort to the widow. Keep her company. The wake, attended by Lewis, would be a social gathering, and food and drink would be served prior to the sealing of the coffin and its "removal" from house to hearse to be carried to the chapel for the service and thence to the graveyard. He knew it was all to offer immediate and constant support to the bereaved, but Barry found the whole idea of an open coffin with Lewis Miller's face in full view macabre. Would that indeed be a comfort to his widow? To each his own. "That's good," Barry said. "It's important you're not on your own, Gracie."

"She'll not be, Doctor. And when all the formal things is over here, Mammy's coming til live with us in Portrush until she's back on her feet, so she is." Joy looked fondly at her mother. "We'd already built a granny flat for her and Daddy, and all."

Gracie turned to her daughter. "Doctor Laverty and his fiancée came to look at the house, Joy. As you know, Doctor, Lewis and me, we were planning to sell here and move in with Des and Joy. But och." She glanced at the photo in her hands. "Now . . . now all my memories is here. I want to live out my days here. I'm sorry to disappoint you, Doctor. I know you and Miss Nolan liked the wee house."

"We did, but I understand." And unless Barry could mend fences with Sue, Gracie's decision might now, from his point of view, be of academic interest only. If things did work out, though, getting another house would not be impossible. Finding another Sue would.

"Could you not persuade Mammy til move in with us permanently, sir? We'd love to have her," Joy said.

Barry shook his head. "I'm sorry, Joy, and I can understand how you'd feel. But I can see how you want your familiar things round you too, Gracie. I'd suggest you do move in with Joy for a while, see how you like it, then decide what's best."

Gracie nodded, brushing away a tear. "Aye." She sipped her tea. "That makes good sense."

Barry read Joy's smile as one of thanks.

He rose with care, returned the photo to Gracie, and put another briquette on the fire. A spasm hit and he grimaced.

"Poor Doctor Laverty has a sore rib," Gracie said.

"Och dear." Joy tutted and said, "It was quare nor decent of you, sir, dropping in to see how Mammy was, like. But if you're stiff and sore, run you away on home and put your feet up. We'll be fine. Honest."

Barry nodded. "Thank you." Two grieving women had time to be concerned about him. Humbling. He said, "Once again, my condolences to you both." He put a hand on Gracie's shoulder. "Is there anything else I can do for you?" He knew a lot of GPs would give recently bereaved people sleeping pills, but after his experience with Eileen Lindsay he was hesitant. There was chloral hydrate if Gracie really needed something.

"No, Doctor. It was thoughtful of you to call. Thank you, but I'll manage."

"Don't hesitate to ring if you do need us."

"I don't think I will, Doctor," Gracie said. She smiled at Joy. "Sure amn't I going til have my wee girl here and then my whole family about me? Like I told you. Family's the most important of all, but you don't have to live in each other's pockets. When I get my feet under me, I'll be right as rain on my own back here."

She looked fondly at her only daughter. "And sure doesn't Des have a motorcar and isn't it only about an hour and a half from Portrush to Ballybucklebo?"

23

Days When Work Was Scrappy

"Is it the Duck you're heading for, Doctor?" Barry had parked outside Number One, as it was usually the very divil to find a spot outside the pub. As he passed the front door, Kinky had appeared.

"I am, Kinky. You for home?"

"I am. It's just a wee doddle and I thought the walk would do me good, so I didn't get Archie to pick me up." She fell into step beside him. "And how's your chest, sir?"

"Bit sore. Thanks for asking."

"I do hope it won't be long until you are well mended. It is a good thing Doctor Fitzpatrick is on call tonight and you can rest up."

"Thanks, Kinky. I will once I've had a pint with Doctor O'Reilly."

"Himself left ten minutes ago with the dogs. Saving your presence, but the apple never falls far from the tree. You're getting more like Doctor O'Reilly every day."

"I thought that saying applied to fathers and their children." He glanced over at Kinky. What with Anne Galvin worried about her sons and Gracie's talk of family, he'd thought of little else on the drive here. Perhaps his reservations were wrong. Of course, both Anne and Gracie had been giving the mother's perspective. Maybe fathers felt differently?

"It usually does." She laughed and her chins wobbled. "But only if the fathers work at it. My own raised four of us near Beal na mBláth in County Cork on a shmall little farm. We did be poor farmers, but us children never went without, always had shoes on our feet. Da worked like a slave, but he always had time for the four of us. Taught my brother

Tiernan road bowling. And I've watched Doctor O'Reilly work with you, sir, teaching you."

"Only if fathers worked at it," she'd said. Was Barry willing to work? He shrugged. "I could do worse than Doctor O'Reilly. Mind you, my own dad's not a bad example either." Could he ask his father's advice? The answer was of course no. Sue had said she would say nothing to anyone else and asked him to do the same. They were to let all their arrangements stand. He was duty-bound to respect that and indeed take some comfort from it. The hope was there that they could work it out and their wedding would proceed without anyone except Jack Mills and Fingal being any the wiser. He knew he was bending the rules talking to his friends, but he needed their counsel. Least said soonest mended.

"He must have been, or you'd not have turned out so well." Before waiting for a reply Kinky said, "We do be at the traffic light, and it's in your favour. Trot along now. I'll see you tomorrow, sir. Take care of yourself, bye."

"Night, Kinky. Safe home." Barry crossed the road, and went in through the swing doors. This would not be a good place for Anne Galvin. The tobacco fug would have gagged a maggot. And yet the place did not seem to be as busy as usual. The hum of conversation was muted. Only an occasional burst of laughter.

O'Reilly, briar belching, sat with Dapper Frew and Donal Donnelly, whose left hand was neatly swaddled in bandages. Arthur Guinness and a leashed Kenny lay under a table. Barry noticed the pup taking an experimental sip of Smithwick's and wrinkling his nose. Arthur, as usual, was tucking right in.

Barry joined the men. "Evening, everybody."

He was greeted in return.

"How's the rib?" O'Reilly asked.

"Not too bad." Barry looked over to Willie Dunleavy and nodded. Willie nodded back. He would bring over a pint of Guinness once it had been poured. "It'll ache for a few weeks, but if I'm careful it's tolerable. Could have been worse."

"Good."

"Quiet tonight," Barry said. "Must be because it's a Monday."

"No, sir," Donal Donnelly said, surveying the room. "Take a look around. There's Dapper here . . ."

Barry decided this was neither the time nor place to tell the estate agent he'd probably lost a sale. It was unlikely the news of Lewis Miller's death would be common knowledge in the village yet. Barry remembered Gracie's eyes, full of longing and grief. He sighed and Kenny got up and put his head on Barry's lap.

". . . and youse two doctors. But near everybody else is in farming or works for the Harland and Wolff shipyards. Lots of work there, so there is. They're on schedule with the *Myrina*. She's the first supertanker ever to be built in the U.K., and there's an oil-drilling rig, *Sea Quest*, being put together on three separate slipways."

"Doctor Laverty." Willie set down a pint.

"Thanks, Willie." Barry pulled out his wallet and Kenny returned to the floor to sniff suspiciously again at the Smithwick's. "Cheers." He took a pull and looked round. Many of the familiar faces were indeed missing. "So what's going on?"

"Mister Bishop's men are pulling their horns in. We thought we'd be at work next month, but now we can only start in June." He shrugged.

"Any idea what's causing the holdup?" Barry asked.

"Och," said Donal, "the ministry's being slow producing the permits, that's all. Just the usual oul' load of red crêpe."

"Tape, Donal," O'Reilly said.

Despite his mood, Barry found it hard not to smile.

"Right enough. Tape. They're just a big bunch of bureaucratic bollixes. Couldn't organise a piss-up in a brewery. But it's holding us up from earning our crust."

"And is that why you're only drinking a half-pint?" O'Reilly said, indicating the slim glass.

"I have til cut back on the spending until we do get back til work," Donal said, "but I miss the *craic* so I like to pop in and see my pals. Anyroad, I suppose the timing's good in a way, with this hand of mine. Doctor O'Reilly here stitched me up on Sunday morning. Got lifted for taking game out of season."

Dapper said, "It's a pity Malcolm got close enough to pull off your balaclava. The Peelers can't arrest you unless they've identified you properly."

Donal laughed. "You mean like the two fellows down from Belfast that Malcolm wanted to do for drunk and disorderly last year? Says he til one, 'What's your address?' and your man says, 'No fixed abode.' So Malcolm turns til the other. "How about you? Where do you live?' He staggers a bit then says, "Ossifer, I lives in your man's first-floor flat, so I do.'"

Barry had to cut his laugh short when his rib protested. But he was still full of admiration at Donal's skills as a raconteur. Barry took a drink of the bittersweet stout as O'Reilly and Dapper joined in the mirth.

"To be more serious," Donal said, "I felt like a bit of cheering up, so Julie says I should come down here."

Wise move, Barry thought. He'd needed the same, and already his mood was lighter.

"So I did. It was good to see Dapper. You're a good head, Frew. He said he'd stand me a pint but," Donal shrugged, "I asked Willie for a glass of water. He's a sound man too. Heart of corn. Says he, 'I'll stand you a pint the night.'"

"So, Donal, you wouldn't accept a pint from a friend, but would take one from the publican? What's the difference?" Barry asked.

"Och," said Donal, "a good publican like Willie buys all his regulars a drink once in a while. It's like advertising to keep your trade, so you don't feel obliged to him like you would to a friend."

"I see. That makes good sense."

"So then I asked him, could I please have a half-pint tonight and put the other half in the stable for next time I'm in." He finished his glass. "That half-pint may have to do me til June when Mister Bishop hopes to get the road building under way." He rose. "Anyway, I'm for home. Good til have seen youse, sirs."

"I hope you do get work soon, Donal," O'Reilly said, and Barry saw the sincere concern in his senior partner's face. And something else too.

"If I don't, I've a half notion of a way til raise a bit of dosh," Donal said, "and I may need medical advice. But not the night, sir. Not the night."

Dapper stood and sank his drink. "I'll give you a lift home, Donal. You can put your bike in the boot. Night, all."

O'Reilly shook his shaggy head. "Incorrigible, that Donal. What the hell's he cooking up now?"

"No idea," Barry said, and took another pull, "but with Donal Donnelly, it's bound to be a corker. I wonder why he might need medical advice?"

"Beats me," O'Reilly said. He frowned. Looked thoughtful. "Even though they get their unemployment benefit, maybe it's Bertie's crew of ten who are going to be needing Kinky's four hundred pounds."

Barry had quite forgotten about Kinky's winnings. "Maybe," he said.

O'Reilly's pipe had gone out so he relit it. "So tell me, how was your afternoon?"

Barry could feel his spirits lighten even more as he said, "Anne Galvin was so glad she's not got cancer she's going to try to quit smoking." He looked hard at O'Reilly's fuming pipe and was studiously ignored. "But I'm afraid poor old Lewis Miller died last night. Gracie's daughter is there keeping her mum company. The funeral's later this week."

"I'm sorry to hear he's gone," O'Reilly said. "Truly, but *'Media vitae morte sumus.'*"

"'In the midst of life we are in death.' I know. We learned quite early in our clinical training that if us doctors-to-be were to break our hearts over every death, we'd not remain sane for long."

O'Reilly smiled. "True. But there'll always be those that stick in your mind. I lost a man called Kevin Doherty when I was a student. Rheumatic heart failure. I still think about him now and then." He took a deep pull from his pint. "We can't do anything for them anymore when someone's gone, but we must care for the bereaved, and we also have a duty to the living."

"I know."

"And I don't just mean when they get sick. It's getting a bit concerning that Bertie Bishop isn't able to get started. I'm worried about both Bertie and his crew. I owe Bertie Bishop for all his help with that council business this spring."

Typical O'Reilly, Barry thought. Carries the whole village and townland on his broad shoulders.

Kenny stuck his head out from under the table and O'Reilly patted it. "I was teaching the pup here to retrieve the other day and I met John MacNeill. I've remembered something he said that gave me an idea when we were talking to Donal. Maybe John can help. Kitty and I are invited for a meal. We're going next Wednesday. I'll ask him then."

The swing doors opened and Barry looked up to see who had come in. Good Lord. Doctor Ronald Fitzpatrick? What the hell was he doing here? He was meant to be on call. Maybe he'd come to seek advice about a patient.

Fitzpatrick raised his arm in greeting and weaved over to their table, where he sat heavily, knocking his pince-nez askew. "My 'steemed— 'steemed colleagues. A ver-very good ev'ning. How—how do you both do this f-fine ev'ning?"

"God almighty," O'Reilly said, leaning forward and sniffing the man's breath. "Ronald, you're full as a goat. What the hell have you been doing?"

"I have come . . ." He swayed in his chair. "I have come seeking assistance. I have made anerrorin . . ." He blinked and shook his head. "I have made—an erreh in judgement, and am a little unwell."

"Unwell? Unwell?" O'Reilly spoke sotto voce. "You're bloody well stocious."

Barry realised the room had gone quiet. Everyone was staring.

"Fingal. We've got to get him out of here. He's ruining his reputation."

"You're right, and with a bust rib you're in no condition to help oxtercog him. Can you bring the dogs home?"

"I can."

"Lenny," O'Reilly called to Colin Brown's father. "Could you come over here, please."

Lenny, a plater at the shipyard, stood and moved toward the doctors' table.

O'Reilly raised his voice. "Doctor Fitzpatrick has taken a turn. I'm going to ask Lenny here to help get him to my surgery, so quit your rubbernecking." He took off Ronald's pince-nez and stuffed it in the man's jacket pocket. "Having a turn could happen to a bishop."

An unidentified voice called, "Aye, a bishop that's got at the communion wine."

There was general laughter.

"What do you want me til do, sir?" Lenny asked.

Barry left his pint unfinished, rose, and, taking Kenny's leash, said, "Come."

Both dogs obeyed. He held open the swing door as O'Reilly and Lenny marched past with Ronald Fitzpatrick's skinny arms draped over their shoulders. "I'll see you at Number One," Barry said and set off, the dogs obediently at heel. They were both, under O'Reilly's tutelage, well behaved. Would it take the same, Barry wondered, for Ronald Fitzpatrick to behave himself?

Barry had left the dogs in the back garden, happily tucking into the remains of two deboned lamb chops. He opened the front door to Fingal, Lenny, and their burden.

"Bring him into the surgery, Lenny."

"Right, Doc."

Barry followed.

O'Reilly, with Lenny's help, hoisted Ronald Fitzpatrick up onto the examining couch, where he lay reclining at an angle of forty-five degrees. "Thanks, Lenny."

Fitzpatrick muttered, "Thank you both."

"Can I do anything else, Doc?"

O'Reilly shook his head. "We'll look after him now. Can you let yourself out?"

"Aye, certainly."

"And Lenny? Do me a favour. Could you make light of this incident back at the Duck? I've never in my life seen Doctor Fitzpatrick in this condition, he hardly touches the stuff, and I've known him since 1931."

"I believe you, Doctor. Sure anyone can get full once in a while." He grinned. "And the Duck crowd aren't the ones til be pointing fingers, so they're not. I'll do my best. Good night."

O'Reilly said to Barry, "Remember the night he came to the Duck a couple of weeks ago and said 'I could get a taste for this stuff'? I think he has. Have you, Ronald?"

"I am very—hic—sorry. Very sorry. I don't t'ink—hic—I've a head for drink. I do—hic—apog—apog—apologise."

Barry shook his head. He couldn't claim to know Ronald Fitzpatrick well, but this poor drunk was a far cry from the punctilious man he usually appeared to be.

O'Reilly said, "Can you tell me exactly what happened?"

Fitzpatrick's hiccups had stopped. "Yes. And I am very," he sighed, "very ashamed. I prom'sed I'd not start gambling 'gain, but . . ." He hung his head and gave O'Reilly the look of a chastised puppy. "I've been bad."

"Go on," O'Reilly said.

Barry heard the coolness in his senior partner's voice.

"I did rather well 'is af'noon at Ladbroke's, the bookie's. I'd no surgery. No home visits and I wasn't s'posed to be on call here until five. I nipped into the Old Priory in Holywood to cebel—celebrate." He hung his head. "I t'ink. No. No. I know, I had one over the eight." He hung his head. "I'm sorry."

"And so you should be," O'Reilly said. "Just how much and what did you have?"

"A nice man helped me cebe—he—No, I bought them. We had what he called horses' necks."

"That, Barry, if you don't know," O'Reilly said, "is a pint with a whiskey in it. The Yanks call it a boilermaker."

Ronald Fitzpatrick counted on his fingers. "I think I'd six." Then to Barry's horror, Doctor Ronald Fitzpatrick began to cry. Great heaving sobs. He stuttered. "I knew I c-c-c-couldn't take call, no one answered your phone, s-s-so I took a taxi here to Number One."

"At least you'd the wit not to drive," O'Reilly said.

"There was no one in so I tried the Du-Du-Duck."

"I'm glad you did," O'Reilly said. "If you'd tried to take care of a patient in your condition you could have killed somebody."

Barry was aware that O'Reilly's nose tip had gone white. A sure sign his mentor was on the verge of exploding.

O'Reilly said, his voice level, "As a colleague and a friend I'll try to help you. Compulsive gambling's a disease like any other. And you're right. You've no head for drink, so stay away from it. No reason why you can't. It takes practice to become an alcoholic and you've only been at it a couple of weeks."

Fitzpatrick's sobbing increased in volume.

Barry had no handkerchief so offered the man a small surgical towel to dry his tears.

"Thank you. Never thought I'd use one of th-these as a hanky."

"Now. Barry here is suffering from a cracked rib and I wanted him to rest this evening. I'll run you home to the Kinnegar, Ronald. And once I get back I'll take over, but Barry, you'll have to take call while I'm gone."

"I will," Barry said, silently thanking Fingal.

"Thank you both. And I'm sorry, Doctor Laverty." Fitzpatrick honked into the towel.

"Ronald Hercules Fitzpatrick"—O'Reilly's voice had dropped and Barry heard pure venom—"if you ever, ever come within a mile of putting any of our patients at risk because you've been drinking, you're out of the rota and a letter will go to the General Medical Council, and your licence will be in jeopardy. Is that clear?"

Fitzpatrick's "Yes, Fingal" was practically inaudible.

24

Lords Have Their Pleasures

The sculptured trees flanking the drive up to Ballybucklebo House, once the pride of the topiarist's art, looked to O'Reilly, he could think of no other words, as if they needed a haircut. Leaves and branches straggled here and there. John MacNeill was having to cut back on staff. The gravel crunched under the Rover's tyres as O'Reilly swerved to avoid hitting one of his lordship's peacocks and the bird's dowdy consort. He had to work hard to avoid skidding. "Stupid birds," he yelled.

The sapphire-cloaked, silver-winged, and fan-tailed cock heaped scorn on the insult by screeching at the top of his voice in tones that would have cut tin.

O'Reilly laughed. "They usually only do that immediately before, during, or after copulation," he said.

Kitty solemnly asked, "Do you think, in the words of one of your old Dublin patients, the peacock was hinting that you should feck off?"

O'Reilly guffawed. "Trust you, Kitty O'Reilly. That's one of the very many reasons I love you. You are a thoroughly earthy woman." He parked outside the broad sandstone steps up to the front door.

"Only in private," she said with a grin. "And certainly not in tonight's company."

Despite John and Myrna's graciousness, Kitty, O'Reilly knew, still felt a little overawed to be dining with two titled people. John MacNeill's rank was only one lower than a duke, after all, and senior to a duke was only Her Royal Highness—and God.

Before O'Reilly could walk round the car, John MacNeill, twenty-seventh Marquis of Ballybucklebo, had come down the broad front steps and opened Kitty's door. He made a small bow. "Good evening, Kitty. You're looking particularly lovely tonight."

Kitty got out and dropped a small curtsey. "Thank you, my lord."

John, of course, was right. O'Reilly had had his breath taken away back at Number One as he had draped her camel hair coat over a silver, sleeveless, V-necked cocktail dress with a wide sash to cinch her waist and a just-above-the-knee skirt. The colour complemented the silver tips of her raven hair. Dark nylons, silver dress pumps, and a silver clutch handbag completed her outfit.

"Kitty O'Reilly," John MacNeill said, "it's John, and you know that perfectly well."

"Evening, John," O'Reilly said, rubbing his hands. He could see their breath on the evening air. "Nippy tonight. There'll be frost."

"Indeed. Let me get you both into the warm." He offered Kitty his arm, and O'Reilly followed them up the steps and into the spacious, thickly carpeted hall. O'Reilly noticed another hint that the number of servants had been reduced. A cobweb ran between the arm and breastplate of one of two suits of plate armour flanking the corridor. Each grasped a massive broadsword, its point resting on the floor between pointed iron *sabatons* for covering the feet. The mediaeval suits stood beneath crossed pikes hanging on the mahogany-panelled walls. Overhead soared a high, black-beamed ceiling. Portraits of previous marquises and their ladies, one with a Cavalier King Charles spaniel on the lap of her voluminous skirts, stared down with haughty miens.

"In here," John said, stepping aside to let Kitty precede him to where Finn MacCool, a red setter, lay asleep in front of a fire in a huge grate beneath a tall mantel. Over it hung an enormous oil painting, in the style of Sir Joshua Reynolds, of a peer of the realm in his ermine-trimmed robes.

Lady Myrna Ferguson, the marquis's sister, sat in an armchair. "Hello, Fingal. Kitty. Lovely to see you both." She held a sherry. "Do come and sit down beside me, Kitty."

"Kitty, let me take your coat," John said, did so, and held an armchair for her.

She sat and crossed her legs.

O'Reilly parked himself in another chair beside her. He opened his mouth to ask where Lars was, then thought better of it. Perhaps he would come later. O'Reilly was bursting to know how things were going with Myrna and his big brother and was concerned that the answer was "not well." Lars was reticent by nature and didn't always tell his brother about important things, particularly if he was hurting. O'Reilly wanted to know, but he hesitated to ask outright. In these circles, one didn't pry into another's social life.

"And what would you both like?" John said.

"Gin and tonic, please," Kitty said.

"Neat Jameson for you, Fingal?"

"Please."

"It's Thompson's night off. Cook will look after us. She'll be serving at seven fifteen."

O'Reilly was disappointed about missing Thompson. He always enjoyed seeing the marquis's valet/butler, who had been a gunnery chief petty officer on HMS *Warspite*, O'Reilly's old ship during the war.

"So I'll do the honours." John draped Kitty's coat over a chair back, walked to an ornate sideboard, and poured. He headed back with the drinks. "I hear the Americans landed their Surveyor 3 on the moon last Thursday."

"At least they got a nice clear day for it," Kitty said, deadpan except for an upcocked right eyebrow.

John MacNeill laughed so hard he nearly spilled her drink. "Here, Kitty," he said, still chuckling as he handed it to her. "And here's yours, Fingal." John took a chair beside O'Reilly and picked up his own whiskey and water from a three-legged wine table.

Myrna said, "Big day today in Montreal."

"Oh?" said Kitty, sipping her gin.

"Opening ceremonies there for Expo 67. It was in today's *Belfast Telegraph*. The Canadian governor-general, Roland Michener, made the proclamation and their PM, Lester Pearson, lit the flame. It'll be open until October."

O'Reilly heard Freddy Eynsford-Hill in *My Fair Lady* saying to Eliza

Doolittle, "It's the new small talk. You do it so awfully well." The British upper classes were adept at making a conversation run on perfectly safe grounds devoid of any risk of controversy, and the MacNeills were remnants of the old Protestant Ascendancy.

Myrna was certainly avoiding any reference to Lars. O'Reilly was still hoping his brother would appear, but his hopes were fading. And fading fast.

"So, Doctor," John said. "You know I've been at Westminster for the last few days." His smile was wry. "You have no idea how positively riveting a debate about sewage disposal and coastal pollution can be." He sipped his drink. "Ballybucklebo can't boast an Expo like Montreal, but what's happened in the village while I've been away in London?"

O'Reilly reckoned he'd been given a way to introduce one of the matters he wanted to discuss tonight. He laughed. "Bit of excitement early Sunday morning. You know Donal Donnelly?"

"Carpenter? Works for Bertie Bishop?" Myrna said.

"That's him. Sometimes Donal can be about as bright as a beach ball." Everyone chuckled.

"He stupidly got himself nicked early on Sunday morning. He'd—er, borrowed a couple of cock pheasants."

"On the estate?" John MacNeill asked.

O'Reilly shook his head. "No. In a coppice that marches with the estate."

"Pity," John MacNeill said. "If he'd taken them here, I'd have had the charges dropped. Our birds, after all."

Kitty said, "That would have been very decent of you," she hesitated, "John."

The marquis shrugged. "Kitty," he said, "if it had been a stranger I would not have interfered. Let the law run its course. Serve the blighter right. But, damn it all, Donal's one of our villagers."

O'Reilly hid a smile. He loved how John MacNeill still regarded the locals as his ancestors might have. Feudal possessions who must defer to their betters, but to whom the lord of the manor owed loyalty and a strong protective duty.

"It would have helped," O'Reilly said. "Donal's not a wicked man, but he's short of cash because he and the other nine of his mates are un-employed."

Myrna frowned. "I thought he worked for Bertie Bishop?"

"They all do, but the building of the new road's been delayed until June." O'Reilly sipped his whiskey. He glanced at John MacNeill, who was frowning.

"I'd heard," said John, "but didn't quite realise the implications locally. I'd like to help, but I'm afraid there's no seasonal work on the estate at the moment."

"I actually think you might still be able to do something."

"Oh? Do tell, Fingal."

"Last time we met, you told me two of your labourers' cottages were going to the Ulster Folk and Transport Museum and you were meeting with the museum people to arrange transport. I know for a fact that buildings going there have to be taken apart brick by brick, each com-ponent numbered, transported to their new sites, foundations poured, and the cottages rebuilt. I'd say that's pretty labour intensive."

Kitty said, just as she and O'Reilly had planned she would, "And I'd say it would be a great job for Bertie Bishop's building company."

O'Reilly cocked his head to one side and waited.

"By Jove," John said. "There's a thought. Yes, indeed. What do you think, Myrna?"

Myrna inhaled and sighed. "The museum has agreed to take the cot-tages. The estate can't afford to pay for their move. I imagine the museum folks have their own contractors."

John, drink in hand, stood, paced across the room, then came back. "They do, and they were to start work here mid-May. They're moving an old church at the moment and won't be free until then, but I don't see that we can lose anything by asking the museum to give the job of our cottages to Bertie Bishop. Don't you think so, Fingal? Unless there are contractual difficulties."

"I agree . . ." He saw another opening. "So why don't we ask my brother to find out. I'm sure he'd be delighted to do so. I'd imagined he'd be here tonight."

John MacNeill cleared his throat and refused to meet O'Reilly's eye.

Myrna put her drink down and crossed her arms, tucked her chin down.

As innocently as he could manage, O'Reilly said, "Did I say something wrong?"

The marquis was quick, too quick, to offer reassurance. "Of course not." He smiled and O'Reilly knew the smile was forced.

Myrna took a deep breath. "Unless you've been speaking to your brother recently, Fingal, and by the way you asked about him I don't think you have, you'll not know that he and I came to a parting of the ways a couple of days after we fell out at Kirkistown. Too many differences."

"No," O'Reilly said. He had been dreading it. "I'm sorry to hear that." There had been friction at the races, but O'Reilly had been forced to concentrate on taking care of the driver who had crashed and fortunately had only sustained minor scratches and bruises.

"So am I," Kitty said. "It's none of my business, I know, but the pair of you seemed so . . ." she was clearly looking for *le mot juste*, "so comfortable with each other when you got back from Villefranche."

Lord, O'Reilly thought. The wheels are coming off Barry and Sue's romance. Now Lars's was falling apart. And Fingal was pretty much helpless when it came to doing much for either couple except offering sympathy, but he could try. "Is it hopeless?" he asked. "Can't you two work things out?"

Myrna shook her head. "We are both pig-headed, stubborn people." Her words were clipped, clearly with irritation, but her eyes were moist. She looked away.

There was an uncomfortable silence, broken by John saying, obviously to change the subject, "So I'll get our family solicitor, Mister Simon O'Halley, to talk to the museum people to see if they could use Bertie Bishop's firm instead of their usual contractors."

O'Reilly, deciding it would be unwise to pursue matters any further, said, "That would be terrific if you would. It could make life a lot easier for ten families and Bertie and Flo Bishop."

"I understand," John said, "and I also understand the urgency. I'll phone Simon first thing tomorrow, and I'll have a word with one of the museum's senior staff. I was, after all, on the steering committee that set the thing up and, damn it all, they are my cottages."

O'Reilly nodded and finished his whiskey. "Thank you," he said. "Will you keep me posted, please?"

"Of course." John looked at Fingal's empty glass. "May I refresh that, Fingal, or would you rather wait for dinner? We'll be eating in five minutes."

Kitty said, "The last time Fingal and I were here with La—" Kitty paused, looking flustered; she must have realised what she'd almost said. "The last time we were here, Cook delighted us with a beef Bourguignon. May I ask what we can look forward to tonight?"

"What? I'm sorry, Kitty, I wasn't paying attention," Myrna said. She was twisting the stem of her glass with taut fingers.

"She's wondering what's on the menu for tonight, old girl," John said.

"Right. Cook and I discussed it as soon as we knew you were coming. We'll be starting with melon balls and ginger, then a prawn cocktail, roast glazed Ulster ham with pineapple and seasonal veggies, crème caramel for dessert, then a cheese plate. There's an Alsatian Gewürztraminer with the fish, and a Moulin aux Vent Beaujolais for the ham. John has a Graves if you'd like a sweet wine with dessert, and to complement the cheese a 1924 port our father laid down."

O'Reilly thought about the feast to come and felt a pang for his brother, probably home alone with a book and his housekeeper's shepherd's pie. And he thought too, of the bedraggled topiary and the spider's web on the suit of armour. He marvelled at how John MacNeill, groaning under the massive expense of keeping the estate running, could still entertain like a king and find time to be concerned about Donal Donnelly and Bertie Bishop and his men. "You really are doing us proud," he said, quite loudly to try to hide the gurgling of his tummy. "And with wines like those to come, I think I'll wait."

25

Accidents Will Occur in the Best-Regulated Families

"The young medical gentleman you were expecting has arrived, so." Kinky stood aside to let Doctor Connor Nelson into the dining room. She handed O'Reilly a slip of paper. "And here does be your list."

"Thank you, Kinky." O'Reilly pocketed the list of patients who needed a home visit and, from where he sat at the head of the table, said, "Come in, Connor. Welcome to Number One Main Street."

Connor Nelson's receding ginger hair was neatly combed. He wore a dark blue two-piece suit, the trousers crisply creased, a white shirt with enamel cuff links, and a Royal Victoria Hospital staff tie done in a neat half-Windsor knot. A tiny sun was reflected from the toe of one of his highly polished black shoes. He carried a black leather doctor's bag. "Thank you, sir."

O'Reilly said, "May I introduce you to the real boss around here, Mrs. Maureen Auchinleck? Kinky to her friends, owing to her previous name of Kincaid. And, Kinky, this is Doctor Connor Nelson. As you know, he'll be attached to the practice for the next year."

"And I am sure that will be very good for the practice, so. Doctor O'Reilly, you should be slowing down, and I am sure Doctor Nelson will help you to. I am very pleased to meet you, Doctor Nelson," Kinky said.

"The pleasure's m-mine, Mrs. Auchinleck," Connor said, making a small bow.

That tiny stammer.

"Aye, so. I'm sure you'll do very well. I'll be off, gentlemen, there's hoovering to do, and can I expect four for lunch?"

"Please, Kinky," O'Reilly said.

"Grand altogether, and because today is the first Monday in May it does be Beltane," Kinky said.

O'Reilly saw a puzzled frown cross Connor's face, and said, "Lá Bealtaine. Old Celtic festival. Celebrating the first day of summer in the Celtic calendar. Kinky's very well up on her Irish myths and legends."

"That is true, sir, for as you know I do have personal knowledge of the Little People and what must be done to keep them happy. In olden times, the Celtic folk lit bonfires and held feasts, and some of the food and drink was given as offerings to the Aes Sidhe, the faerie people of the mounds. We'll not be doing that today, so, but I do have a special lunch planned." Before Kinky left, she added, "So do not be late. One o'clock sharp."

O'Reilly smiled and shook his head. "Have a pew, Connor. That Kinky? She truly is one of a kind. And she cooks to beat Bannagher. It would take a nuclear blast to make me late for one of her specials."

Connor cocked his head. "And would I be right in guessing that an explosion is precisely what you'd get from Mrs. Auchinleck if you were late?" He sat to O'Reilly's right.

"Perceptive, Connor. Very perceptive. In deepest County Cork where Kinky's from, she'd be called a 'powerful woman.'" He laughed. "Now, would you like a cup of coffee before we start the working day?"

"Please."

As O'Reilly poured, he began explaining the way the practice worked, with one doctor running the surgery, one making home visits, while whoever had been on emergency call last night was having the morning off. He handed Connor the cup and nodded at the milk and sugar.

Connor ignored the milk but put in three spoonfuls of sugar. "I've a terrible sweet tooth," he said.

O'Reilly chuckled. "Me too," he said. "Enjoy your coffee. Then we'll be off. This morning Barry's taking the surgery. Nonie Stevenson was on call last night, but she'll be holding a well-woman clinic this afternoon, and we're making the home visits. The doctors leave a note if they want one of their patients followed up. Folks phone in and Kinky decides who's most urgent and adds them to the list. Then I try to work out a way of seeing them that involves as little backtracking as possible.

You'll soon learn the local roads." He fished out the list and scanned it. "Right," O'Reilly said. "Nobody on this is in extremis, so if we head off soon we'll have time to give the dogs a run first, and then Barry wants me to look in on one of his patients who was discharged from the Royal nine days ago. Make sure she's not having any more trouble with her porphyria. Eileen Lindsay had an acute attack brought on by Nembutal fifteen days ago."

"I'm ready when you are, Fingal," Connor said, setting down his cup and rising.

Together the men headed for the kitchen and back door. From overhead came the sounds of a vacuum cleaner.

"Porphyria?" Connor said. "Interesting and rare condition. I've read that it probably afflicted King George III of England and Vlad III of Walachia, better known as Vlad the Impaler. He was the model for the Dubliner Bram Stoker's Dracula."

"Now that's something I didn't know," O'Reilly said, opening the back door and waiting for Connor to limp through.

"Mammy always said I should learn something new every day. I did a brave power of reading when I was l-laid up."

O'Reilly closed the door.

Two Labradors charged from the doghouse. Both without bidding halted in front of O'Reilly and sat awaiting his instructions.

"Good," said O'Reilly. "Good. The big fellah's Arthur Guinness. He and I have been together for years. The little lad's Kenny. He's four months and learning, but he's a quick study."

"I h-hope I'll be one too," Connor said.

"Heel," O'Reilly said to the two dogs. "Come on, Connor. The car's in the garage." He walked more slowly than usual to allow for the man's limp, clapped him on the shoulder, and said, "Quick study? I'm sure you will, Connor. I'm perfectly sure."

"Good morning, Doctor O'Reilly," Maggie Houston said as she opened her front door. It was an informal morning. She wasn't wearing her teeth.

Her hat, hanging on a hat stand, had fresh bluebells and yellow broom in the band.

The Houstons' dogs could be heard barking from the kitchen.

"Morning, Maggie. This is Doctor Nelson. He's working with me. Training to be a GP. Doctor Nelson, Mrs. Sonny Houston."

Connor inclined his head.

"Pleased til meet you, sir," Maggie said. "Come on on in." She led the way.

O'Reilly let Connor go first into the sitting room.

"If youse have come til see about Sonny's anaemia, he's out. He ran Eileen's chisslers til school and he's doing some messages in Bangor." She indicated a couple of armchairs.

O'Reilly and Connor sat. "I'm sorry we've missed him." O'Reilly turned to Connor. "Sonny—Mister Houston—has controlled pernicious anaemia," O'Reilly said. "Doctor Laverty made an astute diagnosis without needing to send Sonny to see a consultant."

"Good for him," Connor said. "It usually needs a bone marrow biopsy."

"It does." O'Reilly was pleased with Connor's knowledge. "And no, Maggie. We've come to see Eileen."

"She's in the kitchen. Will I get her?"

"Please."

Maggie headed off.

O'Reilly said, sotto voce, "I know you've a sweet tooth, but if Maggie offers you her plum cake, avoid it or you might break a tooth."

Connor chuckled. "That bad?"

"Worse."

"Here's Eileen," Maggie said.

O'Reilly and Connor both rose as was fitting when a woman entered a room. Pleasantries and introductions were exchanged.

"I'll leave youse alone," Maggie said. "I'll make us a cup of tea in our hands for when youse is finished. I just poured a pot but it needs to stew a bit longer."

O'Reilly's head shake to Connor was nearly imperceptible. He said,

"Take a pew, Eileen," and waited until she sat down on a high-backed chair. He noticed that her brown hair was neatly brushed and her blue eyes were bright and full of life. He and Connor sat. "How are you feeling, Eileen?"

"Rightly," she said. "I was already getting well mended when they discharged me from the Royal on the twenty-third, and I don't think I could be much better than I am now. Mister and Mrs. Houston have been dead on. I don't know how to thank them enough for looking after me and the weans."

O'Reilly smiled. "I've known them both for a lot of years. The only thanks they'll want is for you to get better." He leant over and took her pulse. "Perfect," he said. "Doctor Laverty really just wanted us to pop in to make sure you were all right and not having any more symptoms. And you're not, are you?"

"Nary the one, thanks be."

O'Reilly turned to Connor. "One thing about country folk like Eileen, she'd need to be at death's door before she'd call us out. That's why it's part of the routine to pop in like this."

"I understand. I suppose I'm more familiar with city folks." Connor smiled. "I think, Doctor O'Reilly, a GP here could get much closer to his patients—"

"Here we are," said Maggie, carrying a tea tray. She set it on a table. "Just let it stew a wee bit longer," she said. "For when youse doctors is finished."

"We're pretty well done, Maggie," O'Reilly said. "When are you due back at the Royal, Eileen?"

"Two weeks for blood and urine tests, but Doctor O'Reilly, sir, I need to get back to work—and me and the kiddies need to get back into our own home. The sick leave money Doctor Laverty got for me's not bad, but . . ." She pursed her lips and shrugged.

"Eileen's a shifter in a mill in Belfast," O'Reilly explained. "Do you think we could let her start work again, Doctor Nelson?"

Connor rubbed his chin with the web of his hand. "There's not much point examining you, Mrs. . . . ?"

"Lindsay, sir."

"Once the acute episode's over, and clearly it is, there's really nothing to find. Do you feel well enough, Mrs. Lindsay?"

She nodded. "Aye, sir, I do."

"And you're sure there's no more abdominal pain, no confusion, no pain in your arms or legs."

"No, sir."

"And no heart palpitations, or vomiting."

"Not at all, sir."

Connor rummaged in his bag and fished out a sphygmomanometer. "Just to be on the safe said," he said, taking her blood pressure. "Perfectly normal."

O'Reilly approved of the young man's thoroughness.

Connor asked, "And you'd let us know at once if you started feeling sick again?"

"I would, sir. Cross my heart."

"Doctor O'Reilly," Connor said, "I don't see why not."

"I agree." It seemed Eileen, who might have become a candidate for some of Kinky and Archie's Grand National winnings, would not be in need once she was back at work.

"Honest to God?" Eileen's smile was vast.

"Now, excuse me interrupting," said Maggie, "but you and yours is welcome til stay here for as long as yiz like, you know."

"Oh, Maggie, you and Sonny have been so sweet, but I'd like til get home."

"Never you worry," Maggie said. "I'll help you get your stuff redd up and Sonny'll run you home after he gets back. And he'll bring the kiddies to you after school's out. He's a few things he was getting for Hester Doran. Her husband's going across til Scotland, to Stranraer on the Larne ferry, to some big agricultural show, and Sonny offered to do some shopping for her while he was out." She started to pour tea. "Poor oul Hester's still getting over them bruises, but she's nearly back on her feet."

O'Reilly turned to Connor. "Hester Doran is a bit accident-prone, I'm afraid. Has been since she was a little girl. She fell off a stool in the kitchen two weeks ago and broke her wrist and blacked her eye. The cast made her a little off-balance and a week later she had another wobble and a few more bruises. But Sonny and Maggie have been keeping an eye on her and I'm glad to hear she's getting better, just like you, Eileen. And as to you getting back to work, today's Monday. Give yourself a day or two to get back into your home routine. You'll likely need to buy groceries, things like that, then off you trot. Say on Thursday?"

Eileen's smile was vast. "That'll be great, sir, so it will."

"And to celebrate," said Maggie, "we'll all have a cup of tea and some of my plum cake."

O'Reilly was at a loss for an excuse. He inhaled deeply and was about to accept a cup when the front door opened. Moments later Sonny appeared, helping Hester Doran into the room and onto the sofa. Not waiting for any introductions, Sonny said, "Doctor O'Reilly, I don't know why you are here, but your presence is most fortuitous. Hester's had another accident."

26

Be Bruised in a New Place

O'Reilly stopped reaching for the offered cup of tea. He moved to the couch where Hester Doran, wearing a calf-length floral smock with buttons the whole length of the front, sat propped up on cushions that Sonny had arranged for her. Sonny had stepped back, putting his arm protectively round his wife's shoulder. Eileen sat silently watching.

"In the wars again, Hester?" said O'Reilly. Barry had splinted her broken wrist the day she had fallen off a stepladder and then he'd sent her to the Royal for treatment. He had told O'Reilly about her at dinner that evening.

She nodded but said nothing.

The bruise of two weeks ago beneath her right eye had faded. O'Reilly glanced at the cast on her left forearm. What would have been pure white when the surgeon at the Royal had applied it was a muddy grey now. Working on a farm was not the cleanest of pursuits, and O'Reilly knew that Hester was a hard worker. He knelt beside the couch and looked into her eyes. He spoke softly. "You've not had a good two weeks, Hester, you poor thing. You fell and broke your wrist and blacked your eye, then a week later you came to see Sonny and Maggie because you'd taken another tumble, isn't that right?" This recapping of her recent history was for Connor's benefit.

She whispered, "Yes, sir."

"And what happened today?"

She nodded, pointed to her left breast, and stared at the floor as she spoke. "I was in the byre. Someone had left a hay rake on the floor. It was half hidden by straw. I stood on the tines and the handle flew up and hit me a right dunder, so it did."

"But you didn't fall down?"

She shook her head. "No, sir."

"Certain? It's important."

"Yes, sir. Honest til God."

O'Reilly was satisfied that she'd not lost consciousness, but for Connor's benefit he asked her the requisite questions to establish that she was fully orientated in space and time, then asked, "Are you sore anywhere else?"

"No, sir."

"Sonny, can you add anything?"

"Not really, Doctor. I let myself into the house with the things she'd asked me to get in Bangor. Hester was sitting at the kitchen drying her eyes."

O'Reilly could imagine the initial pain of such a wallop.

"I brought her here first so I could let Maggie know what was going on, and then I was going to bring Hester to see you in the surgery."

"Thank you," O'Reilly said. "Now, Doctor Nelson and I will need to have a look . . ."

"Come on, Maggie," Sonny said. "We'll leave the doctors to their work." They and Eileen left.

"Can I see your arm, please?"

Hester offered it. O'Reilly examined it and repeated his findings to Connor. "Cast is tight, but not too tight. Hand is warm. Fingers are not swollen. Can you wiggle them, Hester?"

She did.

"So the wrist seems to be coming along. Time to take a look at the sore spot. Can I help you with the buttons?" O'Reilly asked.

"Please," she said. "It's tricky with this here cast."

Soon Hester was uncovered from her neck to her waist.

"I see," said O'Reilly, peering at an angry-looking purple bruise right in the centre of her left breast. It was larger than he'd have expected, but bruises could spread quickly, and this one had. "See that, Doctor Nelson," he said, and grimaced. "That must have hurt, wouldn't you agree?"

Connor Nelson nodded his head once but said nothing.

"I'm just going to squeeze your chest, Hester." And putting one hand behind her back and one beneath her left breast, O'Reilly pushed them toward each other. "Did that hurt?"

"No, Doctor."

"Then you're not likely to have a broken rib."

"I'm very glad about that. This bruise and a bust wrist are enough to be getting on with."

"Indeed they are. On the bright side, bruises usually heal pretty quickly and you'll be out of the cast in another four weeks. So just to be certain, Hester, are you sore anywhere else? Anywhere at all?"

She shook her head.

"Doctor Nelson, is there anything you'd like to ask Mrs. Doran?"

Connor said, "Mrs. Houston mentioned that Mister Doran was going to Stranraer? He wasn't at home when you got hurt?"

Her eyes were downcast, but her voice was emphatic. "No, I was all alone in the byre, so I was. He left first thing this morning. He'll not be back 'til Saturday. He's booked on the noon ferry from Stranraer."

"Thank you," Connor said. "That's all I wondered about."

O'Reilly nodded. "Now let's get you dressed." He helped her, then opened his bag and fished out a free sample that had been left by a pharmaceutical company's representative. "Here's some Panadol. It won't cure your bruise, but one every six hours'll make the pain less."

"Thank you very much, Doctor O'Reilly," she said.

"And," he said, glancing at the tray with its teapot, cups and saucers, milk and sugar, and a crockery plate of Maggie's armour-plated plum cake, "I'm sure the tea's cold by now, but I know Maggie will be happy to make another pot after we've gone. I want you to rest up here for a few hours."

Maggie stuck her head round the door. "Did someone say more tea?"

O'Reilly wondered if Maggie had been listening in. He'd not put it past her.

"I'll see til that, so I will," said Maggie, "and you can stay til the cows come home, Hester dear."

"Thank you, Maggie. I'm feeling a bit peely-wally."

O'Reilly was not surprised that she felt out-of-sorts. "Doctor Nelson and I have to be running along." He looked at Connor and inclined his head toward the door. "If the pain doesn't get any better in a few days and the bruise doesn't start to fade, give us a call. Otherwise, pop into the surgery in about a week and one of us will see you."

"I will, Doctor," she said. She cast her eyes down. "And then," she said with a deep sigh, "and then after a wee cuppa and a rest, I suppose I'd better be running along home. I've chores to attend to. The eggs won't collect themselves, so they won't."

When they got to the car, Kenny was standing on the backseat of the Rover, paws against the window, nose pressed to the glass. Arthur Guinness was asleep on the backseat. Kenny gave a delighted "yip" as the two men approached.

"Hop in, Connor," O'Reilly said, then let himself in and started the engine. "Poor old Hester. She's been clumsy since she was a wee girl. But she'll be all right."

O'Reilly took a sidelong glance at Connor, who seemed to be deep in thought. O'Reilly had hoped for a more sociable companion, but he had to remember it was only the lad's first day. He drove down from the Houstons' house toward the Bangor to Belfast Road. Ahead was Belfast Lough, shimmering in the May sunshine. Overhead, a few puffy clouds hung. Lapwing staggered across the cerulean. O'Reilly found himself enjoying the calm until Connor said, "I'm not so sure she will be."

"Come on. It's only a bruise. She'll be right as rain in no time."

Connor half turned in his seat. "Doctor O'Reilly, may I ask you a q-question or two?"

"First of all, it's Fingal, and second, how the blazes do you expect to learn if you don't?" He braked—hard—for a hare, its great hind legs pumping, who had made the wrong decision about when to cross the road. "Eejit rabbit," he roared out the window. "You nearly got yourself killed." He accelerated. "Go on, Connor."

Connor Nelson inhaled, then said, "Where did you grow up, Fingal?"

O'Reilly frowned. "Holywood in County Down and later in Balls-bridge, Dublin. Lansdowne Road to be precise. Why?"

"I told you when I was wee my daddy was out of work for a b-brave while, and when he got a job and we left the country, our house was on Rydalmere Street in Belfast. Ballsbridge is where the toffs live in Dublin, and no harm to you, but that would include you, Fingal. Rydalmere Street wasn't upper class."

O'Reilly stopped at the junction with the main road and waited for a gap in the traffic. "I'm not sure I'm following." What the divil had their differences in background to do with Hester Doran? He admired Connor and how he had got himself through medical school despite his poverty, but he hoped the youngster wasn't going to make a song and dance out of it. "And if the implication is that I've no insight into how the other half lives, I spent a year as a GP in the Liberties in Dublin. It doesn't get any rougher."

"Aye," said Connor, "but you didn't live there. You may have been respected as a physician, but you were an outsider, a 'blow-in' as far as the people who did live there were concerned."

He thought he had been respected and well liked, but O'Reilly was willing to concede the point. He nodded. "True. I'll grant you that. But I still don't see—"

"Y-you've just told me about your patient Hester Doran. Three accidents in two weeks? That's a b-brave lot. How many women in the Liberties did you see with a history of frequent repeated trauma like that?"

"Trauma? That might be overstating things, don't you think? It started because the poor woman fell off a stool trying to reach something on a top shelf."

O'Reilly found a gap in the traffic and turned left, heading back toward Ballybucklebo. "But to answer your question, people were always having accidents, and what the natives there called 'ruggy ups,' street brawls, were ten a penny . . ." He slowed behind a Dale Farm Dairy lorry stacked high with aluminium churns heading to the facility so their contents could be pasteurised, bottled, and crated for delivery by milkmen like Archie Auchinleck. "But the locals didn't run to the doctor, even if the dispensary doctor didn't cost them anything, for bumps and bruises, so, honestly? I don't believe I ever saw anyone like that. Not three times in two weeks." Was Connor Nelson suggesting there might be some underlying causative medical condition that O'Reilly and Barry were missing? O'Reilly shook his head. He could think of nothing that would cause an adult to step on a half-concealed hay rake. He said, "Most of the cuts and bruises I patched up came from brawls." He laughed. "And there were some pretty good women fighters too." He smiled remembering Aungier Place and the surrounding roads like Peter Street and Francis Street. "I did a bit of boxing back then. There were one or two local members of the gentler sex I'd not like to have gone three rounds with."

"I knew you were a rugby international . . ."

No doubt the young man had made enquiries about his potential mentor before applying for the job.

". . . but I didn't know you were a boxer, Fingal."

O'Reilly laughed. "You thought I was born with my bent nose and cauliflower ears? It might surprise you to know that your highly respected teacher, Mister Charlie Greer, broke my schnozzle in 1935." He grinned. "Made an awful crunching noise when it went."

Connor laughed. "Mister Greer played rugby too. I wasn't able to, but despite my leg I was pretty good at table tennis. I don't know too much about b-boxing." There was a seriousness to his next question. "If a fighter stood facing his opponent and let go what I believe is called a straight right, and the defendant failed to b-block the punch, where would he get hit?"

O'Reilly managed to get past the slow-moving dairy lorry. "He'd have a bloody great bruise round his left nipple."

"That's what Hester has."

O'Reilly shook his head and smiled. "I don't think the country women of the Ballybucklebo townland go in much for street fighting. They're too busy trying to keep the farm going."

"I think a rake handle would make a much narrower bruise." Connor cocked his head. "What about her husband? What kind of a man is he?"

O'Reilly's lip curled. "He's a bully and an unmitigated bastard and he'd run faster than that hare I just missed before he'd put his fists up." O'Reilly snorted. The very thought of Hubert Doran boxing? It would make a cat laugh.

"I don't mean that," Connor said. "What if it was her husband who h-hit her today—and was the cause of her earlier injuries too? Do you think he's that kind of a man?"

O'Reilly could think of nothing to say. Connor's words had hit him the way that rake had hit Hester. Or had it? He needed to think. Now. Did Connor Nelson, courtesy of his working-class background, have special knowledge O'Reilly himself lacked?

He saw a lane a few hundred feet ahead, pulled into it, turned off the engine, and hauled out and lit up his pipe. Could Hubert Doran be beating his wife? "Six or seven years ago I was out on the Houstons' property next door to the Dorans'. I heard a ferocious howling and there he was, the bastard, holding a golden retriever bitch by her ear—her ear—and beating the tar out of her with her own leash. He was screaming at her and he punched her. I ran over and, damn it all, I was furious. He set up to hit her again so I grabbed his arm and I decked him. He was out for about two minutes. When he came to, I told him if he ever—ever— laid hands on a dog like that again, I'd thrash the bejasus out of him."

"Sounds like the type," Connor said. His gaze, which he fixed on O'Reilly, was wistful. Sad. "Friday nights on Rydalmere Street were," the young man paused, "eventful. The men at the match factory got paid their wages at knocking-off time. Some went to the b-boozer, got pissed, and some of them came home and beat the living bejasus out of their wives. My mammy ran an amateur first-aid station—the women wouldn't go to the hospital, swore b-blind they'd had a fall, bumped into something."

"I don't believe it," said O'Reilly. He found the whole idea of an Irishman raising his fist to a woman incomprehensible. He saw a crestfallen look on Connor's face and realised it sounded as if he doubted the man's veracity. "Sorry, Connor," he said. "I'm not calling you a liar. You're telling me that men in Belfast beat their wives. Their own wives? I never heard the like."

"Why would you, Fingal? You just said the people of the Liberties didn't run to the doctor for bumps and bruises. And the men were usually smart enough to hit where it didn't show."

O'Reilly eyes widened. "Like Hester's bruise today?" He said quietly, "And it was wider than I expected."

"That's right. I wanted to see how she'd react when I asked about her husband. Did you hear her voice?"

"I did. It was . . ." He struggled for the right word. "Defiant? Defensive?" Connor was onto something here.

"They always were like that on Friday nights at our house too. The poor women think they're to b-blame, that it's their fault. They're ashamed of themselves, don't want to let their husbands down in public, and wouldn't dream of going to the authorities," Connor said. "There's even a song about it.

> When I was single I had a plaid shawl
> Now that I'm married I wear none at all
> But still I love him I'll forgive him
> I'll go with him wherever he goes.

" 'I'll forgive him,' and they do. They do. Over and over. When you asked them outright, they'd deny it. My mammy knew, and she taught me that a man should never hit anybody, especially a woman."

O'Reilly shook his head, let go an enormous cloud of pipe smoke. If Connor's right, he thought, something must be done. He started the Rover and backed out onto the road. "So how do we find out what's going on?" he asked as he turned the wheel and headed for Number One Main.

Connor shrugged. "We could ask Hester, b-but I don't think she'll tell tales. Even if she does, I've no notion about what to do next."

"Nor me," O'Reilly said, "but," he nodded to himself, "a few weeks back I had to treat my brother and remarked then that it's useful to have a doctor in the family. Sometimes it may be useful to have a solicitor too. There's got to be some legal recourse." He puffed, blew out another blue cloud, and said, "Right. We'll nip into Number One, let the dogs off.

I'll phone my brother and get advice, and head straight back to the Houstons' before Hester goes back home. I want to put it to her—gently, of course. But I want to see if she'll confide in her doctors at least. She's safe for now. Doran's at that farm thing in Scotland. But this can't go on. And since Eileen and the chisslers are going home, perhaps Maggie and Sonny can put Hester up once Doran returns, just until we figure out what's to be done."

"She probably won't stay, but if she tries to, her husband will likely come and take her home anyway," Connor said. "I've seen it happen."

O'Reilly indicated for the left turn into his back lane. He owed Connor an apology. "I was wrong, Connor Nelson."

"About what?"

O'Reilly ignored the question. "Any time, lad, you think I'm making a mistake about one of the customers, don't hesitate to say so. Not in front of them, mind. But tell me, just like you did today. You did very well."

Connor laughed. "Thank you." His voice became more serious. "I've heard tell, Doctor O'Reilly, that you always put the patient—or should I say customer—first. That's the kind of doctor I want to be too."

O'Reilly guffawed. "Good man-ma-da." He parked. "Now, let's do what we have to here and then get moving to see what we can do for Hester Doran."

Connor whispered, as if to himself, "If anything."

27

He Would Bet You Which One Would Fly First

"Morning everybody." Barry opened the waiting room door and was greeted by a small chorus of "Good morning, Doctor Laverty." Now that cold and flu season was well over, the room was half empty and Barry felt disappointed. He'd still had no word from Sue, and work might take his mind off that constant ache. Put it away, he told himself, and get on with your job.

"Who's first?"

Donal and Julie Donnelly rose.

"Morning, Donnellys. Come on, then." Barry headed back toward the surgery. He'd last seen Julie in early April. She'd been twenty-seven weeks. Now, on Monday, May 1, she'd be one day short of thirty. He took them in and closed the door. "How are you doing, Julie?"

"Can't complain, sir. Usual aches and pains. Backache. Lots of kicking."

"When he grows up, the wee lad'll be playing for Manchester United, just like Georgie Best," Donal said, taking one of the wooden chairs. "I can't wait til show him how til pass a football." He pulled his duncher from his pocket, gesturing with it as if it were a ball and grinning.

George Best, a Belfast native, was rated one of the world's top players of all time. Donal Donnelly was still convinced his offspring was going to be a boy, and, Barry thought with a smile, a boy his father was clearly going to enjoy playing with.

"One thing about kids. They keep folks young," Julie said, and gave

Donal an indulgent look and shook her head. "Here you are, sir." Julie handed Barry a small plastic bottle.

"Thanks." Barry took the bottle and set it on his desk. "Let's get you weighed, Julie." He helped her onto the scale. "You've put on eight pounds." That was a couple of pounds more than Barry would have liked, but he wasn't going to make a fuss if everything else was all right. He helped her up onto the examining couch. As she adjusted her clothes so Barry could examine her belly, he tested her urine. No albumin. No sugar. Good.

Barry satisfied himself that all was going according to plan. Her blood pressure was holding at 130 over 85, up a tad but not enough to cause concern. No swelling of her ankles. Add that to a blood pressure that was only slightly elevated and no albumin, he could exclude pre-eclamptic toxaemia, a condition that threatened both mother and child.

She was certainly carrying high, but he could detect no sign of an excess of amniotic fluid, a condition known as polyhydramnios. The foetal heart rate was normal and this time the baby's head was at the lower end of the uterus. He smiled. "It looks A1 at Lloyd's," he said. "Please get dressed."

Julie sat up and tucked in her blouse. "And I went til the post office last week," she said, "eleven weeks before my due date, just like you said to, Doctor, and collected my first maternity allowance. Three pound seven and six. And I'll get the same this week. Every wee bit helps." She sat up and Barry helped her down.

"Aye, it does," said Donal. "And I suppose you heard, Doc, that I got lifted?"

"I did indeed, Donal. You told us last Monday in the pub. Remember?"

Donal shook his carroty head. "D'y'h know, I'd clean forgot, so I had. I must be getting magnesia."

"Amnesia," Barry said.

"Aye. Right enough. Anyroad, it was just a bit of bad luck. That's when I cut my hand, but it's all better now." He held it up, palm out. "See. Healed up a treat"—the new scar was clean and pink—"but I'm up in court on June the twelfth and I know I'll get a fine. I just hope it's after Mister Bishop gets us all back til work."

"Still no word on the road contract?"

Donal shook his head. "Not a dicky bird, but him and me and the marquis were on the estate on Friday. There's two cottages til be moved til the museum. The marquis asked Mister Bishop til tender for doing it. He brung me along for carpentry advice. If he gets the job, it'd keep us busy until we get going on the road building. Be a lifesaver, so it would."

"Any idea when you'll hear?"

Donal shook his head. "But I hope it'll be soon. Mind you," Donal looked wistful, "being off work's got its advantages. I've all the time in the world to play with wee Tori. We took her up til Belfast last week, til the Templemore Avenue swimming baths. You should see her in the water. Like a wee seal, she is." He turned and put a work-roughened hand on Julie's. "Our own wee selkie." They smiled at each other. "And the gurgles and chuckles of her? It made me laugh so hard I near drowned. But Julie came and saved me." He grinned his buck-toothed grin.

Barry tilted his head. "You enjoy being a daddy, Donal."

"I do, Doc. Even more than I thought. You'll see for yourself one day," Donal said. "There's going til be another one after this wee lad."

Julie said, "That's right."

"Good for you, but let's get this one here first," Barry said, and sat at the rolltop desk to fill in a form. "Now, I need you to get some routine blood work done just like in your last pregnancy, Julie, before I see you in two weeks. Nip down to Bangor Hospital." He stood and handed her the form, indicating the consultation was over, but added, as he did with every patient, "Have you any questions for me?"

Julie shook her head.

Donal said, "I've a wee one, so I have."

"Fire away." Hadn't Donal remarked last Monday night about "a way til raise a bit of dosh," and needing medical advice? What was coming?

"You reckon Julie's due on July the twelfth, isn't that right, sir. Like I told you before, if the wee lad arrives dead on time he'll get called William."

"For King William of Orange?" Barry smiled. "The twelfth's the due date, all right."

"What are the odds she'll have the wean on that day?"

Barry frowned. "Odds? I'm not sure I understand."

Donal cocked his head. "Look, sir, out of a wheen of women who got pregnant on the same day, not counting them who miscarried like poor Julie did with our first"—he flashed her a look of deep sympathy—"of one hundred that kept going, how many would deliver exactly on time and how many wouldn't?"

"Uh-huh, I see. Well, you know that doctors count the length of a pregnancy in weeks?"

"Aye. And Julie's near thirty now, aren't you, love?"

"That's right," she said. "Not long to go."

Barry closed his eyes and summoned up the figures he'd learned years ago. "People who study these things have calculated that of your hundred women, approximately ten will deliver before thirty-seven weeks . . ."

Donal had fished out a notebook and a pencil and was scribbling. "That leaves ninety."

"The rest will have the baby somewhere between the start of the thirty-seventh and the end of the forty-second weeks. Only five will hit the bull's-eye, the exact day, and the specialists don't like women to go more than ten days past it, so they induce labour in those women." What the hell was Donal going to do with this information? Even he wouldn't dare lay odds on his own wife's due date, would he?

"And that's it, sir?"

"Best as I can remember."

Donal's facial expressions changed as rapidly as wind-driven cloud shadows dashing over a field, a sure sign he was indulging in a series of mental contortions. "So, if I've got this right, that's six weeks or forty-two days, but the doctors don't let a woman go more than ten days over? Forty-two take away four, that's thirty-eight days when the wean can come, and nobody can tell exactly when that'll be?"

Barry nodded.

Donal grinned and said to Julie, "Didn't I tell you, love, that Doctor Laverty is a learnèd man and would know?"

She smiled and nodded.

"What you are saying, Doc, is that the due date is pretty inaccurate. Only five out of one hundred? That's odds of twenty to one, so it is. I'd not back a horse at them."

Barry laughed. "It's not exactly a horse race, you know."

Donal ignored the comment. "Dead on. Thanks a million, Doc." He rose.

"Not so fast, Donal Donnelly," Barry said. "What's all this about?" There were only a few patients to be seen. He'd all the time in the world to satisfy his curiosity.

Donal blushed to the roots of his carroty hair. Frowned. "You'll not tell nobody, sir? At least not until it's out in the open?"

"Donal, what a thing to ask," Barry said. "Of course not."

"All right. I'm going til run a sweepstake."

Barry had quick flashbacks to a long line of Donal's escapades that included a fixed raffle for a good Christmas cause, a disguised racing greyhound, and selling fragments of Brian Boru's war club. He supposed betting on when Donal's wife would give birth made a kind of Donnelly logic too.

"I'll start selling tickets when Julie reaches thirty-six weeks. Folks don't like to wait too long for the results. Each day from the start of her week thirty-seven will be numbered from one til thirty-eight. That would be til forty weeks and ten days like you said, sir."

"And?" Barry was beginning to see how it would work.

"A pound buys you a day, and no day'll be sold to more than one punter, but anyone can buy as many days as they like."

"Sort of like the Irish Hospitals' Sweepstakes and Julie here is the horse. So it is like a horse race."

"I suppose so, sir." Donal eyed Barry. "Do you not think it's a good idea? It's not illegal, mind. And if I sell all thirty-eight days, that would be thirty-eight quid."

"I think it's a fine idea. How much does the winner make?"

"Whoever has the winning day gets ten pounds."

Barry whistled. "That's a fair bit of money."

Donal winked. "Sure aren't you a fisherman, sir?"

"I am."

"Then you'd know that if you want til catch a fish, you have til use the right fly."

Barry nodded. If this worked out, Donal stood to make twenty-eight quid, there'd be one happy bettor, no one who lost would suffer drastically and, being Ballybucklebo, Barry was sure Donal would reach full subscription if only because he was a popular man and the villagers were renowned for their willingness to support each other. "You, Donal Donnelly," Barry said, "missed your calling." If he'd had the education, stockbroker might have been more Donal's avocation.

Julie said, "There's no curing him, sir," but her smile was gentle and loving. "Come on, love. Doctor Laverty's a busy man, so he is. I'll see yiz in two weeks, sir." She rose and together they left.

Barry chuckled. Incorrigible, but not a hair of harm in the man. Donal Donnelly was definitely one of a kind. And it was clear he doted on children. Barry was missing Sue as a man might miss his right arm. Damn it all. Enough. He'd call her today. If surgery finished soon enough, he might even catch her at morning break time at MacNeill Memorial Primary.

He was smiling on his way back to the waiting room and laughed when he had to step aside for Lady Macbeth who, clearly beset by the demons that intermittently affect all felines, tore past him at full speed, cornered on two legs round the banisters' newel post, and raced up the stairs.

"Right," he said, looking into the waiting room, "who's next?" and was surprised when Anne Galvin stood up. Surely she must be the last one to have arrived? Yet there were no protests from any of the other patients. "Come along then," he said, hoping her chest wasn't playing up again.

They started down the hall and she cleared her throat. "I told all the others I just wanted a wee question answered," she said quickly. "I promised not to take up your time for more than a wee minute, sir. They said til go ahead. Decent folks."

"They are that," Barry said, going into the surgery. "So what can I do for you?" He closed the door.

"I came til tell you I've not had a smoke since I seen you last, and that was a week today, so it was. And I'm coughing even more . . ."

"That's to be expected. It'll get better soon."

She put her hand in her pocket and produced a small paper bag. "It's clove rock. When I really want a smoke, I gobble one of these sweeties. I've saved a pound already. I was doing my shopping today so I was in the village anyway and I wanted til spare you the trouble of coming out to see me. That's all, sir." She smiled. "We all know youse doctors are busy."

"Anne, that's wonderful about the smoking. Wonderful. And very thoughtful of you to drop in," Barry said. "Thank you. Now keep up the good work. It'll get easier and easier as the days go by."

"I will, sir, and I'll let myself out so you can see who's next." She headed for the door.

A touched Barry Laverty shook his head. There were more benefits to being a GP here in Ballybucklebo than the salary he got from Fingal. He headed back to the waiting room.

He could hear Kinky busily hoovering upstairs. Barry was just about to call for the next patient when O'Reilly rushed from the kitchen and into the hall. It was clearly urgent because without as much as a hello, O'Reilly went to the hall telephone. "Have to talk to my brother," he said.

And he was talking as Barry returned with his next patient, but then he put the receiver down—hard—and galloped off. Barry frowned. O'Reilly usually worked on the *festina lente,* or "make haste slowly," principle. When dealing with patients, he only ran for severe pain or bleeding. His brother was forty minutes away in Portaferry. So what in the name of the wee man was going on? Barry shrugged. He'd just have to wait to find out.

He looked at his watch. Eleven fifteen. It would be morning break time at the school. "Go on into the surgery, John," he said. "I've a phone call to make. Only be a minute." John Gallagher was one of Bertie Bishop's crew and by the way he had a hand in the small of his back, he probably wanted a disability certificate so he could draw sickness benefit.

"Right, sir."

Barry picked up the phone, dialled, and had the operator at the school connect him with the staff room. "Hello? Yes. It's Doctor Laverty. Is Miss Nolan there, please?"

"Hang on."

He could hear the hum of background conversation, then, "Barry?"

He thought he'd had momentary cardiac arrest just from hearing her voice. Was she excited to hear from him? "Sue. I—"

"You'll have to speak up. There's a terrible row in here." Her tones were matter-of-fact. Of course she'd not want to let her feelings show in front of the other teachers.

"I-I understand." He raised his voice. "Look, it's been eight days, Sue. I have to see you. I'm off tonight. Will you have dinner with me?" He realised if he didn't relax his grip on the receiver he might crack the Bakelite. He waited, his breath caught in his upper chest.

"I'm sorry, Barry. I can't. I've a meeting. You remember my old Campaign for Social Justice?" She didn't wait for an answer. "It's been replaced. On April the ninth we formed the Northern Ireland Civil Rights Association. I'm on the steering committee. We have meetings all this week. This weekend, I have to go down to Broughshane to see how Dad is. And right now I have to get back to class. I'm sorry."

What could he say? He exhaled.

"You still there?"

"Yes."

"Barry, I'll call you next Monday. I promise." And with that she hung up.

Barry replaced the receiver. He was trembling and without thinking whispered, "But Sue, I love you." He had to wait for five more silent minutes before he felt well enough collected to go and see John Gallagher and feign sympathy for what was probably a nonexistent condition that could not be refuted and would require a certificate of disability.

28

In Quietness and in Confidence

O'Reilly, with no Kitty to restrain him, was driving with his old reck-lessness, narrowly missing a cyclist and roaring down the country lanes, eager to get back to Hester as quickly as possible. "I got through to my brother, Connor," he said, "but he wants to look into it more, and there are some family matters he and I need to discuss too. We've got until Hester's husband gets back from Scotland, so Kitty and me will go down there on Wednesday. I'll get it straightened out then." He turned to Connor.

"You're the b-boss, boss," said Connor with a fleeting smile. "Y-you did see that cyclist, right?"

"Of course I did," roared O'Reilly. "Now, Lars says there doesn't seem to be much in the way of legal protection for her, but he'll find out what he can. I think it's going to be up to us to do something."

"I agree," Connor said.

O'Reilly honked at a man trundling along on a motor-assisted bike, who pulled right over so O'Reilly could speed past. O'Reilly turned right on the road up to the Houstons' house. "What do you reckon's the best way to get the truth out of Hester, Connor? I'd like your advice. You say you've seen many wives who were beaten by their husbands."

There was sadness in the young man's voice when he said, "Too bloody many."

What might go on behind the velvet curtains of exclusive places like Blackrock in Dublin or the Malone Road in Belfast? O'Reilly wondered. Come to think of it, he had from time to time seen a wife of one of the highheejins with bruises or a black eye, always blamed on an accident. And he'd always accepted the explanation. Upper-class boys, and he was one, were trained from childhood to believe that women were the weaker sex and should be treated with the utmost respect and protected. Any so-called "gentleman" who would raise his fist to a woman had forfeited the right to be called a man.

"We've got to get to the bottom of this. Do you think if you saw Hester on your own, you'd be more likely to get the answers? Know the right questions to ask? Pick up the clues?"

Connor frowned. "I probably do have a better notion what to look for, but . . ." He pursed his lips, inhaled, then shook his head. "No. I d-don't think so. You've been her doctor for years, haven't you?"

O'Reilly nodded. "On and off. She and her husband left the practice after I decked Hubert over that dog business seven years ago. Hardly surprising. But what was surprising was that she rejoined last month on her own."

"If she'll confide in anybody, it'll be you."

"You know I can't help but feel I've let her down. That I should have been aware of a pattern. She said herself she was accident-prone even as a little girl. I wonder if she took a lot of beatings at home. Country folk are big on 'Spare the rod and spoil the child.'"

"Aye," said Connor, "and grew up believing getting thumped was the norm?"

"You could be right." The more O'Reilly saw of Connor Nelson, the more he appreciated the man's depths. "These recent episodes aren't the first ones I've treated for her. But she always had a good reason for it. A cow kicked her. Or one of the pigs shoved her. Farming is physical work." He shook his head.

"You had no reason to suspect what was going on," Connor said gently. "You go on in, Fingal. And b-better you see her alone. Both of us there might give the impression the medical profession's ganging up on her. I'll wait in the car." He smiled at O'Reilly. "Good luck."

"Thank you." He parked outside the Houstons'. The hedge was glowing with the bright green of spring, and birds twittered in its leafy shelter. He left his bag in the car and headed for the house, to be greeted by Maggie. "Boys-a-dear," she said over the usual canine chorus, "two visits in one day? That's great, so it is. Sonny'll be quare nor sorry til have missed you, sir. He's just away off running Eileen home, but Hester's still here."

"Good," said O'Reilly. "There's something else I need to ask her."

Maggie grinned her toothless grin. "You can tear away, sir, and ask all you like. She seems to be feeling better. And you're just in time for a wee cup of tea in your hand too. I made another pot for Hester and me just a few minutes ago and it's rightly stewed now, so it is."

"Not today, thank you, Maggie," he said. "Kinky's making a special lunch." Oh God, and he'd not left word that he and Connor might be late. He imagined he could hear the BBC weather forecaster on the kitchen radio saying, "North cones, an indication to sailors of the approach of stormy weather, have been hoisted over Ballybucklebo." He hoped it was just meteorologically and not metaphorically.

Maggie smiled. "And we all know how Kinky is if folks don't finish the grub she's made. She stepped aside. "Come on on in."

"Maggie," O'Reilly said quickly, "I want you to leave me alone with Hester for a minute or two."

"Aye, certainly," Maggie said.

"Thank you."

She stopped outside the lounge door. "And is that nice young Doctor Nelson not coming in?"

O'Reilly shook his head.

"I'll take him a cup out while you're with Hester, have a bit of *craic* with the young doctor then." She opened the lounge door. "Hester, see who's come to see you again?"

Hester looked up from where she sat on the same chair she'd been in when O'Reilly and Connor had left earlier. She smiled politely at O'Reilly, but behind the social smile O'Reilly thought he saw fear, perhaps even suspicion. "Hello, Doctor," she said. "Thank you for coming earlier. I'm feeling much better now. I'm just finishing up my tea then I'm going to run away on home."

"Do you know what the nice young doctor takes in his tea?" Maggie poured a cup and put a slice of plum cake in the saucer. O'Reilly recalled the three spoons full of sugar in Connor's coffee earlier this morning. "Three sugars," he said, and hoped Connor had remembered his warning about Maggie's cake as he watched her head for the front door.

O'Reilly sat in the chair beside Hester. "Are you sure you're feeling well enough to go home? You've got a nasty bruise."

"Och, aye," she said. "It still pains a bit, but I've got a brave wheen of chores needing doing at the farm, but thanks for asking."

"Fair enough." O'Reilly cleared his throat. "Hester," he said, "just one more wee question. How long have you been my patient?"

She frowned. "We come til your practice in 1946 just after you come back to Ballybucklebo from the war, and we stayed until 1961 when you and Hubert had thon falling out. I'm sorry about that," she said, "but when he gets his mind made up, he's like a terrier on a rat. He won't let go."

"It must have taken a lot of courage for you to come back as a patient to my practice last month," O'Reilly said. He looked her straight in the eye.

She sniffed. "I never agreed with him about you, sir. Him saying bad things and all. You were always very kind til me when I was sick, so you were, and I trust you, so I do."

A humbled O'Reilly inhaled deeply, then exhaled past pursed lips. This wasn't going the way he'd hoped. He did not want Hester to think he was trying to get information he could use to discomfit her husband. "Hester," he said, "as far as I'm concerned, what's between Hubert and me's over and done with. I'm concerned about you. You've had a lot of accidents lately."

Her giggle was falsetto and, O'Reilly thought, forced. "Sure amn't I just an awkward one? I was too when I was a wee girl."

This, assuming he was right, was exactly how Connor had predicted she would react. Deny everything. Shield her husband even before any accusations were made. O'Reilly decided to try to overawe her by using the great and actually unfounded belief of country folks that doctors knew very much more than they actually did. He kept his voice low and level. "Hester, when I examined you this morning I didn't want to say anything in front of anyone but you. That's why I came back, so it would be just between the two of us." His fingers were firmly crossed behind his back. Such an action, it was believed in the country, would lessen the sin of a deliberate lie or negate the binding of a promise made under duress. "You did not walk onto a hay rake. Someone thumped you today. That's what brought me back. Us doctors can easily tell the difference between a hit by a rake and a punch." He was quite sure Hester Doran would not have the courage to ask how, which was a good thing, because in reality he had not known the difference. But Connor had. "I want to make sure you're all right." And that was the gospel truth.

Her eyes flew wide. Her right hand went to her mouth. "Nobody never did." Her voice rose. "Never did. I walked onto a rake. I did. I did." Her shoulders started to shake. The tears flowed. She whispered, "I did."

O'Reilly's instant instinct was to put his arms round her to comfort her, but he simply said, "No, Hester. Hubert punched you. And it's not for the first time, is it?" He waited.

She looked at him, her face as crumpled as a discarded paper bag. Her sobs were wracking, her tears a torrent. "God forgive me, it's all . . ." sobbing, "it's all my fault."

"The poor women think it's their fault. That they're to blame." Connor's words came back. He'd been spot on. But the question now was what to do for Hester.

"I burnt his breakfast eggs. He was rushing to get to the ferry in Larne and he lost his temper, but he's not like that . . . usually. He's-he's not."

She was pleading, but was she trying to convince O'Reilly—or herself?

He said gently, "Another wee question, Hester. Did you get the strap a lot when you were wee?"

"Och, sure, Doctor, don't all kiddies? And I only got it when I'd been very bad. Da was a great one for a quick clip on the ear for wee things."

And grew up thinking getting thumped was the norm. O'Reilly nodded to himself before saying, "Tell me. Has it got worse since you came back to my practice?" Unless she said it only started at that time then either "yes" or "no" would confirm that this had been going on for a long time.

"It's no worser, sir. Honest. This is my doing. It's my own fault." She bit her lip and tried to wipe away the tears, but more took their place.

It was all O'Reilly needed to know. Now he rose, squatted before her, and took one of her hands in both of his, looking her right in the eye. "It's all right, Hester. It's all right. It's not your fault. It's not your fault."

She looked into O'Reilly's face. He saw the hope there.

"It is not your fault," he repeated.

The sobbing was subsiding. She sniffed and dabbed at her eyes with one of Maggie's white linen tea napkins. "Thank you, sir. It-it helps to talk a bit about it," she said shyly. "I've never told no one."

"I appreciate your honesty, Hester." His voice was firm. "But it's got to be stopped. No one's ever going to thump you again."

She shook her head. "No, sir. I know what you're thinking. But this is to stay between you and me. I'll not shame myself and I'll not have Hubert shamed. Let us be. It's between a man and his wife. That's all. Let it be. It's to go no farther."

O'Reilly clenched his fists, but what could he do? What had Connor said about women not wanting "to let their husbands down in public," women who "wouldn't dream of going to the authorities." Connor Nelson knew these painful truths from bitter experience. He'd have to. There was absolutely nothing in any medical texts that dealt with wife beating. "All right," O'Reilly said, "but will you let me do one thing? And believe me, it'll go no farther. My colleagues will have to be told."

"No," she whispered. "Please, sir."

O'Reilly shook his head. "If I'd been treating you for . . ." He sought a good example and thought of Anne Galvin. ". . . acute bronchitis, my colleagues would have to know so that if they were on call and you needed them, they'd be up to date with your history. That's all."

"And they'll keep it to themselves?"

"They have to. It's the law." And, he thought, that same confidentiality existed between physicians and other professionals too, so in that sense Lars was a colleague. But O'Reilly'd not scare this poor creature any more by telling her that on Wednesday he was going to seek legal advice in Portaferry from Lars Porsena O'Reilly, his brother—and solicitor at law.

"All right." She sounded resigned.

"And one more thing. How'd you feel about staying for a few days with the Houstons once Hubert comes home. Just for a little rest?"

"Och no, sir. Leave the farm? I can't. There's too much to do. And besides, I'm happier in my own home." She shook her head. "No, sir."

"Fair enough, Hester," O'Reilly said. "But you call if you need us, and I'll pop out on Saturday. See how you're doing." And, he thought, I'll be armed with advice from my brother and have Connor Nelson along for support and as a witness. One way or another, this had been the last time a certain Hubert Doran would raise his fist to his wife.

"I'll be off. Look after yourself, Hester. Try to rest as much as you can."

"Thank you, sir—for everything."

"Hester. Hester." O'Reilly's knees creaked as he rose. "Doctoring's not just about colds, and flus, and broken bones. It's about looking after people. It's our job."

There was gratitude in her eyes and a small smile on her face.

He smiled and glanced at his watch. "Now I'd better run on. I might just get home in time for Kinky's special lunch."

29

Hence Horrible Shadow!

Barry turned his Volkswagen onto the council estate road. He had not enjoyed the drive from Number One. He'd barely been able to think about his driving.

Ten minutes ago he had been in his quarters affixing the first tiny mahogany outer plank to the completed under-hull of his HMS *Victory* model. Glue first, then tiny brass nails. Fiddly work. He was off duty this morning and the need for intense concentration on the delicate task kept his mind from worrying about next Monday, when he would hear from Sue again. He had been interrupted by a sharp knock on his door.

Kinky had been in better form at breakfast than she had been yesterday, when O'Reilly and Connor Nelson had shown up late for her special Beltane lunch. But she was now clearly concerned and said, "I do have Mrs. Anne Galvin on the phone. Will you speak with her please, sir? She does sound very agitated, so, and the other doctors are busy."

"Of course." Barry went to the telephone extension on his bedside table, usually only activated when he was on night call, pushed a button, and lifted the receiver. "Doctor Laverty."

"Doctor, it's Anne again. Guffer's at work and I'm coughing up more blood. Great dollops. Please come quick."

Blood? Not good. "Hang on, Anne. I'm coming right over. I'll be there in ten minutes."

He had driven through the village, struggling to understand why she would be bleeding again. Three weeks ago he'd been confident in his diagnosis of acute bronchitis, and she had recovered in jig time, confirming his confidence. O'Reilly and Kenny had seen her nine days ago for some bloodstaining of her sputum, but it had not recurred and her X-ray had been clear apart from some emphysema and that old healed TB scar. Only last Monday, Barry and Kenny had brought her the good news and yesterday she'd popped in to tell him she hadn't had a smoke for a week. And now this? What the hell was going on? To him, "great dollops" sounded ominous. What had he and O'Reilly missed? He hit the steering wheel with his fist.

And now here he was parking outside the familiar grey-stuccoed, two-up two-down terrace house with the brown peeling paint on the door. He turned his coat collar up in a half-hearted attempt to shield himself from the downpour, strode through the gloom of the estate to the Galvins' front door, and knocked.

Anne opened it, clutching a bloodstained hanky. The harness for the bellows from a set of uilleann pipes was strapped around her waist and right arm. "Come on in out of that, sir." She stood aside, closed the door behind Barry, and took his wet Burberry and paddy hat. "We'll go into the parlour."

Barry crossed the linoleum-floored hall after her.

She sat on the sofa of the old maroon three-piece suite and coughed. It was a dry, hacking sound that Barry could almost feel in his own chest.

"Poor Anne," Barry said. "I'm so sorry you're not so good." He crossed the floor to stand by her side. He noticed the rest of her uilleann pipes—bag, regulators, and chanter—on the sofa beside her. "Can you tell me what happened?"

She coughed again, holding the hanky to her mouth. "I had the house til myself. The housework was done and I was having a wee practice. I was in the middle of a reel, 'Rakish Paddy,' when I had til cough. I've been doing more of it since I quit the smokes." She looked up at him and he saw the fear in her pale blue eyes as she offered him her hanky. "I brung up this."

The linen was soaked with what must have been scarlet blood. It was now turning brown. This was no bronchitis, not the simple irritation O'Reilly had suspected. Anne Galvin had bled into her lung, and her recent X-ray had ruled out one probable cause, active pulmonary TB. In Barry's mind, there was only one other possible diagnosis.

"Is it bad?" Anne said.

"I honestly don't know," Barry said, realizing that while it was the truth, he lacked the facilities to get the answers he so badly wanted in that moment. "I can't do much here and I'd only be going through the motions examining you, Anne. Honestly. I want to get you specialist help. The consultant will want to examine you himself."

"If you say so. I trust you, sir."

Barry wondered why she still did after he had clearly missed her diagnosis. "I'm going to phone Kinky. Let her know I'm taking you to the Royal so Doctor Stevenson can take over in Ballybucklebo for me this afternoon. I'll get Kinky to talk to the chest doctor's secretary. It can take a while to get through, so we can get going straightaway. Can you pack a wee bag? Toothbrush, hair brush, nightie. You know the sort of things you'll need."

She stood and took off the pipes' bellows. "So I'm going til have to stay in?" She sighed. "But surely it can't be that serious?"

We all do it, Barry thought. Try to deny potentially bad news. He inhaled. This was not the time for comforting prevarication.

She frowned and spoke more softly. "Can it?"

"Anne," he said, and looked into her eyes, "I honestly don't know for sure"—he steeled himself for what must come next—"but I am worried."

She caught her breath, took a step back, and tossed the bellows onto the sofa. "I'll go and get my things, sir, and let Myrtle, her that lives next door, know so she can tell Guffer what's happening. Poor man, he'll go spare if he gets home and I'm not here."

"What time does he get back from the shipyard?"

"Six."

"I'll try to be here then to explain."

Her tears started. "That's very kind. He'll appreciate that." She coughed and sobbed. Her voice broke as she said, "And if it is bad, how are him and me going til tell our boys? I can phone Pat in Dublin, but Seamus . . ." another shuddering sob, "Seamus is far, far away." She looked at Barry with pleading in her eyes. "I thought if I saved up all

An Irish Country Practice   255

the money I was not spending on smokes anymore, never mind new curtains, I'd have enough in a few years til help him with a plane ticket, but
och . . ." She wiped her nose on her sleeve. "I may never see him again
now. I know it. I just know it." She was begging to be told she was wrong.

And Doctor Barry Laverty, for all his training, for all his wish to comfort Anne Galvin, could not in all honesty contradict her. All he could
do was hold her as the tears flowed and her body shook.

"That wasn't too bad, was it, Anne?" Barry asked. He was guiding Anne
Galvin along with a hand under her elbow and holding in his other hand
an envelope containing her chest X-ray films. They left the department
of radiology and walked along the main corridor. Mister Bingham's secretary earlier had been most helpful when they arrived. Barry had been
instructed to take Anne directly for an X-ray, then to ward 16 where
she'd be seen by a senior registrar who was training to be a thoracic
surgeon.

"No, sir." She managed a tiny smile. "But I think they keep the bit of
the X-ray machine in the fridge that they put fornenst your skin."

Barry thought back to his student days. That had been the complaint
then too. And about certain gynaecological instruments. One nurse had
put woolly oven mitts over the stainless steel stirrups where women were
expected to put their bare feet. He glanced round. The Royal Victoria
Hospital seemed ageless. Changeless. Same smells of disinfectant and
floor polish. Same bustle of nurses and medical students in their bum-
freezer white jackets, their heels clacking on the marble floor. Porters,
cleaners, and patients' relatives filling the long, echoing main corridor
where the blue plastic double doors of the twenty wards slapped each
time they closed.

He stuck his head into the nurses' station. A corridor ran between
the paired male and female wards, 15 and 16. A long desk behind a glass
partition stretched the entire width of the unit, giving a panoramic view
along the length of the ward to high French windows at the far end. More
light was admitted by a series of skylights. Twenty-four full beds were

lined up in two rows facing each other across a central open area. A single bed was at the end of the ward in front of the French windows. Women, some sitting up in bed jackets, others either sleeping or sedated, filled each bed. Many of the patients had intravenous drips running. Tables bearing vases of cut flowers stood along the central space. Several beds were screened by closed curtains on overhead rails. Staff, student nurses, and medical students went about their duties. Snoring and moaning rose above the muted sounds of the staffs' voices.

The ward's senior sister, recognisable by her dark red dress beneath a white apron, sat at the desk writing in a chart. Unusual. Nurses hardly, if ever, sat down when on duty. She looked up. "Barry," she said, "we are expecting you. Mister Bingham's secretary phoned. Is this Mrs. Galvin?"

Barry nodded. "Hi, Betty." Betty Adair had been a junior sister three years ago when Barry had been a houseman here. "Anne, this is Sister Adair."

"Pleased til meet you, Sister."

"Doctor Laverty, will you please take Mrs. Galvin into the side ward?" She was formal now. "I'll bleep Mister Strachan. He'll be looking after your Mrs. Galvin on behalf of Mister Bingham. You can give Mister Strachan the X-rays."

"Thank you, Sister," Barry said.

"One of my nurses will be along to do the admitting paperwork, and I'd like you to put on a nightie, dear, and get into bed."

"Yes, Sister."

In a short time, Anne Galvin's chart held the required information—name, age, address, phone number, next of kin, religion—and the bed in the single-bedded side ward, usually reserved for patients who needed to be isolated, held Anne Galvin.

Barry sat on a plain chair beside the bed.

The door opened and Alan Strachan came in. "Doctor Laverty," he said, and smiled.

"Mister Strachan," Barry said. If Anne had not been there, it would have been "Alan" and "Barry." They had worked together in 1964 when Alan had been halfway through his general surgical training. He had passed those exams and now was specialising further. "This is Mrs. Galvin and here are"—Barry handed over the envelope—"today's X-rays and the ones taken on the twenty-fifth of last month."

"Thank you." He set the envelope on the end of the bed.

Barry listened and watched as his friend took a detailed history and carried out a thorough physical examination, including much work with a stethoscope all over her chest. He paid particular attention to the hollows above her collarbones. Barry knew he was looking for enlargement of the scalene lymph nodes, a common site of metastasis, or spread, of lung cancer.

"Right, Mrs. Galvin," said Mister Strachan. "Doctor Laverty and I are going to look at your pictures."

"Thank you, sir," she said. The look she gave Barry would have melted tungsten steel.

"I'll come back and explain to you soon, Anne," he said, dreading what he was pretty sure he was going to have to tell her. He followed Alan out and into the adjacent ward office where the surgeon had already switched on a wall-mounted viewing box. He slipped the plates side by side under the retaining clips with practised ease. "There's sweet FA in her history except for the recent bleed and I can find nothing else by examining her. No abnormal chest sounds. No consolidation, no finger clubbing when the fingertips are thickened in severe pulmonary disease. Not a sausage," Alan said, then scrutinised both X-rays over and over, making a series of noncommittal grunts. He stepped back. Shook his head. "I'll be damned. Take a gander at that, Barry." He stepped off to one side so Barry could get a good look.

"See. The first plate seems to be clear as a bell. Emphysema. Healed TB. What Teddy reported was gold in the bank. You and Doctor O'Reilly have nothing to feel sorry about. That X-ray showed nothing amiss. Then this. Look." He pointed with his index finger at the recent film.

Barry leant forward. He had no difficulty recognising structures in varying shades of grey: the clavicles at the top, the spine running from top to bottom, the curved ribs encasing the chest cavity, and off to the left the great triangular shadow of the heart. The ringed cartilages of the central trachea, the windpipe, ran down into the chest before diving into the right and left main stem bronchi, each of which in turn branched into a veritable tree descending and ascending into the tissues of the lungs.

"See?" Alan said. "That small blurry darkness on the wall sticking into the inside of the first right upper lobe bronchus just after the main division? That little dark devil is what's bleeding."

Barry stared at the thing. "Cancer?" he asked, thinking about the Greek word *karkinos,* the crab, because as they spread through the tissues, some cancers looked like crabs' claws. "Are you certain?" He knew that, like Anne earlier, he was grasping at straws, hoping beyond hope that his friend was wrong.

"No, I'm not certain," said Alan, "but we're going to have to be sure one way or the other. I'll schedule a bronchoscopy and biopsy as soon as I can get her into the operating theatre."

Barry felt his shoulders slump. "Alan, how the hell could that thing blow up so quickly? Bad chest thirty days ago. Recurrence but clear X-ray last week. Cancers don't develop that fast from nothing, do they?"

Alan shook his head. "No, they don't. It'll have been growing for years. But from her history, the first really solid clue was her frank bleeding today."

Barry felt some shame that, despite his deep concern for Anne, he could still feel relief that he was not responsible for getting the diagnosis wrong at first.

"And X-rays are not infallible. The first one failed to pick the lesion up." He peered at it again. "It's a small one. It may be curable."

Barry knew his friend was offering words of comfort. Lung cancer, particularly in a woman so relatively young, was nearly universally lethal. "Thanks, Alan." Barry stepped back from the box. "If you don't mind, I'll go and break the news. It may be a little easier coming from me."

Alan clapped Barry's shoulder. "I'm truly sorry, Barry. Will you be home this evening?"

"After seven. I've promised to talk to her husband at six." He could feel his stomach flip over at the thought of telling Guffer Galvin what had happened today.

"I'll phone. Let you know when the bronchoscopy's on. Your mate Harry Sloan, the pathologist, has developed a special interest in lung cancers. I'll get him to read the slides. That's the best opinion you'll get in Ulster. We'll get on to you with the results as soon as possible."

"I'd appreciate that, Alan. Very much." Barry headed for the door. "If you'll excuse me?"

Anne Galvin was sitting up in bed. "It's not good news, is it, sir?" Her hands, which lay palm down on the blanket, were trembling.

Barry sat on the bed beside her and took her right hand in both of his. It was clammy. "We don't know for sure, and Mister Strachan's the expert. The X-ray shows a wee spot on your right lung . . ."

Her eyes widened and her left hand flew to her mouth.

"Mister Strachan needs to do another test called a bronchoscopy. They'll put you to sleep . . ." He regretted the expression, a euphemism for putting a sick animal down, but he ploughed on, "And slip a narrow tube into your windpipe. They'll take a specimen."

"Excuse me, sir, is that what's called a biopsy? I use til watch *Doctor Kildare* on BBC until they took the programme off last year."

"That's right, and we'll not know for sure what's wrong until we get the results." He squeezed her hand. "Mister Strachan and I have worked together in the past, Anne. He's going to get things going as quickly as possible. I'll see Guffer tonight."

"And tell him not til worry too much. Please, sir." She stared through to his soul. "I'll tell him and the boys all in good time."

Barry was struck with admiration for Anne Galvin's courage, but also recognised that it was going to take time for the probable gravity of her condition to sink in.

"It's like Mister Robinson the minister tells us," she said. "We're til hope for the best, but get ready for the worst." She nodded to herself. "Now, sir. Thank you very, very much. You've been dead on bringing me here, and all. Run you away on. And don't you worry your head about me." She picked up a Mills & Boon romance from the top of the bedside locker, and Barry was certain she was sparing his feelings by pretending to read.

"I'll be in touch," he said, releasing her hand and standing.

It wasn't until the door had been closed behind him that he heard the muffled sounds of a woman in tears.

30

Dusty Purlieus of the Law

Lars O'Reilly opened the door of his big grey house on the shores of Strangford Lough and shook his brother's hand. "Finn," he said, and then hugged Kitty. "Lovely to see you both. Come in. Come in." He ushered them into the spacious hall and took them through to his lounge, which counted among its decorations a turbulent skyscape that Ma had painted back in Dublin in 1936, the year the boys' father, Professor O'Reilly, had died of leukaemia.

O'Reilly thought his brother was starting to show his sixty years. Greying hair. A slight stoop. His neat moustache, which had been dark, was turning pepper and salt. And there was no spring in the man's step.

"Sit down. Sit down. What can I get you?" he asked.

"G and T, please," Kitty said.

"Neat Jameson, Finn?"

"Please."

O'Reilly and Kitty sat beside each other in two of four armchairs arranged around a large fireplace. A single purple orchid sat in a small Waterford vase on the mantel. The seating was arranged in such a way that three seats gave panoramic views over Lars's garden, dominated by a huge horse chestnut tree decked with white candle flowers. A window cleaner was washing the glass of the large greenhouse where Lars cultivated his orchids. Out on the Narrows in their strong tidal current, the little ferry crabbed across to Portaferry from Strangford Town.

To O'Reilly's right lay the 820-acre Castleward Estate, originally

Carrick na Sheannagh and home of the Earls of Kildare. It had been
the seat of the Ward family since 1570 almost to the present day.
O'Reilly never ceased to marvel at the comforting sense of perma-
nence such places gave to his country. The estate's trees were verdant
with fresh spring leaves and trimmed lawns ran down to the lough's far
shore. A window was open and O'Reilly, even at that distance, heard
borne on a northwesterly breeze the harsh cry of a cock pheasant. A
syndicate led by a Mister W. J. McCoubrey of Ballynahinch rented the
shooting rights from the new owners, the National Trust.

Lars gave them their drinks and took another armchair. He raised his
glass. "Welcome to Portaferry."

"Cheers," O'Reilly and Kitty said in unison.

"Now, Finn," said Lars, "you sounded pretty frantic on the phone,
so apart from enquiring about Kenny—"

"Growing and learning fast," O'Reilly said. "Arthur Guinness and I
are training him."

"I'm glad to hear it. I'm going to dispense with the usual pleasantries, tell you I'm fine . . ."

Which O'Reilly doubted, considering Myrna and Lars had parted,
but they'd come to that later.

". . . and assume you are both well. But it must be said that, Kitty,
you are looking particularly lovely."

"Thank you, sir."

"Now, I'll get on with trying to answer your telephone query, Finn.
Both of you, please feel free to interrupt if you have questions." He managed a small smile. "Lawyers can be a bit dry sometimes."

O'Reilly chuckled and sipped his whiskey.

"In a nutshell, Finn, you believe a man is beating his wife?"

"I don't believe it anymore, I damn well know it," O'Reilly said. "After
I spoke to you on Monday I went back and she broke down and admitted it. Not that she had anything to be ashamed of. The unmitigated
bastard is beating the living daylights out of the poor woman, and I
want to try to understand what the law can do to protect her."

"I see. Do you think she'd go to the police? Lodge a complaint?"

Hester's words came back verbatim: "No, sir. This is to stay between you and me. I'll not shame myself and I'll not have Hubert shamed. Let us be. It's between a man and his wife." O'Reilly held up his hand. "No, I don't. I explained I'd have to tell my colleagues, and why. Kitty has been told. She is a colleague, and so are you, big brother, although I'd prefer that Hester doesn't know that."

"No reason why she should, Finn. I don't appear in court. I'm useless as a public speaker. She'd need a barrister in a criminal case anyway." He sipped his drink. "All I can do is advise you what the law says." He shook his head. "And that's precious little in this country. I'm afraid there are only three options. I'll explain." He took a mouthful and continued, "English common law, even before the rule of Charles II, allowed a husband to give his wife 'moderate correction,' but specifically forbade beatings. Historically, the U.S. was ahead of Britain in that. The Massachusetts Body of Liberties ruled in 1641 that 'Every married woman shall be free from bodily correction or stripes by her husband, unless it be in his own defence from her assault.' In 1878, under the Matrimonial Causes Act of the United Kingdom of Great Britain and Ireland, a woman could use wife beating as grounds for divorce."

O'Reilly shook his head. "That's not going to happen. You know how country folk feel about divorce."

Lars's smile was faint. "I'd starve if it was my only practice." Lars glanced at Kitty. "You look puzzled."

Kitty set her glass on a small round wine table on tripod feet. "What about the 'rule of thumb'? I thought a man could beat his wife with a stick, provided it was no thicker than his thumb."

Lars chuckled. "That canard arose because in 1782, James Gillray, the English satirist who succeeded Hogarth, published a cartoon lampooning a judge, Sir Francis Buller, for reputedly ruling that. But there's no written record of Sir Francis or any other judge making such a statement. Not one word."

Despite the seriousness of the matter, O'Reilly couldn't resist teasing Kitty. "Damn," he said with a grin. "I'll never get Kitty to behave now."

She smiled back. "This from a man who asked me to drop the word 'obey' from our wedding vows because, and I quote, 'No wife of mine is going to be subservient.' Sometimes, Fingal Flahertie O'Reilly, I don't think you trying to hide the fact that you are a pussycat under that fake carapace always works."

O'Reilly snorted. "There's nothing fake about my wanting to stop Hubert Doran in his tracks." He turned to his brother. "What else can you tell us, Lars?"

"You, or at least Hester, has three possible lines of defence. Two in civil and one in criminal court. She can apply for a nonmolestation order and, if necessary, an occupation order. The first is self-explanatory, the second means a judge can turn Mister Doran out of the family home. Order him to stay away from her. And she can even apply *ex parte* so the defendant does not have to be in court so she won't have to face him. He'll be notified in person by the RUC. That will only be a temporary measure until he can appear. It's used in emergencies. And depending on her personal income, she may be eligible for legal aid provided she'd be willing to initiate proceedings."

O'Reilly shook his head. "Fat chance."

"Theoretically she still has recourse to the criminal courts. Wives aren't specifically included, but the Offences Against the Person Act of 1861 is the foundation of all criminal prosecutions for anyone's personal injury short of homicide. To use that, she'd need to report it to the police. Show the police doctor her injuries. Bring witnesses if possible."

"That would be me and Doctor Nelson, but only if she'll go, there's the rub." O'Reilly frowned. "And that's it?"

Lars nodded. "'Fraid so. Sometimes I don't think our society, sorry Kitty, takes women too seriously. Do you know it's only thirty-eight years since the Privy Council, the highest legislative body in the British Empire, recognised five Canadian women as 'persons' in their own right and not mere chattels of their husbands?"

"Huh," said O'Reilly. "Pretty pathetic if you ask me." He inhaled deeply. "There should be more we can do, but I'm not exactly sure what. Somewhere women could go to be protected, maybe? Some kind of mandatory treatment for battering husbands? Laws explicitly dealing with wife beating." He stared at the floor, then said, "I suppose it's folks like you and me, Lars, who are to blame for the lack of facilities, special laws.

I certainly wasn't aware of wife beating in Ulster. It wasn't a subject covered at medical school."

"And I've just explained that what law there is, is pretty sketchy," Lars said.

"I don't want to start a battle between the sexes here," said Kitty, "but it is mostly men who sit in Parliament. Make the laws. I'm a traditionalist. I don't agree with everything she says, but there's that American woman Betty Friedan who published *The Feminine Mystique* in '63. She identified this great gap between the rights of men and women. We can't forget that it was only forty years ago in this country that all women were even allowed to vote. Mrs. Friedan, and more and more women like her, are beginning to agitate for better treatment. Equality."

"And," said Fingal, "I'll wager when they get it, there'll be a great deal more attention paid to wife beating. Better laws. More facilities. But for the moment, I'm powerless to use the law as it exists to help Hester unless she cooperates?"

"Certainly within the current legal framework," Lars said.

O'Reilly took a healthy swig, swallowed, frowned, and said, "There was an old RAF expression during the war, 'Bullshit baffles brains.' Is there no way I can scare him enough with some legal gobbledegook?"

Lars managed a tiny smile. "I don't know one, and what little I do know of the subject, even court orders to cease and desist are more often broken than not. From what you say, they're not likely to go to a marriage-guidance counsellor, and I wonder if that would even be of any use in cases like this. I know of colleagues who have obtained nonmolestation orders for their clients, the wife has moved back to her family, only to have the order ignored and the wife dragged, for want of a better word, 'home,' anyway."

"That really is appalling," Kitty said. "Poor Hester. Fingal, you've simply got to do something."

"Aye," said O'Reilly, shaking his shaggy head, "but what?" He took a thoughtful sip of his drink and turned to Lars. "Thank you. I'll have a word with her before Hubert gets back from Scotland, and if she won't talk to a lawyer or the police . . ."

"It seems," Lars said, "your efforts may all be for naught."

O'Reilly shrugged. For "naught"? His mouth opened. His eyes widened. A glimmer of an idea was taking shape. He looked out to the Narrows. He'd need to consult Connor on the most recent medical jurisprudence he would have learned in his forensic medicine lectures. The kind of stuff only doctors, not lawyers, would have to know. He'd say nothing, but there might just be a way to put the fear of God so deeply into Hubert Doran that he would behave—and go on behaving.

O'Reilly had finished his whiskey. He looked at Lars, down at the empty glass, and back to his brother.

Lars stood. "Sorry, Finn. Let me refill that." He did so and gave the glass back to O'Reilly, who said, "*Go raibh mile maith agat, deartháir,* and thanks for the legal advice." He hesitated, glanced at Kitty. "And you, Kitty, for a woman's perspective."

She inclined her head.

"Lars, there is one more thing, and you are perfectly free to tell Kitty and me to mind our own business, but we had dinner with John MacNeill and Myrna a week ago."

Lars sat heavily. "It's perfectly all right," he said. "I know I've been keeping you in the dark, Finn, but I didn't want to admit," he sighed deeply, "that Myrna and I are not seeing each other anymore. I don't think we will be. Not for some time."

"We are so sorry, Lars," Kitty said, and leant over and patted his knee. "Is there anything Fingal and I can do?"

Lars shook his head. "I don't really think so." He sipped his drink. "I was always awkward with women. I don't think I ever got over a girl called Jeannie Neely." He looked at O'Reilly as if asking him to continue the story.

"Kitty knows that you proposed to her on Christmas Eve 1933 and she turned you down."

"Said she couldn't bear to leave Dublin and live the life of the wife of a country solicitor," said Lars, staring into his drink.

"I do remember, Lars," Kitty said. "Miss Neely's father was a judge, wasn't he? I was walking out with Fingal then. He was very cut up about it too. He felt he should be doing more for you, but didn't know how."

"Finn did the only thing that could be done. He listened. Finn has always been there when I needed him," Lars said.

"And Lars for me," O'Reilly hastened to add. "It was Kitty and I who talked you into telling Myrna that you were worried she wouldn't want to be wooed by a commoner. I thought it took courage for you to approach her, not wanting to be rebuffed again. That was in February. Were we wrong?"

Lars sighed. "Not at all. I did think I was in love with her. I was over the moon when she said she had feelings for me. And we seemed to be able to work comfortably together when we were getting things organised about giving the estate to the National Trust once John's gone." He stared out the window.

"Fingal and I were very happy for you both," Kitty said. "We thought wedding bells were in the offing."

Lars inhaled. "I thought . . . well, I had hopes. We had our differences about my work for wildfowl preservation and her huntin', shootin', and fishin', but we agreed to disagree on that. We mostly had a wonderful two weeks in Villefranche, but every so often there'd be friction. Usually over trivial things. Like which restaurant to go to. I can't stand Italian cooking. She loves it. My musical tastes run to the classical. She thinks the Rolling Stones' 'Satisfaction' and the Hollies' 'Bus Stop,' of all things, are two of the greatest songs ever written. Things like that. And Myrna's never wrong—about anything. Anything. Ever." He glanced down at his highly polished brogues.

O'Reilly remembered her at Kirkistown a fortnight ago falling out with Lars about motorcars and whispering in Fingal's ear, "Sometimes, Fingal, I think your brother and I are more different than I originally believed."

"I can't remember who said it, but I once heard an adage that every partnership, and marriage is a partnership, has to have a sun and a moon. Myrna is a sun." Lars sucked in a very deep breath. "You remember the way it was with Father and Ma, Fingal? Father, very Victorian. Very much the head of the household. The paterfamilias. That's always been my idea of what a marriage should be like."

"Maybe." O'Reilly smiled. "I'm not so sure Father was the boss, even if Ma let him think he was. A very astute woman, Ma. But it seemed to work for them all right."

Lars managed a weak smile himself. "You and Kitty seem very happy together."

"We are," Kitty said, "even if I didn't have to promise to obey the old bear."

O'Reilly knew he was grinning like a mooncalf.

Lars's smile faded. "The trouble is, I've been a bachelor man all my life. I was worried that I might be a bit too set in my ways. The law is very precise. I am very precise and I, well, as much as I hate to admit it, I hate being wrong too." He looked directly at Kitty, then at O'Reilly. "It seems that I am set in my ways, and I want to be a sun too. And frankly, I'm too old to change." There was a tone of finality in Lars's last statement. "For the rest of the weekend after Kirkistown we seemed to be rowing over everything. We decided to call it quits, and Myrna not so much walked as stormed out."

"Blue blazes," said O'Reilly. This did not sound good at all.

"But," Kitty said in her most reasonable voice, "that was only twelve days ago. Is it not worth trying to talk it over? See if you can patch things up?"

Lars shook his head. "I'm no great believer in predestination, but somehow I feel I was never really cut out for marriage. You, Fingal, you love people."

And with a few exceptions like Hubert Doran, and Bertie Bishop before his recent reformation, O'Reilly knew it was true.

"You have to do what you do day and daily. I think you got that from Ma. Father, except for his family and tight circle of friends, preferred the world of his work, the great writers in the English language. I take after him. I like ferreting out obscure legal documents, pottering with my orchids, working for the Royal Society for the Preservation of Birds, the National Trust. I'm sorry I had to let Kenny go, but I don't miss him the way I miss old Barney. I think the single life suits me fine. And honestly, I don't seem to be missing Myrna as much as I had anticipated." He managed a smile. "I think I can face approaching old age with a certain amount of equanimity. Honestly."

O'Reilly glanced at Kitty. She was frowning. "Are you sure, Lars?"

"Pretty much," he said. "I think in a few more weeks, Myrna will have calmed down enough that we might still become friends, but I'm not in a rush."

O'Reilly shook his head. He was not as concerned for his brother as he had been when they walked in. How Lars controlled himself, O'Reilly did not know. He looked again at Kitty. Dear God, if he lost her he didn't know what he'd do. He said, "We don't want to interfere, do we, Kitty?"

She shook her head.

"We only wanted to see if we could help."

"And it's greatly appreciated. I've always known I could call on you both, and I still do. Thank you. Thank you very much."

O'Reilly, who had been nipping at his drink as Lars unburdened himself, finished it. He was aware of how much the atmosphere in the room had lightened. He noticed too, that his companions' glasses were empty. He rose. "I don't know about anyone else," he said, "but I'd not mind stretching my legs with a stroll along Lough Shore Road."

"Not by any chance in the direction of the Portaferry Arms?" Kitty asked.

"Mind reader," said O'Reilly, "and, Lars, I know you are feeling grateful—so I'll let you buy the drinks."

31

Patience Under Their Sufferings

"Good luck, Anne. You'll be going off to sleep soon." Barry stood by her side, gowned and masked, holding Anne Galvin's left hand. Alan Strachan had been true to his word. He'd managed to squeeze her in at the end of Thursday's operating list only two days after her admission on Tuesday. She lay under a blanket on the operating table gazing up at him, drowsy from the pethidine and atropine she'd been given as pre-medication. The narcotic would calm her, and the atropine would dry up secretions in her respiratory passage that might hinder the procedure. An intravenous drip of saline ran into a vein on the back of her right hand. Doctor Richard Clarke, the consultant anaesthetist, was inject-ing sodium pentothal into the drip's tubing.

Alan was wearing a tube-gauze surgical cap and was masked, gowned, and gloved, and the theatre sister, similarly clad, stood on the opposite side of the table's head. A rigid bronchoscope and long biopsy forceps lay on a sterile towel on a trolley at the head of the bed. The scope was attached by rubber hoses to the anaesthetic machine. It was too large to permit any other tubing in the trachea but would itself conduct the gases and oxygen.

"First bronchoscopy was in 1897, Barry," Alan said. "A German doctor, Gustav Killian, used one to remove a piece of pork bone from a patient's right bronchus. A British doctor, Negus was his name, im-proved on Killian's design and it's a Negus instrument I'll be using today."

Anne's eyes fluttered and closed.

"Right," said Doctor Clarke. He lifted a laryngoscope and deftly exposed her larynx. "Pop it in, Alan."

Barry inhaled the antiseptic odours of the operating theatre, listened to the rhythmic pumping of the bellows on the anaesthetic machine.

Alan Strachan, bending to put his eye to the eyepiece, guided the bronchoscope with its built-in lighting system into Anne's mouth. He gave a running commentary. "Vocal cords look good, I'm past them. Trachea. Nothing wrong there. I'm at the carina."

The ridge where the right and left main bronchi diverged, Barry thought.

"Looking to the right into the upper lobe bronchus . . ."

Barry held his breath.

"There's the little devil, Barry. Take a gander."

Barry exhaled and moved to beside Alan, who held the telescope steady. Barry bent and peered in. He could see two oval tubes, one going up into the upper right lobe of the lung. The tubes' walls were nacreous with a tingeing of pale pink. Little bubbles formed in the natural secretions and moved back and forth with the in-and-out flow of the anaesthetic mixture. A dark red craggy mass stood above the surface of the wall of the bronchus supplying the upper right lobe. "What do you reckon, Alan?"

"Sorry, Barry, but I don't like the look of it," Alan said. "We'll know in about twenty minutes once the biopsy has been done. Move over in the bed."

Barry stepped aside. Surgeons, he thought. All the same. Masking serious concerns with flippant remarks.

Sister gave Alan long biopsy forceps with jaws at one end and scissor grips at the handle. He slid them down the bronchoscope, manoeuvred his right hand, closed the grip, and withdrew the scope. "Here, Sister." He deposited the specimen in a specimen bottle Sister held for him. He stared down the scope. "Very little bleeding. Mission accomplished, I'd say."

"If you like, I'll take it across to pathology," Barry said. "I'd like to see Harry, and I'm anxious to hear his opinion."

"We'd be grateful," Alan said as he withdrew the bronchoscope and

Richard Clarke slipped in an endotracheal tube. Anne would be kept under a light anaesthetic. Mister Bingham, the consultant thoracic surgeon, had been happy enough for the trainee to do the bronchoscopy, but he was waiting in the surgeons' lounge so if the results were bad, an immediate removal of the entire right lung and all the lymph nodes in the centre of the chest could be performed. Cancer cells often spread by way of the lymphatic system. Barry shuddered. It was the kind of macabre figure that stuck in his mind: One in ten such patients did not survive the procedure. He accepted the specimen jar from Sister. "Thanks again, everybody," he said, heading for the changing room. He sighed as he took off his theatre clothes. Not long now until he had the answer, and he was sure he wasn't going to like it.

"Nyeh, how are you, Barry?" Harry Sloan, Barry's old classmate, now almost fully qualified as a pathologist, prefaced many of his sentences with that peculiar nasal noise. He looked up from a binocular microscope.

His room, third on the left in the department of pathology, always stank of stale cigarette smoke, which stifled the usual smells here of floor polish and formalin. A half-smoked fag smouldered in an ashtray. "I'm fine, Harry." Barry handed over the requisition form and specimen. "But I'm worried sick about the patient this came from."

Harry took the specimen. "Bronchial biopsy? Needs a frozen section. No problem. Alan Strachan told me about it." Harry stubbed out his smoke. "Make yourself at home. I'll only be a minute. I just need to pop this in the cryostat." Harry left.

Cryostat? Barry guessed it was the device that froze the specimen. He sat down. Looked around. Two tomes, each of a thousand-plus pages—Boyd's *Pathology* and Muir's *Pathology*—sat on a bookshelf surrounded by monographs and pathology journals. Harry's desk was cluttered with papers—and an ashtray full of butts. The last time Barry'd been in this office, he'd been trying desperately to get the results of the postmortem of a patient whom he'd misdiagnosed. The man had died and his widow had been threatening to sue. Harry, bless him, had speeded things up and Barry had been exonerated by the medical evidence.

Harry came back. "The technician will bring them in as soon as they're done. I'll read them." He took his seat and pulled out a packet of Capstan Full Strength cigarettes, looked at Barry, smiled, left the packet on the desktop, and said, "Given what we're hoping not to find, I think smoking might be a bit tactless."

Barry sighed. "The poor woman was on her way to having quit when she bled. I'm no preacher, Harry, but . . ." He let the sentence hang.

"Nyeh, you're dead on, Barry. And I will. One day. Honest."

Barry shook his head. Addicts were all the same. For a moment, he wondered how Ronald Fitzpatrick was doing. Certainly there had been no complaints on the two occasions in the last ten days when he'd been on call.

Barry and Harry passed the time in catching up. Harry was still single. His profession, he said, was not to every woman's tastes, and he lived in hope of meeting someone unfazed by the way he spent his days. He thought Jack Mills was probably in love at last, pronounced Helen Hewitt a right corker, and congratulated Barry on his engagement. Barry kept his present difficulties to himself but wished Monday would hurry up and come. When Harry asked about Sue, he answered briefly and then steered the conversation back to the biopsy. "I was never the world's greatest student of pathology. You read Boyd. I used the much shorter *Lecture Notes on Pathology*. I don't know much about frozen sections."

Harry sat back in his chair. "Nyeh, they're pretty useful for a case like yours, to help the surgeon decide to carry out more surgery under the same anaesthetic, particularly in an open case like an ovarian tumour. Spares the patient being closed up and then reoperated on. Takes about ten minutes to prepare the slides for examination. The regular method is much more accurate, of course, but takes sixteen hours. We only make a final diagnosis from the specimen from the excised organ. But if the frozen section is clearly malignant or clearly benign, that's practically always confirmed by the second examination. Borderline cases are more tricky. They're quite often wrong."

"I hope Anne's is clearly benign." Barry sat forward and, despite his concern, was interested in what his friend was saying. "I used frozen sections once in a while for ovarian tumour cases during my year in the Waveney Hospital in Ballymena. But I guess like most clinicians I'm not well up in the technical details. How long has it been around?"

"A Doctor Lois Wilson at the Mayo Clinic developed the technique in 1905. The key is the cryostat. We put the biopsy in the machine, freeze it to between minus twenty and thirty Celsius, embed it in a special gel, then a built-in microtome automatically cuts the tissue and gel into wafer-thin slices. Mount them on a microscope slide. Stain them, then the pathologist—that's me today—takes a look-see."

Barry smiled. "Takes me back to those pathology classes with John Henry Biggart. He'd project those blue-and-red microscope slides onto a screen. They all looked the same to me."

Harry laughed. "Nyeh, we're still using that haematoxylin and eosin dye."

There was a knock on the door.

"Come in."

A technician wearing a white coat entered. "Your slides, Doctor Sloan."

Harry took the box. "Thank you, Kearney." He pulled out a slide, set it on the stage of his microscope, and fiddled with the focussing wheel, muttering to himself.

Kearney left.

Barry reckoned he was feeling like the accused when the foreman of the jury stands to give his verdict. He held his breath.

Harry stood. He pursed his lips, shook his head. "I'm sorry, Barry. It's not good. Want to take a look?"

Barry exhaled and shook his head. Despite all his training, he couldn't bring himself to look at a piece of the thing that was putting Anne's life in jeopardy. "Just tell me, Harry."

"I'm afraid it's an undifferentiated oat cell tumour."

Barry's screwed his eyes shut. Inwardly he was screaming "No." He opened his eyes and looked at Harry. "I see. I thought they often secreted hormones, but Anne has no sign of any endocrine disorders."

"The ones with well-developed cells usually do, but this one has tiny, completely undeveloped cells."

"And as I remember they are the worst?" He could hear one of his teachers saying, "Do not get emotionally involved with your patients," but this on top of Lewis Miller's demise only nine days ago wrung his heart.

" 'Fraid so."

"I know it's only on TV that the doctor says, 'I'm sorry, you've only got six months to live.' That we can't be as accurate in real life, but—?" He took a very deep breath.

Harry put a hand on Barry's shoulder. "But we can guess. I'd say with one like this, she's got eight to eleven months. I'm sorry, Barry, I really am."

Barry's head drooped. Poor Anne, poor Guffer, and poor Pat and Seamus.

Harry said, "I need to get word to the theatre." He picked up the phone and dialled. "Theatre? Doctor Sloan. Please tell Mister Strachan it's an undifferentiated oat cell lung cancer. Thank you." He put the phone down. "I am sorry, Barry. We can't win them all. Don't blame yourself."

"Thanks, Harry. I'd best be running along."

"Good to see you, pal. If you'd like my advice, I'd pop into my local on the way home. Have a stiffener."

"Thanks, Harry. I might just do that." And as Barry left he decided he would take his old friend's advice.

Barry walked through the Duck's doors into its usual fug of smoke and alcohol fumes, friendly clinking of glasses, and buzz of conversation. Immediately, the tension in his shoulders relaxed a little. Dapper Frew was chatting to Gerry Shanks, but there was no sign of Donal Donnelly and not as many men as usual sat at tables or stood at the bar.

"Evening, Doc. Bout ye, Doctor Laverty."

Barry wasn't sure who'd spoken, but replied, "Evening, all."

"Hello, Barry." This from O'Reilly, who sat alone at a table near the door. Arthur Guinness and Kenny lay beside an empty dish that would have contained their Smithwick's, for which Kenny had now developed a taste. "Come and have a pew." He turned to Willie Dunleavy. "Pint for Doctor Laverty, please."

Barry sat. He didn't speak.

"Bad?" asked O'Reilly in a low voice.

Barry nodded and replied, also sotto voce, so as not to be overheard, "Couldn't be much worse. Undifferentiated oat cell."

"Bugger," said O'Reilly.

"She's having her right lung and mediastinal lymph nodes removed as we sit here," Barry said. "Sometimes I wonder what would be kinder. To slip away under anaesthesia or be granted a few more months of life?"

"Only twenty-five percent of those surviving the surgery are alive five years later," O'Reilly said, "and I know the average is much lower for oat cell."

"Much," said Barry. He looked up. "Thank you, Willie."

Willie set a pint before Barry.

O'Reilly paid.

"I don't feel much like saying cheers," Barry said, and stared at his pint.

"Just sup it, son," O'Reilly said, and Barry heard the compassion in the big man's voice. He took a pull and put the glass down. The stout was bitter. "I'll just have the one," Barry said. "I'm going to nip round and break the news to her husband. He's usually home by six so I'll be late for tea."

O'Reilly shook his head. "No need. I know he's going straight from the shipyard to the Royal during evening visiting hours. Gerry Shanks was in here earlier. He told me. The staff on duty will give Guffer the news."

"Well, at least I'll phone the ward and see how she is. Set my own mind a bit at rest," Barry said. "Poor Anne. Her big concern is getting her son Seamus home for a visit."

O'Reilly took a deep swallow. "It's a brave way from Palm Desert. It won't be cheap."

Barry was aware that someone was standing by their table. He looked up.

Bertie Bishop said, "I don't want til intrude, like, but could I have a wee word?"

Barry, still preoccupied with Anne, would rather the man would go away, but O'Reilly said, "Have a pew, Bertie."

Bertie lowered his bulk into a chair. "I just want til let youse know that the Folk Museum is going til use Bishop Contracting til move them cottages. We'll start next Monday and I've just heard too, that all the permissions will be in place for the road building to start on Tuesday, June the sixth. Earliest the museum can let us in. The lads is going til be very pleased, so they are." He looked round. "None of them's in tonight. I'd hoped til pass the word, but my office'll send out letters in the morning."

"I'm pleased too, Bertie," O'Reilly said.

Barry forced a smile and nodded. "That," he said, "is very good news. For everyone. They'll all be relieved to know the money's going to be coming in again."

"Aye," said Bertie, "and not just my lads. Willie's take'll go up and it'll be the same for the rest of the shopkeepers."

Those words got Barry thinking.

"This," said O'Reilly, whose glass was empty, "calls for a pint. You'll have one, Bertie?"

"Please, but my shout," Bertie said. "Doctor Laverty, will I put one in the stable for you?"

Barry shook his head. "Kind of you to offer, but not tonight, thanks." He hesitated then said, "May I ask you a question, Mister Bishop?"

"Aye, certainly."

Willie brought the pints and Bertie paid.

Barry had time to wonder, should I not discuss my idea with Fingal first, but decided no.

"Cheers," said O'Reilly, and drank.

"Good health," said Bertie. He was still grand master of the local Orange Lodge and saying *sláinte* in Irish would be anathema to him. "Now, Doctor Laverty, your question?"

"Nearly the whole village and townland pitched in in February and March, signing the petition."

"That's right. My Flo and Alice Moloney organised it."

Barry glanced at O'Reilly, who was sitting with his head cocked to one side. Looking puzzled, Barry thought.

"I'm not breaching any patient confidentiality, but someone who lives in the village is very ill and needs money. Do you think Flo would be willing to organise a whip-round?"

"In the Liberties in Dublin," said O'Reilly, "they used to pass round a sugar sack in pubs to help pay for wakes."

Bertie nodded. "I could ask her, let you know, Doctor." He took a pull on his pint.

"Thank you," Barry said. "Thank you very much." He'd come in here feeling absolutely helpless, defeated, but now his spirits were lifted. He may be powerless to help Anne, but he could at least contribute in a small way to helping the rest of her family. He sat back and took a pull on his pint. The Guinness, it seemed, was somehow tasting less bitter.

32

Justice Is Truth in Action

Connor and O'Reilly watched the two dogs bound away over the springy grass of Hubert Doran's pasture, then share a companionable leak against a large erratic boulder that sat in the middle of the field. O'Reilly knew rocks such as these were thought by the locals to be the home to the Dubh Sidthe, the Doov Shee, or dark faeries. "I'm in a hurry to get to the Dorans', Connor, but I wanted to give the animals a chance to cock a leg first."

From a nearby beechwood, where the new-burst leaves were the pale lime colour of early spring, came the laughing call of a green woodpecker. Its name in old English was "speight," which also meant "to despise." The bird had been the emblem of his ship, HMS *Warspite*.

"Come," he called sharply, and both dogs raced back. "Good," he said, "now, in you get." He closed the car door behind them as a movement overhead caught his eye. A huge hooded crow flapped past, giving a series of harsh caws. He had enjoyed the few moments of pastoral peace, but now he and Connor must go and confront a violent man and hope to God he could be stopped.

Little was said until O'Reilly parked in the Dorans' farmyard. "He shouldn't be home for a while. We've plenty of time to see Hester on her own first."

O'Reilly knocked on the farm door, looked over to see Doran's golden retriever cowering in a kennel near the house, then back to the door. It was a typical one, split in the middle so the top half could be opened to see who was there without letting the chickens, which had the run of the yard, into the house.

Hester opened the top half and smiled. "Och, it's yourself, Doctor O'Reilly." She squinted at Connor. "And Doctor Nelson?" Her smile vanished and the lower half of the door remained shut.

"Doctor Nelson has come up with a way to maybe help you." It wasn't entirely true, but there was no question the young man's more up-to-date knowledge had been helpful, and O'Reilly saw no reason not to improve Connor's standing with Hester Doran. "He is a very smart young man."

"I'm sure he is. All right," she sighed as she opened the bottom half of the door. "Come in, the pair of you."

She closed the door and they found themselves in a typical Ulster farm kitchen: red-tiled floor, plain wooden table surrounded by six chairs, a great black range against one whitewashed wall, a deep sink beneath a window looking out over the farmyard to the outbuildings, a long sideboard on a third wall, and a door leading to the rest of the house in the fourth.

"Come and sit down," she said. "I was expecting you, sir, but not the young gentleman."

"Doctor Nelson is fully qualified, bound to keep anything about a patient in strict confidence, and knows a deal more about your kind of trouble than I do. He's here to help when Hubert comes home."

"Hubert?" she said, and her eyes widened. "Dear God, if he catches you here there's going to be hell to pay. Doctor O'Reilly, I'm all healed up, and my arm's near better." She held up her cast and wiggled her fingers to show him. "I think the two of youse should go away. Right now."

O'Reilly shook his head. "Hester," he said, "we really want to help you. Please let us try. Please?"

She sighed deeply, pulled out a chair from the table, and slumped into it. "I'll listen til what you have to say, but I think you and the young doctor should be on your way by the time I expect Hubert home at"—she glanced at the clock—"three thirty. That's twenty minutes from now."

"That's plenty of time. All I need to know is this: Are you still bound and determined to say nothing? The court can order him to stop, you know. Or you can press charges with the police. Doctor Nelson and I would be willing to bear witness to what we saw on Monday."

"I'm so tired," she said, burying her head in her arms on the tabletop. O'Reilly heard her gentle sobs. He moved to her. Put a hand on her shoulder. "Hester? It's all right."

She looked up at him. "Doctor dear, I know you're trying to help, but no. I'll say nothing til nobody but you, sir. Just leave it be. Please."

As she spoke, a car pulled into the farmyard. "Oh, dear God," she said. "It's him. He's early."

O'Reilly glanced at the door. "Hester, go you through to another room. Doctor Nelson and I need to talk to Hubert in private. And," he stepped up to her, put a hand on each of her shoulders, and looked into her eyes, "I'll not say a word about what we've discussed. As far as he's concerned, I'm just here to see my patient, that's all he need know about this. No one's going to get hurt and he's never going to hurt you again. Never. I promise." This time he was so confident of his plan he did not cross his fingers. "Now be quick, and we'll come and get you soon."

Hester left through the inner door without a word, closing it behind her.

The other door swung open. "I was dead lucky. Second off the ferry—" Hubert Doran stood just inside his kitchen, setting a suitcase on the tiled floor. A short man, sallow complexion, oiled black hair with a centre parting. "What in God's name are you doing here, O'Reilly, and where's my wife? I should have known it was you as soon as I saw the beat-up old Rover."

"Shut the door, Doran, and—"

"The hell I will," he shouted. "Not until you and whoever that man is are off my property. Youse are trespassing, so youse bloody well are."

"I don't think so, Hubert. Hester's my patient and I'm making a home visit to make sure she is recovering. She is, I'm happy to say, and she's in your sitting room. This, by the way," he inclined his head to Connor, "is my colleague, *Doctor* Nelson."

"I don't care if he's physician to the bloody queen." Spittle flecked the man's lips. His face was flushed and he clenched one fist, but thrust an outstretched finger in O'Reilly's direction. "If you've finished your visit, get out of here. This is my house and I'm not your patient. I see that Doctor Fitzpatrick. He's as odd as two left feet, but a decent enough doctor for all that. But I will never set foot in your surgery again after what you done til me, O'Reilly." He pointed at the open door. "Now get the hell out."

O'Reilly kept his voice level, low, and spoke slowly to Connor. "Mister Doran and I are not friends and," he turned back to Doran, "I've recently discovered that not only does he thrash golden retrievers, he beats his wife too."

Doran spluttered. His eyes bulged. "It was my dog, so it was. You had no right to interfere, and as for the other, I've no idea what the hell you're talking about." He folded his arms across his chest.

O'Reilly walked over, closed the door, and turned back to Hubert Doran. There was ice in O'Reilly's voice. "Not only did Hester not stand on a rake on Monday, you punched her. Later that day, Sonny went over to drop off some groceries for her, knowing you'd taken the car and gone to Scotland. Sonny found she was hurt, brought her to his house. Doctor Nelson and I happened to be there seeing another patient—"

"Dancing attendance on that Eileen Lindsay. Wee hussy couldn't even keep her man."

O'Reilly decided to ignore that remark. "Your wife was in pain. We examined her. We both saw the bruise. A fist had made it. We'd both take our oaths on that." O'Reilly let the unspoken threat of legal action sink in before saying, "You hit her. And not for the first time. I haven't asked him, but Doctor Barry Laverty can attest to her broken wrist and black eye that you gave her." O'Reilly strove to keep his voice level, to refrain from swearing, but inside he was boiling.

Hubert Doran sneered. "But you can't prove it. All you can do is give an opinion. That opinion would be open to 'reasonable doubt.' It'd never hold up in a court of law without witnesses. And Hester won't testify. She's too good a wife." His fist unclenched and he was no longer shouting.

"Who you reward by beating." O'Reilly shook his head and curled his lip.

"What happens between a man and his wife in their own home is

nobody's business but theirs, so away off and chase yourself, *Doctors*."
This last was sarcastic. "You don't frighten me. Not one toty-wee bit."

"Correct me if I'm wrong, Hubert Doran," O'Reilly said, "but I don't
remember saying anything about going to court."

Doran frowned. "Are youse not threatening me with legal action?"

"Not as you understand it," O'Reilly said. He hardened his voice,
moved over to stand very close to Hubert Doran, and towered over
him.

Doran backed away. Held up an arm in front of his face. "You lay a
finger on me, O'Reilly, and it'll be you in court for assault. I'm good at
getting people intil court. Your man Donal Donnelly found that out."

O'Reilly ignored the remark about Donal, but said, "I'd not dirty my
hands a second time. Doctor Nelson, will you please explain?"

"Mister Doran," Connor said, "doctors are t-trained in aspects of
medical jurisprudence—"

"What the hell's that? I know youse doctors think youse can bam-
boozle people. Well, you're not fooling me, so you're not."

"Medical jurisprudence," Connor said, "is the law as it is applied to
matters medical."

Doran's frown deepened. "I don't understand."

"But you know where and what the 'Burn' is in Belfast?" O'Reilly
asked.

"Purdysburn Hospital off the Saintfield Road? The loony bin? Aye.
What about it?" He cocked his head and slitted his eyes.

"I think a more respectful term," O'Reilly said, "is mental hospital,
but that's right. How would you like a holiday in there?"

Doran took another step back. "What are you talking about? You
need til be astray in the head til have til go in there, so you do."

"And you don't think beating up your wife is a sign of a mental disorder?"

Connor said, "The Mental Health Act of 1959 thinks so."

"What?" Doran's voice rose an octave. "What's he blethering on
about?"

"Under that act," O'Reilly said, "if, in the opinion of a policeman, or
if two doctors are of the opinion that an individual is at risk of injuring

themselves or another person—like Hester—the individual can be involuntarily committed to a mental institution on their say-so."

"I don't believe you."

O'Reilly pulled a folded form from his inside pocket and gave it to Doran. "You'll see that's headed 'For the Involuntary Commitment—'"

"I can read. It's got my name on it and youse two's signatures." His eyes widened. "Bejezzis, youse are serious."

"Never more so," O'Reilly said. "All I have to do is pick up a phone, call Purdysburn, and they'll send out an ambulance with two very large male psychiatric nurses who'll be quite happy to put you in a straitjacket if you try to fight them." He held out his hand. "May I have the form back, please."

Doran thrust it behind his back. "No. I won't. I won't give it back."

"All right," said O'Reilly with a smile. "Keep it to remind you." He produced an identical form from inside his jacket. "I have a spare."

"Oh, Jaysus." Hubert Doran tottered to the chair Hester had so recently vacated and sat, head in hands.

O'Reilly sat on a chair in front of the man. "Look at me, Hubert Doran. Look at me."

His head slowly rose.

O'Reilly stared at the crumpled face. "You can avoid a trip there, you know. It won't be hard."

"What happens between a man and his wife in their own home is their business." This time the words came out slurred by quiet sobs. "It's none of yours, O'Reilly."

"You've made it my business, Hugh Doran. Your wife's health and welfare is my concern. Now, what is it going to be? You can avoid a trip to the Burn. But you have to do what I say."

"What do I have to do?" The defiance was gone, his voice expressionless. He wiped his eyes and then looked at his hands.

"One. The beating will stop. Right now. I know men like you often promise not to, but we'll be watching you. Break that promise, even one small slip, and we'll use our form. Understand?"

The man grunted, but said nothing.

"Do you understand, Hubert?"

The words were muffled. "I do."

"I didn't quite hear you, Hubert."

"Yes, Doctor, I do."

"Two. I'm not your doctor, but I often take call for Doctor Fitzpatrick, who is. I will make an appointment for you at the psychoneurotic unit at Newtownards Hospital. They may be able to help you. I'm told sometimes calming medication and counselling helps. You will keep that appointment and any others or—"

Hubert Doran nodded. "Yes, Doctor." He fished out a hanky and blew his nose.

"Three. On Monday, you will go to your bank with Hester and change your existing accounts to joint accounts. At least if you do fall from grace, she'll be all right financially and can clear out if she needs to. I don't trust you, Doran. For the time being, I'll take Hester's word for it that it's done, but as soon as they are printed, I want to see a void cheque with both your names on it."

"Ah, Jaysus, all right."

"And four, from now on, you will remember that I am not 'O'Reilly' to you. I am Doctor O'Reilly. And as a doctor, you have my and Doctor Nelson's promise of confidentiality. Connor, would you go and get Mrs. Doran, please. She's next door."

Connor left and returned with Hester in tow.

"Please sit, Hester," O'Reilly said. "Your husband and I have been having a little chat. I explained that Doctor Nelson diagnosed a punch bruise. Hubert hasn't confessed directly, but since our little talk, he has promised to mend his ways, go for treatment, and change his existing accounts to joint accounts so you yourself'll have a few bob if you need them. I want you to phone Kinky and confirm it's been done. Isn't that right, Hubert?"

He looked at O'Reilly, Connor, and then to his wife. His face softened a little and then he looked away. "That's right, Doctor O'Reilly," Hubert Doran whispered, "and thank you, sir."

"Good," said O'Reilly. A thought struck him. Had he and Connor helped Hester enough that Kinky's money would have to be going to some other worthy cause? He wondered what that might be, then wondered if he and Connor were naïve to think they could leave now and trust Hubert Doran not to take what had just transpired out on Hester.

"Hester, are you going to be all right? Are you sure you don't want to come stay with the Houstons for a while?"

"I'll be all right, Doctor, thank you." Her voice was quiet but he thought he heard a new strength there.

"I'm delighted to hear it, Hester. Don't be afraid to call me any time you need me. And Hubert? Do go to Newtownards. They'll send me a letter when you've been, but follow up with Doctor Fitzpatrick." He turned to Connor. "Now, Doctor, I think we've done all that needs doing here, so we'll be off. Time to give the dogs a real run." He looked back at Hubert Doran and said, "I'm getting better at bringing them to heel."

By the way Hubert Doran flinched, the words had not been lost on him.

Nor was the look of compassion in the eyes of the man's wife lost on O'Reilly. As he closed the door behind him, words from an old Buddy Holly song ran in O'Reilly's head. "Love is strange."

33

The Prisoners of Addiction

O'Reilly hurried through the kitchen and knocked on the door to Barry's quarters.

"Come in." Barry was smiling as he took off a binocular jeweller's loupe mounted on a spectacle frame and put it on his worktable. An almost completely planked hull of the bluff-bowed HMS *Victory* was clamped to a modeller's vice. "Hello, Fingal. What brings you in here on a sunny Sunday morning?"

"Fitzpatrick."

"What now? He's not stocious on a Sunday, is he?"

"Nooo, I wouldn't say that," he said.

"Is he sick?"

"I'm not sure. Nonie's just off the phone. She's at his house. She says he's very upset. He won't tell her what it is, but he felt he couldn't go on seeing patients today. He's got her to take his call. She's staying at his house so phones ringing won't disturb us."

"That was decent of him. And at least," Barry said, "he had the nous to make sure the patients are getting looked after."

"Nonie says he's talking about feeling lost . . . at sea. Panicky. He needs a friend to talk to."

"So naturally you're going round to see him."

"No—we're going round to see him, if you don't mind. We're all in this. I want your opinion too. I want to get to the bottom of what the hell's got into him."

"I understand, Fingal," Barry said. "Of course. Let me get a jacket."

"Thanks, Barry." O'Reilly took a deep breath. "It sounds like that man needs our help. I'm not sure what for, but he's struggling."

Barry shrugged into a sports jacket.

"Come on then." O'Reilly headed for the back door. "We'll take my car."

"Later, pups," O'Reilly told Arthur Guinness and Kenny as they bounded across the grass.

O'Reilly let the Rover find its way down to the Kinnegar, like an old horse that has travelled a road many times, while he tried to anticipate what was the matter with Doctor Ronald Fitzpatrick. His home was in the middle of a long terrace of slate-roofed, pebble-dashed, two-storey houses and seemed to be like the man himself—a bit grey, a bit gangly. All the houses faced low front-garden walls and with nothing between them and Belfast Lough but the street and the seawall, they would have uninterrupted views of the Antrim Hills and the water with its ever-changing moods.

O'Reilly parked the Rover and, opening the garden gate, walked with Barry past a pocket-handkerchief lawn to the grey front door, which was offset to his left with a single sash window above and two large bow windows on each floor to his right.

He rang the bell.

An unshaven Ronald Fitzpatrick answered, wringing his hands as if he'd been waiting at the door. "Fingal. Thank you so much. And you've brought Barry. Good. Good. Please come in." He rushed inside as if ashamed to be seen with his colleagues and slammed the door. "Doctor Stevenson is making a home visit. I'm rather glad. I would prefer to see you both and no one else."

O'Reilly took in the bags under the man's bloodshot eyes, the frown lines on his narrow forehead, the gold-framed pince-nez perched on the bridge of his nose, and the repeated bobbing of his large Adam's apple. He held something like a rosary in his right hand. "I need help," he said. "Dear God, I need someone to talk to. I—"

"But not in the hall," O'Reilly said through pursed lips. He expected a colleague to have better self-control. He nearly said, "Pull yourself together, man." Only years of training restrained him.

"No. No. Of course not. Sorry. Sorry."

O'Reilly noticed long paper scrolls covered in oriental ideographs hanging on the wall. He peered at one.

Fitzpatrick tried, and failed, to smile. "I'm afraid my calligraphy's not very expert." His hands were trembling and his voice was shaky, but he seemed to be making an attempt to control himself. He opened a door to the right and ushered O'Reilly and Barry into a well-furnished living room. Several examples of the *netsuke* he collected were arranged on a mahogany mantel beneath a wall-hung pen-and-India-ink rendering of what O'Reilly assumed to be the Yang-Tse Gorges.

A musical instrument like a small grand piano sat in one corner. The varnished walnut lid was propped open.

Fitzpatrick must have seen O'Reilly looking at it. "My harpsichord," he said. "I'm particularly fond of the works of Byrd, Scarlatti, and J. S. Bach. I find their precision calming."

O'Reilly glanced at his long bony fingers and could imagine them flicking across the ivory keys as the strings were plucked. Another facet of this strange, shy man.

"I-I'm forgetting my manners," Fitzpatrick said. "Please sit down."

O'Reilly and Barry took armchairs as Ronald Fitzpatrick began to pace up and down. His voice cracked when he said, "I'm sorry to bother you, both, but I can't go on." A single tear trickled. "I just can't." His larynx jerked up and down. *Click.* He had moved a bead on his rosary.

O'Reilly was immediately sympathetic and regretted his initial irritation. He would treat Ronald as he would any upset patient. "Tell us what's bothering you, Ronald."

Fitzpatrick inhaled once, then said as if clinging to his last shred of self-respect, "I've kept one promise. I haven't touched a drop of drink, not one since that evening nearly two weeks ago. And I won't. Ever."

"Good man," Barry said.

Then it's got to be the gambling, thought O'Reilly, but he didn't want to ask leading questions. The man needed to spit it out without prompting.

"I told you I'd wrestled with another weakness years ago." He seemed to be having difficulty carrying on, but O'Reilly chose to wait.

Click. Another bead was moved along the string. "Fingal, you know I lost my parents in China when the Japanese invaded in 1931?"

"I do. It was hard for you."

"I didn't know, Ronald," Barry said, "but please accept my condolences."

"Thank you." Fitzpatrick nodded. "I found it extraordinarily difficult to find solace. I-I felt it had been my fault. They'd sent me to Dublin to an aunt so I could go to Trinity." He inhaled deeply. "I felt I'd abandoned them." He stared at his scuffed shoes, shoes that usually gleamed, and, O'Reilly noted, the man needed a haircut. "Although my parents were Christian missionaries, my growing up in the East led me to an interest in Buddhism. Even back then when I really didn't know much about it, some aspects could give me peace of mind." He stopped pacing. "If only I could have stayed with it." He stared into space; more tears trickled. He snatched out a hanky and dabbed his eyes, blew his nose.

O'Reilly waited, then prompted, "But?"

Ronald dropped into an armchair facing O'Reilly. "You remember Bob Beresford, Fingal?"

"A close friend when we were students," O'Reilly explained for Barry's benefit. "He died in Singapore during the Japanese occupation." O'Reilly missed him yet. "I remember him very well," he said.

"Bob loved going to the horse races. I was bored one day." He blew his nose again and managed a small smile. "You remember how unutterably dull social medicine was. Well, on a whim I cut class and went to Leopardstown with Bob, and God help me, I bet on a horse . . . and it won." His eyes lit up. "I'd never known such excitement. Never. I bet again. And won again. It was wonderful. Wonderful. All that afternoon, all I could think of was my next bet, and the intense elation that I'd experienced lasted well into that night. I felt happy for the first time in years. From then on I found I couldn't stop going to the horses. The dog racing." Ronald Fitzpatrick stared out the window, but O'Reilly could tell that the man wasn't seeing the view.

"But, Ronald, you told me you"—an American phrase from a movie came into O'Reilly's head—"kicked the habit back then."

Ronald Fitzpatrick nodded. "I did. I did." He hung his head and inhaled deeply. "Until recently. Now it's worse than ever, and nothing I do is working this time."

Barry said, "Why not?"

Ronald Fitzpatrick swallowed. "I don't know. I've been finding life very flat ever since my neck surgery last November." He sighed. "You'd think I'd be happy I came through it so well, thanks to you, Fingal. And yet, I can't seem to . . ." He shook his head. "I never, never should have bet on the Grand National last month. I've thought about nothing else ever since and I've been trying to increase my four thousand, four hundred and forty pounds. I don't need the money. God help me, I think I need the excitement." He closed his eyes and clicked three more beads before saying, "And now all I've done is lose money since. Then I feel terribly guilty about it. Going betting again comforts me for a while, takes away the guilt, but the feeling doesn't last. Sometimes, dear Lord, I've thought—I've thought of—That it's not worth going on." He shook his head violently. His face screwed up in pain.

"I'm trying to understand," O'Reilly said, "and it's not a medical condition that doctors can deal with, but I've seen enough gamblers lose their jobs, their families, everything they owned, and still not be able to quit."

Fitzpatrick's voice trembled. "I know. I know." Then he yelled, "Tell me something I don't know, O'Reilly."

"Steady, Ronald. Yelling at me isn't going to help."

"Neither is mouthing platitudes. I need help. I can't cope." The man's eyes moistened.

O'Reilly stifled his irritation. A man as disturbed as Ronald Fitzpatrick had to be given a fool's pardon if he lost control. "Barry?" O'Reilly said. "We've got to help Ronald. Any ideas?"

"I—" Barry took a surreptitious look at Ronald and then shook his head. "None, I'm afraid."

The lad looked taken aback by Ronald's outburst. This was not the Ronald Fitzpatrick Barry had known for these past two years. O'Reilly wondered what he could offer in the way of comfort. "I didn't tell you, Ronald, and I should have, how proud of you I felt when you told us you'd quit once before. Are you sure you can't again? All your friends in Ballybucklebo will help, you know."

Ronald Fitzpatrick shook his head from side to side. "I can't. I can't. Not on my own. I've tried."

"Then tell us exactly how you quit the last time? Maybe it could work again?"

Fitzpatrick closed his eyes. His lips moved silently. Every few seconds a bead would click and be shifted along the string. He opened his eyes, looked straight at O'Reilly, stopped moving the beads, and said, "I got my strength from the East by—" He lapsed into silence.

This was a critical moment. O'Reilly leant forward to show he was paying attention. "Please tell us how you got your strength."

"The Buddha, the awakened one, taught that his followers could end suffering by eliminating ignorance and perhaps, more importantly, cravings, by following his teachings." He looked to O'Reilly, who nodded encouragement. "I succeeded in eliminating my craving as a student and I recognized it for what it was this time and tried to use the same principles. Lord knows how I tried." He sniffed. "I've failed. I need help. I keep telling you, I can't do it on my own."

That remark about needing help pleased O'Reilly. If compulsive gambling was anything like alcoholism, the first step was for the victim to recognize they had a problem and needed help. "Whatever we can do, Ronald," he said, but he recognized that medicine had no answers.

Barry said, "There's an organization for drinkers called Alcoholics Anonymous. They support each other. It seems to work quite well for some people."

Fitzpatrick leapt from his chair and said with vehemence, "I am not a bloody alcoholic, you idiot."

Barry kept his voice calm. "I know you're not. I just wondered if there was a similar group for people who gamble."

O'Reilly admired Barry's self-control.

"In America," Fitzpatrick said, "but not here."

"Would you—" Barry said, "I know it sounds a bit daft, but would you consider going to America for help?"

"I—I've looked into it. I believe it might work for me, but . . ." He shook his head like a punched prizefighter. "Who'd look after my patients here?"

The pleading in his voice made O'Reilly think of a small child begging to be excused from a visit to the dentist.

Barry said, "You're willing to put your patients before your own needs?"

Fitzpatrick's reply was halfway between a snarl and a groan. "I don't have any choice, and how much help I am to them when I'm all at sixes and sevens myself I'm not sure, but what else can I do?"

"Bravo," O'Reilly said. "I'm proud of you, man, for recognizing that, and you're right. We have to get you back on your feet." He frowned, rubbed the web of his hand over his upper lip. "So, you were able to control the gambling as a student using Buddhism. Please tell Barry and me exactly how. And why not sit down."

Fitzpatrick lowered his lanky frame into a chair. He swallowed. "Very well. I'll try." He held up his rosary. "This is a Tibetan *mala*. We use it like a rosary. There are one hundred and eight beads. We use them to count our mantras. It's very soothing. These beads are made from the wood of a *bodhi* tree." By merely talking about his interest, Ronald Fitzpatrick seemed to be calming down. "I used to chant to myself in my rooms at Trinity every time I got the urge to gamble. It's a form of meditation. It worked." His face cracked. "But it's not working now."

He rose again and started pacing, clicking his beads with metronomic regularity. "I even built myself a shrine to try to get closer to the Buddha's teachings. Would you like to see it?"

O'Reilly looked at Barry, who nodded and said, "Please."

"Follow me." Fitzpatrick went up a flight of stairs to a small room. The smell of incense hung on the air. The walls were painted in a soothing light pink. A single sash window gave a view across Belfast Lough to the Antrim Hills and the Knockagh monument. There were no paintings. No furniture. A soft beige carpet covered the floor.

Fitzpatrick pointed to the far end of the room to a structure consisting of three wooden shelves arranged one above the other. Objects had been placed on each. Fitzpatrick explained, "The top shelf has a statue of the Buddha. No other images may be displayed higher. The second shelf has a little Budai . . ."

O'Reilly recognized a pot-bellied laughing figure similar to the one Ronald Fitzpatrick had presented to Fingal and Kitty.

"And three stones are arranged to resemble a *stūpa*, a kind of pagoda. The lowest shelf has offerings."

O'Reilly saw a small bowl of water, two sticks of incense, and some fresh flowers.

To O'Reilly's amazement, Fitzpatrick dropped to the floor and sat facing his shrine. The man's back was straight but relaxed; his long skinny legs were twisted into a pretzel shape, his right foot placed on his left thigh, left foot on right. Each hand lay palm up on his knee.

"This is the lotus position," Fitzpatrick said. "It was hard to learn at first, but now I find it very relaxing." He intoned, *"Om mani padme hum,"* and clicked a bead of his mala. As suddenly as he had assumed the position, the only word O'Reilly could think of to describe it was that Ronald Fitzpatrick had unwound. He stood, pince-nez askew, facing O'Reilly. "I just want you to try to understand."

O'Reilly's heart went out to this strange man. "Please go on, Ronald," he said.

Fitzpatrick adjusted his spectacles and said, "There are two main branches of Buddhism . . ."

I hope they're not at each other's throats like our two main branches of Christianity have been and could be again, O'Reilly thought.

"Theravada, which seeks Nirvana by following the eightfold path, and Mahayana, whose adherents seek enlightenment by the cycle of reincarnation. In the last few years I have been investigating another branch, Vajrayana, which is practiced in Tibet and Nepal." He smiled. "I do tend to run on," he said. "I don't want to be a bore, but—"

"No, no, I'm intrigued," O'Reilly said. "This is all new to me. Go on."

"Vajrayana puts a lot of stock in the Triple Gem: The Buddha himself, Dharma, which is teaching, and Sangha or community."

O'Reilly hesitated to interrupt, but he'd seen a glimmer of hope.

Barry must have seen it too. He asked, "Is there one in Ireland? A Buddhist community, I mean?"

Ronald shook his head. "Not that I've been able to find."

"Is there some way Kitty and Barry and I could make something like one for you?"

For the first time Ronald Fitzpatrick managed a smile. "That is very considerate, Fingal, and Kitty would be most welcome. There are Buddhist nuns, but I just don't see you, my friends, wearing saffron robes, turning prayer wheels, and chanting mantras to transform an impure body into a pure one."

The picture of himself with a shaved head amused O'Reilly, but he kept a straight face. "This may sound crazy, but you said you'd made enquiries about Gamblers Anonymous in America. Have you ever thought of going to a Buddhist community in the East for a while?"

Ronald Fitzpatrick said softly, "You mean join a community of lamas?"

"Yes, that's exactly what I mean. I'll bet you'd find it hard to locate turf accountants in—in Tibet, for example."

Barry began to laugh, but when he saw the look on Fitzpatrick's face, he turned to the shrine and began studying the statues there.

"Why, I wouldn't be able to gamble in a monastery, would I, and they could support me so I could work toward annihilating my craving." He sounded embarrassed, yet O'Reilly heard longing in the man's voice. "I believe that would work for me. In fact, I think it could be wonderful." His face crumpled. "But the question remains. Who'd look after my patients here? I can't abandon them."

O'Reilly reached out a hand to his friend's shoulder. "I think I may be starting to see a way to help you. Look." As he spoke he counted off points on his other hand. "One. You keep on gambling. Two. Practising Buddhism helped you once before . . ."

Fitzpatrick nodded.

"And three. The solitary efforts aren't working. You need the help of a community. But, the stumbling block is you're tied to your practice." He turned to his young partner. "Any ideas, Barry?"

"I do. A very simple one. Yours isn't the biggest practice in the world, Ronald. Fingal, I reckon if you and Nonie and Connor agree, we could cope for a while, but we'd have to ask them."

"I've no objection," O'Reilly said.

"Do you mean it?" Ronald Fitzpatrick's eyes moistened.

O'Reilly leant forward and now put both hands on Fitzpatrick's shoulders. "Yes, Ronald. We do. We want you to get better."

Fitzpatrick heaved a shuddering sob before saying in a low voice, "In all my fifty-nine years I've never had friends like you two. I don't know how to thank you." He offered a hand, which O'Reilly shook and, humbled by the man's sincerity, inclined his head.

"We'll ask the others first thing on Monday. Let you know."

"I've dreamed of going to visit the Haeinsa monastery in Seoul. They say it's one of the most beautiful of all the Buddhist monasteries, but I've also had some correspondence with the abbot of Tengboche Monastery in the Khumbu region of Nepal. As soon as you find out, Fingal, I'll write to him again."

"Tengboche? I've heard of that," said O'Reilly. "It's in Sherpa country. Near Mount Everest. Sir John Hunt had his base camp there for his 1953 expedition."

"And," Fitzpatrick said, "it has links to the mother monastery in Tibet where Tenzing Norgay, one of the first two men up Everest, was given his name. I'd have liked to go there, but Tibet's been part of Communist China since 1951."

"You've done your homework," O'Reilly said.

Ronald closed his eyes and clicked three more beads before saying, with the tiniest bit of pride mingled with enthusiasm in his voice, "I haven't lost all my money. I have some invested and I won't touch it, and I probably have enough left to fly to Nepal, spend six months to a year there if I lived very simply, make a donation to the lamas to defray their costs in having me, and fly home when I feel I'm ready."

"I'll be damned," said O'Reilly. "It takes a very big man, Ronald Fitzpatrick, to admit to his faults, and a bigger one to work on plans to overcome them."

"Thank you both. The Buddha said in the *Dhammapada,* 'Virtuous deeds are a shelter,' and may your shelters, Fingal and Barry, be strong. You are good men."

O'Reilly cleared his throat, tried not to blush, then said, "Thank you,

Ronald. We're only trying to help." And, he thought, perhaps there might be a way I could help more. "There's something else," he said. "I'll need to talk to a colleague in Belfast, but I see an even more efficient solution to running your practice." He looked at Ronald Fitzpatrick. "I think your practical problem here can be solved. I'm sure your way of beating your devils will be of great help too. Even getting it off your chest and explaining about Buddhism has made you look a lot calmer, my friend."

"Thank you both very much," Fitzpatrick said. "I am already feeling better."

"Good," said O'Reilly. He squeezed Fitzpatrick's hand, smiled, and said, "Now, would you like to come to us for dinner tonight? You could even sleep at Number One. I don't think we should be leaving you on your own."

"That's very generous, but I'd rather . . ." He lifted his *mala* and inclined his head to his shrine. To O'Reilly's surprise Ronald Fitzpatrick chuckled his rustling-dry-leaves laugh and said, "And you needn't worry about me tonight. It's Sunday and all the bookies are shut."

34

Reconciles Discordant Elements

Barry knew he was behaving like a sixteen-year-old on his first date. He had bathed after work, shaved for the second time today. He had out-grown the teenager's propensity for using Old Spice aftershave, but he had brushed his teeth before putting on his best, indeed his only, suit of charcoal-grey worsted over a clean white shirt. His Old Campbellian tie, black with two thin diagonal stripes of green and one of white, was done in a neat half-Windsor. Kinky herself had starched the collar.

"Someone looks like they're going courting," she had said as he left his quarters. "I thought, sir, you had already secured the young lady." She smiled a knowing smile and cocked her head, her double chins wagging. "Still, it never hurts to treat your *muirnín,* your darling girl. There'll be a dozen red roses waiting for you at the flower shop, I'll wager, so," she said.

"And you'd win, Kinky," he said, "and I'd better run on. The last thing I want to do is be late."

Now he was in Holywood after a nervous drive over and was glancing in the rearview mirror, straightening the knot of his tie and using his right hand to try to flatten the tuft in his fair hair. Barry took a deep breath, lifted from the passenger seat the dozen red roses Kinky had guessed about, and got out.

He inhaled, rehearsing again what he was going to say, but other words intruded. "Why anybody, anybody in their right mind, would have a brood of bloody rug rats is utterly beyond me."

He sighed and shook his head. They'd been long, these last sixteen days. When his mind wasn't occupied by his work he'd thought of precious little else but that one sentence and its aftermath. A tight-lipped Sue saying, "I love you, Barry, but I couldn't face a childless future."

Sue had kept her promise to phone today, Monday, and had suggested he come to her flat at six. Now it was two minutes to six, make-or-break time. He stood on the pavement plucking up his courage, steeling himself for possible disappointment. God, it was like staring at an envelope containing dreaded examination results. The outcome was preordained, but as long as the envelope remained sealed he wouldn't know if he had failed.

As soon as he'd rung her front doorbell, he could hear Max, Sue's lunatic springer spaniel, barking furiously. Barry raised the roses above his head and dropped his left hand in front of his crotch. He didn't want a repeat of his last visit here. Max had damn nearly gelded him. Tonight was no time for slapstick comedy.

The door opened.

Dear God, but she was beautiful, and—and she smiled when he gave her the roses. How he had missed that smile.

"How lovely. Thank you. Come in, Barry. I've locked Max in the kitchen." She pecked his cheek as he passed her. "We'll go into the sitting room."

She wore no perfume. No makeup. But her burnished hair was freshly washed and loose around her shoulders. In the sitting room, a table was piled high with exercise books and papers headed "Northern Ireland Civil Rights Association." That was definitely not a topic for discussion tonight.

She indicated an armchair, not the sofa they usually sat on side by side. "Would you like a drink?"

Dutch courage? He shook his head. "No, thank you." He waited until she had laid the roses on her desk. Clearly this wasn't going to take long, because Sue was usually concerned about getting cut flowers into water. She took an armchair opposite and Barry heard a rustling of nylon as she crossed her shapely legs. She wore flat heels.

"You—you went home last weekend. How's your father coming along?"

"He's doing well. Able to get about a bit more every day. He's doing light chores on the farm now."

"I'm pleased to hear it."

"Sometimes I can't quite believe he had a heart attack in February. So much has happened since then." Sue's voice trailed off and she looked down at her shoes. Barry glanced down at his own highly polished brogues. Inside he was screaming, "Tell her you love her, you fool," but he couldn't bring himself to move the conversation toward more serious topics.

"Did you ride Róisín?" He could hear the sound of Sue's little Irish Sports horse cropping the grass as he and Sue had made love in a bluebell wood.

"We had a nice canter along the banks of the Braid, thank you." She sat back. "And how are you getting on, Barry?"

Breaking my heart for you, he thought, but said, "Pretty well. Jack and I went sailing a couple of weeks ago." He grimaced and pointed to his chest. "I cracked a rib."

Her hand flew to her mouth. "I'm so very sorry. Does it hurt much?"

He shook his head. So much for Jack's suggestion of using the "old wounded soldier" ploy.

"I'm glad." And she did sound as if she was.

Barry had once read that in many cultures before serious business was discussed there was always a long ritual of exchanging general and usually meaningless pleasantries. At the time he'd thought how foolish it was, but here they were doing the same thing.

The silence was starting to lengthen.

"I . . ." he said.

"I . . ." she said.

They both smiled.

Her smile, he thought, had broken the ice. "Sue, I've been doing a lot of thinking. A lot. You called it soul-searching. And I've been missing you—a lot."

"Me too," she said quietly. She leant forward. "Please tell me, Barry, what have you decided?"

He swallowed and held her gaze with his. His voice was steady.

"Sue, I love you from the deepest part of my soul. I don't want to get divorced."

She frowned, inclined her head, then a slow smile spread. "I remember. You said, when we were alone in the farmhouse the day after Dad had his heart attack. You said that after our night together in Marseille you felt completely married anyway and it will be ' 'til death do us part,' ceremony or no ceremony." She inhaled. "Barry, Barry I love you. I feel married too. I know what you mean, but . . ." Her eyes glistened. "But, I'm sorry. I don't think it's enough." The tears trickled, sparkled in the sun's rays. "I do want children. I know you're uncertain . . ."

Like a court of law, it had to be the truth, the whole truth, and nothing but . . . "I still am, Sue . . ."

She hung her head. Her in-drawing of breath was as sharp as a razor cut, her voice hushed as she whispered, "No. No."

Barry ploughed on, discarding all his thoughtfully prepared arguments. "But, I remembered what you said about a little boy by the Braid being taught to fish by his daddy . . ."

Sue began to raise her head.

"I broke my promise to keep quiet. I cried on Jack's shoulder. I'm sorry. Old Don Juan really surprised me. He said he thought there'd be a great deal of satisfaction seeing your offspring take their first steps, speak their first words."

She dashed her hand across her eyes. "Yes, there would be."

"He knows I enjoyed teaching junior students. He thinks I'd get a kick out of watching kiddies playing sports. Teaching them to sail, fish, swim. Watch them do well at school, learning how to play the bagpipes in the school band . . ."

Sue managed a weak giggle. "I'm not so sure of that last one, but he's right, Barry. Jack's right."

Barry stood. "You know Fingal's been my father confessor since I came here in 1964?"

She nodded.

"I asked his advice too."

"That's all right," she said.

"He told me that he'd had a conversation with his first wife just after they were married about starting a family. It was in 1940 when it looked like Britain might lose the war. He hadn't been keen on the idea. She'd had to talk him round."

Sue shook her head. "Barry, I wouldn't want to do that. I couldn't. It's got to be your decision. Nobody else's."

He loved her for that. He moved to stand in front of her, put his hand under her chin so she had to look up. "Fingal said he regretted to this day he never had children." Barry swallowed recalling why that was. Poor Fingal. It was not something Barry was going to tell Sue. He squatted in front of her. "Neither one of my friends told me what to do. It is my decision." He took one of her hands in both of his. "Sue Nolan, you told me you were a country girl and that you'd be proud to be a country doctor's wife and mother of his children. Mother of his children. Our children. Will you, darling? Please? I want you to. Very much. I promise."

Together they stood, arms round one another. He inhaled the scent of her copper hair, kissed the last tears from her eyes, tasted her lips, and when their kiss broke she said, "I will, darling. I will."

And despite the gnawing ache in his rib brought on by her loving hug, Barry Laverty's smile was as broad as that of his bride-to-be.

Their lovemaking was tender and gentle and all Barry wanted to do after was hold her and never let her go. And he would have too, if that bloody Max hadn't started howling.

"That was a great meal, Sue," Barry said, pushing aside his empty plate. "Really great." After Sue had thrown on a dressing gown and gone to quieten her imbecilic dog, Barry had lain on his back thanking his lucky stars, drowsily sated, deeply in love. Then he'd arisen, dressed, and combed his hair. The face looking back at him from the mirror could only be described by one word. Elated. He'd not bothered putting on his tie.

He'd gone through to the kitchen and, useless cook that he was, his sole help with preparation of dinner—prawn cocktails followed by beef stew with suet dumplings—had been to uncork a bottle of Châteauneuf-du-Pape.

He sipped from his glass, savoured its fruity richness, inhaled the fragrance of the roses which Sue had put in a vase in the middle of the kitchen table, and drank in the loveliness of her sitting across from him, still in her tartan dressing gown and fluffy slippers. Her copper mane hung around her shoulders. "Thank you, darling, for loving me." He stretched out a hand and took hers on the white tablecloth.

"I do," she said. "Very much." She grinned at him. "And I'll be happy to say 'I do' in the First Broughshane Presbyterian Church on July the seventh. It's only nine weeks away." She squeezed his hand. "And then off to Villefranche. Fingal's brother's a pet letting us have his place for our honeymoon."

Barry laughed. "And you'll be able to speak with the natives. I can just see us. Breakfast. Coffee and a fresh crusty loaf . . ."

"Café au lait et une baguette," she said, "unless you'd prefer *un croissant.*"

"Anything with you, pet, would be heaven." He let go of her hand. "I think," he said, "you were very wise, not telling anyone about our—our difficulty."

She pursed her lips. "I'm sorry I sent you away. I missed you so much, but I've seen you around kids like Colin Brown, Mickey Corry. Barry, you will be a great daddy. I know it now and I knew it then. I think I've known it all along. You just had to see sense, that's all."

Barry shook his head. "Sometimes, Miss Sue Nolan, you can be a tad Machiavellian, but, damn it, I love you." He blew her a kiss.

"And you, Doctor Barry Laverty, can sometimes be a bit otherworldly, wrapped up in your work. Lucky for us, my mum is a super organizer. All you'll have to do is sort out things like the groom's guest list, best man—"

"Jack Mills."

"Ushers, buttonholes, rent morning suits, buy a ring, and show up on time."

Barry guffawed. "Like Stanley Holloway in *My Fair Lady*? I promise I will. And I thought it was the bride's job to be a bit late." His heart sang. He raised his glass. "To us, pet. You and me."

Together they drank.

"One thing," Sue said. "About the Millers' cottage. I know Mrs. Miller was having some second thoughts about selling when we looked at the place together before. Any chance she might have come to a conclusion?"

Barry's smile fled. He frowned and drew in a deep breath. "I'm afraid Lewis Miller passed away in hospital a fortnight ago."

"Oh no. Barry, I'm so sorry. How's Mrs. Miller?"

"Upset. Very upset. Living in Portrush with her married daughter, Joy, and her family."

Sue hesitated. "Barry, I'm sure Gracie must be very unhappy. They'd been married for a very long time."

"They had. Since 1907. She's taken it very hard."

"Oh dear. Now, please don't think I'm soulless, but knowing you, you softhearted old thing, I'll bet you didn't even mention if she was ready to sell, did you?"

Barry shook his head. "She told me she was going to stay with her family for a while, but when she was good and ready, she'd be coming home. That she couldn't bear to leave all her memories behind. I'm sorry. I know you'd your heart set on that bungalow."

Sue smiled. "No," she said, "I'd my heart set on you, my love. That's all that really matters."

And inside him Barry Laverty's heart swelled up. He stood, walked round the table, helped Sue stand, and kissed her, gently, possessively. "I do love you very much, Sue." He held her at arms' length. "Fingal says we can use my quarters pro tem."

"It's all right. Max can go back to Broughshane for a while."

"Thank God for that," Barry said. "The image of a confrontation between Arthur Guinness, Kenny, and Max hardly bears thinking about, and Lady Macbeth would probably hang, draw, and quarter your poor Max. Fingal christened her Lady Macbeth because he reckoned she'd kill for her kingdom."

Sue laughed. "You're right, and Max won't mind being on the farm."

"But I know you'd rather have him with you, so tomorrow first thing I'll get on to Dapper Frew. See if he's got anything else up his sleeve. A fit home for Doctor and Mrs. Laverty and family who, at least for a start, but only a start, will include Max returned from exile."

35

To Sit in Sullen Silence in a Dull Dark Dock

"Six days, that's all it took to win a war and call a cease-fire with the Egyptians last Saturday. Took us six bloody years against the Germans," O'Reilly said as he swung the Rover into Bangor's bustling High Street and reversed into a parking spot. "I'd like to have had the Israelis running my war so efficiently."

"I'm sure my dad would agree with you, Fingal," Barry said, and smiled.

"And here we are two days later on a Monday morning, and I've to give evidence in magistrate's court in the matter of *Regina versus Donnelly.*" He switched off the engine and opened his door. "Come on if you want to see what happens to Mister Donnelly."

Barry joined Fingal on the footpath and they walked downhill toward the four-faced sandstone McKee Clock on the far side of Quay Street fronting Bangor Bay.

A gentle breeze carried the salt tang of the sea and wafted dark smoke inland from the funnel of one of Kelly's little red and rusty coal boats as she discharged her cargo at the Central Pier. Barry remembered being taken there as a small boy by his father to see an exhibit featuring Hermann Goering's bulletproof car, then treated to a run from Bangor Bay to Ballyholme Bay and back in an army-surplus amphibious DUKW. Times had been hard for ex-servicemen after the war. Some had seen ways to try to earn a bit of cash. Two had even tried making a go of offering high-speed rides in a Whaleback air-sea rescue launch. But the huge engines had consumed enormous amounts of petrol and the venture had failed.

Barry pointed across the road. "That's the Togneris's Coronation

Café on the corner. One of their sons, Joe, taught me to sail when I was thirteen. I wonder how he is?"

"Haven't seen him for a while?"

"I pretty much left home after I qualified in '63. Hardly get down here to Bangor much." Barry shrugged. "I'm off this Saturday. I'll nip down and see him. Take Sue. Joe'd be tickled pink to meet my fiancée." I've been feeling guilty about Joe, Barry thought. You shouldn't neglect old friends.

They swung right onto Quay Street and passed the Palladium amusement arcade with its penny-in-the-slot games and the risqué *What the Butler Saw*. Put a penny in the slot, peer through an eyepiece, and crank the handle. As a series of cards flipped over, a buxom Victorian lady stripped off her voluminous garments until she stood in only her "unmentionables."

Barry and Fingal came to number 6, a grey two-storey Italianate building. Fingal stopped to admire it. "They built this place in 1866, the year an Irish horse, Salamander, won the Grand National."

Barry grinned. "Enough, *Encyclopaedia Britannica*. I've had my fill of horse racing this year." He looked at five rectangular bow stucco first-floor windows, each with a low balustraded base. On the ground floor, pairs of rectangular windows flanked a Tuscan doorframe. "It is a handsome building, I'll give you that," he said.

"Opened as a branch of the Belfast Bank," O'Reilly said. "Then it became Bangor Courthouse. In 1888, when petty sessions were held here to try minor criminal offences, they were overseen by three lay justices of the peace. Then in '35, the panel was replaced by a properly qualified magistrate." He headed for the door.

Barry followed, shaking his head and smiling at his senior partner's love of trivia.

Their heels clacked on a marble floor.

"Courtroom two," said O'Reilly. "The summons said two thirty, June twelfth, Magistrate Michael Carson." He pointed to the number hanging above a closed door. It was flanked by two plain benches. Constable Malcolm Mulligan, his bottle-green RUC uniform neat and clean, boots shining, his revolver holstered, cap on his knees, sat rigidly on one. He greeted the new arrivals with a nod.

"Officer," Barry said to the constable, and turned to O'Reilly. "If Malcolm's here, I'm sure it's the right place."

"And," O'Reilly said, "there's no show without Punch." He nodded to where Donal Donnelly sat on the other bench. Julie must have worked hard. His black brogues were polished, flannel pants creased and held up with a snake-clasp belt. A tweed sports jacket covered a white shirt. His tie was neatly knotted and his carroty thatch was clipped short back and sides and combed with a left side parting. "Doctors. How's about ye?" He patted the bench beside him in an invitation to join him.

Barry followed O'Reilly, who said, "Ready, Donal?"

"Indeed I am, Doctor. Indeed I am. It shouldn't take long. I'll be charged. I'll plead guilty. It was a fair cop, guv."

Barry smiled. Donal sounded just like the petty criminals in the BBC programme *Dixon of Dock Green*—good sports who, if they thought they had been fairly arrested, surrendered at once and with a smile.

"I don't need the expense of a solicitor if I do that. I'll get fined, I know, but Julie's getting her maternity allowances, the wages was good shifting them cottages and even better on the road building." Donal bent forward and lowered his voice. "Mister Bishop's happy as a pig in you know what and he's more contracts for when the road's done, so he has."

"I'm glad to hear it," said O'Reilly.

Still sotto voce, Donal continued, "And I'll be getting the lottery going next Wednesday." He sat straight, grinned a bucktoothed grin to himself, and said, "I can see the loot at the end of the tunnel now."

"You know, Barry? This time one of Donal's Donalisms has hit the nail on the head. I like that, the loot at the end of the tunnel."

The three men were laughing when the door to courtroom two opened. A long-faced-looking defendant was being taken away by a police officer. A few spectators straggled out.

A man with a slight squint, wearing a dark three-piece suit, appeared. "Constable Mulligan, please."

Malcolm rose. "Mister Hoey." The constable went into courtroom two.

"Doctor O'Reilly? I'm John Hoey, the clerk of the court."

O'Reilly and Barry stood.

"Mister Donal Donnelly?" Donal got to his feet.

"Will you all please come this way?"

Barry followed the little party into a plain, oak-panelled room smelling of dust. It was the first time in his life Barry had been in a courtroom. His only brush with the law, years ago, had been a fine of five pounds for not having had a taillight on his bicycle. It had been delivered by mail—on his birthday.

Sunlight poured in from two windows. The floor was carpeted. Rows of chairs, some occupied by a handful of folks who had nothing better to do than rubberneck and thought they might find the proceedings amusing, faced the bench. A man sat near the front with an open notebook and a yellow pencil. He'd be a court reporter for the *Belfast Newsletter*. Barry looked straight at the soberly dressed officiating magistrate. Michael Carson sat behind a plain table set on a slightly raised platform. Large framed photographs flanked the dais. One was of Her Majesty Queen Elizabeth II wearing a diamond-encrusted tiara, the sash and star of some order of chivalry over a long gown, and His Royal Highness the Prince Philip, Duke of Edinburgh, in his Admiral of the Fleet's uniform with a star of the Order of the Garter beneath his rows of campaign ribbons. In official buildings, it was de rigueur to remind the citizens they were in Northern Ireland, a part of the United Kingdom, not the Republic of Ireland.

The clerk asked Donal to take a seat in what Barry reckoned would be the dock, to the side of and half-facing the magistrate. Constable Mulligan and Barry and O'Reilly were seated in the front row where, to Barry's surprise, he saw John MacNeill, Marquis of Ballybucklebo. Now, what the hell was the marquis doing here? It wasn't his land Donal had been on.

The magistrate banged a gavel and the clerk of the court said, "Please rise."

Everyone did.

"Hear ye. Hear ye. To all interested persons here today, be it known that this is case six, *Regina versus Donnelly*, before His Honour Mister Michael Carson LL.B. Q.C., Barrister at Law. God save the Queen. Be seated."

QC? Queen's Counsel. Barry had been taught about ranks of lawyers in his medico-legal course. This man was a barrister, the most highly qualified type of attorney. He had, in legal jargon, "taken silk," because in a more senior court he would wear a silk gown and horsehair wig.

There was a rattling of chairs.

The magistrate turned to Donal. "Please state your name and address."

Donal beamed at the little audience. "Sure everyone knows I'm Don—"

"Stand up when you address the bench," John Hoey snapped.

"Right enough." Donal stood. "I'm very sorry, your worship."

"Address the magistrate as 'Your Honour' or 'sir.' "

Donal's blush clashed with his carrotty hair. He bobbed his head. "Your Honour, I'm Donal Donnelly of Dun Bwee cottage in the townland of Ballybucklebo off a wee lane off the main Belfast to Bangor Road. Me, and Julie, and wee Tori live there, so we do, and—"

"That will be sufficient, Mister Donnelly," Mister Carson said.

Barry wondered if Donal had been taking advice from Cissie Sloan.

"Have you any counsel, Mister Donnelly?"

"Yes, Your Honour. We do. Mister Bishop and Miss Moloney's on it, but I don't see what the borough council has til do with this."

Barry had difficulty smothering a grin.

The magistrate whipped off a heavy set of tortoiseshell-framed spectacles to reveal a pair of hard blue eyes beneath a set of bushy eyebrows. The corners were bereft of any crow's-feet or laugh lines, but his forehead was the possessor of three deeply etched frown lines. "This is a serious matter. Counsel. A lawyer. Do you have one?"

"No, sir."

O'Reilly whispered to Barry, "I hear he's a tough one. A real hanging judge."

The magistrate read from a sheet of paper. "Mister Donnelly, you have been summoned to answer to two charges under the Northern Ireland Game Preservation Act of 1928 that on the early-morning hours of Sunday, April twenty-third, in the year of our Lord nineteen hundred and sixty-seven, you did knowingly trespass on the property of one Thomas Bowe, and you did take by unlawful means, out of season, two of his pheasants." He set down the paper. "I have read Constable Mulligan's statement, duly signed by you, in which you admit to these offences. You are lucky he did not confiscate your means of transport."

Donal sent a smile of gratitude to PC Mulligan, who kept his face deadpan.

The magistrate said, "I see here in court the good Doctor O'Reilly," he inclined his head in Fingal's direction, "who, if necessary, under oath will attest to having sewn up a cut in your hand that morning and having witnessed your properly performed arrest by Constable Mulligan and the corpses of the unfortunate birds in question."

Donal Donnelly said, "Yes, Your Honour. And," he held up his left hand, "the doctor made a right good job of my hand, so he did."

The magistrate cleared his throat. Frowned so his eyebrows tried to meet. "Donal Donnelly, how do you plead? Guilty or not guilty?"

"Och, Your Honour, sure didn't Malcolm catch me red-handed? I'm guilty as sin, so I am."

"And just exactly how guilty is sin, Mister Donnelly?"

Donal's brows knitted. He pursed his lips and scratched in one ear with a fingertip.

"Never mind. Your plea is accepted. Under section eight of the act, I pronounce you guilty of trespass and taking game birds out of season. You are also responsible for reimbursing Mister Bowe for the value of his property, the two pheasants, at fair market price. Both offences carry level-two penalties on the standard scale of fines not to exceed ten pounds, and in addition I can impose a jail sentence of up to three months for the taking out of season."

Donal's eyes flew wide. "Jail? Och, you wouldn't, sir. My Julie's going til have a wee boy next month and—"

"Be quiet, Mister Donnelly, or I'll find you in contempt of court."

Donal Donnelly clapped a hand over his mouth.

"Have you anything more to say before sentence is passed?"

Barry saw the marquis rise. "If it please the court, may I be permitted to give evidence as to the character of the defendant?"

Mister Carson sat back, peered at the marquis. It was possible that this was the first time the magistrate had had a peer of the realm in his courtroom. "It's irregular, but yes, my lord, please continue; but first," he inclined his head to where the clerk sat, "you must be sworn in. And you may be seated, Mister Donnelly."

After providing his name and address to the clerk, and with the Bible held in his right hand, the marquis intoned the words ending in ". . . and nothing but the truth," and relinquished the Bible. "Your Honour, I have known Mister Donnelly for nearly twenty years. He is a hard-working, highly skilled carpenter by trade. He is involved in all aspects of life here in Ballybucklebo, never failing to volunteer in any times of need. He is a devoted family man and as you heard is expecting to in-crease his family very soon. But lately he and his workmates have fallen on hard times. The Bishop Building Company, for whom he has re-cently earned the job of foreman, has been unable to provide work for its crew. Men have been unemployed for several weeks, and I believe Donal Donnelly took those birds, in essence birds of mine which had strayed onto a neighbour's land, he took those birds to provide for his family. I have already told the doctor that had Donal taken them on the Bally-bucklebo Estate, I would not have required recompense, not have pressed the trespassing charge, and fully recognising that he is in con-travention of an act for which penalties must be applied, would remind the court he surrendered peacefully to Constable Mulligan, admitted his offence, and has today pleaded guilty. A jail sentence would be a terrible blot on his character, and as Mister Donnelly is just beginning to recover financially, I would ask the court's leniency in levying fines. If it please the court. That is all." The marquis returned to his seat.

"Eloquent, my lord," Mister Carson said. "Eloquent." He managed a small smile. "You must have taken a lesson from Portia in *A Merchant of Venice*." He turned to Donal. "I still must ask if you have anything to say before I pass sentence."

Donal bounced to his feet. "No, Your Honour."

"Very well. Donal Donnelly of Dun Bwee of the townland of Bally-bucklebo, I find you guilty as charged on both counts. You are ordered to pay the sum of six pounds, fair market value for two pheasants, as well as five pounds on the charge of trespassing and five pounds for taking game birds out of season. The clerk of the court will accept payment of the money."

Barry whistled and received such a gimlet eye from Magistrate Carson that he could feel his face reddening.

Barry looked over at Donal, who hung his head and whispered, "Yes, sir." It could have been much worse, but sixteen pounds for a man like Donal was more than three weeks' wages.

"You may step down, Mister Donnelly. Case adjourned." The magistrate rose and left.

Donal went straight to the marquis.

Barry had no trouble overhearing the conversation.

"Thank you very, very much, my lord. That was quare nor decent of you, sir, so it was."

John MacNeill smiled. "Sorry I couldn't do more. Doctor O'Reilly had mentioned your troubles, so I kept an eye on the court diary in the *County Down Spectator*. But from now on, Donal"—he looked Donal straight in the eye—"from now on, keep coming and beating for me during our shoots and you shall have plenty of game for your table, but leave the rest alone. Now please forgive me, but I must be running. Bye, Doctor Laverty, and say my good-byes to Doctor O'Reilly."

"Of course, sir."

Barry turned to see O'Reilly bending over John Hoey's desk, straightening up, and replacing something in an inside pocket. He turned and walked back to where Barry stood with Donal. O'Reilly grinned. "No," he said, "I am not one of the Sisters of Charity. I am not Santa Claus come early. I am lots of things, but I am not a philanthropist."

Oh no? Barry thought.

"You, Donal Donnelly, owe me sixteen pounds. And I hope your lottery is fully subscribed. I'll wait until you announce the winner. But not a day longer. Now, are you here on your bike or would you like a lift home?"

36

The Future's Not Ours to See

O'Reilly sat in the upstairs lounge waiting for Kitty to join him. Lady Macbeth was curled up in front of the unlit fire, her fur a dazzling white in a sunbeam that poured itself through one of the bay windows.

Kitty came in dressed for walking, light blue cardigan over a high-collared white blouse, knee-length tartan skirt, and low-heeled brogues. "You know, Fingal, I really am getting used to having more free time with you."

And one day soon, he hoped, when he had persuaded her to work part time, she'd have even more.

"I didn't like it when Ronald left for Nepal in mid-May and you were back to working one in three nights and weekends."

"It wasn't so bad, and that didn't last for long." He stood. "Come on. It's a lovely day. Let's go and get the dogs."

Kitty picked up the little netsuke Budai figurine that Ronald had given them as a present after his operation last November. "I'm glad Ronald has found some solace for his troubles, even if he did have to go all the way to Nepal to get it. I have to say, when he came here to say good-bye, it was a bit fraught. He came very close to tears."

"I reckon that man has carried an unspoken torch for you since we were students."

"Don't be silly, Fingal," Kitty said. "I think he's one of those men who is just not really cut out to be happy round women."

O'Reilly laughed. "I don't think that's going to be much of a problem in a monastery in Nepal. And his last letter was pretty cheerful."

He chuckled. "Ronald Fitzpatrick with a shaven head? Doesn't bear thinking about."

Kitty giggled. "Golly. You're right. Ronald, a baldy-nut?"

They walked down the hall into the kitchen. "Just a tick," Kitty said. "I want to leave out that salmon steak John MacNeill gave us to have for our dinner tonight." She fussed round the fridge and then with a covered plate so her ladyship would be deterred from getting at their dinner. "I wonder if we'll ever see him back?"

"He's holding on to his house for six months until he's certain, but if he does decide to stay he asked me before he left if I would ask Dapper to handle the sale. I simply don't know what'll happen. Time will tell, but from the purely practical point of view, Professor George Irwin was very decent agreeing to let Connor Nelson work independent of supervision after the first of this month. That young man is turning out very well. Very well indeed. He's doing four surgeries a week in the Kinnegar. It spares Ronald's old patients that need to be seen in a surgery the trouble of coming here and doesn't clog up our waiting room. Ronald's calls out of hours are routed here for whoever's on call."

"And," she gave him a less-than-chaste kiss, "means you are working only one in four again. I do like that."

He returned the kiss, then said, "Definitely a fortnight in Paris for us, Mrs. O'Reilly, once Barry and Sue are back from Villefranche." He took down Kenny's leash from its hook and opened the back door.

The morning sun of the mid-June Saturday was warming the sea-salted air. Donal Donnelly had been round earlier and had cut the grass, and the scent of its new-mownness filled O'Reilly's nostrils. The broad seven-fingered leaves of the big horse chestnut tree in the garden had turned from the lime of spring to the shamrock of early summer. The white candle flowers were gone and sticky buds were forming in their places.

The pair were greeted by Kenny, who charged over and without bidding sat at his master's feet.

"Good," said O'Reilly.

Kitty knelt and petted the pup. "Who's a good boy?" Kenny wagged his tail. "Who's a big boy?"

"Come on," said O'Reilly, "heel."

The six-month-old pup, who now weighed close to fifty pounds, tucked in like a prize entry at a dog show.

Old Arthur Guinness lay outside his doghouse. He grinned, raised his head, and cocked it to one side, but did not get up.

O'Reilly said to Kitty, "I think my loyal friend's saying, 'Will you and the youngster please go on, boss? I've taught him all I can and it's so restful lying here in the sun.'"

"I think you're right," she said.

He knelt by Arthur's side and patted the big dog's square head, seeing how grey his muzzle was, how cloudy his eyes. O'Reilly recalled a line from Kipling's *His Apologies,* "Master, pity Thy Servant! He is deaf and three parts blind." O'Reilly said, "Your years are passing, my friend. You take your ease, big fellah. You've earned it."

Arthur sighed and lowered his head onto his paws.

O'Reilly was convinced he could feel the dog's gaze follow them to the garden's back gate. Old age, he was sure, had very little to recommend it, and he knew his own was approaching.

"Heel." He clipped the leash to Kenny's collar. "Now's the time in a pup's development when, like human adolescents, they want to widen their horizons, exert their independence. Kenny might appear to be perfectly trained in the quiet of his own garden, but it could be a different matter round other people, other dogs. The last thing I want is for him to rush out into the cars on our way to the shore."

He moved to walk between Kitty and the traffic and set a steady pace. "I wonder how Barry and Sue are getting on? Dapper Frew's taking them to look at a house right now."

"I hope they find something soon," Kitty said. "It's only three weeks until their wedding."

"Morning, Alice," O'Reilly said as they approached Miss Moloney. "Lovely day."

"It is, indeed." She stopped abruptly. "Doctor O'Reilly?"

"Yes, Alice."

She blushed. "I wonder if you've heard from that nice Doctor Fitzpatrick?"

"As a matter of fact I have. I got a letter last week. He says he's settling in very well and the monastic life is suiting him to a T."

"I am happy for him," she said, but her face was sad. "He seemed such an interesting man. I did enjoy talking with him about the East." She sighed. "Thank you for telling me. Now I must be running along." And away she went with short little steps.

"I can't help but feel sorry for Alice," he said to Kitty. "Losing her first love"—he took Kitty's hand—"and not lucky enough, like me, to find it again, the way I found you."

"You are sweet," she said. "Old bear."

O'Reilly grinned and gave her hand a quick squeeze. "I wonder how the whip-round Alice and Flo Bishop organised to raise money for the Galvins is going? I saw Flo yesterday. They stop accepting donations at noon today. Then they're going to pop round to give me the money to give to the Galvins so they can start working on getting their son Seamus home from Palm Desert."

"That would be wonderful for them," Kitty said.

They crossed Main Street at the traffic light. "Oh, my," said Kitty, "speak of the devil and he's sure to turn up."

O'Reilly recognised the couple approaching. Guffer Galvin's bald pate was half hidden under a tweed duncher. He was walking slowly along the Shore Road toward the O'Reillys. Anne leant on his arm. Her pale grey-blond hair was tucked under a head scarf. Despite the warmth of the day, she wore an overcoat. Her National Health Service wire-rimmed granny glasses covered her pale blue eyes. Her cheeks were sunken. Barry and the district nurse Colleen Brennan had been keeping an eye on her since her discharge from hospital seven weeks ago.

"How's about youse," Guffer asked, raising his cap in the presence of a lady.

O'Reilly and Kitty stopped and Kenny sat. "We're fine, thank you," Kitty said. "How are you, Anne?"

O'Reilly heard the genuine concern in his wife's voice. Truly caring for her patients and about her patients was one of the things that made her such a fine nurse.

"I'm doing bravely, so I am," Anne Galvin said. "My wound's healed rightly and the pain's all gone." She paused and took her time breathing deeply. "I get short of puff, but sure that's til be expected with only one lung." She managed a small laugh. "Good thing I play the uileann pipes. They have bellows. The Brian Boru ones, and those great Highland ones you have til blow into. Still," she said, "Guffer and me goes for a walk every sunny day, and I can go a wee bit farther each time." Her last words were defiant. "I'm mending, so I am. Mending rightly."

But for how long? O'Reilly wondered. The outlook with oat cell lung cancer was grim.

Guffer said, "She's a brave warrior, so she is, my Annie, and, Doctor and Mrs."—he lowered his voice—"she kept things til herself until she was certain sure, but then she told me and the whole family, indeed when Cissie Sloan asked Anne why she'd been in hospital . . ."

O'Reilly knew what was coming next.

"Now all of Ballybucklebo knows what ails her." He shook his head. "Our Pat and his ones has been up from Dublin three times. Seamus writes every week. He's trying til raise the dosh to fly home, but och . . ." Guffer shrugged.

"How much would it be?" Kitty asked.

"He wrote it all down in one of his letters," Anne said. "I'm not very good at exchanging pounds for dollars, but the way he explained it, his yearly carpenter's wage is about ten thousand dollars a year before the government takes their share, and the fare's about nine hundred here and back. That's a brave chunk of his wages."

"Living in the USA's far more dear than living here," Guffer said. "Even a haircut's about ten times what it is here."

"Seamus reckons nine hundred dollars works out at about six hundred pounds," Anne said.

O'Reilly glanced at Kitty and saw her looking back with one eyebrow raised. Kinky and Archie's four hundred pounds were untouched. Would two and two make four—or rather the sterling equivalent of nine hundred? They'd have to wait and see.

"I'll just have to bide," Anne said, "and hope for a miracle." There was a crack in her voice. She squatted down unsteadily, Guffer bracing her against him, as she put her arms around Kenny's neck, leant her face on his fur. "You used to be a wee dote. Now you're a great big one, so you are."

And the great big dote wagged his tail and licked her hand.

"Number 10 Shore Road's not much til look at from the outside," said Dapper Frew as he held open the door of his Ford Cortina for Sue. "But it has good points inside, and it's just a wee doddle from Number One Main and your work, sir, and you could walk til MacNeill Memorial Elementary, Miss."

The three of them had been looking at a series of disappointing alternatives to the Millers' bungalow every weekend that Barry had been off duty since the beginning of May. Ballybucklebo, it seemed, had a spectrum ranging from relics of the 1800s, all badly in need of being dragged into the twentieth century, to a small estate of two-bedroom, prefabricated bungalows with asbestos walls that had been not so much put up as hurled up by the borough council as stop-gap measures immediately after the war. Dapper had apologised for even asking them to have a look but had wondered if one might do in the short term? It wouldn't. Nor would two monstrosities that could have housed a family of eight and several servants.

Barry already knew what a great salesman Dapper was and what an optimistic fellow he was generally. He could probably find something positive about a trip to the dentist. Barry stared up at his latest offering: the second in a row of identical two-and-a-half-storey narrow-fronted Victorian terrace houses in an unappealing shade of industrial grey. The front door of one was immediately adjacent to the one next door, separated only by thin brick walls. He wondered how soundproof it might or might not be. A single ground-floor sash window flanked the entrance. Immediately above was another sash window and at its side an angular bay window was supported on timber brackets.

Dapper laughed. "That there kind of window's called a canted oriel. Dead popular in the 1880s when these houses was built, so they were"— he pointed up—"and see you the sash window on the second floor? That wee pointy roof over it's called a gablet—sort of like a mini-gable. There's a neat wee attic up there." He put the key in the lock. "Come on on in."

Barry stood aside to let Sue go first. He followed. Immediately he smelled boiled cabbage. The hall light was on, otherwise the narrow corridor would be dark. Brown linoleum covered the floor.

Dapper opened a door to the right of the hall. "Dining room," he said.

Sue went in. It was a simple small room with a fireplace at the far end. There was a musty smell and Barry was certain he'd noticed a damp patch behind a strategically placed chair. The sash window gave a view—of pavement, Shore Road, and an identical terrace opposite. His friend Jack Mills had described such streets as "being laid out so you could sit in your front room and stare directly into the red-rimmed, hate-filled eyes of your cross-street neighbour."

"There's a very good coal house in the backyard," Dapper said. "Be cosy in here in the winter with a nice coal fire."

And nice heavy buckets of coal to lug in and ashes to carry out. "Like that one on Croft Street," Barry said, "with only a fireplace in the lounge—on the second floor and a very steep staircase."

"Fair play, Doc," Dapper said, "but them Victorians weren't big on central heating, so they weren't."

Barry, who was becoming frustrated and very disappointed for Sue, thought, Even the bloody Romans had hypocausts, under-floor hot-air heating, about two thousand years ago. But he kept the thought to himself. Dapper was doing his best. Barry looked at Sue. She shrugged and said, "Not very big, is it?"

"No." Barry nodded and thought of the spacious lounge/dining room in the Millers' place—and the view from the lounge window. "What else is on this floor, Dapper?"

"Come on, I'll show you."

Back to the hall. A carpeted staircase ran up along the right-hand wall. The hall led to a kitchen. An old kitchen. The floor was tiled. A chipped enamel sink with exposed plumbing sat beneath a sash window. An elderly washing machine with hoses to be attached to the sink's taps was stored beneath and off to one side. No sign of a spin dryer.

"The machine may be ancient," Sue said, "but at least there is one.

The last place had a washboard. I can't see myself as 'The Irish Washerwoman.' "

Dapper started to whistle the opening bars of the familiar Irish jig and they all laughed. "I thought washboards went out with cigar box guitars and musical saws when Skiffle bands packed it up in the fifties," said Barry.

"Oh, I liked your man Lonnie Donegan," Dapper said, "and his 'Does Your Chewing Gum Lose Its Flavour on the Bedpost Overnight' and 'Grand Coulee Dam.' "

Barry crossed the room to look out and saw a small backyard with a central square grill for drainage in its concrete surface. A shed, presumably the coal house, stood at the far end. A meat safe with a wire-mesh door hung from one wall. A single clothesline supported in its middle by a wooden pole drooped from the back of the house to the coal house. Shadows from the surrounding houses and the high, pitted, and moss-encrusted redbrick wall made the place gloomy in midmorning. "I suppose," he said to Sue, "you could put a pram out there on a sunny day."

"I suppose," she said, and he knew she was pleased by his mention of a family, but not happy with the shady yard. She turned and scrutinised the rest of the place. "No fridge."

That accounted for the meat safe.

"Gas stove. Ancient," she said, and shook her head when she saw a mangle propped against a wall. She walked round opening and closing doors. "Cupboard space is all right and"—she opened a tall door and switched on a light—"good-sized pantry and . . . oh dear God." She took two quick paces back as a brown rat scuttled across the floor.

Barry grabbed a broom, opened the back door, and went and stood protectively in front of Sue.

The animal must have recognised its chance to escape and raced to and through the door, which Dapper slammed shut. "Are you all right, Miss Nolan? That was desperate, so it was. I'm awful sorry, so I am."

Barry put an arm round Sue's waist. "You all right, love?"

She took a deep breath and said, "Please, Dapper, don't worry. No need to apologise, and yes, Barry, I'm fine. I'm not actually scared of rodents. It startled me. That's all."

"Me too," Barry said. "I'm glad you're okay." But this house was not for them, that was for sure. "Come on, let's get out of the kitchen." And he propelled Sue to the door to the hall.

Dapper, who followed, shaking his head, said with a distinct lack of enthusiasm, "I've been in this business a brave wean of years. I'm not going til come within a beagle's gowl of selling youse this house, am I?"

Barry looked at Sue, who shook her head. "Dapper, I think that would have been the case even without our furry friend. We really would like something a little brighter and a little less, well, Dickensian—with a view if possible."

"Aye, I know," Dapper said. "I've nothing like that on the books in Ballybucklebo at the moment, but we could look at places in Holywood or Cultra, even Carnalea if youse like?"

Barry said, "It may have to come to that. What do you think, Sue?"

"I'd prefer Ballybucklebo, if possible. I've got used to commuting from my flat in Holywood to school, but I work from nine to three. It wouldn't be so bad for you, Barry, in the daytime, but I know you won't want longer drives to your patients if there are emergencies at night."

He nodded. "Dapper," he said, "we understand you're doing your very best. If we have to, we'll use my quarters with Doctor O'Reilly and Kitty for a while. Or maybe use Sue's flat in Holywood. I could use Fingal's attic to take night call. Let's not go at it like a bull in a china shop yet."

"Fair enough," Dapper said, holding the front door open. "My oul Ma used til say, 'Buy in haste. Repent at leisure.' I hear you, sir. And you never know, we may have a bit better luck soon."

There was something in the man's voice that caught Barry's attention, but he knew Dapper well enough to understand that he'd say nothing until he was good and ready.

Barry climbed into the passenger seat.

As Sue got into the back of the car, she said, "At least if we do hold on to my flat in Holywood, Max wouldn't have to stay on the farm when we get back from France."

"That's true," Barry said with a forced grin and thought, Oh, goody. He loved Sue dearly, but he wasn't at all sure about Max, the mad springer. And because Sue couldn't see him in the front seat, he raised his eyes to the heavens.

37

Kindness in Another's Trouble

O'Reilly had been expecting Flo Bishop and Alice Moloney at four, so he was surprised when someone knocked on the door of the upstairs lounge at three thirty. Folks usually rang the doorbell. They must have let themselves in. "Come in," he said, and looked at Kitty, who lifted her head from her book, Jan de Hartog's *The Captain,* and raised an eyebrow.

Kinky poked her head round the door. "May we come in, sir?"

"Of course, Kinky," said O'Reilly, rising. "What brings you—"

Archie followed her.

"—and Archie here on a Saturday? And please, both of you, have a seat."

Kinky, who was wearing her best green hat and a green dress, settled in an armchair, but Archie remained standing at his wife's side.

Kitty closed her book and laid it on the coffee table with a smile. "Lovely to see you both."

"Thank you, Mrs. O'Reilly," Archie said.

"Doctor O'Reilly, will you please sit down?" Kinky said. She sat straight-backed, knees together, hands in her lap holding her handbag. "You are not in the presence of royalty, so."

O'Reilly smiled and sat. But she was wrong. As far as he was concerned, Kinky Auchinleck, née O'Hanlon, had been the queen of Number One Main Street for many years until she had graciously abdicated in favour of Kitty.

"We do be very sorry to intrude, uninvited, on a Saturday."

"Kinky Auchinleck," O'Reilly said, "who said anything about intruding? You and Archie are always welcome here at Number One."

"Thank you, sir." She beamed at him and rummaged in her handbag.

Kitty said, "Would you like a cup of tea?""

Archie shook his head. "That would be very kind, but no thank you, we are not a direct part of what your guests are coming to discuss."

O'Reilly frowned. How did Archie mean, and how did he know—

"No, sir. I have not used my gift," Kinky said. "It does be common knowledge that money is being raised for a very good cause." She smoothed her dress over her knees.

"I'll come to the point, so. You will remember a Saturday in this very house, ten weeks ago, when a certain Foinavon, the wee dote, won the Grand National?"

O'Reilly chuckled. "I do indeed. I'll remember it for a long time."

"Fingal lost twenty pounds," said Kitty, "and you and Doctor Fitzpatrick did very well."

Poor Ronald, O'Reilly thought. Much good had the money done him. Still, judging by his letters from Nepal, he was finding some peace at last.

"That is true," Kinky said, and from her bag produced a wad of ten-pound notes held together by a red rubber band. "I told you then that I was raising the money for a need which was going to arise in the village."

And I've wondered over those ten weeks, O'Reilly thought, what that need was going to be. At first he'd wondered if Eileen Lindsay, with her three kids to raise on her own and a serious illness to contend with, might be the recipient. But Barry, whose patient Eileen was, had reported last week that she'd had no recurrence of porphyric attacks and was fully employed at the linen mill. He'd also remarked that she'd said she'd been sleeping better since her stay in hospital, away from all her stresses. Then O'Reilly'd thought it might be Bertie Bishop's unemployed workers, but the moving of the marquis's cottages had provided temporary work until the bypass construction had begun. And Hugh Doran had been true to his word, opening accounts at the bank in Hester's name and steadfastly keeping his appointments at the psycho-neurotic unit at Newtownards Hospital. Even Donal Donnelly, with his near-ready-to-deliver wife and an impending court case, had not filled the bill. Ballybucklebo's arch schemer had got off relatively lightly.

"That need is now." She handed the notes to O'Reilly. "It would greatly please Archie and me"—she smiled up at him and he put his hand on her shoulder—"if you, Doctor, and Mrs. O'Reilly would add this to whatever amount the whip-round has raised."

"Bless you, Kinky," O'Reilly said, accepting the money. "You are going to make someone—"

"Forgive me for interrupting, sir, but it does be the Galvin family. We all know that. But we don't want them to know about Archie and me. We told you when we won the money that when the need came for it to be spent, we did not want it known that it came from our wager, or indeed from us."

"And I said then," Kitty said, "that it was very gracious of you. It is. Thank you, Kinky and Archie. Thank you."

"Och, sure it is only a shmall little thing, so." She glanced at her watch. "Your guests will be arriving soon. Archie and I have no plans for this afternoon. It would please us greatly if we'd be allowed to prepare and serve your afternoon tea."

O'Reilly caught Kitty's eye. He made a tiny movement with the tip of his right index finger toward his breastbone, meaning, let me deal with this.

Kitty nodded.

"I don't think so," he said, "and hold your horses, Kinky, until I explain. Afternoon tea would be lovely, but you will not serve. How am I going to explain you being here on a Saturday? Doesn't everyone and his dog know you get the weekends off?"

"Wellll . . ." She glanced up at Archie, who squeezed her shoulder.

"But," said O'Reilly, "there's nothing to stop Mrs. O'Reilly and me having our friends round for a cuppa, is there? Even if, as you put it, Archie, you are not a direct part of what is to be discussed?"

"True, sir."

"So," said O'Reilly, "by all means make the tea—and, if you please, there's lots left from the baking you did yesterday, so give us some of your Guinness cake with Jameson cream icing, ginger bickies, and ginger bread. They are all exceptional." Kinky rose and he could see she was glowing. And this would also give her and Archie the opportunity to see the effect of their donation to the amount of money raised by the organisers of the whip-round. "And while you're down there, why don't you ask Doctor Laverty to join us. He was out earlier with Sue, looking at houses with Dapper Frew. She's had to nip home to Brough-shane to help her mother with some arrangements, but I heard him come in ten minutes ago. The whip-round was his idea. I'm sure he'd like to see at firsthand what happens next."

"Come in, come in." O'Reilly greeted Bertie and Flo Bishop at the front door. Flo's hat was a feathery confection that clung to her head. "Where's Alice?"

"She's on her way," Bertie Bishop said. "It's such a nice day, Flo and me walked here, and when we were passing her shop she stuck her head out and said she'd be coming as soon as she'd finished with a customer."

"Good," said O'Reilly. "Go on up to the lounge. I'll wait for her here."

He chuckled as he watched the portly pair heading upstairs. Tweedledum and, forgive me Lewis Carroll, Tweedledess.

A breathless Alice Moloney arrived on his doorstep. "Sorry I'm late."

"Come in, Alice, and not a bit of it." He closed the door and followed her upstairs to where Barry and the Auchinlecks were seated taking tea and Kitty was pouring for the Bishops.

Greetings were exchanged and a chair found for Alice. She said, "Oh, my. Is that Kinky's Guinness cake?"

"It is, bye," Kinky said, and offered Alice a slice.

She took a bite, closed her eyes, chewed, and swallowed. "Kinky Auchinleck," she said, "that is the food of the gods."

Kinky smiled and nodded.

O'Reilly picked up his cup and saucer from where he'd left them on the mantel. "Now, I know everybody would like to blether on and enjoy the tea and Kinky's baking, but we have some business to transact. I believe, Flo, you were chairwoman of the whip-round. We're all busting to know."

There was a murmuring of assent.

"How did you do?"

Flo stood and rummaged in her handbag. She produced a notebook and a fat envelope. "People have been very generous."

"I'd expect no less in Ballybucklebo," Bertie said.

"Wheest, dear," Flo said. She cleared her throat and consulted the book. "We have raised a great deal, but I fear it will not be nearly enough. How much will a ticket on an aeroplane cost, Doctor O'Reilly?"

"Mrs. O'Reilly and I ran into Guffer and Anne this morning. They reckon somewhere close to six hundred pounds."

"Oh dear," Flo said. "We only came up with one hundred and thirty-seven pounds, fourteen shillings and thruppence."

O'Reilly heard the disappointed "aahs" and wondered if his sense of showmanship would best his compassion for the disappointed friends in his sitting room. He allowed the moment to stretch out, but then had to say, "All is not lost." He produced Kinky's wad of ten-pound notes. "This very afternoon a donor, who is insistent on anonymity"—he kept a surreptitious eye on Kinky—"came around and handed me the princely sum of four hundred pounds."

There was a communal indrawing of breath.

"My God," Bertie said, "that's ferocious, so it is. Dead on. That comes til—" By the way he was frowning, it was clear Bertie Bishop was doing mental arithmetic.

"It's a veritable king's ransom," Alice Moloney said.

"Aye," Flo Bishop said, "and who round here has that kind of money? Not me and Bertie. Maybe the marquis?"

Archie said, "If the donor wishes to be anonymous it's not our place to pry, but to give thanks."

O'Reilly saw the tiniest of smiles flit across Kinky's lips. *More power to your wheel, Kinky Auchinleck. You're a saint.*

Bertie said, "Archie's right, and we now have five hundred and thirty-seven pounds, fourteen shillings and thruppence, so we're still sixty-two pounds, five shillings and nine pence short."

"Fifty-two and change," Barry said, digging into his jacket pocket and producing his wallet. "Here's another tenner." He handed O'Reilly a note.

"Forty-two and change," Kitty said, reaching down for the slim black leather handbag at her feet. "Nursing sisters do get paid too, you know." She handed O'Reilly another note.

"Twenty-two and change," O'Reilly said, adding to the wad.

Bertie Bishop said solemnly, "Flo and me's no family and there's no pockets in a shroud." He gave O'Reilly a final twenty. "But I've no change."

Archie said, "Milkmen always do, so their customers can settle up on Fridays. Here's two pounds five and nine, sir." The coins rattled in O'Reilly's hand.

"And that's that. Six hundred pounds exactly. Well done, everyone," O'Reilly said. "There's only one more thing to do. Get this money to the Galvins." He held the wad and change in his great paw.

Archie produced another thick red rubber band. "Put that there round the notes, sir, and then put the notes and change in the envelope."

"Right," said O'Reilly, and did so. He looked straight at Barry. "Anne's your patient. The collection was your idea. I'd like to suggest that Doctor Laverty be the bearer of glad tidings—and the lolly."

Everyone applauded.

"Thank you, Doctor O'Reilly," Barry said. "I'd like that." He accepted the bulging, jingling envelope.

Bertie Bishop, as befitted his station as councillor and worshipful master of the local Orange Lodge, stood and tucked his thumbs under the lapels of his dark blue double-breasted suit. "And may I just say, congratulations to my Flo and Alice Moloney for raising what they did, a big thank-you to all who have contributed, including those here today, and an enormous thank-you to the anonymous donor." He beamed round the room. "Now youse all know me and Flo goes til church every Sunday, but I'm not a deeply religious man. Nevertheless, nevertheless

I'm going til ask youse all til stand, close your eyes, and bow your heads, and say a silent prayer for Anne Galvin and her family."

All rose.

The silence stretched.

"Thank you," Bertie said.

"And now," said O'Reilly, "everyone is invited to stay and enjoy the tea."

People sat, but Barry remained standing. "If you'll all excuse me?"

"Off you trot," said O'Reilly, handing Barry the money, "and I know Guffer and Anne will be flabbergasted."

"They'll likely near take the rickets," Flo said, "but when it sinks in they'll be so happy."

O'Reilly said, "They will that, and, Barry, take Kenny with you. That'll make Anne feel even better."

"Doctor Laverty?" Guffer half opened the door. "Is something the matter? God knows you shouldn't be out here on a Saturday afternoon. We never sent for you, so we didn't."

"I know," Barry said, "but"—he pointed to where an impeccably mannered Kenny sat at his feet—"Kenny and I have some news for you and Anne. May we come in?"

Guffer took a deep breath. "I don't like the sound of this, Doctor Laverty. What kind of news?"

"Something I know is going to make you both very happy. I promise. Honestly."

Guffer, still sounding uncertain, opened the door and said, "All right. I hope so."

"I'd not lie to you, Guffer," Barry said. "It's just I want to tell you both together."

"Fair enough." He stood aside. "Me and Anne was playing Monopoly." He lowered his voice. "She can't play for toffee, but I'm letting her win. It cheers her up, so don't you be saying nothing."

Barry smiled, shook his head, and wondered at the love that sentence held. He himself would certainly do the same for Sue if they were in like circumstances. Love, he thought, is as much in the little considerate things as passionate embraces. "Not a dicky bird," he said. "By the way, how is she since I saw her last?"

Guffer shrugged. "About the same. She has her good days and her bad days, but all in all I'd say she's bearing up bravely. Like she likes to say, 'One day at a time.'" He ushered Barry into the hall.

In the living room, the ceramic mallard still clawed for height above the fireplace. Anne sat at a baize-topped card table where a Monopoly board was dotted with tiny green houses and red hotels. It looked like someone had hotels on both Mayfair and Park Lane. A small silver racing car pursued a black boot round the squares. Two dice lay on the board. Anne shrank back.

All patients were convinced, Barry knew, that an unannounced visit by a doctor presaged bad news.

"See who's come til see us, love," Guffer said. "And never you worry your head. He says he has some good news, that's all. He's promised it's really good, but he wants you til hear it first, like."

"Doctor dear," Anne said, "and Kenny. I seen him this morning with Doctor and Mrs. O'Reilly. The wee pup's certainly growing into his paws and ears."

"Call him," Barry said.

"Come."

Kenny trotted over.

"Sit."

"Good." Anne Galvin patted Kenny. "Thank you for bringing him, sir. Can you and him stay for a wee while? Would you like a wee cup of tea in your hand?"

Barry smiled. "No thank you. I've just come from afternoon tea at Number One. I'd be awash."

"I'll not twist your arm," Anne said as she continued to stroke Kenny, "but take a pew anyroad, sir."

Barry sat in an armchair facing her as Guffer stood beside his wife and put a hand on her shoulder. He said, "You've news for us, sir? Fire away."

Barry said, "I'll get to the point straightaway. You'd like to see Seamus, I know. Everybody in the village knows."

"I'd so love til see him."

"And you shall. Here." He handed her the envelope. "A group of people in the village and one anonymous donor have raised six hundred pounds." She stared at it. Shook it. Opened the flap. "Oh my God," she said, "it's full of money, so it is. Here, Guffer you take it. My hands is shaking too much." She tried to haul in an enormous breath, but she gagged and coughed. She swallowed. Shook her head. Tears welled. "I don't believe it. It can't be true. Six hundred pounds? Six hundred?"

Guffer, who had peeped into the envelope, patted Anne's shoulder and said, "There's a brave clatter of notes in here, pet, so there is, and Doctor Laverty'd not have us on about something so important."

"That's right. The money comes from your neighbours and a donor who wanted the gift to be anonymous."

"I don't know what to say," Anne said. "Such kindness. Doctor, I'm not for asking you til tell a secret, but if you know who that person is, please tell them thanks very much."

"Of course."

Anne patted Kenny. "Do you hear that, Kenny? We're going til get til see our wee boy again." She kissed the dog's head. "We're going til see our Seamus."

And Kenny, the best-behaved of dogs, must have sensed her joy. He let go a "woof" that made the rafters shake.

When the laughter had died down, Barry said, "I don't want to spoil your excitement, Anne, but please put the cash somewhere very safe for now. First thing on Monday, go and bank it and ask the manager how to get it to Seamus. Then nip into the post office. Send him a telegram so he won't get a shock when the money arrives."

"We'll do that, Doc, right enough," Guffer said, "and Annie? I can spring for a few bob to put an ad in the *County Down Spectator* til thank all the people who gave. Jaysus Murphy, Doctor, how can we thank you enough?"

Barry said, "I didn't do anything. I'm just the delivery boy, but in truth it's made my day to see you both so excited. So happy." And it had.

He'd had enough gloom in the last weeks with Lewis Miller's death, Anne's cancer, his spat with Sue, losing the bungalow.

"Aye," said Guffer, grinning like a slice of watermelon, "and you know how at Christmas we all give the postie, and the milkman, and the bread man a wee present, like?"

"Yes." Barry wasn't sure what Guffer was getting at.

"Doctor Laverty, yiz has made our Christmas come in June. So wait you there a wee minute. If you're just a delivery man, you're for getting your present early. I'll have one. Anne'll have one, and, sir, you're going to take a wee half with the two happiest people in Ballybucklebo."

"I'll be glad to. Thank you." And he sat and watched Anne quietly crying tears of joy into Kenny's fur.

Barry Laverty let himself be lulled by the deep warm sea of happiness that at least for a while in this house was drowning out any thoughts of sadness that might yet come to pass.

38

A Baby Brings Its Own Welcome

"You don't mean to tell me your dad got married in that morning suit twenty-eight years ago and it fits you to a T?" Sue said as Barry modelled the black, double-breasted tail-jacket and black trousers with white pinstripes.

"I do, and he did, and it does," Barry said. "Might as well use it again. It's one less to rent."

He was on call tonight so they were confined to his quarters at Number One for the evening. The wedding was only ten days away and they were planning seating arrangements at the reception and trying to decide if the florist in Ballymena, who would be arranging the flowers in the church, should also provide the groom's party buttonholes. It was good practice for Sue, Barry thought, to be together during call. She was, after all, on the verge of becoming a country GP's wife.

The evening had not been interrupted until Miss Haggerty, the midwife, had phoned at five past ten to say that Julie Donnelly's waters had broken eight hours previously, that her contractions had gradually increased in strength and intensity and were only three minutes apart, and that the cervix, the neck of the womb, had been dilating at the anticipated rate. The midwife had been present supervising the labour all along.

"That was Miss Haggerty," Barry said as he put down the phone. "Julie Donnelly's in labour. She'll call when it's time, probably in another hour or so."

"Oh, Barry. How exciting. Well, then, I'd better get on home. It's after ten and I've school tomorrow."

"Stay," Barry said. "Come with me, why don't you, when it's time."

"I couldn't, could I? I mean, it's a private time for the family. Wouldn't the Donnellys mind?" She looked both excited and alarmed by the suggestion.

"Not at all. I can't bring you in for the delivery, but Donal will be glad of your company. And it will give you a better feeling for my work."

"All right, Barry. I will. I—I'd like to be there. After all, I'm going to be a doctor's wife," Sue said. "And a mother—someday."

She looked at him shyly and he gathered her into his arms and pressed a kiss on her hair but said nothing. "Why don't you take a nap until Miss Haggerty calls again. I'll keep working away at this seating arrangement for the reception."

Sue was soundly asleep, curled up on his small sofa, when the extension in his quarters rang again.

"Laverty?"

"Miss Haggerty here. It's time, Doctor."

"Be right there," he said, and replaced the receiver as Sue opened her eyes and smiled at him. "Hello, sleepyhead. Hang on. Just realized I was still in this monkey suit. It'll only take me a tick to change."

In minutes he was wearing jeans and a sweater. "Come on. Miss Haggerty'll have all the equipment there. I'll tell you all about Julie on the way."

The Volkswagen had the pitch-dark country road to itself. Fluttering moths and low tree branches were the only things the headlights picked out.

"I thought Julie wasn't due until July 12, the anniversary of the Battle of the Boyne. I remembered the date. You told me that Donal was going to call a wee boy William, after King William of Orange."

Barry laughed and said, "I think he's more favouring soccer players now."

Sue chuckled. "What if it's a girl?"

"We'll just have to see."

Sue sounded more serious. "Are you worried about her being two weeks early?"

Barry shook his head. "Being two weeks early is not going to be a concern. I've been following her with regular prenatal visits, and apart from the fact that she's put on a bit more weight than I would have liked and at her last visit her ankles were swollen, not unusual in late pregnancy, all as far as I can tell is proceeding according to Hoyle."

"Good," said Sue, "and it's not as if pregnancy was some kind of disease. It's a natural event, isn't it?"

Barry, who had seen or read about enough pregnancies going wrong, but who was not going to scare Sue, kept the thought to himself that no pregnancy was uncomplicated until a healthy newborn was in the cot and the mother was recovering. "I'm sure you'll sail through our first one," he said, "and second ones are even easier," and was rewarded with a quick squeeze to his thigh.

A screech pierced the night and a ghostly white shape floated across the headlights' glare.

Sue jumped.

"Barn owl," Barry said.

He pulled off the main road and in moments was standing, Sue at his side, when the door to Dun Bwee was opened by an unshaven Donal Donnelly. "I heard your motor, sir. Come on on in, the pair of you." He hustled them into the hall. "Come to keep me company, have you, Miss Nolan?"

"I hope you don't mind, Donal. Barry and I were making some last-minute plans for the wedding when he got the call."

"Mind? Would a kiddy mind if Santa Claus popped in for tea and brung one of his elves? I'm dead happy to have you both in our home, so I am. I'll enjoy your company, Miss, when Santa here," he inclined his head to Barry, "is at his work. Miss Haggerty says Julie's doing great, so she is. She's in our bedroom." He nodded his head along the hall. "Away you go, Doctor, and Miss Nolan, come you into the parlour and I'll make you a cup of tea."

"Thanks, Donal," Barry said, and headed off.

The odours of disinfectant and amniotic fluid filled the small bedroom.

Barry, wearing a red rubber apron, masked, and gloved, stood to Julie's left. Miss Haggerty stood at Julie's head as she struggled to sit up to see her newborn. The second stage of labour had progressed smoothly over the twenty minutes Barry had been in attendance.

He held a baby covered in white *vernix caseosa,* the waxy waterproofing that protected the infant's delicate skin and helped ease its passage through the birth canal. Julie lay on the rubber sheet that Miss Haggerty had put underneath to protect the bedclothes. The wee one registered its disgust at leaving its warm secure nest to face the perils of the big wide world by giving rise to a series of powerful yells and passing green meconium, the first bowel movement of a newborn's life. It was a good sign. Some babies were born with bowel obstruction, but fortunately very rarely. This one clearly did not have that condition. "Time, please, Miss Haggerty," Barry said. The date of birth was required for the birth certificate, and it must be close to midnight.

"Eleven fifty-six," she said. "Still Tuesday, June the twenty-seventh."

"A beautiful wee girl for you and Donal," he said, holding the little one up for Julie to see before wiping the child off with a green towel.

"Och, look at the wee mite. She is beautiful." Julie giggled. "But she's not going to be called Danny George, is she?"

Barry chuckled. Though not a soccer fan, he knew Donal had been suggesting first names of famous players for his boy. Danny Blanchflower and Georgie Best were two outstanding players from Ulster. "No, this little one doesn't look like a Danny or a Georgie. More a Danielle or Georgina," he said, clipping and cutting the cord and handing the newborn to Miss Haggerty.

"I'll go and let Donal know soon," Barry said. "I hope you don't mind, but I brought Miss Nolan along tonight."

"Why would I mind, sir? Isn't she practically your wife, and doesn't Doctor O'Reilly sometimes bring his missus along?"

"True enough," Barry said, not mentioning that Kitty was a qualified nurse and Sue was not.

"And don't you worry your head about Donal not getting a wee boy," Julie said, staring with love in her eyes at her new daughter. "He'll be just as chuffed. You've never seen a daddy love a wee girl like my Donal loves Tori. And," she said, "seeing it is a wee girl, we agreed I'd get til pick her names. I'd been thinking of Susan, I've always liked the name, and seeing your Miss Nolan's here and all, sir, if that's all right, and Brigit. It means 'powerful' and 'strong'—and our wee girl will be." Julie lay back on her pillows.

The smile on her face made Barry Laverty's heart grow two sizes and her sublime assurance that Donal Donnelly would love his new daughter added to the confidence Barry had gained from Jack Mills and Fingal as he had wrestled with his own feelings about fatherhood.

He put his hand on the uterine fundus, thinking how delighted Sue would be to know the Donelleys' new baby would have her name—and then frowned.

Oh-oh. Now that the baby was gone, the womb should be shrunken to half its full size, hard and firm. That muscular action would loosen the afterbirth, which would then be delivered. But the uterus was still full size. He couldn't have missed—?

Julie moaned. "Unnnuh," and Barry felt a contraction begin, as strongly as any of the recent ones. He immediately examined Julie vaginally. Och, blether. His fingers encountered the firmness of a second foetal head. He *had* missed diagnosing twins. Blast. Blast. "Miss Haggerty," he said with the confidence he did not feel, "there's another one."

"Right," she said, setting Susan Brigit into a cot and supporting Julie again. "Push, love. You have a twin for Susan Brigit." Barry felt the head descending well into the pelvis. Thank the Lord for that. It was not uncommon for the second twin to come bottom-first as a breech—a much more technically difficult delivery. The contraction passed.

Miss Haggerty lowered Julie onto her pillows. "You're doing fine, Julie."

"Will the baby be all right?"

Barry heard the fear in Julie's voice.

"Wheest, love. Doctor Laverty's doing everything he can, and I need to examine you." Miss Haggerty moved round and began to palpate Julie's stomach. "Longitudinal lie, back on the right. Head well into pelvis," she said, putting the bell of the Pinard stethoscope to Julie's belly and bending to listen through the flat earpiece. "One hundred and forty-four," she said.

"That's a relief." Now, instead of berating himself for having made a mistake, Barry concentrated on his work. "Your baby's coming along well, Julie."

And it was. Within fifteen minutes, between them Julie, Miss Haggerty, and Barry, giving thanks for his extra obstetrical training, had delivered a second healthy little girl and one placenta without any postpartum haemorrhage, always a greater risk with twins. The single placenta meant that the girls would be identical. He had given Julie intramuscular Ergometrine to make the uterus contract more firmly and prevent any further bleeding. Miraculously Julie had not needed any stitches.

Miss Haggerty had put twin one in a crib while she saw to cleaning and wrapping twin two to keep her warm. Both had received silver nitrate eyedrops to prevent eye infections with gonorrhoea if the mother were to be herself infected. The drops were a statutory requirement to prevent blindness. Now, with Miss Haggerty's help, Julie Donnelly was sitting propped on her pillows with one twin cradled in the crook of each arm.

"I'm tired," she said, "but they're so beautiful. My wee girls." Her eyes glistened, she swallowed, then began to croon the "Ballyeamon Cradle Song":

> Rest tired eyes a while
> Sweet is thy baby's smile
> Angels are guarding and they watch o'er thee

The lump was so big in Barry's throat he could only nod. It could have been a catastrophe, he thought, looking at the two little bundles tucked safely beside their mother. So many things could go wrong with multiple pregnancies. But they hadn't.

He reassured himself by reciting silently the precise line from *Donald's Practical Obstetric Problems*: "The only sure diagnosis [of twins] rests on adequate X-rays sufficiently late in the pregnancy, nevertheless one does not, as a routine, do X-rays." He took some comfort from knowing he had been thorough in his antenatal care, and even though perhaps the weight gain and swollen ankles might have tipped him off, both were very common in singleton pregnancies. Yes, he'd missed a twin pregnancy, but Providence had smiled, and with the help of a skilled midwife, an experienced mother, and his own extra training in obstetrics, they had brought matters to a successful conclusion. He would not let Miss Haggerty accept any responsibility for his failure. She was a superb midwife and if Barry could be fooled, so could she.

He cleaned Julie's nether regions, removed the rubber sheet, stripped off his gloves, untied his mask and apron, and palpated the uterus once more to ensure that it was firmly contracted before covering her feet, legs, and belly with a blanket. He moved to the head of the bed. "Well done, Julie. I'm sorry we've all had a surprise. I should have—"

"Och, wheest, Doctor dear," Julie said. "Nobody's perfect"—she gazed from baby to baby and smiled—"except my beautiful wee girls."

"Thank you," he said. Country patients? Salt of the earth. "Now," he said, "I'll go and let Donal know." He headed for the door.

"By the way," Miss Haggerty said, "twin one is six pounds two and twin number two is five pounds four. Good weights for twins born two weeks early. Twin two arrived at twelve twenty-one on Wednesday the twenty-eighth." She smiled at Julie. "You can have two separate birthday parties every year."

39

Surprised by Joy

Barry crossed the hall and opened the lounge door.

Sue and Donal leapt up from where they had been sitting in armchairs, each cradling a cup of tea, the Ulster panacea for everything from having lost sixpence to imminent nuclear attack.

"How's Tori's wee brother?" Donal asked, setting his cup and saucer on a nearby coffee table. "She's at her granny's and she's been busting to know about him, but she'll have til wait til morning."

"Sit down, the pair of you," Barry said, and waited until they had. He wanted to be tactful and break the news gently. "First of all, Julie's fine, but I'm afraid Tori's going to be disappointed. There's no brother."

As wind gusts ruffle a lake, expressions flitted across Donal's face. "You mean it's not a wee boy?" And before Barry could break the rest of the news Donal grinned from ear to ear and said, "Another wee girl? That's wheeker, so it is. If she's got half the get-up-and-go of Tori she'll be another cracker."

Clearly Donal was not one bit fazed that the baby was not a boy. "And Donal—" Barry began, but was interrupted by Sue, who said, "Congratulations, Donal, a wee sister for Tori. And you really don't mind you have another daughter?"

"Mind?" Donal said. "Mind? I'm over the moon. I'm Daddy to two little girls."

Sue looked at Donal with a gentle smile on her face and then looked over to Barry, who knew what she was thinking.

Donal said, "Can I go through til see Julie and the wean?"

Barry glanced back at Sue then began, "Donal, Susan Brigit's a fine healthy girl, but . . ."

"Aye?" Donal frowned.

"Susan Brigit has a sister." He saw Sue's eyes widen and Donal look puzzled.

"Och sure, Doc," Donal said, "didn't I just tell you Tori's asleep at her granny's." He chuckled and began to rise.

"Tori has another sister too. Julie gave birth to twins."

"What?" Donal eyes flew wide. "What? Och, go on, Doc. Pull the other leg. I've seen women with twins. They're always like the side wall of a house this late in pregnancy." But there was dubiousness in his voice when he said, "Isn't that right?"

"Usually," Barry said, "but not this time. Julie fooled us all. You've got two beautiful little girls, and they are both fit as fleas. Susan Brigit's six pound two and her sister's five pounds four." Which could account for some of Julie's extra weight gain, Barry thought, but hadn't been enough to make him or Miss Haggerty suspect a twin pregnancy.

"Are you pleased, Donal?" Sue asked quietly.

Donal swallowed, frowned, then said, "It'll take a wee minute til get used til the notion, but . . ." His buck-toothed grin was vast. "Do you know, Miss Nolan, there's no happier man than one wearing his wean's arm for a neck scarf, and I'll have three scarves til choose from. I couldn't be more pleased."

"And we're pleased for you all," Barry said.

Donal said, "Them's lovely names Julie picked out for the first one."

Barry said, remembering how thrilled he had been when Seamus Galvin had called his firstborn son for the doctors who had delivered him, "The Susan's for you, Sue."

"For me? Honestly?" Sue said.

Barry nodded.

"How lovely." Sue grinned.

Donal said, "Julie and me never discussed girls' names, and I like the ones she's given the first one, but I'd like the second one to have Abigail as part of hers. Abi for short. I had an aunty called that. It means 'her father's joy.' And she will be, I know it, so I do."

For a fleeting moment, Barry thought of another Joy, Lewis and Gracie Miller's daughter, and wondered how Gracie was getting on in Portrush. He said, "Donal, you trot along and see your new family, I'll be with you in a minute."

"I'm off," Donal said, "but bring Miss Nolan too. She needs til get a look at her namesake."

Donal left.

Sue moved closer to Barry. "You are a very lucky man, Doctor Barry Laverty. Thank you for bringing me. Golly, how flattering to have a baby named for me." She smiled at him. "It must feel good to be able to help bring such happiness."

Barry nodded. "It is." He kissed her. "And I'm a lucky man because I'm in love with you, Sue Nolan, and yes, if Donal Donnelly can be so elated about daddyhood, I see no reason why I'll not be."

She kissed him. "Thank you for that, darling. Now go and see to your patient and I'll make a fresh pot of tea. I'm sure Julie's tongue's hanging out."

"Good idea, pet," Barry said. "Bring it through when it's ready."

While Miss Haggerty had seen to lining an empty drawer with blankets to make a cot for the unexpected second arrival and tidying up the equipment, Barry had examined each newborn thoroughly, then filled in the birth certificates.

Sue arrived with a tray, cups and saucers, milk, sugar, and a teapot under a woolly tea cosy. She set the tray on the dressing table. "Mrs. Donnelly," she said, "congratulations on your babies, and thank you very much for naming one for me."

Julie said, "That's Susan Brigit in the wee cot. Would you like to hold her, miss?"

Sue glowed. "May I?" She turned to Barry. "I've never held a newborn."

"You go right ahead," Julie said.

Sue bent over the cot and lifted the tiny blanket-wrapped bundle.

Susan Brigit made a soft mewling noise.

Sue cradled her, and rocked her. "She's so beautiful. Oh look, her lips are like a little rosebud."

For someone who's never handled a newborn, Barry thought, Sue's certainly got the knack. And he'd never seen her smile so fondly. His bride-to-be was made for motherhood. And whatever made Sue happy made him rejoice.

Miss Haggerty poured tea for Julie and herself. She said, "Now, folks, it's nearly one thirty—Julie and the bairns need their rest. Let me have wee Susan."

She took the wee one from a Sue who seemed reluctant to let go, and put the baby back in her cot.

"I'm going to chase you, Doctor and Miss Nolan."

Sue said, "Night, night, Mrs. Donnelly."

Barry said, "You're right, Miss Haggerty. We'll say goodnight and well done, Julie, and thanks as always, Miss Haggerty." He followed Sue out, leaving Donal alone with Julie and the girls to say his goodnights.

Donal appeared in the parlour a few moments later. "I've left the tea for Miss Haggerty, but"—he dropped a slow Donal wink—"I've a bottle of Black Bush, Bushmills premier whiskey. Would youse stay to wet the babies' heads with me?"

Barry shrugged. "Why not?" He was off duty after nine o'clock and could catch up on his sleep. "Sue?"

"I'll have to be getting up in a few hours—but why not indeed. Love one."

They each took an armchair.

"Right," Donal said. "Jaysus, that's been quite the night. Twins? Twins, begod? Like an ould pal of mine once said, 'I would not of had of believed it if I had not of would've been there.'" He grinned. "But it is dead on, and seeing there's two babies, it's doubles all round." He poured one glass, but Barry said, "Single for me, please, Donal, we really do have to be on our way."

"Me too," Sue said. "Whiskey's not my usual tipple, especially not at one thirty in the morning."

"Fair enough." Donal poured two much smaller measures. "That there whiskey comes from the oldest legal distillery in the world. King James the First gave them a licence in 1608. Now," he raised his glass, "to the Donnelly twins. May they both live lives of Riley—and have huge funerals."

"Funerals?" Sue said. "Donal, have you taken leave of your senses? They've only just got here."

"And, miss, amn't I wishing my girls riches and a full life packed with friends? Could I ask for anything better?"

"Not a thing," Barry said.

"Well, when you put it that way, Donal. Yes, let's drink to a life of riches and good friends for Susan Brigit Donnelly and Abigail—"

"Just Abigail Donnelly for now," said Donal. "Julie said she likes that, but she wants til give a middle name a bit of thought." He scratched his head. "Now, can youse wait one more wee minute? I want you to know before you go, sir, the thing you advised me about has worked like a charm. I sold all thirty-eight tickets. One for each day from the start of her week thirty-seven til forty weeks and ten days. Sold every single one."

"Good for you," Barry said. "Sue, Donal ran a lottery on what day Julie would be delivered." He winked at Sue, who grinned, and said, "Donal Donnelly, what will you think of next?"

"Och, Miss, I've always got an eye out for things that might make life better for me and mine."

It was then Barry realised that he was going to have to upset Donal's applecart.

"Today is day twenty-eight, so Lenny Brown is ten quid better off," Donal said.

"Good for Lenny."

"That'll leave twelve quid for me." He grinned. "See, I was fined five for taking the pheasants, five for trespassing, and I'd to pay your man Bowe six for the birds." He shoved his hand in his pocket and pulled out and counted off several notes. "There's the sixteen I owe Doctor O'Reilly, if you'd not mind giving it til him, sir."

"Certainly." Barry accepted the money.

"The family budget's still up by twelve pounds. Near two weeks' wages."

"Um, Donal . . ." Barry said, steeling himself to break the news.

Donal grinned. "At the heels of the hunt it's only money. I'm mostly in it for the *craic*, anyroad. The important thing is Julie's fine and we've got another two wee girls. I can hardly wait to push them in their pram and have ould ones like Aggie Arbuthnot and Mrs. Flo Bishop cooing all over them."

A smiling Sue nodded her agreement.

The man's enthusiasm was infectious.

"You're not a daddy yet, sir, but I've seen you with our wee Tori when she's been sick. You have a way with kiddies. You'll be a star, so you will."

Barry smiled. "I do hope so," he said.

"I agree," Sue said. "Looking at you tonight, Donal, there must be a lot of rewards for being a daddy."

Barry said, "I'm sure you're right, Sue." He coughed. "But look, Donal, I don't want to sicken your happiness, but I'm afraid I have some bad news for you too."

"What? What's wrong? Is one of the girls not right?" Donal's voice rose in pitch.

Barry realised he'd been clumsy. "Nothing like that," he said, "but you see, Susan Brigit was born before midnight. She arrived on Tuesday the twenty-seventh."

"Oh," said Donal. "Oh." He looked at his watch, then scratched his head. And looked at his watch again. Clearly the implication was sinking in. "Oh. Now there's a thing." He frowned and looked at Barry. "I don't suppose you'd consider . . ."

Barry was about to explain that he really couldn't fudge the birth certificates when Donal said, "That's a daft thing for me til say, so it is. You'd get your head in your hands if anyone found out, sir, and a bargain's a bargain. The rules was that if you got the date of birth right, you'd get a tenner. Colin Brown's going to be a happy wee lad. His daddy bought a ticket for him too. For the twenty-seventh."

"You," said Barry, "are a sound man, Donal Donnelly. I'm proud to know you."

"Och, sir," Donal said, "isn't it the right thing to do?" He shook his head. "Sure everyone knows that."

Barry, well experienced in the ways of bigger cities, was at no pains to disabuse Donal of his belief.

Donal said, "And never mind that. I'd like you til do another wee thing for me too."

Barry sipped his whiskey. "Of course."

"Until we got the job on them cottages in May, the cash had been a bit tight at Dun Bwee." He stared at the table. "I didn't give nothing til help out the Galvins. I'm desperate sorry, so I am."

"There's nothing to be sorry about, man."

Donal shook his head. "There is. You've been here long enough, sir, to know we all helps each other."

"True, but I can promise you, Donal, the Galvins have got exactly what they needed. I presented it to them ten days ago." He had since heard that Seamus's arrival was imminent.

Donal laughed. "It's easy til see you're a doctor, sir, not a builder. You can have as many quantity surveyors as you like on a job; them's the experts that work out how many nails and planks and screws you're going til use. They always get it wrong. Julie'll understand when I tell her. We've got all we need." He handed over two pound notes. "We'd like them til have that for what we call in my trade 'cost overruns.' We want to do our bit. If the girls hadn't come on two separate days it would have been a fiver."

Barry accepted the notes. "That, Donal," he said, "is very generous. But that would have been your only profit."

Donal shrugged. "Do you know, sir, 'Money is the root of all wuh—'" He frowned. "I was going to say 'weevil,' but that's not right."

Barry chuckled and said, "But close enough. Donal, on behalf of the Galvins, thank you. Now . . ." He finished his whiskey. "We have to be heading for home." He rose.

"Right," said Donal. "Run you two away on. And me and the Bally-bucklebo Highlanders pipe band will see youse on your wedding day, July the seventh. Dapper Frew's got Mister Bishop til lay on a bus til run us til Broughshane."

"Thank you, Donal," Barry said, wishing Dapper Frew could lay on a house for the newlyweds, but as he closed the front door and walked to his parked car, he found himself singing a madrigal—off-key, of course—from *The Mikado,*

> Brightly dawns our wedding day
> Joyous hour we give thee greeting

Before he got into the car, Sue snuggled up to him and said, "Thank you for bringing me, Barry. It was great learning about your work, amazing that Julie would name the baby for me, and, oh boy, when I picked up that wee mite," she gave a shudder of pleasure, "I came all over broody."

"I know. I saw the look on your face when you were cuddling Susan Brigit." He kissed her. "And I know just what a great mother you'll be."

"In time," she said, "in time," and kissed him right back.

40

End My Days in a Tavern

"So I'll see you and Archie on Friday, Kinky," Barry said. "Two days from now. Eleven o'clock sharp. Broughshane First Presbyterian Church on Raceview Street. Just past the Ballymena golf course."

"We'll be there, sir," Kinky said. "Doctor and Mrs. O'Reilly will give us a lift, so. It does be a bit far for Archie's electric milk float." She dusted flour off her hands—she'd been making the pastry crust of a rhubarb pie, and soon Barry was enveloped in an enormous hug fragrant with the perfume of Kinky's kingdom. She gripped him tightly, let him go, and stood back looking at him. "I do ask you to forgive my taking that liberty, sir, but along with himself and Kitty tying the knot, and me and my Archie getting wed, the thought of you and that lovely Miss Nolan going to be man and wife. Och *achara*"—she used the back of her right hand to brush away a tear—"it does be the happiest thought of all." She sniffed. "I've never been a ma, more's the pity, but you've been like a son to me these last three years and I hope it won't be long until I can be like a granny to your wee ones, bye."

"Thank you, Kinky," Barry said. "I'd—that is, Sue and I'd like that very much, but you'll have to be patient." He was now fully reconciled to the idea of, and indeed looking forward to, parenthood, but he was also looking forward to having Sue all to himself for a while.

"Don't I know that, sir?" She went back to her work, pushing a rolling pin with long, steady strokes. "But remember, a baby brings light to the house, warmth to the heart, and joy to the soul, so."

"I will remember, Kinky," he said as he opened the back door. "See you on Friday." He was officially off duty from now until July the twenty-fourth. The tickets were booked to London, where the newlyweds would spend Friday night in the Ariel Hotel at Heathrow Airport before flying the next day to L'Aeroport Côte d'Azure west of Nice and only thirteen kilometres from Villefranche.

Kenny appeared, looking hopeful. "Not today, pup. Sue's Max will be enough dog for one afternoon."

He piled into Brunhilde and headed for Holywood. He'd already put the clothes and toiletries he would need in France in a case in the boot. Later this evening he was heading to Ballyholme to spend the night with his folks before heading to Ballymena tomorrow for a night in the Ballymena Arms, where Jack Mills would also be staying. Barry might not be a superstitious man, but there was no way he was risking his future happiness by seeing his bride-to-be the night before the wedding on Friday.

As he drove through Ballybucklebo, past the familiar sights of the maypole, the Mucky Duck, and the tall-spired Catholic chapel, he could feel himself relaxing. So much to look forward to and no medical worries for two and a half weeks. The schools had broken up for the summer holidays last Friday, but Sue had stayed on to clear out her classroom so painters could come in next week. He had promised to drop by her flat this afternoon and give her a hand loading her car, mostly wedding presents from her fellow teachers, for the forty-five-minute run to her parents' farm in Broughshane. It was traditional for the immediate family to view the wedding presents displayed in the bride's family home the night before the big day. Silly, he thought. They'd just have to be lugged back to her flat after their return from their honeymoon.

Barry made a left turn onto Church Road. Dapper Frew had done his very best, but no suitable house had turned up. It was a real pity about losing the Millers' bungalow, but at times like this he found himself remembering the little homilies Fingal was so fond of. If a thing couldn't be cured it had to be endured. Don't cross your bridges until you came to them. Sound advice on both counts.

Barry parked outside Sue's flat. Let's get Sue organised and on her way, he thought, then he was meeting Fingal, Connor Nelson, and Jack

Mills in the Duck for a send-off drink. While Barry and his best man, Jack, would have a quiet dinner tomorrow night, they had agreed to forgo the pleasures of a traditional stag night. Neither wanted to stand at the altar the next day bleary-eyed, muddle-headed, and stinking of stale alcohol.

He rang Sue's bell and braced himself for a Max attack. If the bloody dog could fly, he would have made a fine kamikaze pilot the way he hurled himself at people.

"Darling." Sue grabbed him, pulled him into the hall, and kissed him long and hard. No Max.

"Love you too," he said when he got his breath back after they parted.

"The brute is in the kitchen," she said.

A series of yaps and barks from that direction confirmed her words. Thank the Lord for small mercies, he thought.

"And I'm sorry I'm such a mess," she said. And in truth Sue was not at her most elegant. Her copper hair was bundled up under a scarf; a blue, dust-stained, sleeveless cotton sweater was half tucked into a pair of jeans which were torn over the right knee. "I've been packing like billy-oh."

"You're still a vision of loveliness to me."

"Thank you, eejit," she said, and kissed him again before continuing, "flatterer. Now, we've work to do. All I need now is a hand carrying things to the cars."

"Cars?"

"Yes. I've got my trousseau in two suitcases. I thought if we put them into your car now, they'd be ready for when we leave after the reception." She raised one eyebrow. "I do hope you like black silk negligees and sheer stockings."

Barry swallowed as erotic pictures of things to come flashed through his mind. Memories of their first love-making in Marseille. He cleared his throat.

"Oh, good," she said, and winked. "I have a separate case for my going-away outfit too, but I'll take that with me today."

"Good idea," he said, trying to banish thoughts of Sue in a black silk negligee and get on with the job in hand. "So what have I to carry?"

"The boxes in the sitting room go in my boot, the cases in your car, and after you've gone, I'll put Max in my backseat."

"Right," he said, heading for the lounge, "Bob at your service."

"Bob?" She frowned.

He lifted a parcel. "Also known as B. O. B. Beast of burden," he said, and headed for the car still hearing Sue's contralto laughter.

Half an hour later, both cars were loaded. Barry stood beside her in the hall. "That's it, then," he said. "Next time I see you, I'll be wearing a morning suit and you'll be in white." He moved closer to her, feeling the warmth of her breath. He took her hands in his and looked into the depths of her green eyes. "Sue Nolan," he said, "thank you. Thank you for loving me. Thank you for forgiving my uncertainty about children. Thank you for agreeing to be the wife of a country GP in Ballybucklebo." He kissed her, long, hard, insistently. "Thank you for being you, you wonderful woman whom I shall love to my roots— now and forever."

Barry entered the Duck and immediately through the tobacco smoke haze saw O'Reilly, Connor Nelson, and Jack Mills sitting at a table for four. O'Reilly's briar was doing its best to make the place look like a scene from an old Sherlock Holmes film.

Regulars called "Evening, Doc," or "Bout ye, sir," and Barry replied in kind. There was a wonderfully familiar comfort in this bastion of the male side of his Ballybucklebo family. Glasses clinked and the conversational buzz punctuated by laughter filled the room.

O'Reilly pointed to the empty chair.

Before Barry took it he peered under the table. Arthur Guinness was asleep and snoring, but Kenny and Brian Boru, Mary Dunleavy's Chihuahua, were tucking into a bowl that could only contain Smithwick's.

All three men were drinking pints and, judging by O'Reilly's, with only two white tide marks above the creamy head, they had not been here long. "Yours is on the pour, Barry," O'Reilly said. "Willie'll bring it over. And your money's no good this evening."

"Thank you, Fingal," Barry said. "It was good of Nonie to agree to take call while we're here. And thank you all for coming to have a jar with me before Sue and I tie the knot."

Connor Nelson nodded his ginger head. "Nonie said since you weren't having a stag, you still needed a bit of a boys' night out, before the big day. We all wish you every happiness, don't we?"

Two heads nodded in agreement. In Ulster, congratulations were not offered to one about to be married.

Connor said, "And it truly has been my pleasure to have been taught by you, Fingal, and worked in harness with you and Nonie, Barry."

"Happy to have you, Connor," O'Reilly said.

"Thank you. And I'm flattered you've the confidence to let me run Doctor Fitzpatrick's practice unsupervised. I couldn't wish for better colleagues or a better place to work. It's made those three years trying to get into medical school all the more worthwhile."

"You've earned it, Connor," O'Reilly said. "And as far as I'm concerned you can stay as long as possible."

"Hear him," Barry said. He raised his glass. "To you, Connor, and to colleagues, and to Ballybucklebo."

They drank.

Barry gave a thought to Ronald Fitzpatrick in his monastery in Nepal. Yesterday Fingal had had another cheerful letter. Apparently, Ronald was hinting that he might like to stay there permanently. Barry glanced at Connor. Might he take over Ronald's practice? From what Barry had seen of Doctor Nelson, they could do a lot worse than having him in their rota.

"All set for the big day, Barry?" said Jack.

"Pretty much." Barry rummaged in his pocket. He handed his oldest friend a small, grey, velvet-covered box with a domed lid. "Here," he said, giving Jack the box. "Don't forget this."

"Aye," said Jack, his Cullybackey accent thick as Kinky's champ. Jack's hometown was only fifteen minutes from Broughshane. "I'll no', and just between the three of you, I hope you'll be doing the same for me, Barry, once Helen's qualified."

"Do you mean?" Barry said.

"No' yet, hey." Jack's country face split into a grin. "I'll have to wait until she's closer til she's finished at Queens."

Barry grabbed his friend's hand. "You'll not regret it, Jack. Helen's a lovely girl."

"I'll drink to that," said O'Reilly and, with Barry and Connor, did.

Jack frowned. "I only hope her being Catholic and me a Prod won't be a problem."

Oh-oh, Barry thought. Alan Hewitt was a staunch Catholic with Republican leanings and Jack Mills' family was Presbyterian. There might be choppy waters ahead. Maybe Sue with her involvement with the Civil Rights folks might have some suggestions—but later. Not tonight.

Barry felt a presence at his shoulder and turned to see Bertie Bishop. "Good evening, Doctor," Bertie said, handing Barry a parcel. "Just a wee something from Flo and me for you and Miss Nolan. I was going til drop it off on my way home."

Barry rose. "Thank you, Bertie. And please thank Flo too. We will be writing proper thank-you letters once we get home and settled in."

"Och, never you rush yourself, Doctor Laverty. Now sit you down. I'm going til finish my pint, then head for home." He wandered off to, Barry was surprised, a table where Donal Donnelly was sitting, also enjoying a pint. Barry supposed that as Bertie's permanent foreman, Donal had, in Bertie's opinion, climbed the social scale.

Willie arrived. "Your pint, sir, and it's on the house."

"Thanks, Willie," Barry said, then lifted his glass and said, "Cheers," before taking a mouthful.

"Cheers," was echoed three times and then a fourth as Donal approached the table.

"I reckoned you'd be in the night, Doc," he said. "It's a week now since the wee twins was born, and your Doctor Stevenson called round this morning. She's a dead-on wee lady doctor so she is. She says the weans are coming on a treat and my Julie? See my Julie? Never stops grinning. I just wanted til say thanks a million and"—he proffered a box—"we all know you're getting wed, sir, but that's not a wedding present. That there's a wheen of flies—black butchers, renegades, mayfly, William's favourites, woolly buggers. It's just a thank-you from the Donnellys—all five of us." He touched the brim of his duncher.

"Thank you very much, Donal," Barry said. Three years ago, at Seamus Galvin's leaving party, Seamus had given Barry a box of hand-tied flies for the same reason, the birth of Seamus's baby boy, Barry Fingal Galvin. Later that afternoon, Donal had asked Barry how he liked Ballybucklebo and he'd replied, "I don't think 'like' is the right word. I love it here." And three years later he saw no reason to change his mind.

"Maybe one day you'll be teaching a wee lad til fish," Donal said, "and them flies'll remind you of a pair of Donnelly twins."

"Indeed I might," Barry said, and relished the thought, "and they will, and"—he lowered his voice—"they'll also remind me of a damn fine sportsman who paid up twice on his birthday lottery. I heard Colin Brown's invested part of his ten pounds in a tortoise."

"I see the lad's still crazy for animals. And him going til Bangor Grammar this September, I'll bet—"

"Donal," Barry said, "you'd bet on anything."

Donal laughed. "A pound says he'll go on til be a vet."

Barry cocked his head. "Right," he said, offering a hand. "Right, you're on. And I hope you win."

Donal grinned and shook. Then said, "And this business about me being a sportsman for paying up? Och, Doctor, no harm til ye, but away off and chase yourself, sir. I done what's right, that's all."

The swing doors made their familiar *boing* as the springs swung them shut. Dapper Frew came in beaming, made a beeline for Barry's table, but stopped when he saw Donal. "How's about ye, oul hand?"

"Rightly, and so's Julie and the twins."

Dapper said with a smile, "Well done, you great bollix. It's hard enough to shoot one bird, but to get one with each barrel? A right and left? Must be powerful cartridges you're shooting."

Barry laughed.

Donal's skinny chest swelled with pride. He grinned and shook his hands above his head like a victorious prizefighter. "I must be quare nor puerile." Chuckling, Donal added, "I'm away off til finish my pint, Dapper. Are you coming over?"

Dapper shook his head. "Later. I need a wee word with the doctor first."

"Which one?" came a chorus from a nearby table, and then laughter.

"Doctor Barry Laverty, if you please." Dapper grabbed an empty chair, swung it round, and parked himself beside Barry. "Please excuse the intrusion, Doctors," he said, "but I asked Mrs. Auchinleck where I'd find Doctor Laverty. I've something really dead on til tell him and it won't keep."

Barry held his breath.

"You mind the day we seen the house on Shore Road. With"—he chuckled—"what you called our furry friend?"

Barry shuddered. "I do."

"And I said, 'You never know, we may have a bit better luck soon'?"

Barry leant forward, drink ignored. "Yes." He had wondered about that remark.

"We've had it. I've been keeping in touch with Gracie Miller, and—"

"Go on." Barry felt his nails digging into his palms.

"It's been a little over three months since she went til her daughter Joy in Portrush. She phoned me this morning. Says she's loving it there. She's still sad that Lewis is gone, but she wants a new start with her family. She's changed her mind about selling, wants time to collect some of her memories, like her pictures and bits and bobs like the coronation mugs, but if you want the house, Doctor . . ."

Barry's immediate feeling was relief that Gracie was picking up the pieces, but perhaps selfishly greater relief that he was going to get the bungalow after all. "If I want it? Good God, man, you know we do."

"She'll let you have it for four thousand, nine hundred . . ."

Barry frowned. "That's more than you originally thought."

"Aye," Dapper said, "it is, but there's a bonus, like. For that you get the house and contents, lock stock and barrel. Gracie says they bought some new furniture when the grandkids started coming over, new beds and dressers for the bedrooms and such, and there's some nice Victorian pieces in there, a good bog oak sideboard and dining table. You could move straight in whenever you like once you're back home and not have to furnish it nor nothing."

"Oh Lord." Barry sat back, eyes closed, imagining him and Sue driving down to the little peninsula, parking their cars, and himself carrying his new bride over the threshold. "You are serious, Dapper?"

"In soul I am."

Sue was going to be over the moon, and Barry had a wicked thought. Perhaps he'd not tell her. Surprise her when they got back from France, just carry her over the threshold, but on second thought would it be worth having her worry for an extra two weeks? Nah. But what a lovely thing. Gracie starting to heal and Barry and Sue going to get the bungalow.

Dapper produced a few sheets of paper. "If you can sign these . . ." He indicated where.

Barry took a deep breath and looked around the table. Jack and Connor seemed to be having an animated conversation about rugby, but Fingal was observing him, his big hands wrapped around his pint. "My dad always said to read carefully any document you signed," said Barry to Fingal, "but I trust you, Dapper."

Fingal nodded. "Aye. I trust him too."

"It's a standard contract, no hidden clauses," said Dapper. So Barry scanned them, signed them, and handed them over to Dapper, who checked the signatures, scribbled the date, and said, "Dead on. Now all I need is a cheque for ten percent."

Barry said, "Oh-oh. I need to sell some shares my grandfather left me in his will to raise that. I'll make the arrangements first thing tomorrow, but it'll be a day or two before the money's in my account. Can you wait for a few days?"

"Aye, certainly. Today's the fifth. Make it out for the tenth."

Barry enquired, "To whom?" was told, and scribbled a cheque for four hundred and ninety pounds. "There."

"Great. Me and Mrs. Miller's solicitor and your solicitor'll get all this sorted out before you get home."

Barry said, "I don't actually have a solici—"

"Don't worry," O'Reilly said. "Brother Lars owes me a favour. Leave it with me, and I'll get my bank manager to approve a mortgage for you. I know how much you make a year." O'Reilly chuckled. "I should. I pay your wages."

"Thanks a million, Fingal."

"Great," Dapper said. He handed Barry a key. "I'll give you the rest of the keys when Gracie's finished, but this one means you can go straight from the airport when you're back from France, and I've got a local cleaning lady laid on til redd the place up before you get home. That's my wedding present. Now I'm away to have a jar with Donal." He rose.

"Thank you, Dapper." That he had just bought his dream home was getting through to Barry. "Oh boy," he said. "Oh boy," then on impulse yelled, "Willie?" Damn it all, Barry was getting married on Friday to the most wonderful girl in the world, Jack Mills had proposed and been accepted. Connor Nelson was fitting into the practice like—like a key in a lock, and they were among good friends.

"Yes, Doctor?"

"Champagne and four glasses."

"Right away."

"Looks like you've got yourself a house, Barry Laverty," said O'Reilly, "which means Kitty and I will be getting Number One to ourselves except for the nights Nonie's on call."

"Give you more chances to work on getting Kitty to slow down," said Barry, giving his senior partner a sly wink.

Fingal shook his head and laughed. "I'll miss having you about the place, Barry, but I'm very happy you and Sue will be starting married life in your own home. Just you take care of that girl. She's one in a thousand."

"Thanks, Fingal, and I promise."

Boing.

Barry looked at the pub door to see who had arrived. Guffer Galvin and a stranger—no it wasn't, it was Seamus Galvin, three years older and with a suntan like a film star.

Guffer was squinting through the fug until he recognised Barry. He and his son walked to the table. "Excuse me," he said, "but Seamus here got home three days ago. He was banjaxed with that there jetlag, but he's getting better, so the night my Annie says til me, says she, 'Take you our boy down til the Duck. You bought him his first pint there and I'm sure he'd like a real Guinness. See some of his old mates.'"

Fingal was the first to rise from his chair, pull up two more chairs, and offer a hand to Seamus Galvin. "Welcome back, Seamus."

"And how is Anne, Guffer?" Barry asked.

Guffer smiled. "Since the moment Seamus here set foot in our house she's been like a dog with two tails." He bent and whispered in Barry's ear, "We all know what she has is dead serious, but she does seem to be mending so we're living for the minute." He straightened up. "I've never seen her so happy."

"I'm delighted." Barry wished he could make her disease go away, but at least he could take some comfort in having had a hand in making Seamus's visit possible.

Guffer looked all round the room. "If you'll excuse me, sir, for just a wee minute?" He put two fingers in his mouth and let go such a piercing whistle that Arthur Guinness and Kenny both howled. "If I could have youse's attention, please. Please."

Conversation died.

"Youse all know me."

"We do, Guffer Galvin," Bertie Bishop said, "and we're all sorry for your troubles and hope Anne's doing better."

"She is, thanks to you good people and others not here. Ballybucklebo give us the money for our younger son, Seamus here, til come home all the way from California til see his ma. Say thank you, Seamus."

Barry grinned. It looked like this being a daddy was a job for life.

Seamus said, "I do thank youse all so much, and so does my Ma."

"There are no words," Guffer continued, "til tell youse how grateful we are. Not one. But thank you all very much. Thank you. Thank you."

There was a solid round of applause, then what Barry could only describe as an embarrassed silence, before scraps of conversation began again.

Willie arrived, set four coupes on the table, and began uncorking the bottle.

"Sit down, you two," said Fingal as he sat himself. "How are things in America, Seamus?"

Seamus beamed. "It's a pretty swell place, Doc. Maureen loves it and"—Barry noticed a nasal quality to Seamus's speech—"the one you delivered, Doctor Laverty, Barry Fingal, is getting mighty big. Mighty big. He's knee-high to a grasshopper already."

"Glad to hear it," Barry said, hearing Seamus's American twang and idiom. He half expected John Wayne to belly up to the bar and drawl, "Lookee here, Pilgrim."

"And, Doctor O'Reilly, I always wash my feet when I go to his office to ask my doctor about a sore ankle." Seamus laughed.

Barry pictured with clarity the flight of a terrified Seamus Galvin from the front doorstep of Number One Main into a rosebush, and a great ogre of a man, Doctor Fingal Flahertie O'Reilly, hurling a shoe and sock after the victim and yelling those very instructions.

"Good for you, Seamus," O'Reilly said.

"I hear you're getting wed, Doctor Laverty. Donal says the Highlanders will be playing and he's got a spare uniform for me. My ma taught me how til play when I was a chissler."

Anne had been surrounded by her set of uileann pipes on that horrible afternoon when she'd really started coughing up blood. "I'd appreciate that, Seamus," Barry said quietly, thinking of that day nearly eleven weeks ago.

"Willie?"

Willie Dunleavy stopped wrestling with the wire cage. "Yes, Doctor O'Reilly?"

"Their first pint's on me as a welcome home for Seamus."

"Thanks very much," Seamus said, and offered his hand, "and I've no hard feelings about you chucking me out, sir. Honest to God."

O'Reilly laughed and shook. "I know. Sure didn't you come and apologise and give me a brace of lobsters? Away on, Seamus, and enjoy your pint."

Barry Laverty sat and watched, marvelling at how his first glimpse of a patient and Doctor O'Reilly in Ballybucklebo would also be his last as a single man with Fingal and the self-same patient, Seamus Galvin, builder of rocking ducks, who had just crossed some five thousand miles and three years to be here with his sick mother.

It was an odd feeling, thinking of Anne Galvin as Barry heard the sound of a champagne cork popping and then Willie pouring him a full glass of bubbles. Barry could not be sad right now. His own happiness was complete, and damn it all nobody could predict for sure what the future held for Anne Galvin. Suffice that her beloved son was home and she was happy too.

Was it really three years since she had last seen Seamus? Three years since Barry had joined Fingal? How much had happened in those years? And what more did the future hold?

He lifted his glass and said to his friends, "Never mind me getting married, never mind my getting my house. Think about what you've seen here tonight. Neighbours thanking neighbours for their help in a time of great need. I want us to drink to something wonderful, immutable, permanent. To Ballybucklebo, the best village in the thirty-two counties of the best country in the world."

And four Ulstermen drank to what was simply the unassailable truth.

After adding recipes to eleven books by your man Patrick Taylor, and spending a year writing my *Irish Country Cookbook* I think I'm getting the hang of this. Here I am again in my own kitchen, pen in fist ready to add more recipes that I hope you'll enjoy. Archie and I only got home yesterday, Saturday, July 8, 1967, a day as warm and sunny as the Friday before it. We stayed that night in the Ballymena Arms after the reception for young Doctor Laverty's wedding to that lovely Sue Nolan, and proud we were to have been part of the groom's party. Doctor O'Reilly looked splendid in a top hat, tails, and a dove-grey waistcoat. In truth, he does clean up well when he sets his mind to it, so. Or mebbe it's Kitty that cleans him up. Lord knows it was always a struggle for me when he was a widower man. You'd think then by the yolk stains on them he used his ties to eat eggs with.

Kitty, Lord love her, could have stepped out of a bandbox, pillbox hat on her just-done glossy hair, cream tailored suit with an above-the-knee skirt, dark hose, and patent leather pumps. Doctor Laverty's best friend and best man, Doctor Jack Mills, had brought Helen Hewitt, his lady friend. We're so proud of her here. She is going to be the first doctor ever from Ballybucklebo. And a lady one too, so.

The First Broughshane Presbyterian Church doesn't have a steeple like ours, but it does be neat and tidy and the florist had it decorated with pink and white roses and under their perfume was a hint of jasmine. Archie agreed that Doctor Laverty's folks, Mister and Mrs. Laverty, are a lovely couple, and that Tom Laverty was an old shipmate of Doctor O'Reilly's from the war. I nearly wept when Mister Selbert Nolan walked his only daughter up the aisle, her in white. Her dress did be strapless, and with shoulders like hers why should she not show them off? Close-fitting, it was, but then it flared at the knee to a floor-length train all round. Oh, she did look so glamorous. When I was a girl they called a woman's hair her crowning glory and Miss Nolan's, well Mrs. Laverty as she is now, was done up in all its copper beauty, with only a filmy veil to cover her face.

When the minister had finished and said, "You may now kiss the bride," Mrs. Barry Laverty threw back her veil and, forgive my familiarity, Barry kissed her and the place was as filled with soft love as a pillow is with down feathers. And if there was a dry eye in the church it would only be because—and I know about it because Doctor O'Reilly had such a case—someone had blocked tear ducts, so.

And what a procession to the Nolan farm for the reception. The Ballybucklebo Highlanders had come in a bus hired by Mister Bertie Bishop. They paraded, bagpipes in full tune, with Seamus Galvin, home from America to see his mother who taught him how to play the pipes, and Donal Donnelly marching side by side. The happy couple followed in a wee cart pulled by a donkey. That rig had been laid on at Doctor Jack Mills's request by—? You guessed it. Donal Donnelly.

I'll not bore you with any more details, but the happy couple will be in France now. I did ask Mrs. Laverty to keep her eye out there for new recipes for me.

Och well. For the rest of their lives may the roof above them, which will be the Millers' old cottage by the sea when they come back from France, never fall in, and those beneath it never fall out.

And may I stop rabbitting on and put pen to paper for the first of five recipes, including my very own version of eggs Benedict. Please enjoy them all.

Parsnip and Apple Soup

2 oz. / 55 g butter
2¼ lb. / 1 kg parsnips, peeled and chopped
1 lb. / 450 g potatoes, peeled and chopped
12 oz. / 340 g onions, peeled and chopped
20 oz. / 680 g Bramley apples (or other sharp-flavoured variety),
    peeled, cored, and chopped
40 oz. / 1.2 litres chicken stock
20 oz. / 570 mL milk
Salt and freshly ground pepper
Parsley and maple syrup to garnish

Croutons
2 slices of thick white bread, buttered

Melt the butter in a heavy-bottomed pan, then add the chopped parsnips, potatoes, and onions.

Season with salt and ground black pepper. Cover with parchment paper and the pan lid and sweat gently on a low heat for about 10 minutes, checking often to ensure that the vegetables are not sticking. Remove the parchment and add the chopped apples and the stock and cook for another 10 to 15 minutes until the vegetables are soft. Liquidise with a blender and return to the heat. Thin to the required consistency with the milk and check the seasoning. Garnish in individual bowls with parsley, croutons, and maple syrup.

Croutons
Butter slices of thick white bread. Cut into cubes and place in a hot oven, 375°F / 190°C, for about 10 minutes until golden brown.

POTTED HERRINGS

It is handy to have these ready in the refrigerator when the doctor is on call and I could never be quite sure when he would return from his home visits. I think they do indeed taste even better the following day after you prepare them, so.

8 herrings, cleaned, scaled, and wiped dry inside and out, with heads and tails removed
1 onion, chopped
4 bay leaves
1 teaspoon pickling spice
Freshly ground black pepper
Equal parts malt vinegar and water

Preheat the oven to 325°F / 160°C.

Roll the herrings from the tail end and place side by side in an oven-proof dish about 8 inches by 6 inches so that each one supports the other and prevents it from unrolling. Cover with chopped onion, bay leaves, pickling spice, pepper, vinegar, and water. Cover the dish with a lid or with aluminium foil and place in the oven for about 35 minutes. Leave to cool before serving with buttered wheaten bread, or baby new potatoes cooked in their skins and slathered in butter.

These will keep for several days in a refrigerator and taste even better after leaving overnight.

Herrings are members of the sardine family and have lots of little bones. Somehow they just seem to melt when cooked like this.

KINKY'S EGGS BENEDICT WITH SODA FARLS

4 fresh eggs
4 rashers bacon
1 tablespoon white wine vinegar
Boiling water

HOLLANDAISE SAUCE
3 large eggs
2 tablespoons white wine vinegar
1 tablespoon lemon juice
Salt and freshly ground black pepper
4 oz. /113 g butter
2 Soda Farls (recipe below)

Make the soda farls first. You can have these ready in the freezer to use at any time. You will need only half a farl per person, unless of course you are giving everyone 2 eggs each.

Bacon
Grill or fry the bacon and keep warm.

Hollandaise Sauce
Now make the Hollandaise sauce.

I do this in a blender but you may want to use a whisk. Separate the egg yolks and egg whites.

Heat the vinegar and lemon juice in a small saucepan and reduce to about half. Put the vinegar mixture into the blender and gradually add the egg yolks and salt and pepper with the blender running slowly. Melt the butter in the same pan that you used for the vinegar and with the blender still running add the melted butter to the egg yolk mixture. The sauce will start to thicken and if you think it is too thick just add a little hot water.

What you have now is a traditional Hollandaise sauce. I like to make more than I need so that I always have some in the freezer and am pre-pared to make a quick Benedict. However, the traditional Hollandaise does not freeze at all, so what you have to do is to beat up your leftover egg whites until they form soft peaks and fold them into the Hollanda-ise mixture. Freeze in individual portions and when needed just thaw and heat gently in a bain-marie or in a microwave on very low power for just a few seconds.

Poached Egg

For a soft poached egg, bring a pan of water to the boil, then add the vinegar and reduce to a gentle simmer. Crack the egg into a bowl. Using a spoon, swirl the water in the pan to create a whirlpool, then carefully pour the egg into the centre of the whirlpool. Poach for 2 minutes, or until the whites are just set, then remove and place in a bowl of iced water until you are ready to use. To reheat the eggs just put into hot water for a few seconds and drain with a slotted spoon and paper towel.

To Assemble the Egg Benedict

Cut the farls in half and toast and butter them. Place the grilled bacon on top, then the lightly poached egg. Finally, pour the Hollandaise sauce over the top and serve straightaway.

SODA FARLS
Makes 4
8 oz. / 227 g all-purpose flour
½ teaspoon baking soda
½ teaspoon salt
1½ tablespoon butter
10 oz. / 295 mL buttermilk

First, warm a griddle or a large frying pan over a moderate heat and dust with a little flour. This will stop the wet dough mixture from sticking to the pan.

Sift the flour, baking soda, and salt into a bowl and rub in the butter. Now make a well in the middle and pour in about three-quarters of the buttermilk, stirring quickly. (The baking soda will react on contact with the buttermilk as the leavening agent, and if you take too long at this step the bread will not rise sufficiently.) Add the remaining buttermilk if needed. While the mixture should be quite wet and sticky it is not as wet as a pancake mixture would be. It should not be too wet and sloppy or you will not be able to shape it. Now if it still looks a little too wet to shape add some more flour gradually until it is like a bread dough and not a pancake batter. Now turn your dough out onto a well-floured work surface and knead lightly, then shape into a flat round.

Cut the dough into four wedges (farls) and place on the griddle. They should take 5 to 10 minutes on each side. Just to be sure they are cooked through to the centre, you could test with a skewer. Now put the farls on their edges and turn them every few minutes so that the side edges are cooked too. This is called "harning." Allow to cool on a wire rack under a slightly damp Irish linen tea towel. These can be frozen until required.

These farls are very quick to make but if you are in a hurry you could substitute vegetable oil for butter and add with the buttermilk. If you cannot find buttermilk in the store you could use sweet milk with the addition of a teaspoonful of cream of tartar and a little lemon juice.

BEEF STEW AND SCONE DUMPLINGS

BEEF STEW
Serves 4
18 oz. / 510 g stewing steak
Salt and freshly ground black pepper
2 tablespoons flour
2 tablespoons canola or rapeseed oil
2 large onions, chopped
2 large carrots, peeled and chopped
1 parsnip, peeled and chopped
1 lb. / 450 g mushrooms
35 oz. /1 litre beef stock
Small bunch of thyme

Cut the steak into 2-inch chunks and coat in the flour, which you have seasoned well with salt and pepper.

Heat the oil in a casserole or pan with a lid. Gradually add the meat to the hot oil and brown on all sides. Don't add too much at a time. When all the meat has been sealed, remove it from the casserole to a plate. Now gradually add the prepared vegetables and a little more oil if necessary. Don't worry about the brown caramelised remains of the meat as this all adds to the flavour. Stir the vegetables around for a few minutes and then return the meat to the dish.

Pour over the stock and cook, stirring to scrape the remains from the bottom. Add the thyme and allow to simmer slowly, stirring occasionally, for 2 or 3 hours. Remove the lid and the thyme stalks and cook for a further 30 minutes or so until the liquid has reduced by about half.

Serve with scone cobbler on top and a side of champ.

SCONE COBBLER TOPPING
3½ oz. / 100 g wholemeal flour
3½ oz. / 100 g plain flour
2 teaspoons baking powder
½ teaspoon bicarbonate of soda (baking soda)
A pinch of salt
1 tablespoon finely chopped rosemary
1 tablespoon chopped parsley
5½ oz. / 156 g cheddar cheese, grated
4 to 5 tablespoons buttermilk
1 egg, beaten

Mix all the dry ingredients, except the parsley, and herbs in a bowl, reserving some of the grated cheese. Stir in the milk gradually to make a soft dough. You may not need all the milk or you may need a little more.

Work quickly on a floured surface and roll out to about 1 inch thick at least. Now cut out round scones, glaze with beaten egg, and cover the surface of the beef stew in the casserole with the scones. Top the scones with the reserved grated cheese, pressing it down a little so that it sticks to the scone.

Bake on top of the beef casserole in a hot oven, 425°F / 220°C, uncovered for 25 minutes or until the scone topping has risen and is golden brown.

Sprinkle some chopped parsley on top before serving.

CRÈME CARAMEL

Serves 4 to 6
3 tablespoons water
8 oz. / 225 g sugar, divided
15 oz. / 425 mL thick cream
1 tablespoon / 15 mL pure vanilla essence or a whole vanilla pod split in half vertically
4 eggs
Grated chocolate and mint leaves to decorate
Butter to grease ramekins

Preheat the oven to 375°F / 180°C.

First you make the caramel by putting the water and 6 oz. / 175 g of the sugar into a pan. Bring this to the boil and cook until the sugar has dissolved—about 4 to 5 minutes. The sugar will now be a caramel colour and will be very hot. Carefully pour this into 4 to 6 greased ramekin dishes, swirling as you go to coat the sides and bottom. Leave aside to harden and cool.

Into the same pan pour the cream and vanilla and bring to simmering point. Then remove the vanilla pod (if using).

Now whisk the eggs, together with the rest of the sugar in a bowl and, still continuing to whisk, add the hot cream. Now pour this through a sieve into the ramekin dishes.

Butter the ramekin dishes and put them into a deep baking pan. Pour enough boiling water in to just come about two-thirds of the way up the sides of the ramekin. Put in the oven and bake until set with a bit of a wobble. Depending on the size of the ramekin this should take about 15 to 20 minutes but may need a little bit longer.

Remove from the roasting pan and leave to cool before chilling in the refrigerator.

To serve, turn out onto a plate, sprinkle with grated chocolate, and decorate with a mint leaf.

Glossary

I have in all the previous Irish Country novels provided a glossary to help the reader who is unfamiliar with the vagaries of the Queen's English as it may be spoken by the majority of people in Ulster. This is a regional dialect akin to English as spoken in Yorkshire or on Tyneside, or the American English as spoken in, say, Appalachia or Louisiana. It is not Ulster-Scots, which is claimed to be a distinct language in its own right. I confess I am not a speaker.

Today in Ulster (but not in 1967, when this book is set) official signs are written in English, Irish, and Ulster-Scots. The washroom sign would read Toilets, *Leithris*, (Irish) and *Cludgies*, (Ulster-Scots). Not all the words defined here will be found in this work's text, but have appeared throughout the series. In light of the number of letters I have received telling me how much the glossaries have been enjoyed, please simply consider the additions as added value. I hope what follows here will enhance your enjoyment of the work, although, I am afraid, it will not improve your command of Ulster-Scots.

achara: Irish. My dear.
acting the lig/maggot: Behaving like an idiot.
ails: Afflicts.
aluminium: Aluminum.
amadán: Irish. Pronounced "omadawn." Idiot.
and all: Addition to a sentence for emphasis.
anyroad: Anyway.

arse: Backside. (Impolite.)

astray in the head: Out of one's mind.

at himself/not at himself: He's feeling well/not feeling well.

away off (and feel your head/and chase yourself): Don't be stupid.

away on (out of that): I don't believe you.

aye certainly: Of course, or naturally.

bairn: From Scots. Child.

balaklava: Knitted face protector like a ski mask with a hole for the mouth and one for each eye.

baldy-nut: Description of a bald-headed man.

banjaxed: Ruined or smashed.

banshee: Irish. *Beán* (woman) *sidhe* (fairy). Female spirit whose moaning foretells a death.

barging: Telling off verbally or physically shoving.

barmbrack: Speckled bread. (See Mrs. Kinkaid's recipe, *An Irish Country Doctor* and *An Irish Country Cookbook*.)

barrister: Senior lawyer who tried cases in court as opposed to a solicitor, who did not.

beagle's gowl: the cry ("gowl," not "howl") of a beagle can be heard over great distances. To fail to come within a beagle's gowl is to miss completely.

beat Bannagher: Wildly exceed expectations.

bee on a hot brick: Rushing round distractedly at great speed.

been here before: Your wisdom is attributable to the fact that you have already lived a full life and have been reincarnated.

between the jigs and reels: To cut a long story short.

bide: Contraction of "abide." Wait patiently.

biscakes: Biscuits (cookies).

bisticks: Biscuits (cookies).

blether/och, blether: Talk, often inconsequential/expression of annoyance or disgust.

bletherskite: One who continually talks trivial rubbish.

blow-in: Someone not born in a village but who has moved there.

boke: Vomit.

bollicking: Verbal chastisement.

bollix: Testicles. (Impolite.)

bollixed: Wrecked.

bonnet: Hood of a car.

bookie: Bookmaker.

boot: Trunk of a car.

bout ye?: How are you. See also How's about ye?

boys-a-dear or boys-a-boys: Expression of amazement.

brave: Very.

bravely: Feeling very well.

break-up: Of schools. Closure for holidays.

bright as a bee: Very alert and cheerful.

brogue: a) A kind of low-heeled shoe (from the Irish *bróg*) with decorative perforations on the uppers, originally to allow water to drain out. b) The musical inflection given to English when spoken by an Irish person.

bull in a china shop/at a gate: Thrashing about violently without forethought and causing damage/charging headlong at something.

burroo: The bureau that paid unemployment benefit.

but: Often tacked onto the end of a sentence instead of where it properly belongs at the beginning. "I'm not going with you, but."

bye: Counties Cork and Antrim pronunciation of "boy."

cack-handed: Left-handed.

candy apples: Apples dipped in caramel glaze.

candy floss: Cotton candy.

can't for toffee: Is not very good at.

casualty: ER department of a hospital.

champ: A dish of potatoes, buttermilk, butter, and chives.

chemist: Pharmacist.

chips: French fries.

chippy: Carpenter.

chissler: Child.

chuffed: Very pleased about.

clap: Cow shit.

clappers (like the): Going very fast.

clatter: Indeterminate number. See also wheen. The size of the number can be enhanced by adding brave or powerful as a precedent to either. As an exercise, try to imagine the numerical difference between a "brave clatter" and a "powerful wheen" of spuds.

collogue: Chat about trivia.

collywobbles: Vague feeling of being unwell.

come-all-ye: Traditional Irish narrative songs which start with the bidding "Come all ye" (for example, "Come all ye dry land sailors . . .").

come on, on in: The second "on" (occasionally third) is deliberate, not a typographical error.

comeuppance: Served right.

corker: Very special.

course: From the ancient sport of coursing, where quarry is started by dogs and pursued by the hunters who run after the dogs.

cowlick: Hair hanging diagonally across forehead.

cowped: Capsized.

cracker: Very good. Of a girl, very good-looking.

craic: Irish. Pronounced "crack." Practically untranslatable and can mean great conversation and fun (the *craic* was ninety) or what has happened since last I saw you? ("What's the *craic*?") Often seen outside pubs: *Craic agus ceol,* Fun and music inside.

crayture: Creature, critter.

cup of tea/scald in your hand: An informal cup of tea, as opposed to tea that was synonymous with the main evening meal (dinner).

currency: Prior to decimalization, sterling was the currency of the United Kingdom, of which Northern Ireland was a part. The unit was the **pound** (quid), which contained twenty **shillings** (bob), each made of twelve **pennies** (pence), thus there were 240 pennies in a pound. Coins and notes of combined or lesser or greater denominations were in circulation, often referred to by slang or archaic terms: **farthing** (four to the penny), **halfpenny** (two to the penny), **threepenny** piece (thruppeny bit), **sixpenny** piece (tanner), **two-shillings piece** (florin), **two shillings and sixpence piece** (half a crown), **ten-shilling note** (ten-bob note), **guinea** coin worth one pound and one shilling, **five-pound note** (fiver). In 1967 one pound bought one dollar and sixty cents U.S.

dead/dead on: Very/absolutely right or perfectly.

desperate: Terrible.

divil: Devil.

do-re-mi: Tonic sol-fa scale, but meaning "dough" as in money.

dosh: Money.

dote: (v.) To adore. (n.) Something adorable.

doting: You are wrong because you are behaving as if you are in your dotage.

dozer/no dozer: Stupid person/clever person.

DUKW: Pronounced "duck" Six-wheeled U.S. military amphibious vehicle.

dulse: A seaweed that when dried is used like chewing gum.

Dun Bwee: From the Irish Dun Buidhe, Yellow Fort.

duncher: Cloth cap, usually tweed.

eejit/buck eejit: Idiot/complete idiot.

fag: Short for faggot, a thin sausage. Slang for cigarette.

fair play/to you: Fair enough/Good for you.

ferocious: Extreme.

fey: Possessing second sight, the ability to see into the future.

fillet steak: Beef tenderloin.

fire away: Go right ahead.

flat: Apartment.

flex: Electrical plug-in cord.

floors: The floors of a house in North America are in ascending order: first, second, etc. In Ulster they are ground, first (North American second), etc.

flying: Drunk.

Fomorians: A race of mythical demons who inhabited Tory Island.

footer: Fiddle about with.

fornenst: Beside.

foundered: Frozen.

fudge: Falsify data. (Or a kind of candy.)

gag: Joke or humourist.

gander: Look-see.

geld: Castrate.

git: Begotten. Usually combined wirth hoor's (whore's). Pejorative.

glaur: Glutinous mess of mud.

glipe/great glipe: Stupid/very stupid person.

goat (ould): Stupid person, but used as a term of affection.

go away with you: Don't be silly.

gobshite: Literally dried nasal mucus. Used pejoratively about a person.

good living: Openly religious.

good man-ma-da: Literally, "good man my father." Good for you. A term of approval.

good skin/head: Decent person.

grass: Inform to the authorities.

half-un (hot): Small measure of spirits. (Irish whiskey, lemon juice, sugar, cloves, diluted with boiling water.)

hames: Literally testicles. To "make a hames of" is to mess up.

hammered: Drunk.

have on: Mislead.

head (good): Decent person.

head in your hands: Be severely chastised.

head (screwed on): Intelligent, practical person.

headstaggers: Take leave of one's senses. Make a stupid decision.

heart of corn: Very good-natured.

heels of the hunt: When all's said and done.

heeltap: Drink much more slowly than the rest of the company, usually to avoid having to buy your round.

hey: Post-sentence verbal punctuation used in County Antrim (see **so** for County Cork and **so it is** for County Down).

higheejin: Very important person, often only in the subject's own mind.

hirstle: A chesty wheeze.

hold your horses: Wait a minute.

HMS: His/Her Majesty's Ship.

home visit: House call.

houl' your wheest: Hold your tongue.

houseman: Medical intern regardless of sex.

how's about you/ye? (bout ye?): How are you?

humdinger: Something exceptional.

I hear you: I understand completely.

I'm yer man: I agree and will cooperate fully.

in soul: Definitely.

in the stable: Of a drink in a pub, paid for but not yet poured.

jackdaw: A glossy black bird, *Corvus monedula* of the crow family.

jag: Jab by an injection needle.

jar: Alcoholic drink.

jerry built: Badly and cheaply constructed.

kilter: Alignment.

knackered: Exhausted like a worn-out horse on its way to the knacker's yard where it would be destroyed.

Knockagh: Irish. "Hill Place." A war memorial in the Antrim Hills above the Village of Greenisland. Based on Wellington's monument in Dublin's Phoenix Park.

laugh like a drain: Be consumed with mirth with your mouth wide open.

learned: Ulsterese is peculiar in often reversing the meanings of words. "The teacher learned the child," or "She borrowed [meaning loaned] me a cup of sugar." "Reach [meaning pass] me thon yoke."

let the hare sit: Let sleeping dogs lie.

lift: Free ride.

liltie: Irish whirling dervish.

lockjaw: Tetanus. So called because the disease causes intense muscle spasms including of the jaw muscles.

lolly: Money.

lough: Pronounced "loch," almost as if clearing the throat. A sea inlet or very large lake.

lug(ged): Ear, kind of marine worm. (Carried awkwardly.)

measurements: All measurements in Ireland were imperial at the time of the Irish Country books. One stone=fourteen pounds, 20 fluid ounces=one pint, one ounce=437.5 grains. It can be seen that one 150th of a grain was a very tiny dose.

meat safe: A box with a wire mesh door to keep out flies, hung outside to keep meat cool in pre-refrigerator days.

mending, well mended: Getting better, recovered.

midder: Contraction of midwifery.

milk float: When milk was delivered door to door the milkman was provided with this electric vehicle to carry his wares.

mitch: Either play truant or steal.

more meat on a hammer/wren's shin: Descriptions of a skinny person.

more power to your wheel: Words of encouragement akin to "The very best of luck."

motor(car): Automobile.

muggy: Humid.

***muirnín*:** Irish. Pronounced "moornyeen." Darling.

National Hunt: The body governing steeplechasing, horse racing over a series of obstacles.

near: Nearly.

neat: Of a drink of spirits, straight up.

no': Scots. Not. Widely used in County Antrim.

no goat's toe: Have a very high and often erroneous impression of one's self.

no harm til you: Disclaimer before either contradicting someone or insulting them. Akin to "I'm sorry, but . . ."

nor nothing: Nor anything.

no spring chicken: Getting on in years.

och: Exclamation to register whatever emotion you wish. "Och, isn't she lovely?" "Och, is he dead?" "Och, damn it." Pronounced like clearing your throat.

off licence: Liquor store.

on the pour: It takes some time properly to pour a good pint of Guinness. One "on the pour" is coming but is not quite ready.

on the QT: Privately.

operating theatre: OR.

ould hand: Old friend.

oxter/oxtercog: Armpit/help walk by draping an individual's arm over one's shoulder.

paddy hat: Soft-crowned, narrow-brimmed Donegal tweed hat.

Paddy's market: Disorganised crowd.

pavement: Sidewalk.

Peeler: Policeman. Named for the founder of the first organised police force in Great Britain and Ireland, Sir Robert Peel, 1788–1846. These peace officers were called "Bobbies" in England and "Peelers" in Ireland.

peely-wally: Scots. Under the weather. Unwell.

pethidine: Demerol.

petrol: Gasoline.

pig in a poke: Make a bad bargain.

porter: A dark beer. It was brewed by Guinness until 1974 when it was replaced by its stronger relation, stout, which, rather than being brewed from dark malts uses roasted barley called "patent malt."

power/powerful: A lot, very strong.

puff: Life.

pull the other leg (it's the one with bells on): You are not fooling me.

puke: Vomit.

quare: Ulster and Dublin pronunciation of "queer," meaning "very" or "strange."

quid: One pound Sterling or a chew of tobacco.

range: A cast-iron kitchen stove fueled by coke, coal, gas, or turf.

redd up: Clean up and tidy.

right: Very or real. "Your man's a right eejit."

right enough?: Is that a fact?

rightly: Very well.

rook: Black bird, *Corvus frugilegus* of the crow family.

roundabout: Carousel.

rubbernecking: Being unduly curious.

rug rats: Small children.

scared skinny: Terrified.

scrip': Script, short for "prescription."

see him/her?: Emphatic way of drawing attention to the person in question even if they are not physically present.

selkie: A magical woman on land who becomes a seal when she enters the sea.

shammy: Chamois leather.

sheugh: A muddy place often fouled with cow clap.

sick line: Medical certificate of illness allowing a patient to collect sickness benefit.

sicken one's happiness: Rain on your parade.

side wall of a house: Very big-bodied.

sidhe: Irish. Pronounced "shee." The fairies.

skinful: One of the 2,660 synonyms or expressions for "drunk." (*Dickson's Word Treasury,* 1982)

sláinte: Irish. Pronounced "slawntuh." Cheers, your health.

sleekit: Untrustworthy. Devious.

so I am/he is/it's not: An addition at the end of a sentence for emphasis.

solicitor: Attorney who did not try cases in court, as opposed to a barrister, who did.

spare (to go): Go crazy.

spud: Potato. Also a nickname for anyone called Murphy.

stammer: Stutter.

sticking out (a mile): Good (excellent).

stocious: Drunk. See skinful, hammered.

stone: All measurements in Ireland until decimalision were Imperial. One stone=fourteen pounds, 20 fluid ounces=one pint.

stoon: Sudden shooting pain.

stout: A dark beer, usually Guinness or Murphy's.

sound/sound man: Good/good, trustworthy man.

surgery: Where a GP saw ambulatory patients. The equivalent of a North American "office." Specialists worked in "rooms."

sweet, sweetie: Candy.

take a liberty: Be impertinent to someone above your station.

take a pew: Have a seat.

take the rickets: Have a great shock.

take the strunts: Become angry or sulk.

take yourself off by the hand: Don't be ridiculous.

taste (wee): Small amount and not necessarily of food. "Thon axle needs a wee taste of oil."

teach your granny to suck eggs: Try to instruct an expert in their business.

tear away: Carry on with my full permission.

terrace: Row housing, but not just for the working class. Some of the most expensive accommodations in Dublin are found in terraces in Merrion Square, akin to low-rise rows of attached town houses.

that there/them there: That/them with emphasis.

the day: Today.

the ton: One hundred miles an hour.

the wee man: The devil.

thole: Put up with. A reader, Miss D. Williams, wrote to me to say it was etymologically from the Old English *tholian*, to suffer. She remarked that her first encounter with the word was in a fourteenth-century prayer.

thon/thonder: That/over there.

thran: Bloody-minded.

throughother: Slovenly. Carelessly untidy.

throw another spud in the pot: Add more ingredients to the upcoming meal because of the arrival of an unexpected guest.

throw off: Vomit.

til: To.

'til: Until.

to beat Bannagher: Explanation unknown, but means exceptionally.

tongue hanging out for: Craving; a drink, a cigarette, something to eat.

toty (wee): Small (tiny).

townland: Mediaeval administrative district encompassing a village and the surrounding farms and wasteland.

Ulster overcoat: Heavy-duty double-breasted overcoat.

up one side and down the other: A severe chewing out.

walk out with: Pay court to.

wean: Pronounced "wane." Little one.

wee turn: Sudden illness, usually not serious, or used euphemistically to pretend it wasn't serious.

wheeker: Terrific.

wheen: An indeterminate but reasonably large number. See clatter.

wheest: Be quiet.

where to go for corn: Completely at a loss as to what to do.

whin: Gorse.

whisky/ey: Scotch is whisky. Irish is whiskey.

worser: Much worse than worse. Antonym of "better."

yoke: Thing. Often used if the speaker is unsure of the exact nature of the object in question.

you-boy-yuh (go on): Words of encouragement (usually during physical activity).

you know: Verbal punctuation often used when the person being addressed could not possibly be in possession of the information.

you me and the wall: In strictest confidence.

your man: Someone either whose name is not known, "Your man over there? Who is he?" or someone known to all, "Your man, Van Morrison."

youse: Plural of you.

Turn the page for a sneak peek at
the next novel in the Irish Country series

Available October 2018

1

Blazes and Expires

Barry Laverty, Doctor Barry Laverty, took his time driving their almost-new 1968 Hillman Imp. His ancient Volkswagen Beetle, Brunhilde, had started to cost too much in repairs, and as a full partner in the general practice of Doctor Fingal Flahertie O'Reilly and with Sue, his wife, still teaching at MacNeill Memorial Primary in Ballybucklebo, they could afford a better car.

He made his way carefully from the top of Bangor's Main Street, past the old abbey founded by Saint Comgall in 558 A.D., and onto the Belfast Road, heading for home in Ballybucklebo.

He was feeling a distinct surfeit of " 'Tis the season to be jolly," and a combination of irritation and sadness at something Barry's mother had said shortly before Barry and Sue had said their goodnights.

Two days ago it had been the 1968 Christmas Eve hooley at Number One Main Street, Ballybucklebo, presided over by Doctor Fingal Flahertie O'Reilly and his wife, Kitty. Archie and "Kinky" Auchinleck had catered the event and Donal Donnelly had served behind the bar.

Christmas dinner had been at Sue's family's farm in Broughshane.

Now, Barry had finished his second Christmas dinner in three days with his parents in their home in Ballyholme, and not only was he feeling full of food, there was a distinct atmosphere between him and Sue. If only his mother hadn't asked over coffee, "So, you two, you've been married for eighteen months. When are you going to make Dad and me grandparents?"

He accelerated slightly. A steady January drizzle was falling, reflecting his own feelings of sadness. He glanced over at Sue in the dim illumination of the dash lights and saw the single schoolmistress with the copper-coloured mane who had attracted him at the school Christmas pageant four years ago. How he hated to see her hurt. "Sue," he said, struggling to offer comfort, "Mum didn't mean it unkindly, you know."

Sue made a noncommittal noise and moved her thick plait of hair from one shoulder to the other. She generally kept a firm control over her feelings. She sniffed before saying, "Please. I don't want to talk about it just now, Barry, thank you. None of it," and turning to stare out the side window. She had been silent since they had left his folks' house. In Ulster, the sun sets before four thirty in early January, and although the town's streetlights had made driving easier, once out in the country the night was pitch black and had been until he'd passed through the lights of the petrol station, the Presbyterian church, the manse, and the Orange Hall at Ballyrobert, halfway to home.

Barry dipped his headlights to accommodate an oncoming vehicle. He just wanted to get back to the secluded bungalow he and Sue had bought from the widowed Gracie Miller in 1967. Old Gracie was still living happily in Portrush with her family, and Barry and Sue had settled into their nest on its little peninsula in Belfast Lough on the Bangor side of Ballybucklebo.

"Be there in about fifteen minutes, love," he said. "I'll get a fire lit and we can talk about things if you'd like."

Sue moved and he sensed she was looking at him. "Yes. I'd like that, Barry. I'm sorry I—"

The clanging of an insistent bell split the night and drew nearer. Its steady tinging was given counterpoint by the rising and falling of a police siren and the flashing of that car's blue dome light. Barry realised they were approaching from behind. He squeezed over to the left-hand side of the road, as did the rear lights of the car in front. Both cars stopped.

The emergency vehicles roared past, heading in the direction of Ballybucklebo or— Barry swallowed. He could now make out that up ahead the undersides of the low clouds were bathed in flickering red shot through with yellow.

Max, Sue's springer spaniel, was moving in the backseat, pacing and whimpering.

Sue's interrupted sentence was forgotten as an ambulance tore past before Barry could drive off.

"Wheest, Max. It's alright. Sit down now," she said.

Barry exchanged a silent look with Sue and accelerated until he reckoned he was giving a fair impression of the driving favoured by his senior partner, Doctor Fingal O'Reilly. It was difficult to judge how far away the fire was, but as the crow flies, Barry was sure the bearing would pass close to if not through where their bungalow was sited.

"I think you should slow down," Sue said in a quiet voice. "I know what you're worried about, but killing us trying to get there won't change anything."

"You're right, love." He let the speed bleed off. Please, God, not our place.

Ten minutes later he approached the hairpin bend and . . . and, he'd misjudged distances. They were still ten minutes from home, but he could see flames off to their right. "Holy Moses, Sue. I think it's at Dun Bwee."

"My God, the Donnellys' place."

Barry slowed, indicated for a right turn, and crossed the road to jolt along the ruts of the lane leading to the cottage. Even with the windows shut, the stink of smoke filled the car. Max was standing on the seat looking out the window, a low rumble of distress sounding in his throat. The police car and a fire engine were parked in the front yard. The blue light flickered around in circles, and beyond, greedy flames poured from the windows and front door.

Barry pulled up beside the police car and a yellow Northern Ireland Hospitals Authority ambulance.

Firemen in wide-brimmed helmets, waterproof overalls, and rubber boots were tending canvas hoses. Two men directed a torrent through the front door, from which a stream of filthy water flowed, reflecting the flames. A second branch was arcing a powerful stream onto a roof that was belching clouds of steam.

Barry said, "Stay here, and whatever you do don't let Max out of the car."

Sue was reaching for her door handle. "But maybe I can—"

"Stay here with Max," he repeated. "At least until we see what's happening."

"Hush, Max. It's okay. Yes, alright, Barry."

Barry nodded and got out into the drizzle.

Immediately a bottle-green-uniformed Royal Ulster Constabulary constable approached, grabbed Barry's arm, and said, "Back in your car, sir, like a nice gentleman. We don't need no rubberneckers, so we don't—"

Barry recognised Constable Malcolm Mulligan, Ballybucklebo's sole policeman.

"Och, it's yourself, Doctor Laverty, sir. That's alright then, so it is." He'd had to raise his voice to be heard over the roaring and hissing of the flames.

"What happened?" Barry undid his jacket buttons. The heat was ferocious despite the drizzle. "The Donnellys, are they alright?"

"Dunno exactly what happened, sir, but you can see what's happening now. When I got here, Donal and Julie and the three weans, all of them in their jammies and nighties, was outside."

Barry exhaled. All of them safe. "Thank God for that."

"The place is a goner, though." Constable Mulligan shoved his peaked cap so it sat perched on the back of his head. His forehead was shiny with sweat. "I was out on patrol near here on my bike and I seen the flames. I pedalled like the hammers of hell to get here."

The two watched in fascination as the all-devouring beast raved and roared, its hungry jaws biting at the thatched roof before dragging it down into the bungalow. Sparks and flames fled to the heavens to hide among the clouds.

"Ould Bluebird, Donal's racing greyhound, was a bit singed, but she's alright." He pointed down to the dog on a leash at his feet, shivering despite the heat of the fire. "Soon as I seen they was rightly, I was going til head for the nearest phone, but Donal said he'd called nine-nine-nine before he got out. Then"—PC Mulligan indicated the emergency vehicles—"the Seventh Cavalry from Bangor come and took over, so they did. The Donnellys is in the ambulance being looked at."

"Thanks, Malcolm. I'll go and see them." Barry turned and went back to his car.

Sue was already out, her face highlighted by the blaze. "What's happening, Barry?"

"I don't know what started it, but Malcolm Mulligan says the whole family's safe. I'm going to see them. They're in the ambulance."

"Can I help?"

Barry shook his head. "I don't think so. Not with the Donnellys, but maybe you could move the car a bit farther back. It's pretty bloody hot here. Just let me get my bag."

"Right."

Barry, bag in hand, left Sue to it and, ignoring the puddles of warm water he had to slosh through, made his way to the ambulance. Its engine was running. He spoke through the open window to an attendant who was sitting in the driver's seat, replacing the vehicle's radio microphone. "I'm Doctor Laverty from Ballybucklebo. I was on my way home when I saw the flames. The Donnellys are my patients. May I see them?"

"Aye, certainly, sir, but they're grand. Upset, naturally, but thank the Lord nobody's burnt. I hate burn cases, especially kiddies."

"So do I." During his houseman's year while working in casualty at the Royal Victoria Hospital, he'd had to treat a number of burn cases from Mackie's Foundry on nearby Springfield Road. Sometimes not even morphine could dull the pain.

The man climbed out, led Barry to the rear of the vehicle, and opened one of the ambulance's twin back doors. "It's alright, Billy," he said to the other attendant, who was inside listening with a stethoscope to Donal's chest. "This here's a doctor, so it is. These folks is his patients."

Billy pulled the earpieces out, moved to the back, and offered a hand to help Barry up the step. " 'Bout ye, Doc."

Barry accepted the hand and climbed in. "Thanks, Billy."

The back of the ambulance was crowded. It was like a small, hot, oblong room on wheels, smelling of disinfectant and lit by a battery-driven overhead light powered by the engine's alternator charging the batteries. The light of the blaze flickered through the vehicle's windows.

Along each side ran a stretcher, with a narrow aisle between them. Julie Donnelly, wrapped in a damp tartan dressing gown, sat in the middle of one. She was in tears. Her left arm encircled an eighteen-month-old Abigail—or was it Susan? And her right arm cradled the other identical twin. Barry had delivered them in June 1967. He still couldn't tell them apart. That both wore pink pyjamas didn't help. Julie tried to smile at Barry.

Donal Donnelly had a blanket draped over his shoulders. His carroty thatch was disheveled and singed at the front, his forehead an angry red. He stood in the aisle holding their three-year-old daughter Victoria, Tori for short, by the hand. She clutched a blue-eyed, flaxen-haired dolly. Her cheeks were tearstained. Donal looked up. "Doctor Laverty?" he said. "How'd you get here? I never sent for you, sir. There's no need."

Since he had first arrived in Ballybucklebo four years ago, Barry had been humbled by how the locals, despite their own troubles, could find time to be concerned about the welfare of their medical advisors. "Never worry about that, Donal. Julie. Mrs. Laverty and I were passing. We saw the flames."

Donal shook his head. "It's bloody desperate, so it is." He sighed. "We've lost everything. We're prostitute."

Barry didn't have the heart to correct Donal, but the man must have picked up something in his expression.

"I mean destitute, Doc. Aye. Right enough. Destitute." Donal dragged in a deep breath and coughed, then said, "I don't know where til go for corn."

Barry put a hand on Donal's shoulder. "I'm sorry for your troubles, Donal. There will be a lot of sorting out to do, but first things first. Are you sure none of you are hurt?"

Donal nodded. "None of us is burnt except me, but it's only a toty wee one." He pointed to his forehead. He coughed. "I'm wheezy, like. And I've a bit of a hirstle on my thrapple. I breathed in a wheen of smoke when I was dialling nine-nine-nine." He tapped his fringe. "Got a bit frazzled, but I'll live." Donal managed a small, bucktoothed smile.

For a moment, Barry was worried. Anywhere between 50 to 80 percent of all deaths in fires were due to smoke inhalation, particularly if hot smoke had burned the lungs, but, he reassured himself, ambulance crews were trained to examine victims and give oxygen to those so affected. Clearly such was not Donal's case.

Billy said, "Mister Donnelly's orientated in space and time. I heard a few sibilant rhonchi . . ."

Those dry sounds were due to constriction of the smallest bronchial tubes because of the irritation of the smoke. But they did not suggest serious lung damage.

"I've finished our routine check, Doctor, and apart from a small first-degree burn on his forehead, Mister D's not badly affected."

"Thanks, Billy," Barry said. "I'll not have to repeat your work."

Donal cocked his head to one side. His voice was tense when he said, "Not badly affected? I'm not done til a crisp, if that's what you mean, but our whole bloody world's gone up in smoke."

"I'm sorry, Mister Donnelly," Billy said. "I understand how you feel. I meant you're not burnt badly and your lungs are fine."

"Fair enough." Donal ran a hand through his thatch. "And I didn't mean til bite your head off, oul' hand, but we've all had an awful shock. Christmas Day only two days back. All the Christmas presents except Tori's new dolly up in smoke. I never thought when we decorated the tree it was going til end up as kindling." Donal wheezed as he inhaled. "If Bluebird hadn't started carrying on. She was in the house because it's a miserable night, and she started whining and scratching at the kitchen door. Me and Julie'd might never have got ourselves and the weans out. They was all tucked up and we were ready til go to bed in about half an hour."

Julie sniffed and said, "It all happened so fast." She pointed at a carrier bag beside her on the stretcher. "At least I managed to grab my baby bag with a few nappies, plastic knickers, baby powder. But that's all we saved."

"But we did all get out," Donal said.

"Any idea how the thing started?" Barry asked.

Donal shook his head. "I opened the kitchen door and all I could see was smoke and flames coming from near the stove. Maybe something electrical had shorted. I knew I'd to get everyone out first. So, I done that. Then I made a quick phone call from the hall, but by then the place was full of smoke and I had til get out myself." He sighed deeply. "I wish I could have done something til put the fire out, but it got going awful quick . . ."

"Don't go blaming yourself, Donal. You did the most important thing." He inclined his head to Donal's family.

Tori pulled her thumb from her mouth and gazed up at Barry. "I was dead scared, so I was, but my daddy was brave and so was my mammy."

"And so were you, daughter," Julie said. "Come and sit with Mammy."

Donal lifted Tori and set her on the stretcher beside Julie. The wee girl pointed to her mother's left. "Abi," she said.

So, Barry thought, the other one's Susan.

"Thanks for saying that, Doc," Donal said, "but poor ould Dun Bwee's gone for a burton. Can't be saved. I know the firemen is doing their best, but och . . ." He leaned over and put an arm around Julie's shoulder. "Try not til worry, love. We're insured. We're just going til live through the next wee while 'til we get ourselves sorted out."

Where would Donal Donnelly and his family live? Presumably insurance would ultimately see to the rebuilding of their cottage, but that was no help in the short term, and certainly not tonight. Barry rummaged in his bag, fished out a bottle of aspirin, and gave Donal two. Barry said, "Can you swallow those dry, Donal? They'll take away some of the pain from your burn." And it was true. Aspirin was an effective analgesic and anti-inflammatory, but it wouldn't ease the pain of the Donnellys' great loss.

About the Author

Patrick Taylor, M.D., was born and raised in Bangor, County Down, in Northern Ireland. Dr. Taylor is a distinguished medical researcher, offshore sailor, model-boat builder, and father of two grown children. He lives on Salt Spring Island, British Columbia.

www.patricktaylorauthor.com